HAUNTED

I returned to the house and shuffled through Judith's stack of maps until I found Colorado, but as I started to retrace my way through the kitchen I heard my mother humming. As an instinctual reaction on my part, I hid myself at the doorway and listened. It was a weird snatch of not-quite music, and hearing it made the hairs on my forearms prickle. I positioned myself so that I could see her without being seen.

She was not alone.

Continuing her humming, she came hesitantly across the room dressed in her bathrobe and she was carrying a purple bath towel. The ghost of Senta Trogler was guiding her by an elbow. My mother appeared at once distracted and yet centered and resigned; Senta Trogler looked hollow and way past crazy. Waiting for the two of them at the utensil drawer was the ghost of Romina Trogler, who rifled through its contents, creating a lot of noise, as my mother watched. It sounds nothing to tell, but being there, observing the threesome, was a totally arresting, totally frightening experience, especially when Romina, her manner darkly knowing and forceful, retrieved a single utensil and handed it to my mother.

Our largest butcher knife . . .

Books by Stephen Gresham

IN THE BLOOD

DARK MAGIC

HAUNTED GROUND

Published by Pinnacle Books

HAUNTED GROUND

Stephen Gresham

PINNACLE BOOKS
Kensington Publishing Corp.
http://www.kensingtonbooks.com

PINNACLE BOOKS are published by

Kensington Publishing Corp.
850 Third Avenue
New York, NY 10022

All Kensington Titles, Imprints, and Distributed Lines are available at special quantity discounts for bulk purchases for sales
promotion, premiums, fund-raising, and educational or institu-
tional use. Special book excerpts or customized printings can
also be created to fit specific needs. For details, write or phone
the office of the Kensington special sales manager: Kensington
Publishing Corp., 850 Third Avenue, New York, NY 10022,
attn: Special Sales Department, Phone: 1-800-221-2647.

Pinnacle and the P logo Reg. U.S. Pat. & TM Off.

First Pinnacle Books Printing: January 2003

10 9 8 7 6 5 4 3 2 1

Printed in the United States of America

One

A Requiem for Innocence

"We're helping blood," my father announced as the plume of dust trailing a black dot neared our farm, rolling past the Trogler place a quarter of a mile east of us. My father was more nervous than I had ever seen him. Twice as we waited he glanced at my frail mother, his face eager to smile through a pinched yet hopeful expression.

The five of us stood there in the gravel driveway bracing ourselves as if change were literally coming like a strong wind and might blow us over. The change was the expected arrival of my cousin, Ilona, recently stricken by a crippling disease. She was to stay with us while her mother recovered from a near nervous breakdown. My cousin's father had left wife and daughter for parts unknown. My older brothers, of course, tried to appear indifferent to change; they jammed their hands in their pockets and sneered at each other. They kicked at small rocks until my mother pitched a frown at them.

It was the summer of 1955.

Deep in those dog days I discovered I no longer wanted to be a member of my family; it was the summer I faced the harsh realities of sexual confusion and learned that only if I re-invented myself could I enter a new world of possibilities. That summer I also woke to the terrifying realization that existence harbors darkness and a cast of horrors I had not imagined. Before the season changed and the tall corn was harvested, I would come to know the only thing about life that counts.

Did I see any of this on the horizon?

Perhaps I did.

I know that as change plummeted toward me like a meteor from the vastness of space I felt small and timid. I wanted my mother to touch me reassuringly and whisper away my doubts and fears. But I was too old for that, and when I looked at her I saw a woman whose maternal strength had nearly all drained away. As we waited, my mother was sighing a lot. She had one arm draped across her sunken stomach and one hand raised to her brow to help her squint into the sunlight. It looked as if her whole body was resisting what was taking place.

My father seemed uncomfortable in the opposite way.

"Teddy," he said to me, "scatter those banties. Sometimes city women are scared of chickens."

As I jumped to obey my father, I heard my mother grinding her teeth and issuing a disgusting noise in her throat; my brothers barked laughter and punched at each other.

"Shoo, biddies," I said. I clapped my hands and a knot of them, five or six at least, clucked their annoyance but gave up the driveway without a fight. A thin, scraggily, gray cat—a stray with cockleburs matted in his fur—happened to be wandering through at the moment and sped to the shelter of the barn, believing I had singled him out for harassment. I had named the stray Oatmeal. In their meaner hours my brothers would threaten to skin and cut up the poor beast and make me eat it. I always tried to ignore them. And with the driveway cleared, I wasn't thinking about chickens and cats.

I was thinking about blood.

About why people refer to relatives as blood and why my father might have used that word—about how he was making it seem that we were about to perform a sacred duty not found on the Christian church calendar.

I thought hard about my cousin.

I hoped she wasn't really afraid of chickens because, if so, my brothers would torture her socks off. They could smell fear all the way from our farm to town. They could be relentless, especially when joined by their sadistic comrade, Mickey Palmer.

My father continued to be on edge, his eyes glued to the approaching vehicle. "Teddy, stay on out of the driveway. John's likely not to be sober."

My mother was grinding out more disgust in her throat—sounding as if she were sharpening knives—and though I wasn't close enough to hear precisely what she said, her words bore a question about why Aunt Juanita couldn't drive herself. The black Chevy was slowing when my father said, "Babe, you heard me say she's got a bad case of nerves."

My mother shook her head and hissed something more, and my brothers broke into a cruel pantomime of retarded people. I felt sorry for my father. He wanted to do something with his hands but did not know what; he wanted to fix the whole situation, and if it had been the belt on our old John Deere tractor or the carburetor on his old Ford pickup, he would have. But not this. This involved people. This involved blood. He looked as helpless as noon at night.

I went over to stand next to him. When the black Chevy turned in by our mailbox, it occurred to me quite suddenly that I needed to know exactly how my cousin had become crippled, but I could tell by the way my father's jaw skidded and his brow crashed that I should not ask. Not right then.

Except for my father, who waved sheepishly, we all stood very still until the car crunched to a halt, then we stuttered a step or two forward into the rising puffs of dust. The passenger's side door flew open, and my Aunt Juanita took a couple of excited hops and pretty much landed in my father's arms, losing her purse and several wads of white tissue. Her eyes were red. Her cheeks, tear-tracked.

"Oh, Norman," she said, "you are the rainbow, the blessed rainbow at the end of a storm."

All my father could do was chuckle nervously and turn his head to see my mother being held in the ugly grip of disapproval.

With contrasting deliberation, Uncle John, younger brother to my father and Aunt Juanita, crawled out from behind the wheel. I studied his dark, sullen face for signs of the bottle, an art I wasn't schooled in, and yet since he hadn't clipped the mailbox or nailed one of the chickens, I figured he wasn't drunk.

When Aunt Juanita peeled herself from my father, she reached for my head.

"Theodore, do you know how many girls would slit their wrists for your red hair? Prettiest mop *I've* ever laid eyes on. Even prettier than your mother's. And just how are you, Kathleen?"

My mother nodded once and blinked her eyes rapidly. Her whisper of the word "Fine" was barely audible.

Aunt Juanita tapped my mother's elbow.

"What you and Norman are doing is a kindness unrepayable. It truly is. I had no one else I could turn to and not heap upon myself another load of worries."

When Aunt Juanita let up on her grasp of my hair, I edged around my father and Uncle John who were fumbling with a slow-cadenced, menfolk exchange flecked with comments about road conditions and distances and the price of gasoline. I was getting impatient.

I wanted to see her. My cousin, Ilona. She was sitting in the shadow-strewn backseat, her head twisted around to survey the road they'd come on. But then I could see that she was actually looking squarely at the Trogler place as if entranced by it. I hadn't seen her for three or four years, and my memory of her wasn't crystal clear. She had always seemed quiet and shy, her nose buried in books, her body always seeming to want to be somewhere else other than kickable reality. I guessed she must be about 16, two years older than me. I also remembered that I had thought her rather pretty, though thin and gangly and pale. But I had overheard my father and mother speak of how she'd changed. My mother, especially, had fanned the flames of my curiosity by whispering alarmingly of some strangeness about my cousin—something beyond her physical ailment, something that had made my mouth go dry.

"She's a Child of the Devil," my mother had declared, adding the perverse suggestion that God, in His incomprehensible ladling out of justice, had personally stricken her so that she could not race among other young adults and tempt them into certain damnation. My father had shushed her. He could not, however, diminish my curiosity or snap me out of my anticipatory trance. As I strained to see what dark metamorphosis my cousin might have undergone since I'd last seen her, I could hear Aunt Juanita and my mother shuffling up behind me.

"It's not really polio," said my aunt. "The doctors say it's similar to polio. But not *really* polio."

In the summer of 1955 polio was more dreaded than cancer and rubbed shoulders with the dropping of a hydrogen bomb as something that could scare the living daylights out of a kid.

"What if something happens?" my mother followed.

"Nothing will. I'll just be a few weeks. I'm checking into the place there in Topeka 'specially for this kind of thing. I'll get rest and relaxation and enough pills to settle my nerves back down. Then I'll come back for her. Mid-August at the latest, Kathleen, I promise."

"I don't know," said my mother.

"She's not much trouble. You'll see."

With that, Aunt Juanita was tousling my hair again, and I could feel her fingers trembling like tiny, frightened creatures.

"She and Theodore here will get to be good buddies," she said. "Maybe Jack and Norman Junior will accept her as the sister they never had. I bet they will." My aunt paused, and I assumed she could feel how I was shaking my head doubtfully, especially about my brothers. They were brutes. Often I wondered how they and I could be related.

"Is she ever going to get out of the car?" I said.

My aunt paused before letting out a high-pitched twitter.

"Heavenly days. Yes, of course, she is. I can't imagine what she's doing in there. Building a nest, I suppose." She laughed a bit too forcefully and started to open the Chevy's back door, but my father's large hand beat her to it.

Light poured into the shadows inside the car.

I remember feeling the oddest anticipation: it was

like waiting for that tug when a fish bites at your line and you become instantly consumed by an interest in hooking it. Then the feeling turned dark; the anticipation was suddenly that of swinging open the door to our storm cellar and being confronted by a pitch black nothingness out of which might emerge the worst things your imagination could dredge up.

Child of the Devil.

I was holding my breath.

Would she have grown horns? Would she look like a witch? I worried that I might, upon seeing her, wet my pants.

My father reached forward to help her swing her legs out. I heard the metallic protest of braces or maybe it was her crutches. I had become a soap bubble of fear and fascination hovering as still as death despite the usual summer gusts of hot Kansas wind. I thought it a real possibility that I might disappear in a nervous little pop and rejoin the cosmos as drops of spittle.

Then I saw her, indistinctly at first, details punching at me so fast that I could not focus. She was wearing a pink dress, and something about that color galvanized the silky sheen of her long black hair.

"There you go, sweetheart," said my father gently.

My cousin pushed to her feet and did not meet the eyes of any of us. Instead she turned to look again in the direction of the Trogler place. Yes, she was locked onto it intensely. It was as if she could see right through its gray-weathered siding into the abandoned house, its rooms empty except for a few mounds of milo that our rural mail carrier, Emmitt Suggs, was storing there. Then she blinked once and widened her eyes as if she had just stepped through the curtain veiling the rest of us from another world.

I stared at her.

I was surprised to find that I thought she was beautiful.

No warts. No horns. No hiss or cackle. Her eyes didn't flame. She didn't carry a pitchfork or ride a broom. She had feet rather than hooves.

I thought I was the one who would, any second, need braces and crutches to be able to stand. My legs were like blocks of ice thawing much too rapidly.

"Theodore," said my aunt, "could you give your cousin a nice big hug? Make her feel welcome? She's not contagious, you know. Those braces won't bite."

As I moved hesitantly forward, I could hear my older brothers guffawing and making snarly, biting noises. My cousin fixed her gaze upon me. Her magnificent blue eyes were brimming like a pail of water on the verge of spilling over. I sensed that she wasn't far from tears. Her face was pale, punctuated with black eyebrows and finely structured with a pointed, yet delicate nose and chin, and thin lips coated with a sheen of pink lipstick.

"Hi, Teddy," she said softly. "You remember who I am?"

I said, "Sur-r-r-re," and my whole body flushed with embarrassment as I pressed the word out as if I were rolling dough with it to make biscuits.

We leaned into a hug.

I'm certain my brothers must have been laughing; I, however, did not hear them.

I closed my eyes and rested my chin momentarily on her shoulder and then pressed her closer and felt how, magically and mysteriously, her more than ample breasts were both soft and firm. I felt the brush of her lips on my neck. She smelled clean. I caught the faintest whiff of Blue Water perfume, the kind most of the other girls I knew had stopped wearing. On her, though, it was right. I held her more tightly;

I bathed momentarily in the warmth of her body before the wrongness of enjoying my cousin's embrace stung me; and yet somehow I knew then that just like a bee sting the wrongness would grow less insistent, less painful.

I suddenly thought of David.

The word *betrayal* floated over me. I was confused. I felt a similar rush of blood when I was close to him. David, his neatly combed blond hair and those green eyes inviting me to enter a secret realm, no password needed, merely a forbidden touch. My life promised to become more difficult than I could have imagined, and I did not have the courage to trust what was difficult.

I could hear my cousin's breathing, almost a purr. When it seemed that our hug had lasted long enough, I reluctantly started to pull away.

But she clutched at me.

Something between us was forever sealed in that next instant.

She whispered the way I imagined an angel come down from heaven would.

"Do you believe in ghosts?" she said.

Her breath was a flutter of wings against my ear.

I was instantly caught up, turned upside down, swinging by my heels from nothingness, a terrifyingly delicious, confusing sensation, and before my brain could stop my tongue, I whispered back, "Yes."

The gospel truth is that before that moment I hadn't thought much at all about ghosts; before that summer I confess that I hadn't thought much about anything—I just lived the questions, letting my brain go mostly idle, sort of like a section of land that has lain fallow. Ghosts? No, they hadn't much crossed the river of my lazy mind. And until that summer I can't say that I was afraid of ghosts, though horror movies at the tent shows in town scared the crap out of me, and my brothers could unsettle me with stories of some hideous monster—something like the Creature from the Black Lagoon—that supposedly lived in our derelict cistern. That cistern, now dry, used to be our only source of drinking water until my father dug a new well closer to the house.

Ghosts?

I think I said "yes" to my cousin's question because I sensed that she wanted me to.

We let go of each other. Because my aunt had been talking away about something President Eisenhower had said at a press conference, no one heard our fateful exchange.

My face felt hot like the first sunburn of summer.

My cousin's smile was quick and sharp like a puppy's yip. Then I couldn't hold her eyes. I stumbled backwards and off to one side, desperately afraid that I would fall down.

"She's as smart as a whip, just like your Theodore," I heard Aunt Juanita say, "and she has a memory like a Kodak Brownie snapping a photo of the Grand Canyon. She could tell you what every sign said between here and Topeka. Couldn't you, Ilona?"

My cousin didn't respond. Her gaze had drifted away from me; it was almost as if her eyes were being pulled by a magnet—a magnet at the center of the Trogler place. I wanted to know what she found so interesting about an abandoned farmhouse.

My mother appeared to be talking to herself, whispering incantations or, more likely, some stale passage of scripture.

"But what if something happens?" she murmured, almost more to herself than to my aunt.

My father put one big hand on my mother's shoulder and one on Aunt Juanita's. "This will work out fine. It'll be fine," he said.

We were going to help blood.

Yet mine was singing wickedly. A requiem for my innocence.

Blood and ghosts.

I felt faint.

I did not know what my cousin's reference to ghosts meant. Was she testing me? Maybe I had given the wrong answer—maybe she thought that only little boys believed in ghosts, you know, the way little kids still believe in Santa Claus and the Easter Bunny.

Yet, she hadn't laughed at my answer.

"Yes," I whispered again. Thankfully, no one heard. I had been converted, only it felt potentially more serious than my confirmation at the Christian Church. Some unknowable realm was opening up. Shadows slithered through me. I felt blissfully chilled. All because of ghosts.

All because of my cousin.

Uncle John eased away from all the awkwardness to the trunk of the car, a move my father noticed. "Teddy, give him a hand with whatever your cousin brought."

I did. There were two heavy suitcases. I hefted one to the front porch, a pretty good distance away, and hoped that my cousin saw that I was strong even though I was not muscular. When Uncle John dropped the other suitcase down next to the one I had carried, he said, with no emotion, "She's a goddamned spooky one. You hear what I'm saying?"

I assumed he meant my cousin. I didn't utter a word. I didn't even look at him.

Back at the Chevy, the parting was underway. Aunt Juanita was hunkered close to her daughter delivering a tight, raspy whisper, the specifics out of earshot.

My cousin did not nod or appear to acknowledge her mother's words in any manner.

"She'll be fine," said my father.

My mother and Aunt Juanita shared a limp, obligatory embrace before my aunt spun around, her hand plunging into her purse. "Norman, I want to help with this."

When my father saw that she was trying to offer him money, he backed away violently, shaking his head and saying, "No, no, no," as if she'd tempted him with sin on a silver platter. His response, I reasoned, must have had something to do with helping blood, and blood and money did not, could not, mix. My aunt did not, could not, merely cry. She blubbered, a horsey sound that sent my brothers into a giggling, gagging fit. My mother turned away in apparent disgust, but my father attempted to console his sister, managing at last to herd her to the passenger side of the car. He did it patiently yet firmly, much as he would our Holsteins at milking time.

My cousin was expressionless throughout the good-bye scene.

She wasn't among us. I mean, she was there, but she wasn't. There was an otherness about her that did not allow her to join us, and as I stood next to her, enchanted and puzzled, I thought I heard something. Like some acoustic trick, sounds—soft, eerie sounds—seemed to rise up from the earth in waves. Some seemed to be coming from inside me. Like my stomach growling. Only weirder. I felt as if my cousin were transforming the air around her. I glanced about, but no one else appeared to detect what I had.

I looked at my cousin and I faintly gasped. Her metal crutches and braces appeared to have thrust up from the ground to close around her legs and arms, trapping her. That image stayed with me. She was like an animal caught in a trap, and though its physical fight has been exhausted, it remains calm and defiant, determined to survive and possibly escape. It was as if she were trapped in this dimension, the so-called real world. It was as if she belonged somewhere else.

Among ghosts?

That possibility scared me. I wanted to hug her.

I thought she was very brave.

I could see that she was trembling ever so slightly. I held my breath, hoping that those extraordinary blue eyes would not spill. I silently begged her not to cry, to be strong. I was still holding my breath when several of the banties wandered up near her feet, scratching in the dusty scrabble for food I could never see no matter how hard I tried. Would she shriek? Would she swing at them with one of her braces?

Suddenly I was breathing again, my hands tingling, feeling good under a blazing sun because my cousin showed no signs of fear. Instead, she clucked. It was a pleasing, teeth against the edges of the tongue sound, low and sort of eagerly contented. It was the language of bantam chickens, and they knew it but didn't let on that it was any big deal to be answering her, if that's what they were doing.

Unfortunately, my older brothers were listening in on the dialogue and began to mock my cousin with obscene antics: clucking, scratching, crowing, then slapping at one another and launching kicks at the other's private parts. When my cousin saw what they were doing, she stopped her clucking. She brushed some long strands of hair from her shoulder, and in a gesture that made my heart slew sideways, glanced at me pleadingly.

In turn, I threw a glare at my brothers.

I would have stabbed them in the face had I courage and a pocketknife that didn't have its point broken. My father was no help, for he was leaning in the car window talking with my Aunt Juanita. My mother was hugging herself and rocking back and forth as if she were ill. Uncle John was smoking a cigarette and studying the remains of a large grasshopper smashed on the windshield, its guts a spectacular spiral nebula.

Junior was spinning a basketball on one finger; Jack was stabbing the point of his javelin into the ground. All the while they continued their display of insensitivity.

Anger and frustration filled me with a hot, sticky desire to get back at them. In a blinding moment of hatred, robbed of all good judgment, I ran at them and screamed, "You crummy, smelly, dirty, sissy dogs! Stop it! Stop it!"

I had wanted to say something stronger, something needing the efficient coordination of lips, tongue, teeth, saliva—something unrehearsed yet convincing and filled with measured passion. Something with a vivid, forceful mix of "God" and "damn" and "hell" and "bastards."

I was obviously no swearer, but for a richly satisfying instant, my brothers froze.

Behind me, conversation ceased.

Before my brothers righted themselves and whooped into a counterattack of inspired vengeance, I imagined my cousin silently applauding her defender, her eyes awash in gratitude, her heart pounding in admiration and newfound affection.

Then I bolted.

I ran as fast as boys run in their dreams, my bare feet punishing the earth, my overalls rubbing hard against the naked flesh of my chest and shoulders. I sprinted into our cornfields, the stalks not yet tall, and I headed, as if unconsciously drawn, toward the Trogler place, and even over my labored breathing I could hear my father yelling for my brothers to abort their mission. I was reasonably confident that they would; however, I was equally certain that some way, somewhere, at some darkly appointed hour they could catch me in that dead zone of unprotected, fatherless territory and exact a swift and terrible revenge. I would suffer bruises and, likely, loss of blood, and the pain would be added to whatever reprimand my father would have given me. He was masterful at shaming me, spearing unfailingly with the blade of his disappointment.

But this time it was worth it.

I ran until my chest burned. I burst from the far edge of our field onto what was once Trogler property, property now deeded to Emmitt Suggs. I bent over to catch my breath, and when I looked up, the abandoned homestead that I had seen a jillion times looked somehow different. But not physically different. The two-story clapboard house was still gray and beginning to sag, giving itself up each day to the elements. Maybe twenty yards behind the house a piled-rock cistern remained where it seemed always to have been, its deep water stagnant and with a mossy, pungent stench. And some fifty yards behind the house a small barn of post rock continued to stand, and beyond it the remnants of an orchard where, out of habit, a scattering of apple, apricot and peach trees continued to bear fruit—the orchard where, years ago, the "bloody Troglers," as they were known, had been ingloriously buried. Beyond the orchard was a small, muddy pond with sapling willows and one mammoth cottonwood tree stitched along its banks. It's where I had gone swimming every summer except this one. I had stopped because my mother maintained that a sure fire way to get polio was to swim in farm ponds. Her words conjured up for me images of polio as a massive snapping turtle taking aim at one's toes, crippling you for life.

I thought about my cousin and her affliction.

I thought about my cousin's apparent fascination with the Trogler house; spurred by those thoughts I walked up to one of the glassless windows and peered in. The house ticked silently as always. *Do you believe in ghosts?* Right then and there—my cousin not being present—I would have confessed that I did not. But I did, however, admit that as I continued rounding the derelict structure, peering in at windows and glancing through sadly opened doors, I felt something. Or sensed something. Not a ghost. No, this was more simply the suggestion of color.

Something blue.

I would catch it out of the corner of my eye as the wind toyed with a rotting window frame or stirred up puffs of dust or carved at one of Emmitt Suggs's mounds of milo in the front room. I would glimpse it as I heard mice scurry up and down within the plaster and lathing walls. I imagined it out of the everywhere into the air of the rooms where no one had lived for so long.

I imagined a blue flame. But I never saw it whole and clear.

Curiously, I was not frightened by that inexplicable specter.

And I remember that I wanted to tell my cousin about it, and yet when I saw her next, I forgot all about it. I didn't return to our house until our mid-afternoon Sunday meal. I slid in at the table between

my mother and my cousin and began to load my plate
with fried chicken, mashed potatoes and gravy and
some of the green beans I'd helped my mother put
up last summer. I didn't look at my father because I
knew there would be disappointment in his eyes. I
wanted to sneak a smile at my cousin in hopes she
would return it, but I decided not to. Across the table
my brothers smirked, confident, no doubt, of their re-
taliation plan. The scene grew quiet except for the
metallic click and clank of silverware against plates
and the tumbling mutter of ice cubes when someone
raised a glass of iced tea to their lips.

When my father could tolerate the silence no
longer, he said, "Cousin Ilona, is there anything special you like to eat? Your Aunt Kathleen is a great
cook."

I wanted that to be true. But my mother was indifferent to both food and the kitchen, and I suspect
that her heart was never in the rigors of preparing a
meal. She had a digestive problem that caused her to
lose a lot of weight; her stomach looked like a deflated football.

My cousin waited until she had thoroughly chewed
and swallowed a single green bean before she said,
"Boiled eggs."

My brothers snickered, and my mother whispered,
"Oh, dear," but my father kept running with the subject: "You'll get plenty of eggs here. We can boil 'em,
scramble 'em, fry 'em up or do 'em any way you
want."

"I like boiled eggs, too," I said, the words easing out
of my mouth as if they represented the truth. I think
my cousin smiled shyly. When my father got up to get
something from the icebox, my brother Jack leaned
forward and said, "We're gonna boil your nuts, Teddy,
and make you eat 'em."

I gritted my teeth through the flush of embarrassment. I hated it that my cousin had to hear his remark. At that moment, I hated being a member of my family. Thankfully, my father changed the subject to crops—the next cutting of alfalfa, to be specific—and to the weather—clear and dry forecast for evening. Mostly he and my older brothers held forth. My cousin, who finished only a half dozen or so bites of her meal, said nothing until my mother brought out dessert—a fresh peach cobbler baked by a neighbor lady—at which point my cousin asked, "Who used to live at that next place down the road?"

I heard my mother whisper, "Oh, dear," again.

Then I said, "The Troglers. But they're long gone."

I was wrong about that.

Junior, my oldest brother, 17 and going to graduate from high school at the end of the coming school year, said, "They haven't lived there since the early 40s. There was an old man and his wife and two grown-up kids, a boy who was kind of retarded and a girl who was a witch—or that was what people said about her. And they had a big mean dog, too."

"Does anyone know what happened to them?" said my cousin. And it was real odd, I thought, but something in the tone of her question made it seem like she already knew a lot about them.

Jack, 16, smiled his greasy smile and said, "They got themselves killed. They got what they deserved."

My father, obviously uncomfortable with the topic, broke in. "Now I don't know that this is what civilized folk ought to be talking about at the Sunday meal." In fact, he was always uncomfortable whenever the topic of the Troglers came up. I had never asked him why. He glanced at my mother who seemed lost in thought, wandering around in the emptiness of herself.

"But our cousin asked," said Junior. And so he continued, explaining that the Troglers had a reputation as thieves, their criminal activity bottoming out one day when they robbed Harold "Red" Suggs and brutally murdered him and his small son, Dwight. Harold's brothers, Emmitt and James—or so the story goes—then took the law into their own hands and created a scene of bloody revenge with the help of several other rugged men of Saddle Rock, our tiny town. They buried the bodies in the orchard. No charges were leveled at Emmitt and James and the others, largely because another account held that the witchy daughter, who had just given birth to an illegitimate child, bludgeoned her parents, stabbed her brother, drowned the dog in the cistern and then committed suicide via poison. The authorities bought that version. Case closed.

When Junior had completed his grisly account of the Troglers, my father chuckled nervously. "Goodness knows the Trogler place has a dark history. Things that happened, well, it goes all the way back to 1921 when the Troglers moved here—nobody knew from where—and they bought that tract of land and built that house. Rolf Trogler had a wife, Senta, and a small boy, Siebert, at that time, and he had this horrible, broken mug—shell blew up in his face in World War I. Terrible, terrible thing."

Jack broke in grinning: "People say he didn't have lips or a nose." He cackled and his eyes became slits as he leered at my cousin.

"He wasn't much of a farmer," my father continued. "Couple of years later his wife had twins—a girl and a boy. The little boy died at birth. Senta, she just never got over it. Never. I've always heard that grief opens up strange worlds. Must be true. Anyway, they sold the place to Red Suggs, pulled up stakes. Moved away. Then moved back in either '37 or '38 and leased the same property. By that time they'd turned bad. Like outlaws." My father's jaw went slack. "Nobody knows the plain facts about what all the Troglers did. Folks just know the stories, but stories are just that—stories. The Troglers are dead and buried and so nothing else matters. The rest is like old Kansas sayings." And there he glanced again at my mother. "Kathleen, you remember don't you, babe, how your grandmother had all those peculiar sayings—you know, like 'If you sing at the table, the Devil will get you before night'?"

At the mention of the Devil my mother blinked back to the present.

Jack, eager to add more, said, "The Troglers had this monster black dog, and they called it Hunter, and it could rip out your throat. The Trogler place, it's haunted. You'll stay away from it if you know what's good for you."

You could see that Jack wanted to scare my cousin; maybe if you looked closely you could see something else: He was smitten with her.

"Ho, now," said my father, "let's us drop all this and enjoy some wonderful pie."

The topic might have died right there had it not been for my mother. After a few heartbeats of conversational silence she suddenly opened her mouth and said, "I knew Senta Trogler. Liked her. The loss of her child set her off crazy and quiet with sadness. And she liked me, I believe. And I knew the Trogler girl. I knew Romina. She almost won me to the side of evil."

My father was more embarrassed than shocked by her words. "Kathleen, what on earth are you saying?"

My mother, as if in some kind of a trance, kept talking—like a confession to herself. "Romina kissed a dead person once and so she never feared anything. She could heal folks with her evil powers. I was always afraid that if I stared into her eyes, she'd take my soul." Then my mother paused, her face shadowed, and she gritted her teeth. "Child of the Devil."

And that last remark was accompanied by a fleeting glance at my cousin.

Then my mother paused again. A smile flickered as she darted her eyes my way.

"But I'm not saying God abandoned Romina entirely. He knew how to use a soul like hers for something good."

In a soft voice of reprimand, my father said, "Good country folks sometimes believe that kind of thing about certain people being evil but they shouldn't. Evil's a strong word. The Troglers—they got vicious in the blood. Things had to be done."

He looked momentarily shaken, a face touched by dark memories. Dark secrets.

It got quiet.

Words started crawling up out of my throat like a spider in a wet gutter spout.

"I believe in ghosts," I said. Then I turned to look at my cousin; I was blazoned with a courage from somewhere. "If there's ghosts at the Troglers, I won't let them hurt you."

The laughter and hooting from my brothers cracked open and spread over our table like an egg into a skillet. But I didn't care.

"Thanks, Teddy," she replied in that angelic voice.

My brothers continued snickering and making kissy noises, but then my cousin spoke up. "When I saw it from the road, I knew it was a bad place." She seemed to offer that remark to all of us before directing the next one at me. "Like your mother said, maybe there was evil." Then she said something more that buzzed in the air like a huge swarm of bees that might come after you if provoked: "Maybe the evil hasn't left that place. Maybe it's soaked down into the earth."

Not taking her seriously, my brothers chorused ghostly moanings and generally acted like fools. My father stepped in again at that point.

"Hey, now, we better quit all this talk of evil and the Troglers or we'll all have us bad dreams tonight."

After the meal, my cousin asked if she could lie down. Typical of my mother's poor judgment, she had given her one of the upstairs bedrooms, and because the stairs were hard for my cousin to negotiate, my father carried her. I trailed along behind, jealous, wondering whether I was strong enough to carry her that same way. I doubted that I was.

Not meaning to humiliate me, my father nevertheless raised the related issues of making sure my cousin knew the path to our outhouse and had a chamber pot available. When my father left, I lingered at the door. My cousin was sitting on the edge of the bed; she looked uncomfortable, though she managed to smile my way.

"Teddy, could you help with my braces?"

I didn't hesitate.

Though thin, her legs were nice.

"Do you hurt somewhere?" I said, squatting in front of her.

"All over. There's not someplace that doesn't."

"Oh, I'm sorry."

Then, out of nowhere, she said, "Does your corn need rain?"

I thought a second. Nodded. "It's been pretty dry."

As I was helping with the braces, the lower edge of her dress hiked up and I caught sight of the white, lacy hem of her slip and my fingers twitched nervously and rapidly as if I were typing on an invisible typewriter. I tried to act as if I'd seen nothing.

When the braces clattered to the floor, she said, "Thanks." She paused, then said, "I have to take off my dress now."

"Oh," I said. "Oh, well, sure."

I hustled out of the room. It was hard for me to understand, but when I closed the door I stayed there in the hallway nearly an hour, a puzzled sentry guarding a mysterious someone I knew had imprisoned my heart.

I thought again of David.

I thought of how he had said we were closer than brothers and more than best friends. I thought about that story of the sinful woman and her scarlet A— David's favorite story—of how our teacher, Miss Sisler, had told us we would understand it better when we were adults. But I wanted to understand it right then. I wanted to understand sin. I wanted to understand how I could—in nearly the same heartbeat—have an attraction for David, as well as one for my cousin. Both attractions would be frowned upon by the God-fearing folks of Kansas.

I stood there, alone, feeling like the greatest sinner of all time.

To the surprise of my family, by early evening the broiling sky had mushroomed thunderheads, their bellies dark blue and tinged with an eerie green which promised hail. Pockets of wind swelled up round and heavy like ripe fruit. My father and brothers stood out in the yard to watch the clouds; they had the right eyes for seeing how destructive a storm might become. I did not. My mother stayed on the back porch, worrying, because that's what she did best. I joined her there, and as I did she murmured something just loudly enough for me to hear it: "They say the child of the Devil can raise storms."

I ignored her remark. But I wondered.

Wind and big drops of rain kicked up after a menacing calm. I went back upstairs to my post outside the door to my cousin's room. I knew my father would call us to the cellar if he saw a funnel cloud. In a matter of minutes, the sky seemed to fall: thunder, lightning, wind, a driving rain of Armageddon intensity and pieces of hail the size of the tip of my little finger.

My cousin slept through the worst of the storm.

As night came on I heard the thud of her crutches. When she opened the door, she just stood there, sleepily, in her slip, not self-conscious at all. I should have averted my eyes, but I didn't. The seductively brilliant whiteness of that slip, the arresting sight of a shadow of cleavage, held me as nothing else ever had.

She smiled.

"I forgot to thank you," she said, "for yelling at your brothers."

She closed the door some, enough to hide everything but one shoulder and the electric whiteness of two straps, the strap of her slip not quite concealing the strap of her brassiere. I turned my back to her slightly and nodded because my mouth had filled with so much saliva I could not speak. I must have gulped audibly. She giggled at my embarrassment and said, "Your brothers belong in a zoo."

I coughed once and swallowed again and over my shoulder said, "I know. But they're good basketball players. Both are going to start on the varsity next season."

"Why does Jack carry around that spear?"

"Spear? Oh, that's a javelin. He throws it in track meets. Went to the district meet last year and got third. Probably win it this year. He can really heave it.

I've seen him throw it all the way across Trogler's Pond and stick it in that big cottonwood. The coach at school lets him keep the javelin over the summer to practice with."

I don't know why I felt compelled to defend either of my brothers. Blood, I guess. I found it impossible to read the look in my cousin's eyes, and so probably out of nervousness I prattled on. "I'm no good at basketball. Can't dribble worth a flip. Can't throw balls or javelins or nothing. And jockey straps give me a rash." I cringed and looked away. My ears suddenly burned. I think maybe she giggled again.

"Oh, Teddy, you're too much," she said.

"No, really, I can't do anything with a ball or a bat. My hands aren't big enough. Can't even kick stuff very well. But I'm pretty good at keeping score."

"I don't like sports," she said.

"Me, neither."

I wanted to tell her that David didn't either. But somehow he did not belong with us.

"There's so much else in the world," she said.

"Yeah."

"School tries to turn you into being somebody you don't necessarily want to be."

I hadn't thought about that. Coming from her lips, it sounded like the gospel truth. "Yeah, you're right."

Then she said, "Here's what I always say: no need to hurry. No need to sparkle. No need to be anybody but one's self."

I didn't know at the time that she was quoting from a literary work.

"I agree."

And I could sense that my cousin had something more on her mind. It shouldn't have come as a surprise that she returned to the issue of the Troglers.

"Has anything strange happened there, Teddy? I mean, where they're buried."

I shook my head. The only thing that occurred to me was that two years ago Jack fell out of the crab apple tree in the Trogler orchard and broke his wrist. Not the one on his throwing arm. But my cousin pressed forward, asking something then that about knocked me for a loop.

"Teddy, have the Troglers—have they stayed in the ground?"

I laughed right out loud. It was funny and weird. To cover being unnerved by her question, I tried to act cool. "Well," I said, "that's the way it works for dead people. They gotta stay where you bury them til somebody digs them up." I sort of laughed again.

"You're right, mostly," she said.

Unsettled as I was, I balanced on one leg and had to hop a time or two to catch my balance. I suddenly thought about her earlier question—about whether I believed in ghosts.

"Have you ever seen one?" I said. "A ghost, I mean?"

"Yes. One goes wherever I go. I call him the Fiery Angel, and he came to me from out of the great somewhere a long time ago. You believe that, don't you, Teddy? You don't think I made that up, do you?"

Her words winged right through me. I felt stupid, but I wasn't about to ask what exactly she meant. I nodded that I believed her and then I looked down at my toenails, and as I did so she negotiated forward and planted a kiss on my shoulder where my overalls didn't cover skin.

"Thank you," she said. "We're going to be friends, aren't we?"

I think I must have shuddered in surprise and delight.

"Sure," I said, breathlessly.

When I stirred up the courage to turn and face her fully, I saw that she clutched something in a fist. I was still thinking about a lot of things but especially that kiss and how it had warmed a spot on my shoulder about the size of a silver dollar.

"What have you got there?" I said.

She worked her lips a moment as if deciding how much she could trust me. Finally she said, "Matches."

"Oh."

I didn't know what to think.

"If evil doesn't burn, it grows. That's the world, Teddy—burning and growing."

In the coming weeks, my cousin would often deliver that kind of cryptic line, the kind of line that left me in speechless agreement though I hadn't the foggiest idea what she was talking about.

"The world's a big place," I said stupidly.

"Teddy," she followed, "I have to ask you something."

"Yeah, what?"

I was suddenly trembling. I forgot about the matches and everything else.

"Are you afraid of me?"

"Afraid—you're just funning with me, aren't you?"

I was swallowing back fire. She shook her head.

I didn't know what else to say; fortunately, I heard my father calling from downstairs. I began to shuffle away from the door to see what he wanted. My cousin's voice stopped me.

"Teddy, I need to tell you a secret, okay?"

I edged back to the door.

"Sure, okay."

"Promise not to repeat it?"

"I promise."

"Swear?"

There was so much hesitation in her tone that I knew I had to be really convincing.

"I swear. I swear as hard as I can and hope lightning strikes my heart and shrivels it down to a walnut."

I waited.

She gestured for me to come closer to the door opening, and when I could feel her breath on my cheek, this is what she whispered: "Sometimes I wake up the dead."

Two

The Mud Room

She called herself Judith.

She insisted that I call her that, too. She would simply ignore me if I called her Ilona, though it didn't matter how anyone else referred to her.

"Why do you want a different name?" I said on her second day with us. You see, I just couldn't figure her out; I feared that she was saying things, making up stuff, to show up my gullibility—like that crazy thing she'd said about waking up the dead. Did she think I was just a stupid farm boy? Dead people don't wake up. They rot. Maggots lunch on them. Finally, they get to be skeletons. It works the same way with animals. Birds, too. Even snakes.

"Because 'Ilona' doesn't fit who I am," she said.

That one stopped me.

"But it's what your parents named you, isn't it?"

She shrugged. A cute frown wormed across her forehead.

"I want to be called Judith because that's the name of Shakespeare's sister."

I had heard of William Shakespeare at school, but I didn't know he had a sister. It made me wonder what else Miss Sisler had neglected to tell us.

"Did she have black hair like yours?"

"Teddy, you're too much," she said. Little lines of exasperation webbed the corners of her mouth.

I stared at her lips. I wanted to kiss them. I would have risked damnation to kiss them.

"No, really, I thought maybe she looked like you or you looked like her."

She pushed a small book in my face, a foxed, dog-eared volume: *A Room of One's Own* by Virginia Woolf. I was not familiar with it. With a mildly impatient smile, she said, "Judith is an imaginary person. She wanted to be an actress, but the world wouldn't let her and so she killed herself. She lives in here, and I think she's neat."

My cousin tapped the book, and I said, "Is she a ghost?"

"Teddy, Teddy," she murmured, shaking her head.

And that was the end of the conversation.

My father had told me that I could make up for my unacceptable behavior on the day my cousin arrived by serving as her guide to the farm and her helper in getting settled into the house. Accordingly, our first days together were spent doing as my father requested. I would hear his truck roar to life shortly after dawn for the drive to Council Grove where he worked as a farm implement mechanic. Fortunately, most days Jack and Junior would head out early, too, both being in demand for farmwork in the area, baling hay or feeding cattle in the massive feedlots dotting the Flint Hills.

That left Judith and me with my mother all day.

It was not a harmonious trio.

My mother was not a morning person. She would rise after my father and brothers had left and sit at our kitchen table sipping coffee in her bathrobe and looking morose, her hair uncombed, her face a stranger to make-up. Her indolence rendered her unlike any other farm wife and mother I knew.

For breakfast, I would boil or poach an egg for Judith and me. To make the offering edible, I would add several pieces of toast slathered with peanut butter and wash everything down with fresh milk pimpled with globs of cream; Judith would eat only the egg and nurse a small glass of iced tea. She never slurped and her swallows were as silent as the moon. My mother would often watch Judith as if she expected her to launch into a spastic fit or drop dead on the spot. Or maybe even change her fork into a toad. About my mother's only words to my cousin were, "You aren't getting sick on us, are you?" I never heard her speak my cousin's name.

My mother turned Judith into a pariah.

No one else was allowed to use Judith's plate and silverware or glass. Her clothing and bedding were washed separately. From somewhere, *Reader's Digest,* I believe, my mother gathered the latest myths and theories on polio and would recite them, not *to* us, but rather to herself in a voice too loud for anyone else in the room not to hear.

"Don't you dare ever drink after her," my mother told me in Judith's presence.

"She doesn't have smallpox," I snapped back. "But she *does* have a name."

At night I would hear my mother complain to my father that "the child" or "the girl" was an impossible burden or a morals-corrupting influence on a Christian household; sometimes she would misquote irrelevant passages from the Bible in support of her backstabbing message. She would conclude with an insistence that my father call and have his sister or brother come get "the child." My father would meet her vile words softly and calmly, somehow managing to assuage her fears and temper her demands.

Things worked best when Judith and I stayed out of my mother's sight, leaving her to ghost about the house doing domestic tasks to fill the hours. When she wasn't reading the Bible (she would even take it to the outhouse with her), she would sometimes sew or iron, both being tasks that put her in a gauzy trance. With my help she would also can fruits and vegetables; she seemed to like the cool, musty confines of the cellar where we kept the Mason jars filled with corn, green beans, and whatever fruit I could filch from the Trogler orchard. One day in the cellar, Judith in earshot, my mother said, "Teddy, don't let that girl teach you to love the darkness."

I suspected that my mother slept a good part of the time. Basic chores such as feeding the chickens, pumping water from our well, and tending the garden were assigned to me. I also helped my father with the evening milking. I never thought of Judith as one of those chores. I tried to make her feel better about her upstairs room, but she could never warm to it.

"I don't mind it so much when I'm asleep," she explained early on.

She put her clothes in the dresser drawers and in the closet and her personal treasures on a nightstand right next to her bed. Those included the Woolf book, a notepad (with pencil attached to it by a string and a thumbtack) and strips of leather knotted up that she called monkey fists. When I asked about them she said that twisting leather into monkey fists helped her cope if her various pains got too severe. She also carried a bobby pin which she had named Slim. She used it to deal with intense itching in her ears. Perhaps elsewhere, too. I didn't let on that I thought it was weird to give a bobby pin a name. She kept her matches hidden.

I saw to it that Judith got our best chamber pot, a pure white enamel number that my father had purchased at the hardware store one winter when our banker and his wife came to our house for dinner. As I recall, it remained unused that night. Judith kept it tucked away discreetly under the front of the bed. She always thanked me for emptying it.

Mornings, before the sun hammered full force down on our farm, I would take her on a tour of "the property" (as my father called it), highlighting a different area each time. We would peer into the shadowy maw of the storm cellar and we would prime our new pump. My father was especially proud of the latter, painting the assembly John Deere green. The well produced clean, cool water, but my father insisted that we store it in a large milk cannister and boil it before drinking it. To help purify the water, my father would dump a cup of Clorox in the cannister. Once, too eager to wait for the water to be boiled and then cooled with a chunk of ice, I dipped into the Clorox-flavored brew. It was godawful tasting. Made my stomach gurgle. Made my pee smell funny. For weeks after taking a big swallow of that water I was convinced I would never be able to father children.

Our old cistern was dry, and the dilapidated windmill straddling it cried out as if in pain when the wind blew and its rusted parts groaned and moaned. Judith feared the cistern, the rotted planks ineffectually covering the opening, and the moldy-smelling darkness, the bottom of which she could never make out. I didn't help matters by mentioning that my brothers often alluded to that Creature from the Black Lagoon–like monster they claimed resided down there. I had gut-flinching, really scary images in my head of that overgrown lizard man carrying off Judith the way he had stolen off with that babe in the movie—you know, the one in the white bathing suit. Judith bit at her lip bravely through the dark encounter with the cistern.

But she loved the windmill.

"I can identify with it," she said.

As was often the case, I nodded at her words, embarrassed at not being able to fully comprehend what she meant.

I showed her the implement shed and gave her a boost so that she could sit up in the metal seat of our tractor. I explained what a plow and a harrow were for. We stepped around chicken shit in the coop, and I demonstrated how to reach up into the nests to gather eggs and yet be mindful of the possibility that a coiled-up bull snake would have beaten one's fingers to the prize. That had happened to me once; never again did I reach into a nest with a steady hand.

"Seems like there's a serpent in every Eden," Judith remarked to my narrative of the encounter with the egg-stealing snake.

Judith liked our banties. If they took a notion to let her pick them up, she would hold their feathers against her cheek and cluck lovingly at them and sometimes even put her nose to their beaks. It was the only summer I ever envied a bantam chicken for any reason.

On days when Judith was not in too much pain, we would venture on longer treks, out into our forty-acre pasture where we'd watch our Holsteins graze and over to the far corner to the family burial plot where my paternal grandmother and grandfather were buried. We didn't get close to it because my mother always told me never to step on a grave or I might go blind. We swung over to the other corner, too, where

Rock Creek meandered, poking an elbow onto our property. The water wasn't deep, except for one hole inhabited by perch and red horse minnows. Then into the cornfield (which Judith christened "the dragonfield"—I loved that name!) and on over to the Trogler's pond where we would sit in the shade of the chorus line of willows and wait for soft-shelled turtles to part the water nose first as if they had been pulled up by pearl-like bubbles and we would marvel at how slithery moccasins could skate so effortlessly across the surface. Remembering my mother's declaration about swimming in farm ponds causing polio, I asked Judith if that's how she got her affliction. She just shook her head. Mostly we would just sit and talk about nothing in particular—mostly I would listen to Judith. I loved her voice. I was certain an angel had touched her vocal chords.

And we would gaze at the back of the Trogler place—the barn and the house.

And at the orchard.

For a score of days, despite Judith's request that we explore the property, I resisted. I can't really explain why. Then one day I said, "If you eat the green ones from those crab apple trees you'll get the trots." I gestured toward the orchard from our customary vantage point.

Judith giggled.

"Do you want to take a chance, Teddy?"

It was a seductively vague question. I led the way on a warm, summer morning.

And that's when a lot of the really strange stuff, frightening stuff first started.

From the second major notch in the crab apple tree I was ruler of all I surveyed. Best of all, Judith, sleeved with her crutches and braces, was looking up at me with something that resembled admiration. I hoped like crazy I wouldn't fall.

"Here's one that's pretty much ripe," I said, tossing a small, hard apple smeared with red on two sides, green everywhere else, down to Judith. It smacked against her palms and bounced to the ground. She shrieked softly and then retrieved it with difficulty. I swear to you it was one of the most innocent scenes you could imagine, but it didn't stay that way. What I recall is that Judith took a modest bite out of that apple and juice ran sensuously from one corner of her mouth. I almost leaped down to her side to kiss away the first dribbles.

"It's really tasty, Teddy," she exclaimed through her delicate chewing. Then it seems to me that she lifted the once-bitten apple up toward me and said, "Here, you take a bite, too, and we'll be just like Adam and Eve."

I remember smiling. I thought my cousin looked sexier than Marilyn Monroe or any other movie star you could name. And I started to climb down to claim my prize (the apple or Judith or both?) when it began: a barely perceptible tremor. The earth beneath the orchard kind of hummed for a moment. It was like some unimaginable machine was cranking up. The ground stirred. Dust puffed up and swirled.

And the look on Judith's face—sounds weird, I know, but in there was an instant flash of disappointment. Like she had been hoping something wouldn't occur but suddenly it *was* occurring. I jumped, and when I hit the ground I could feel the vibration beneath my bare feet. Strangest of all, the wind picked up—which in Kansas is as common as sunrise—but this wind came from *under* us.

A wind carrying something like a voice.

A moan. Several moans. Wind-blown, swirling moans.

I glanced at Judith. I blinked hard and my heart braked like it was about to run into something. I kind of froze at what I momentarily saw: it was a terrifying image of Judith in flames. Like a picture I once saw of Joan of Arc.

A cold burning. No heat from the flames.

Then it passed, and Judith was right there, not in flames, though plenty upset. She was having trouble keeping her balance. Another pocket of dust mushroomed up around her; she shrieked and then she pressed into my arms and I held her and didn't want to let go. I wanted to squeeze her inside me and keep her there. We were locked in that embrace when we heard one other sound ghost up over the windy moans—it was the muted growl of a dog.

The growl of a mean, I-mean-business dog. A threatening growl.

Watchdog growl.

Then silence.

Her face buried in my shoulder, tears in her throat, Judith whispered, "I'm so sorry, Teddy." Then she leaned away and held her stomach like she was sick. "I feel it—I feel something." She pressed her fingertips between her legs.

I was scared.

Then one more sound.

A small explosion of laughter. Very strange. Not like somebody laughing at Lucille Ball or Milton Berle or Red Skelton—no, this was more like the laughter of relief. The laughter of somebody being set free.

I pulled Judith toward the post rock barn; she moved as fast as her braces and crutches would allow. Once inside the cool, shadowy, vacant confines I felt a little better. I think Judith did, too. I might have still been breathing funny—you know, not quite able to catch my breath. Like I'd been punched in the stomach. Otherwise, it was simply good to be out of the orchard. The Kansas wind, I reasoned, had played tricks on us.

"Don't be sorry," I whispered to her.

She swiped at some tears and nodded.

"Maybe they'll stay where they belong," she said.

This probably won't make a lot of sense, but when she said that I got mad.

"Don't say stuff like that. You're talking about the Troglers, aren't you? You're talking about dead people and ghosts, and I don't believe it, and if you're going to stay at our farm this summer, you gotta quit it. Do you hear me?"

I was suddenly shaking, mostly from the jolt of anger, but also maybe from fear and confusion. Lots of confusion. I knew that I had told her I believed in ghosts, but what had happened in the orchard shook me up, made me determined, I guess, *not* to be seduced by overtures from what might possibly be the supernatural. I was digging in my heels, being stubborn and mule-headed.

I wanted Judith ghost-free.

But it wasn't going to work out that way.

After my little anger snit, Judith lowered her eyes. My God, she looked beautiful—like maybe one of those Madonna figures you see in real old paintings. I think I even imagined a halo floating above her head. And I wanted to bark out that I was real, real sorry for yelling at her, but I couldn't. I just couldn't.

Then, as if we had suddenly started all over and everything on both sides was forgiven, she raised her eyes slowly and gazed up into the rafters and, a smile of wonderment rising, said, "Oh, look, Teddy. Do you see them?"

I gritted my teeth, thinking maybe she was pointing at something I couldn't see. And, at first, that was the truth. I saw nothing. But I heard . . . well, like wings flapping very softly. Like the American flag on our flagpole at school when a breeze tugs at it. I started to say that she was just hearing the wind when I began to see them . . . one by one . . . like bolls of cotton blossoming . . . and hovering.

"Gee whiz," I whispered. "Gee golly whiz."

A flock of white pigeons materialized or maybe they had been there all the time and I just hadn't seen them. They beat against the shadows. They held their positions in flight as if they wanted to make certain we saw them.

I looked at Judith and I smiled and she smiled back. And it's going to sound sappy, but I felt all warm and loving—inside, you know. And I reached for Judith's hand and it was warm and a little sweaty—like my own. We continued smiling at each other, and even when we looked up again and the pigeons were gone, we kept smiling. I'm not sure why.

We were leaving the barn headed slowly, uncertainly away from it when both of us turned at about the same time and glanced back into the shadowy darkness. A sound reached out at us like a giant arm: "Who-o-o, who-o-o."

I swallowed, and without looking at Judith I said, though not convincingly, "It's just an ole owl. That's all."

I think maybe Judith nodded. We continued holding hands, bound to each other as if our flesh had been fused or soldered. We stood there, maybe ten feet from the barn, just staring into that big square of darkness. When my eyes adjusted, I saw—or thought I saw—a lot of dust motes swirling right in front of the far wall of the barn. It was like they had swirled up from the dirt floor. Like a dust devil. Only they weren't spinning that fast. I know this doesn't sound very scary, but I'm telling you the truth—it was. I figured Judith saw the dust, too. For some reason, I didn't want to ask her if she did. We were there, rooted to the ground, gripping each other's hand pretty tightly.

We didn't hightail it until the dust motes shaped into something that looked like the outline of a man. We heard that owl sound again, only this time I knew it wasn't an owl. It was a human voice.

I swear it was.

If it had been up to me, we would have chased on home then. We stopped at the Trogler cistern, maybe because I had always considered it good luck to toss a rock into it. The metal tower and windmill had long since toppled and been taken away, and there was no cover on the gaping maw, but unlike our old cistern, this one still had water in it. My father said a spring fed it. I found a rock and was going to let Judith drop it in, but she said she was kind of scared, and so I did it for her.

Geez, did we get a jolt.

The splash we heard was as big as if a grown man had fallen into it.

The creepiest part of my imagination had been kicked into action, and I just wanted to give it a rest. Judith sensed that I wasn't eager to stay on the Trogler property any longer. But she was gazing at the screened door at the rear of the derelict house. Hanging by only one hinge, the door swung out from the house at a drunken angle; the screen itself was ripped in several places; a couple of grasshoppers clung to the crossboard. It was a comically pathetic scene, but something about that sad and always-open door offered an irresistible invitation to enter. To Judith, at least.

Behind us, I heard the cawing of crows. I swung around. A murder of them sat in the top limbs of the massive cottonwood tree at the far end of the pond. That Goliath of a cottonwood was so tall that when you stood at the base of it you got dizzy if you tried to gawk up at the shimmering leaves at its crown. Lightning had scarred that old monster tree, but it remained standing, defiant and wise and somehow holy. When I was real small, I thought God lived down in its roots.

The crows cawed again—five caws; that must mean something in crow talk—and then they took flight.

"It's okay, Teddy," said Judith. "I think my Fiery Angel will protect us."

I whined a weak protest, shrugged and followed my cousin into the house. I remember thinking about the blue flame, and I was itching to ask about her Fiery Angel. I was maybe even a little jealous of him (it?). The reason I didn't say anything was that once I was there inside, in what had been the kitchen, I felt a surge of something like fascination, something beyond what I had felt in my most recent visit. I sensed that Judith made the difference. How so? I don't know. It was as if suddenly the empty, dust-laden house had become more . . . *alert*. Like it was watching us.

I can't explain it.

We spent about a half an hour nosing around in all the rooms and trekking up the stairs that threatened not to hold our weight—it was a real effort for Judith to negotiate them, but she was determined. I regretted not being strong enough to lift her up the stairs the way Charles Atlas would have. After a while, I relaxed. I didn't feel the house was so hostile. It was

fun being there. With Judith, it was fun. And I could
tell she found the place interesting. More than that,
when she entered a new room she would sort of nod,
you know, as if she were remembering it, as if she had
been there before. She saw the place with eyes that
seemed to see the history of things. I wanted those
same eyes. I wanted to know whether all the weird stories I had heard about the Troglers were true. At the
same time, maybe I didn't.

Tired by our rambles, we drifted into the front
room. The ceiling had a gash opened in it large
enough for a horse to fall through. We sat down on
one of Emmitt Suggs' mounds of milo and stared up
through the hole and tried to imagine how it had gotten there. I was feeling pretty good even though I
sensed that Judith remained kind of uneasy about the
place. I silently hoped she wouldn't bring up the topic
of ghosts or dead people. I had experienced enough
things I couldn't fully explain—I didn't want her to
fire up my imagination. Of course, I also didn't want
her to see that the Trogler place had the potential to
scare me back into being a little boy again.

Nope, didn't want that.

We were sitting there talking away about I don't remember what, letting kernels of milo shift through
our fingers like sand in an hourglass. I was drinking
in the odd beauty of Judith's face and she was smiling
shyly at me when all of a sudden her eyes were drawn
to something above. She shivered involuntarily, and a
snake of wind coiled up around us. I blinked away
dust and then I followed the angle of her eyes. Suddenly I saw it, too.

It was a playing card.

It was fluttering down from upstairs, down through
that gaping hole in the ceiling. It fell like a leaf from

an elm tree in autumn: tumble, tumble, spin, tumble, until it landed on the floor.

"Hey," I said, marvel in my voice. "Where'd that come from?"

Judith shrugged. For a score of seconds, neither of us made a move to pick it up. It was face down a few feet from us. All I could think about were the times I had played strip poker with my older brothers. I always suspected that they cheated. Leastwise, it never failed that somehow I ended up naked.

We pushed up from the milo mound; I took a deep breath of courage, but when I picked up the card and looked at it, my whole face frowned. I was expecting a regular playing card, you know—a six of diamonds or maybe a jack of hearts or even an ace. This was a card like I'd never seen before: It showed this guy hanging upside down. He had long, blue hair and wore this colorful outfit—red, blue and yellow, the yellow being the color of something like a skirt he wore, and he had on long, red hose and blue shoes.

"It's Le Pendu!" Judith exclaimed.

When I turned the card the other way, the man appeared to be dancing. Neat trick—one way hanged by his feet; the other way dancing. I looked at Judith; she seemed really intrigued, maybe delighted.

"You know what kind of card this is?" I asked.

"Sure, Teddy, it's a tarot card. This is The Hanged Man."

She explained how tarot cards were used to tell somebody's fortune. Could have been left over from the days of the witch girl, Romina. I scoffed at the idea, but I kept the card because it almost seemed that it had been dealt to me. Maybe I had plugged into the ironic doubleness of what it depicted: dancing and being hanged. Maybe intuitively I saw into the significance of the man with the blue hair. Maybe, in a way, I was his brother. Or would become so as time passed.

Things moved real fast from that point to the moment Judith and I found ourselves at the edge of the dragonfield, huffing and puffing, fear sweating out of us in big drops. Here's what happened: I was standing there studying the card of The Hanged Man, thinking how a guy dressed like that couldn't possibly come to our school and not be thought of as a sissy pants or a queer or both. In the next heartbeat Judith was screaming, and I mean a loud, grab-you-by-the-balls scream.

There was something in the mound of milo.

Something buried there. Something moving.

Something writhing to the surface.

Paralyzed, we watched as it emerged: the filmy outline of a horrible face.

A face of dust.

No nose, no lips.

One eye closed; one savage, fiery eye opened and staring right at us.

When we'd caught our breath from running, I remember saying to Judith that we couldn't tell anybody what we'd seen, especially not my older brothers. They would crucify me with their teasing. Judith sort of agreed, but then she said something that I'll never forget.

"Oh, Teddy, it's started. It has. This is where summer ends."

Though our outings usually exhausted her, Judith would thank me for being her "escort," and frequently she would lean over when I wasn't looking and kiss my bare shoulder as she had that first evening. I could never quite figure out that gesture. Was it merely a "blood" kiss? A harmless kiss that a sister might give a brother? Or was it more?

I wondered how such a seemingly innocent kiss could stir me so.

We stayed away from the Trogler place for several days. Didn't talk, above a whisper, about what we'd seen. I didn't escape having a couple of bad dreams. So it went.

After I'd accompany Judith back to her room, I would help her take off her braces and her sandals, and she would ask me to rub her calves and, on occasion, to massage her just above her knees. I did so with sparks of arousal showering my throat. She never gave any indication that she knew how moved I was. She never gave any indication whether she herself was likewise moved. Then she would announce that she had to take off her dress and lie down—my cue to leave. Once, as I was going, she said, "Teddy, I'm not really crippled. It's more like I'm broken. Do you understand?"

I said I did. And wished I wasn't lying.

On the morning I introduced her to our outhouse I steeled myself to sound matter-of-fact and adult, careful to mask any sign of embarrassment. After all, I reasoned, it was a facility built to deal with bodily functions in a crude yet relatively civilized way. Indoor plumbing for our old house seemed a distant dream. My father had constructed a clean, solid two-holer— nowhere did it leak and, if I didn't neglect to sprinkle lime down the holes every other day, the odor was tolerable. When I had shown Judith how the door hooked and where the rolls of toilet paper were, I felt I had done my job.

"What's the axe handle for?" she said, pointing at

the only object in sight not having an obvious function.

"Oh, that. For spider webs," I said. I took the handle and reamed it around both holes to demonstrate the proper procedure. "Spiders love this place. Black widows, especially. So you have to be kind of careful and keep webs from building up."

Judith listened patiently to everything I told her about our farm, and whenever I would attempt a bit of humor she would reward me with a heartbreakingly shy and lovely smile. Her favorite place was our barn, a fact that generated a serious conflict for me. It was one story of rocks piled high and then cemented with an icing of mortar. At one end of it were the milking stalls and manger and at the other the hay mow where bales of alfalfa created a marvelously cozy fort. Judith found the dark and aromatic area particularly enchanting.

"Oh, I could live here," she said.

"Yes, it's neat all right."

But even as I agreed, I couldn't keep from thinking of David. This was his favorite spot, too. More than that, in these comfortable and sheltered confines he and I had spent hours and hours talking and looking at comic books and sealing our friendship. One day over Christmas vacation he had biked out to our farm wrapped in a blanket, and once we had settled in our lair of hay he surprised me by stripping down to his underwear. He invited me to do the same. At first I was reluctant. But he called me "my little Red," and he stroked my face with the back of his hand. When I became more receptive, he unbuttoned my shirt and licked at my stomach like a friendly dog. We giggled, and I remember how the blood pulsed behind my eyes and how there seemed to be nothing wrong with what we were doing.

It was cold that day. We could see our breath as we huddled, almost naked, beneath the heavy blanket and enjoyed the warmth of each other's body. David's seemed perfect. His skin was the color of honey. His hands were somehow warm and so were his lips. We held each other and he kissed my forehead again and again, sighing and whispering, "You are my little Red and I love you."

I couldn't say it back. Not those words. Instead I said, "I like you, too, David. We're best pals."

A year or two older than me, he was disappointed. He stared at me, and those crystalline green eyes were cold and hard.

"You're not ready for this," he said. "I can tell."

Aroused and frustrated and puzzled each in our own way, we dressed hurriedly and David biked home. During the weeks and months that followed we did not repeat our secretive exchange of affection. We wrote notes, David's longer and more mature than mine. In one he told me that he would give me a chance in the summer to show how my feelings for him had grown. Nothing more was said. The school year ended, and David and his parents and younger sister had gone on vacation, to somewhere in Minnesota, where they were to spend a month in a cabin by a lake.

I was glad that he knew nothing of Judith; and she, nothing of him.

"I bet it's warm here in the winter, just like it's cool here in the summer. And it's a good hiding place." Judith was enjoying herself; she smiled coyly and asked, "Do you ever bring your girlfriend out here?"

It suddenly felt as if I were trying to swallow a hay-hook. But I managed to compose myself, despite the flag of my nerves whipping in the breeze of my discomfort.

"Hey, I don't have a girlfriend."

"You don't?"

I didn't know how to respond to her surprise, perhaps because I was caught between two scenarios burning in my thoughts: the first was of Judith and me stripped down to our underwear and huddled beneath a blanket in the dead of winter, embracing, exploring, enjoying; the other was the same scene with the unexpected intrusion of David.

I felt dizzy and claustrophobic.

"Let's get out of here," I said. "I'll boil you an egg for lunch."

It was fine with me that the curious events at the Trogler place began to fade into that realm of personal fantasy where you tell yourself, "No, that didn't *really* happen." It would have been okay with me, in fact, if we hadn't gone back to the Trogler place the rest of the summer. But fate or the wind-blistered gods of Kansas had something else in mind. Judith might have understood the metaphysics of it—I sure didn't.

One noon hour Jack and Junior came home unexpectedly with their cohort, Mickey Palmer, in tow. Judith and I were on the back porch playing with Oatmeal, the stray cat that was becoming less and less of a stray as summer wore on. He was a pathetic creature, always hungry, always covered with cockleburs and something that looked like mange. Mucus seeped from the inner corners of his eyes. My mother had demanded that he remain on the property only one day. My father was to cart him off somewhere down the road, where he would renew his begging for a friendly voice of welcome and a handout. As I petted the cat wherever I could find a healthy patch of fur, Judith had out her pad and pencil. Curious, I said, "Are you going to make a picture of him?"

"No," she said. "I'm thinking about immortalizing him with a poem. I'll call it, 'Ode on a Stray Cat'."

I chuckled. Don't know why. But the word "immortalizing" tumbled dangerously in my thoughts, its sharp points threatening to draw blood. It sounded like a word I should know. I did know that an ode was some kind of poem and I was about to say that I had read one when the three sweaty, dusty intruders burst through the screen door. They were tall and bronzed and shirtless. Junior, his mind obviously on something else, shoved past us indifferently, but Jack slowed. He was carrying his javelin.

"What you up to, snotlicker?" he said, jabbing at me with the tip.

I had been giving my brothers a wide berth for several days because I knew they still had revenge in mind. They had ratcheted up my anxiety by pretending they had forgotten about my having called them names.

I was about to explain how we'd been taking care of the stray when Mickey, eyeing Judith and grinning malevolently, stepped forward and lifted the cat out of my hands. I hated and feared Mickey, his foul mouth, his offhanded brutality, and his obsession with violence. He was a star basketball player, and I watched him, petrified with terror, as his large hands cupped the cat as if it were a wadded up t-shirt. Those same hands performed wonders with a basketball; those same hands, the gossip went, had abused Wendy Wentworth, his achingly beautiful blond girlfriend and head cheerleader for our high school. As Mickey held the cat, he stared at Judith. He drew in a breath and showed his teeth; his eyelids were hooded and he looked sleepy and very, very mean. Then he glanced at Jack and said, "So, this the polio pussy you was telling me about? This the crippled cunt? Wish I had a cousin with cupcakes like hers." He held his gaze on Judith's breasts, and I felt like I had been kneed in the throat.

White dots of rage spun in front of my eyes like tiny insects. I knew I had to do something, so I lunged at him and stomped my foot and tried to shout through my nearly paralyzed vocal chords.

"It's *not* polio! You don't know nothin'! Leave her alone!"

Mickey and Jack exploded into laughter at my hapless attempt to defend my cousin. I was making a foolish spectacle of myself (as I had before) and risking a thrashing, as well. I dared not look at Judith. All I could think was that she'd leave as a result of this scene. She'd ask my father to take her back to Topeka. Take her somewhere away from this place in which she could not be protected.

My hands had balled into fists and I was shaking.

When the two of them finally reined in their laughter, I anticipated the worst.

Mickey, a cool, dull, gleam of madness in his eyes, put one hand gently on my shoulder and grinned into my face.

"What's the deal here, Teddy?" he said. "This young lady been sucking your weenie for you?"

My haymaking swings struck nothing. In fact, all they accomplished was the spawning of another round of laughter. I was spared from further miles of humiliation and an onslaught of physical injury only by the reappearance of Junior who swept through the room, angrily motioning for the other two to follow. When the screen door slammed behind them, I felt the knots in my stomach relent. Then I heard Judith whisper, "Teddy, they took our cat."

I scrambled to the door and hollered through the screen.

"Hey, give us back that cat."

Mickey was already twenty yards or so away. He wheeled around like a gunfighter, his face contorted with glee. He glanced down at the cat, seemingly surprised that he was still holding it. His voice carried a chilling lilt. "Sure," he said. "He's coming at you."

The thud had an oddly muted yet resonant sound like a firecracker going off in the bottom of a barrel. Mickey punted the animal with his heavy boot, and I heard it squeal once, more like a castrated pig than a cat, and watched it tumble in the air and splat onto the ground, where it writhed in pain. I heard Mickey's laugh grow more distant. I felt Judith's fingers pinching at my shoulder.

Like the coward I was, I waited for my brothers and Mickey to roar off in Junior's old car before I went out to check on the cat, Judith at my heels making soft, distraught noises. It seems that when the cat hit the ground it yowled, rolled around some and then, probably disoriented by its injuries, crashed into the concrete footing of the house, determined to escape to some kind of safety. The initial crash dazed it. When it awkwardly righted itself, it looked our way.

At my shoulder, Judith gasped.

The kick had popped one eye out of its socket; it glistened against the gray fur like a brand new marble. Fearing that we were its enemy, the cat rammed several times more into the footing, hoping to find a hole large enough for it to gain the shelter of the crawlspace.

It was a sickening sight to behold.

At last the cat wheeled, shook its head violently, then sped into the dragonfield.

I believed Mickey Palmer, at that moment, to be the

cruelest person in the universe. The most evil. More
evil than Satan or the communists or the hydrogen
bomb.

"Oatmeal!" I cried.

Keeping a line of sight on the row of corn into
which the cat had disappeared, I ran after it. Judith
was not too far behind. My mind was completely
blank as I chased down the row, the corn stalks whipping at my legs. I continued chasing, stopping only
when I saw that Oatmeal had made it through the
corn and on to the Trogler place, slipping under the
house in a gray blur. Breathing hard, I turned to find
Judith approaching, locked in a vacuous stare. She
didn't cry. In fact, she didn't even speak. She patted
her lips with her quivering fingers, and I went to her
and I held her and told her over and over that I was
sorry.

That horribly injured cat was to haunt us all summer. So was the image of Mickey Palmer's cruelty.
Neither Judith nor I fully comprehended his motiva-
tion. In our weaker moments we would imagine
possible punishments for Mickey—Judith favored
burning him at the stake—but nothing ever sounded
severe enough to me. We concluded that his blood
must run cold and that his heart was frozen. Winging through the intoxicating air of poetry one day,
Judith said of him: "There is no furniture of love in
the empty rooms of his soul."

Not a day passed that we didn't attempt to coax
Oatmeal out from under the old Trogler house. In
the course of our efforts, we learned for certain that
we were to be haunted by something more than the
phantoms of cruelty—something ghostly was stirring,
and I found that I could no longer deny it. Embrac-

ing caution, Judith and I did not go into the abandoned house or the barn or even the orchard. Didn't even throw anything down the cistern. We would hunker down near where Oatmeal had dashed into the crawlspace and call for him. We would fill bowls with water and food and scoot them through an opening resembling a giant missing tooth. Miraculously the cat stayed alive. I told my father about Mickey's mindless act. He shook his head the way a man does when confronted by the darkest mysteries of existence. There was nothing much he or anyone else could do. Mickey's parents were divorced, and his uncle was the county sheriff, a gruff, belligerent man who thought Mickey hung the moon. He loved to brag about the boy's athletic feats.

On nearly each of our trips to tend to Oatmeal—it was as if we were visiting him in prison—we would encounter something strange. Out of the corners of our eyes, we would see movement, something faintly human, or we would hear barely audible voices, the kind of voice that you might hear from someone very weak and fighting to get stronger. Or we would hear the muffled bark of a dog.

And once Judith saw the blue flame flickering in an upstairs window.

But I did not.

One morning Judith and I both saw one half of a man's face peeking around one corner of the house. It scared us. I ran in a wide half circle to see if maybe it was Emmitt Suggs, but this was a younger man, and when I reached a vantage point, I saw no one. Whoever it was had completely disappeared.

"Teddy," said Judith, her fingers twirling strands of that beautiful black hair, "you saw it, too, didn't you?"

I did, but I didn't want to admit it.

Then she put her hand on my shoulder and said, "I don't think I can stop what's happening."

I continued to believe she couldn't possibly have generated the strange goings on at the Trogler place; I certainly didn't hold her accountable for them, and it troubled and irritated me that she sounded so guilty.

Truth is, I was much more worried about my mother's dislike of Judith than I was about ghosts. During the second week of Judith's residence on our farm my mother's preoccupation with getting my cousin permanently out of the house seemed to obsess her. One day we learned her main ploy: pack Judith off to see the county nurse, Mrs. Wallace, and thus validate her notion that my cousin required more competent attention than we could give her.

"This is just a precaution," my mother told Judith. "Your own mother would appreciate us making sure you're not getting sicker or more crippled. You never know when something might happen to someone in your horrible condition."

One weekday afternoon each month our local physician, Doc Gillis, an emaciated octogenarian who reminded me of a snowy egret, gave his office space over to Edie Wallace, who drove up from Emporia to bring our town a slightly more modern and enlightened brand of medical care than Doc Gillis could provide. Mrs. Wallace was a chunky lady in her thirties, brash and flirtatious with black snappy eyes and a throaty voice. She liked to look up and down my body and wink as she popped her gum.

I liked Doc Gillis's office because he always put out copies of *Life* and *Look* and *Time* in the waiting room. I would open myself to the pages, filling my mental storage bins with images of famous people: Marilyn

Monroe, Frank Sinatra, James Dean and President Eisenhower.

"My picture and a big story about me are going to be in these magazines some day," I told Judith as we cooled our heels and my mother talked out of earshot with Wallace.

"Why would you want that?"

"Well . . . because."

"What will you do that'll make them write a story on you?"

"Something . . . something big. You'll see."

I was disappointed that Judith had any doubts about my projections of fame.

Wallace broke up our exchange, asking Judith to come with her. "Let's have a look at you, sweetie."

While they were in the examination room, my mother sat with me. She was rigid with worry and something more. I think she believed I despised her for not showing Judith affection and warmth.

"Teddy," she said, in a thin, anxious voice, "it's just that I'm afraid something will happen."

I gave her a big helping of silence.

About thirty minutes later, Wallace gestured for my mother. I trailed along, determined not to feel like a kid, but not well versed in feeling like a young adult. In the examination room Judith was lying on her back on a table, a sheet covering her from her neck to just above her knees. She was naked under the sheet except maybe for panties. I concentrated my gaze on Wallace as she explained something called the Kenny Treatment.

"In cases like this sweetie's there have been almost miraculous recoveries."

I think I must have fallen instantly in love with those words: *miraculous recoveries*. Something stirred in me as I listened ever so intently to Wallace's spiel about a

woman from Australia named Sister Elizabeth Kenny,
who believed that the diseased muscles of polio pa-
tients should be stretched and exercised after they
had been relaxed through the application of hot
packs. As Wallace talked, I noticed that my mother
edged away from the table, her mouth set grimly.
When Wallace demonstrated how to apply the packs,
which had been heated in a sterilizer and placed in a
washtub lined with heavy rubber sheets, I drew closer.
The sheets really stunk. At one point Wallace smiled
at Judith and said, "Honey, how does this feel?"

In a dreamy tone, Judith said, "Heavenly."

The packs covered her legs like armor.

To my mother Wallace said, "Mrs. O'Dell, this may
allow her to put away her braces and crutches forever.
I wouldn't want to get your hopes up too high, but the
Kenny Treatment once a day may do her a world of
good."

My mother started shaking her head. It made me
want to hit her.

"What if something goes wrong?" she whispered.

"I assure you it won't. You can use strips of woolen
blankets as packs. It does require daily application,
but—"

"No. No, no, no."

It looked as if my mother were fighting off someone
who was trying to tie her up with a rope. But Wallace
pressed on. "I'd recommend it in this case."

"No, I couldn't . . . I couldn't *touch* her. No, no."

I could tell that Wallace was shocked by my
mother's attitude. My response was to plunge into a
pool of hatred. From its depths I resurfaced claiming
to myself that I no longer had a mother. Wallace was
scrambling to keep her composure.

"But surely for the young lady's welfare you
would—"

"No!" My mother's voice pitched high like the cry of some wild bird.

Judith covered her face with her hands.

Wallace was unnerved. She obviously couldn't believe what had been said, and yet swiftly the nurse in her took control.

"Is there anyone else who might be willing? It does take a daily commitment. It's safe and I'm almost certain it would have a positive effect."

My mother's face was awash in bitterness and fear.

I knew that I couldn't bear the awful tension that filled the room. When I pleadingly sought my mother's eyes, she turned away. To Wallace I gestured helplessly with my hands. I felt something like a time bomb ticking in my chest. Wallace's lips were tight. She looked down at Judith and patted her bare foot and then shook her head, and it reminded me of the way my father had shaken his head when I had told him about Mickey Palmer. Knowing intimately my own cowardice, I still felt I had to show I would fight. I would take a swing at the implacable face of the world's evil. I would be brave because my cousin deserved to have someone act bravely in her behalf. But it was with a strained and tremulous and unreassuring voice that I said, "*I* will. I'll do it."

That evening Judith moved her things to the back porch.

My father called it the mud room because it's where muddy boots and clothing could be removed. It was screened-in on two sides. From one wall a large, rectangular closet jutted out, and there we set up a cot for Judith and helped surround her with the belongings that comforted her. The closet had a sliding door to afford privacy. Judith called the inner area her "darkness."

From the mud room you could see the Trogler place. On the night that Judith relocated herself, a nearly full moon was grinning over the top of the much-too-empty house—or, at least, I continued to fool myself into believing it was empty. Judith seemed enthralled by the view.

Overall, I'd say the mud room pleased her immensely.

"It's a room of my own," she said.

My mother, of course, sniffed her displeasure with the idea, fearing, I assume, that with exposure to the night air Judith might catch cold and generate new worries. But my father maintained that we should do whatever was necessary to make our guest comfortable.

With Judith happily situated in the mud room, I developed a secret, nightly ritual. I would rise after everyone else was asleep and go downstairs with a sheet and pillow and lie on the floor next to Judith's cot. I pretended that I was protecting her. I wanted nothing more than to impress her and please her. And just as Judith could never put aside her goal of transcending her pain, I could never free myself of my cousin's sexual pull.

In the blackness, we rarely talked, but I believed that our thoughts somehow greeted and mingled and embraced. We shared solitude and silence, and yet there were nearly always a few sounds: the distant whistle of a train, the wind soughing through the blades of our windmill, and the mewings of pain issued by the mutilated stray cat self-exiled under a possibly haunted house.

One night as Judith and I listened to that trio of

kindred sounds, she spoke. "Hear that?" she said. "Those are the voices of my heart."

I burned to say something poetic in return, but my soul lacked a muse.

That particular night Oatmeal's mewings were especially persistent. It was impossible not to respond, and so we rose and trod through the dragonfield—I was carrying a small saucer of milk—and up to the side of the Trogler place. It seemed larger and more ominous at night. We halted our advance when Oatmeal quite suddenly ceased his mewing.

Judith clawed at my wrist. I think we both knew something was about to happen.

When the barking broke through the air, it shattered the illusion of time and space. The don't-come-any-closer tone of it seemed to encircle us. It was impossible to run. Impossible suddenly to move.

Then we heard something like a shout. It seemed to come from someone walking underground. The barking cut off, but in the ensuing silence we heard more voices, a jangle of them. People talking—confused, troubled, angry talk—not loud. Yet, gaining strength.

"They can't be doing this," I whispered. "The only people here are dead. Buried in the orchard."

"I know," said Judith. "I didn't want this to happen. It's me, Teddy. I'm to blame."

"No," I cried. "Don't say stuff like that. Dead is dead."

I heard her sigh heavily, and when she spoke again it was so matter-of-fact that it was scarier than the ghostly sounds we were hearing.

"But sometimes," she said, "they just don't want to stay that way. They'll be weak at first. Barely visible. Like dust. But they'll get stronger. They'll start looking like flesh and blood people, except they won't be. They'll be made of earth."

My breathing accelerated. Became ragged.

"Earth? You mean, like *dirt?*"

She nodded.

I refused, of course, to believe it. Stupid talk. Idiotic. Except that I had seen something, too.

We were standing there in the moonlight like scarecrows.

When the voices died back, the wind gusted and covered all traces that we had ever heard a single sound out of the ordinary.

Three

The Wife of Pain

I gave Judith the Kenny Treatment every day.

Before we had left Doc Gillis's office, Mrs. Wallace showed me how to apply the hot packs. She promised she would contact us in the coming weeks to see how things were going, and she encouraged us to see her on her next visit to Saddle Rock. Flushed with anxiety, my mother told her, "Someone's coming for the girl. Before something happens, someone will come for her."

I assured Mrs. Wallace that I would follow her instructions to the letter. She hugged Judith, shook my hand and we poured out into the hot sun. At home Judith and I prepared for the Kenny as if we were going to war, a war against an invisible enemy which threatened to cripple her for life. Over time, I began to see that there were certain parallels between the specter of disease and the ghostly entities of the Trogler place—and that Judith was the one who suffered most from both of them.

Wherever she turned, she was haunted.

From the attic I hauled down winter blankets, heavy, woolen ones that had become worn and threadbare, and we cut them into strips with my

mother's sewing shears until our hands hurt. We were
in high spirits as we worked. Judith thanked me several times. "You're a good Teddy," she would say and
often kissed me on the shoulder, and I would blush.

One morning I heated water on the stove in our
big, galvanized washtub and tested some of the strips
on Judith's calves. At first I got them too hot and she
sucked in her breath and winced but didn't complain.
Eventually we found the right degree of warmth. We
set aside a period each day after lunch for the Kenny.
That way Judith could nap once we had finished. I
would leave the mud room while she got ready. She
would lie on her cot—first on her stomach and then
on her back—her body covered from neck to knees
with a thin sheet. She was mostly naked. My mother
observed us only once and that was the first afternoon
we did a complete Kenny. Arms folded against her
stomach, her mouth set firmly in a grim, straight line,
my mother peered over my shoulder and grunted her
characteristic grunt of disgust.

"You shouldn't be putting your hands on her," she
said as I placed heated woolen strips over Judith's
calves.

"Mrs. Wallace thinks it'll do her good," I said.

"Does your father know you're doing this?"

"Yes," I said, which was a lie, but not a whopper because I knew that my father would want us to help
Judith any way we could.

"Does he think you should be putting your hands
on her? What if you catch what she has and get crippled, too?"

"Ma, stop it. I got a polio shot at school. Besides, I
can't catch it from her. I explained to Pop what we're
doing and he said it's okay and hopes it'll help. Mrs.
Wallace says I can't catch something by doing this."

I was startled by how easy and guiltless it was to lie

to my mother. I could feel Judith's body quivering as
my mother and I talked. Mostly my mother simply
stood and watched, but when I pushed the sheet up
a ways to apply strips to the muscles just above Judith's
knees, she exclaimed, "Now that isn't right—what
you're doing there. It's not proper. Nothing good's
going to come of this. Look at where your hands are."
She paused. She was sending out gleams of disapproval like shook foil. "This isn't right. I'm going to
tell your father this isn't right. That girl is just like the
wicked women in the Bible, always luring men. Spider
and the fly, that's what it is. She's leading you down
the path to hell and damnation."

I hesitated as the ugly stream of words poured from
my mother. My hands were trembling, and I felt that
I was trying to keep my balance on a rim of potential
shame. My mother's words stabbed at the goodness of
the procedure. I felt wounded, and I'm sure that Judith did, too.

"We're not doing anything wrong," I said.

Hissing like a snake, my mother left the room and
said nothing more about the Kenny to me and probably not to Judith either. But she had damaged the
moment. I could not, no matter how hard I tried, con-
vince myself that my motives were pure. I wanted to
help Judith. I wanted to relieve her pain. I wanted her
to be able to toss the braces and the crutches away,
and yet the Kenny was also a good excuse for me to
get closer to Judith.

I loved touching her.

While the warm strips were soothing her calves and
thighs, I would massage her feet, sometimes tickling
her toes. Judith would squirm, but no matter what I
did, she would try to keep her eyes closed. She had
the most beautiful eyelids—they reminded me of rose
petals—and her eyelashes were as fine as the brushes

I imagined great painters used on their masterpieces. When my touch especially pleased her, she would smile sweetly, and her lips would part, lips coated with pink lipstick, a fresh application before every Kenny. I never understood why she put on lipstick before every Kenny, nor did I understand dozens of other tiny rituals that belonged to her and that she practiced with such feminine grace.

On occasion, as I rubbed and stretched her muscles, I would gaze at her breasts, the tantalizing outline of them beneath the sheet. They were full and womanly for such an otherwise thin girl. At certain intervals in the Kenny I would notice that her nipples would harden. The first time this caught my attention I found that I had an erection in a few seconds. I stopped what I was doing and Judith blinked awake.

"Teddy? Don't stop yet, please."

"Oh, I won't," I said. "Just a second. My hand got a cramp."

I couldn't tell her the truth. I couldn't tell her how much I wanted to caress her breasts, how much I wanted to put my mouth on those nipples. I sweated shame to have such desires. I had never touched a girl's breasts, never cupped them as prelude to a passionate kiss, though I had practiced such a move on the corner of my pillow at night.

Thinking such thoughts about Judith made me feel like a fraud. I *was* a fraud. Worse, I believed I was a sinner. I was sexually attracted to my cousin. I knew such an attraction was probably wrong. God was watching. It made things difficult. But the most difficult moment of all came the day I was applying a warm strip to one of her thighs and studying her inscrutable expression and suddenly her face became the face of David. I jerked away and told Judith I didn't feel like finishing the Kenny. My stomach was upset. I told her my poached egg must have been bad.

Judith never suspected anything.

She claimed that the Kennys helped her, but I know that most of the time she was in pain, and the pain created problems only she and I were aware of. For example, she developed a startle reflex because intense pain would often steal her moment-to-moment awareness. Noises—the slamming of a door or the backfire of our mailman's pickup—would make her jump out of her skin; the same was true when someone unexpectedly entered the mud room. My solution, though it wasn't fail-safe, was to wear a bracelet of tiny bells so that a soft, friendly tinkling would announce my arrival.

After her post-Kenny nap, she would awaken seemingly pain free.

"Maybe it'll stay away a lot longer this time," I said to her once as she rubbed her eyes and pulled herself from her den of slumber. "I'll help you watch for it."

"But you have to keep up your guard," she said. "Pain is sneaky." I easily adopted her image of pain as something real, something virtually human.

She smiled.

"It's always with me. I'm never completely separated from it. It's like I'm married to it, only it's not a good marriage. It's like one where the wife knows the husband is going to bust her one every day—but she doesn't know *when* he's going to do it."

It wasn't a pleasant image, but I chuckled nervously. How did she come up with such stuff?

"Married to it—that's strange," I said.

"Yes," she said, those brimming eyes reaching into my soul, "I'm the wife of pain."

* * *

I came to believe that Judith grew from some darkness within me. Selfishly, I wanted her back inside. Only then could I truly share her pain. But that, of course, was not to be. In every meaningful sense, she had to face her pain alone. Solitude was her frequent mode. I often shattered upon the rocks of that solitude. It was not her fault. In our evolving intimacy I frequently lacked imagination; it was my most fatal defect. I think Judith understood. She tolerated me, she took pleasure in me because she knew I thirsted—I did not want to live my life untouched.

Judith elevated coping with pain to an art form. Monkey fists—I wonder how many dozens of them she created that summer—were her rosary beads, each one validating the mystery and holiness of pain. She knotted them mostly from leather, but when she exhausted her supply she sought out string or wire or strips of cloth. She also coped through re-conceiving time and ritualizing it in ways only I was privy to. There was "old" time and "before" time and, the one that troubled and frightened me, "angry" time. She would slip into "old" time on those days when pain would sap her vitality and leave her pretty face looking as aged as the visage of my grandmother just before she passed away. I learned that the secret to "old" time was not to fight it; when Judith felt it coming on, she would accept it. "Teddy," she would say, "I'm 112 years old just now." Even her voice would sound old. She would let her pain hold sway and do its best to exorcize her youth, knowing that in the end a blush would return to her cheeks.

"Before" time was a tool she often used mornings when pain would awaken her, promising her a day of hell. It was a mind game on her part. She would pretend that she was the girl she was before her ghastly affliction struck her. "Before this," she would say, "I could outrun my father in a race. I bet I could have outrun you, Teddy." I maintained that she couldn't have, but I didn't press it because I didn't want that twinkle to leave her eyes. Sometimes she really got going: "I could do somersaults and cartwheels, too, and climb any tree around. I could climb your windmill." And I would enter into the spirit of things, too: "But what about our silo? I wasn't brave enough to do that until last summer." Her hands would flutter like birds taking off. "The silo, too. And I could have swum across Trogler's pond faster than any old water moccasin." I liked the exaggerated feel of our exchange so I added, "If you were Jesus, you could walk across it." She smiled and said, "I think I'd rather swim." I told her I thought I would, too.

Right around supper could be the toughest time. Steamrolled by fatigue and tempted by pain to lose her senses, she would lash out at her fate—anger would twist her face until it was hard to recognize her. At such times, she wanted to reach into her body and find the core of her pain and rip it out by its roots like weeds in our garden. "Angry" time caused her to be ashamed; usually she would not let me see her, leaving the mud room without supper and stealing off to some secluded spot. Once, I found her sitting against one of the crab apple trees in the Trogler orchard with a grocery bag over her head. She was crying and slapping at her braces. When she sensed that I was near, she screamed, apparently thinking at first that I was one of the Trogler ghosts. Then, when she knew it was me, she ceased her abuse of the braces and lifted her hands, inviting me to embrace her. She was the proverbial blind man with his cup, and I gave her all of myself that I could give.

"Angry" time often became "teary" time.

The rhythm of her voice broken by sobs, she would

say, "Teddy, count to a hundred and then I'll quit crying."

And frequently she would.

Pain siphoned off her appetite for food; to add insult to injury it would leave her constipated. I would
accompany her to the outhouse for marathon sessions
during which I could wait outside, a discreet distance
away, while Judith tried to coax nature into some degree of regularity. She gobbled Ex-Lax tablets like a
kid munching popcorn at a movie. Sometimes they
helped; sometimes not.

After one especially long sentencing in the outhouse, Judith emerged, smiled weakly and said,
"Thanks for waiting, Teddy. I guess summer must be
about over by now."

She could make me laugh at the most peculiar
times.

I loved her for it.

I wanted to say those words to her, words I somehow
couldn't say to David either.

However brutally pain had treated Judith the day
before, we would always return to the Kenny, just as
we would return to trying to seduce Oatmeal out
from under the Trogler place. We were more successful with the Kenny.

"Is it doing any good?" I asked her one evening.

"A lot," she said.

"I sure hope you get better."

She waited a good while before speaking again. It
got so quiet I imagined I could hear our hearts beating. Then she said, "When I'm strong enough, I'll run
away. I have to, Teddy, because of what I've done to
the Trogler place. It's only going to get worse—and
you and your family will be in danger. I think if I'm

not around, they—you know, the ghosts—they'll go back to being dead."

"That's stupid," I said. "You can't really believe that."

But I knew she did. I didn't want her to run away, or rather, I didn't want her to run away without me. I wasn't ready to say that, so instead, I said, "What would we tell your mother?"

She gazed into herself.

"Just say, 'Judith's gone away with her Fiery Angel'."

I held my tongue, swallowing back as so often before, questions about that guardian creature she held so dearly.

Four

Called Away

Judith was as anxious to see the world as I was.

Compared with my experiences, her travels were extensive because of a trip to Arizona she had taken with her parents several years before she got sick and her father abandoned the family. They had gone to see the Grand Canyon and the Painted Desert, and along the way had passed through the panhandle of Oklahoma and Texas and crossed the shoulders of New Mexico. On the other hand, I had yet to inch beyond the borders of Kansas. My older brothers had gone on a school field trip to Kansas City, Missouri, and had come back talking about it as if it were the greatest metropolis on the planet. My mother and father were not travelers, content instead for the world to come to them over the radio or through the newspaper. It was to be a year later before our household acquired a television set.

The thirst that Judith and I shared to hit the road and chase the next horizon caused us to obsess over maps. We loved them. We couldn't get enough of them. Of course, I knew our motivations were different—my urge was simply to be "away from here," the *here* being Saddle Rock, Kansas; for Judith, the ghosts of the Troglers and the presence of her angelic guardian influenced her desire to make tracks. Maps connected her and me like telephone lines between poles. I particularly adored some brightly colored maps in the junior high world geography book I had salvaged when our school got new texts. I knew the shapes of all the continents and the capitals of many European countries and the names of the bigger oceans and the longest rivers. But Judith knew even more. She had memorized every significant bit of information about places like India, Switzerland and Brazil and could spell "Australia" and "Israel" and "Czechoslovakia" without even pausing to think.

My father fostered our obsession by bringing us state maps he picked up free of charge from the Phillips 66 station out on the highway. Naturally we had several maps of Kansas, but we filled out our collection with ones of the surrounding states: Missouri, Nebraska, Colorado and Oklahoma. We liked the stiffness of a new map as we unfolded it, and though I was no good at folding them back up, Judith was. I begged her to reveal the secret of map folding; however, she was steadfast in maintaining that no such secret existed—you just had to have a feel for the way the folds embraced one another.

Over the summer the mud room became our map room.

Late mornings, before lunch and before the Kenny, we would create a sea of maps covering the entire floor, and we would navigate around on our hands and knees studying the distances from Topeka to St. Louis and from Tulsa to Wichita and Wichita to Omaha. We read our maps slowly and deeply. We circled the point of highest elevation in each state. We learned the most populous cities and challenged each other to memorize the names of all the Kansas coun-

ties. I was no match for Judith. She learned them all
in one day. As you might expect, we were careful not
to lay out our maps any time we thought Jack and Junior and Mickey might be tearing through. We didn't
worry so much about my mother; she indifferently tolerated our map orgies. On wash day she would tromp
through the mud room on the way to the clothesline
with a load to hang out to dry. Judith and I would giggle when she—like Godzilla—would step right in the
middle of Denver or in Governor Docking's face.

I couldn't help noticing that when Judith would
turn the state maps over and study the one of the con-
tinental United States she would frequently trace her
finger from northern Kansas out to Arizona. Seeing
her repeat that route one day, I said, "You sure like
that state, don't you? Arizona, I mean."

She nodded thoughtfully and said, "Arizona has
rocks that crowd the roads and watch your car pass by
just like cattle do around here. Rocks that are curious
but very silent."

"Oh," I said, "that sounds neat."

More honestly, I thought it was another piece of Judith's delightfully enchanting strangeness. It was clear
that she was privy to the spiritual secrets of geography
while I, on the other hand, worshiped them but did
not understand. I would have dropped the subject
had she not said, "I think maybe the Fiery Angel believes I should go there. Arizona or maybe . . . maybe
California. He whispered both states in my ear when
I woke up this morning."

I grew bold.

"Have you ever seen this Fiery Angel? I mean, what
is it? An angel like in the Bible? Wings and halo and a
white robe—maybe one that plays a long, funny trum-
pet or a harp? Or is it just something you made up?"

She looked at me for a long time. It made me nervous.

"Can you keep a secret?" she said.

Of course I said I could. My heart started beating so rapidly that I had to blink my eyes as if I were squinting into the sun. Often when I talked with Judith it seemed that way. She had the burning brightness of the sun shining within her. She could look at me and I could no more hold her gaze than I could have locked my eyes onto the sun.

And she could read the map of my soul.

In contrast, I was never really sure of the distance from her heart to mine.

"Well, you see," she began, "the Fiery Angel isn't a regular angel—not like what everybody thinks an angel is." As she continued speaking, her expression sort of floated or sailed off like a kite lifting in the wind. "He's a creature of light. The purest light you can imagine. And he's constantly transforming from the visible into the invisible, and he's more real when he's invisible."

My mouth was open like a dumb animal. It's a wonder a bug didn't fly right into it and down my throat.

"Is he, you know . . . scary?"

She nodded.

"Sometimes. Sometimes he's very scary because he's just not like us at all. But most times, he makes me feel . . . protected."

"Oh, that's good," I said.

"Teddy, he can see inside your mind. He can shine a bright light into your thoughts, and he can communicate with you without words."

She blinked out of her reverie and challenged me with her expression.

All I could do was softly whisper, "Wow."

"There's more," she said. "Sometimes I have visions

of the Fiery Angel. When I do, it's definitely a 'he,' not a 'she' or an 'it'."

That word *visions* got me flipping mentally through the pages of the Bible. At least what I'd read in it. I associated visions with a kind of holy madness, with white-bearded, fiery-eyed old men seeing into the secret rooms of Hell. The idea of Judith having visions worried me.

"Isn't that what crazy people do?" I said.

I wanted to snatch back those words the second they tumbled from my lips.

She frowned. I think I hurt her feelings, but she didn't let on.

"When I'm in awful bad pain, sometimes he comes to offer comfort and show that I'm not alone."

"Don't I do that?"

"Sure you do, Teddy. It's just that . . . the Fiery Angel is more . . . um-m-m, more personal. Do you know what I mean?"

Of course I didn't, but I said yes anyway and then I said, "Has he come around here lately?"

She hesitated so long I had to squirm.

"Yes," she said eventually. "This morning he was walking around the top of the silo."

"No kidding? Wow, I didn't think anybody could do that. Wish I could have seen him."

I just couldn't process the image of such a feat.

"But you wouldn't be able to because he's a vision. He's my personal vision."

I began to want nothing more in the world than to have a vision, and so I pressed her to teach me how to have one. She wouldn't, or, rather, she claimed she couldn't. Didn't know how. You either had visions or you didn't. The way you either had blue eyes or you didn't. It wasn't like learning to swim or drive a car. But I wasn't ready to give up.

"I bet if you showed me a couple things about it I could have one on my own."

She shook her head.

"Teddy, it doesn't work like that. I told you."

"But *I* show *you* stuff around here. Like the other day when I showed you about milking a cow."

It had been quite a scene—Judith sitting on the milking stool, pressing her head up against Belle, our best Holstein, just the way I had demonstrated, and then her long, slender fingers pulling tentatively and seductively on one teat. I had watched and had gotten aroused by the sight. And I had felt rotten about my response. I wanted to be touched by Judith. I wanted her hands on me. Some days I wanted it so much I thought maybe I was perverted.

"I'm telling you, Teddy, I can't teach you how to have a vision and that's that."

I was disconsolate the rest of the day.

Two days later I was worse than depressed—I was emotionally shaken and physically uncomfortable. Judith, knowing virtually every nuance of my body and soul, noticed. As we folded up our maps so we could help my mother put away clothes, she said, "They got you, didn't they? Your brothers got back at you. What did they do?"

I couldn't spell out the specifics to her. It would have been too humiliating. Besides, it wasn't just my brothers who had unsettled me.

"Nothing," I said.

She brushed aside my lie.

"When did they get you?"

I really hadn't planned to discuss it. Any of it. It was those eyes of hers—she could do what David could do, only better. Something irresistible. Both she and

David could place me dead center in the circle of their attention. Right where I wanted to be. It made me feel incorrigibly selfish.

Caving in, I said, "Yesterday. After your Kenny, when you were asleep."

If I hadn't been lost in fantasy again, it wouldn't have happened.

I told Judith everything.

The summer is long but not long enough when you have maniacal and revengeful older brothers. I had spent a few minutes watching Judith sleep that fateful afternoon, thinking about what it would be like to kiss her lips and recalling the delicious warmth of our embrace the day she arrived. As I drank in her appetizing slumber, I heard something—a cry—drifting on the river of the Kansas wind. Listening more closely, I detected that it was Oatmeal.

I guess I was simply called away. Even those two words now seem haunting.

I was restless, and so, though I knew there wasn't much point in it, I decided to go visit the pathetic cat. It was warm and breezy as I sauntered through the dragonfield. Summer was cooking up a batch of increasingly hotter days. The corn was growing. It was a good afternoon for a swim. If the polio threat represented by the Trogler's pond hadn't been so strong, I would have shed my overalls and dipped my naked self into its cooling waters. But I certainly didn't want anything like what afflicted Judith.

Emmitt Suggs's black pickup was parked in front of the Trogler place when I got there. It was kind of weird because he didn't see me at first—didn't see me as he hustled down the sagging steps of the front porch—then stopped out a few yards from the house and stared back at it. No mistaking, his was an expression of a man who had been frightened. I remember that he lifted his farm cap and wiped his forehead. He almost stumbled as he moved toward his truck, his eyes never leaving the house. I had to smile; in fact, I almost laughed—because that's what you naturally do when you see somebody get scared. Long as it's not you. Well, just like that Suggs happened to catch me out of the corner of his eye. He quickly composed himself and smiled sheepishly and waved. Then he got in his pickup and pulled away pretty fast. I think he was embarrassed. In a way I was glad that maybe he saw something in the house. I guess maybe he'd come to check on his mounds of milo, and he'd seen something. Just the way Judith and I had, and so that meant we weren't imagining things.

I suddenly heard Oatmeal let out one of his painful meows, and it turned my attention to him and I began moving toward the house, creeping right up to the crawl space and peering into its thick shadows. I called Oatmeal's name a couple of times. His meow filtered out to me so mournfully that it made my teeth ache. I looked harder, and I could see his one good eye shining out indifferently or maybe hopelessly. Then the cat moved to where the shadows gave way to a slice of light. I grimaced. Warm acid rose in my throat: the eye that had been popped out of its socket was now dry and brown and rested on his facial fur like a discarded raisin. I just about couldn't stand to gaze at it. But I couldn't *stop* gazing at it either. I was hunkered down there secretly wishing that Oatmeal would die. What kind of life could he have? Pity washed over those thoughts, and I began to fantasize about catching him and somehow fixing that bad eye—I would be responsible for his *miraculous recovery*.

And Judith would think I was a god.

And she would love me. Not a cousin to cousin love—real woman to man love with sex being stirred around in the stew of possibilities.

You can see how I was adrift on a dangerous sea.

What brought me back to the reality was this: The Trogler house groaned.

Just like a sick person might. Startled, I backed up in a hurry. My mouth tasted dry, filled, it seemed, with a handful of salt. Or maybe dust. The house groaned again. Then it shuddered. You could hear its weathered clapboard creak and snap. And one thing more: The incessant Kansas wind died down to nothing, and then it was so quiet I could hear the sun moving higher in the sky.

Four ghostly figures stepped out of the walls.

I stumbled back some more; I cried a short, panicked cry and felt more the rush of incredulous surprise than fear. I took them in with an astonished sweep of my eyes.

They were a family.

I knew that—I could see that—instantly. And they were almost real, almost distinct. There were creatures of dust shifting, struggling to take shape, to materialize, it seemed, as solid, elemental earth.

There was an older man—he of the hideous face— in overalls; he had longish gray hair and a sun-beaten farmer's forehead, and besides missing a nose and lips, he had, right under one eye, another terrible disfigurement—like a giant, comma-shaped indentation where maybe he'd been kicked by a horse or a mule. He was grinding his teeth and staring hard at me. They all were. And at his side he was carrying a sharp sickle or sling blade, and by the look in his eyes he wanted killing. Or worse.

Standing next to him was a grayish-haired woman,

his wife, I supposed, and she had cold, stormy, deadly eyes—the eyes of a blizzard—and she was staring right through me like she was somewhere beyond hate and revenge—somewhere no sane person ever was. Right beside her was a young man, rather large and muscular, with black curly hair, and I thought immediately he was not all there. He was taller, obviously much stronger, than the man and the woman. I say that I immediately thought he was crazy because there was madness in his expression, especially the way he was trying to smile. It was a smile that kept falling off his face. It was like that smile was a knife he was trying to balance on its point. He carried a small sledgehammer gripped tightly, his fingers eagerly kneading the handle.

But the most arresting of the four was the young woman next to him.

She was slender with long black hair; she was rather pretty in a witchy way, firelight flickering in her eyes, a dark mole—like a beauty mark—above her lip . She was spellbinding. Like the older woman—whom I assumed was her mother—she wore a simple feed-sack print dress. I also noticed right away that she was carrying Oatmeal; she was petting him gently, apparently not bothered by that hideous piece of something that had once been his eye. Seeing it closer like that, I almost puked. I would have, but I was so amazed to be in the presence of the ghostly figures that my body just sort of unplugged.

The young woman's eyes signaled for me to approach, a curiously gentle, almost maternal, here-I-have-something-I-want-you-to-see look to her.

I think I shook my head.

Then I watched her as she cupped her long, thin fingers over the cat's head. I thought she was going to strangle it, so I tried to work my tongue and my lips to protest; instead, I swallowed hard and coughed once. Because she did this thing: she lifted her hand from Oatmeal's head and his eye . . . well, it was healed. At least, I think it was. I think that's what I saw: Oatmeal with two good eyes.

I was blinking in wonder when the savage barking exploded up from the ground.

Oatmeal leaped from the young woman's hands and scrambled wildly back into the crawl space. I screamed. I'm sure I did. And I ran. I remember hearing the discordant *chinka-chinka* of my tinkle-bell bracelet.

They say in nightmarish scenes you feel like you're not running at all—not the case with me. I was running pell mell. Running like my life depended on it. Because it did. I sped into the dragonfield, my arms pumping, spittle of fear and exertion foaming at my lips. I only looked back twice. The first time almost caused me to crash down into the dirt and cornstalks. The black dog appeared bigger than a yearling calf, and it had dark sockets for eyes and teeth that seemed as huge as 16-penny nails and a tongue that lolled and dripped from a mouth so hungrily that I could imagine I had already been bitten—that hunks of my flesh had been torn away. That I was prey. That I would be eaten alive.

I ran as hard as I could. Harder maybe. And I yelled for help until my throat burned.

I knew I was doomed. No one would hear me. No one would save me.

But when I glanced over my shoulder a second time a strange kind of tingling warmth began to spread through me because I could see the monstrous dog losing ground. And fading. Fading. Fading into a swirl of dust. Fading until its savagery was miraculously gone. I gradually slowed. Then stopped. I was so shaken that I just stood there in the corn with the hot sun beating down on me, and I cried. Cried like I hadn't cried in years.

Enervated by the terrifying experience, I wandered on back to our barn. Images of the ghosts were branded on my brain. Part of me wanted to go wake up Judith and tell her about them. About the Troglers—I was almost certain it was them—and the horror of a dog that had also been awakened from the dead. I wanted to tell her about Oatmeal—did I really see what I thought I saw? But I was trembling so badly that another part of me knew I couldn't. I wasn't sure I could even talk. Had fear stolen my voice?

In an icy, near-panic mode of anxiety, I climbed onto the gate to our feedlot and practiced whispering my name several ways: "Theodore Lawrence O'Dell," "Teddy O'Dell," "T.L. O'Dell" just to test my vocal chords. Then I whispered Judith's name. Then I said it louder, and I began to feel better. Still thinking about the ghosts, I fell into that trance one falls into frequently when one is alone, and I might have stayed in it quite a while longer had I not been startled by the bull's snort. My dad had agreed to keep Mr. Penner's whitefaced Hereford bull a couple of weeks so Mr. Penner could build a new feedlot and string new wire on his fences. This was a behemoth of a bull, his massive head nearly as wide as a yardstick, his horns—which curled down near his mouth—were as big around as the hitting end of a baseball bat. I calculated that I could probably put my fist inside the iron leader ring in his nose. Judith was fascinated by the creature, too, especially the wavy, white hair on his forehead.

"It looks like somebody gave him a permanent," she had said. "Isn't he a handsome fellow?"

He was. And he had all the physical equipment necessary to perform his procreative duties. I had checked him out.

Well, I should have been paying attention. While I was gawking at Mr. Penner's bull—his name was Brutus—and still thinking about the ghosts and my eluding the hound from hell, my brothers and Mickey Palmer roared in, scattering banties and gravel and dust before parking in the only available slot in the implement shed. They jumped out, popped the hood of Junior's 1949 Ford and crawled halfway down into its metal bowels. I figured they were much too occupied with changing sparkplugs or whatever arcane auto mechanics task they were engaged in to bother with me, so I took off my tinkling bell bracelet and shook it, hoping to turn the head of Brutus.

My blood flow accelerated when he cast his demonic eyes my way.

You would think I'd had enough thrills for one afternoon, but it felt curiously neat to suddenly imagine myself a bullfighter, clad in one of those colorful matador outfits, replete with funny hat and pants that hugged your bottom as tightly as wallpaper on plaster, I would swirl my cape and invite the hairy, horned juggernaut to attack. He would paw the earth and snort and pierce me with his eyes, but when he would charge I would step aside deftly. Again and again the crowd would shout its approval and encouragement—*ole, ole, ole!*—especially the senorita dressed in black lace fanning the heat from her lovely face—the beautiful Judith applauding and tossing me kisses like roses. I would be the envy of every man as my name would echo over and over.

"Shitface, you're dead!"

The hand squeezing the back of my neck was rough and strong. There was no pulling away. I glanced help-

lessly at Brutus; he stared blankly at my stupidity. Jack
yanked me down from the gate and out of my bullfighter's fantasy and held me as Junior and Mickey
walked around to glower down into my face. Mickey's
expression morphed into a psychotic smile, but Junior kept his indifferent deadpan in place. He was
shaking his head slowly, and my empty stomach filled
with the cool air anticipation of pain.

"Teddy, when you ever going to learn to keep your
mouth shut?"

I put on my best whining, weasel-out-of-it voice.

"I promise I'll never call you names ever, ever
again."

"Too late for that," said Junior. "I can't help you.
You just never learn."

Then he walked away still shaking his head as if he
were so disappointed he might have to sit down and
cry. At that moment he reminded me of my father. Junior was mean, but he was also complex and often
seized by an inward brooding that would not release
him. He possessed a difficult subterranean self totally
unlike the superficiality of Mickey. Jack, on the other
hand—Jack was always kind of a mystery to me. I had
gathered that going into the summer Junior was worried about something having to do with Phyllis
Penner, Mr. Penner's only daughter and Junior's
steady girlfriend for two years. Everyone knew they
were hot and heavy, and I knew that Junior kept
matchbooks of rubbers in his glove compartment.
Down deep, I liked my oldest brother and wanted him
to like me.

Then, hissing like a cobra, Jack gave me a burr rub
across my scalp that brought tears to my eyes. Then he
hawked up a mouthful of spit and hit me smack in the
forehead with it. He and Mickey laughed as it oozed
down between my eyes. Junior had gone back to his

car and to whatever else was worrying him. I knew that his disinterest in my plight sanctioned the violence likely to follow.

"Mickey, whatcha think we should do with this sorry little prick?"

There was so much cold, hard anger in Jack's voice that I shivered at his words. But I managed to speak.

"Hey, you guys, listen. I just saw ghosts at the Troglers's—I swear I did. They just walked right out of the walls . . . and . . . and this huge dog—I mean, humongous dog—it chased after me and then it disappeared, and Oatmeal—you know, that stray cat—one of the ghosts healed its bad eye." The words poured from me in an edgy torrent. "I can show you where I saw them. I swear I can."

Mickey chuckled. He scratched his head as he leered at me. There was no intelligence in his eyes, only a blank, implacable madness.

"The hell you say. Ghosts, huh? You hear that, Jacko? Your goddamn little brother here's been seein' ghosts."

"Crazy pissant shithead," Jack murmured.

Obviously they weren't interested in my ghost story.

Mickey was wheezing sort of funny like and grinning a grin that would give you nightmares.

"Jacko," he said, "we have to make Teddy here see that he should never fuck with his brothers and their best friend. We gotta teach him not to make up stories about ghosts—fucking lies." He paused. I closed my eyes, but I could hear Jack grinding his teeth. Then Mickey added, "It's Teddy's mouth that gets him in all the goddamn trouble."

"I agree," said Jack.

Their tone of voice was suddenly disarmingly sane. It was as if I were some kind of machine not working properly and they had figured out that I had a faulty magneto. Or something.

Mickey leaned down to where I sensed his nose was maybe an inch from mine. "The problem," he said, "is that shit comes out of his mouth the same as it comes out of his ass. Open your eyes and look at me, tally-whacker." I did. He smiled and when he leaned away he arched his eyebrows in a self-congratulatory gesture as if he'd offered a profound amendment to the matter.

"I got an idea," said Jack. "Go get the grease gun and let's take him into the barn."

They led me away like a captured soldier. I didn't resist at first. There was no point—there was no one around to help, and over the years of abusing me they had succeeded in making it impossible to tattle about them to our father, an act which would only up the ante of retribution.

In the hay mow they unclasped the hooks of my overalls and ripped them off. Then Mickey tore at my underwear, and I felt one of his fingernails cut a deep scratch low on my back.

"Damn you all to hell," I cried.

I fought back then. I got an arm free, swung at Mickey and missed. I kicked several times, and the second kick caught Jack on the outside of his knee. I had hurt him. He tossed the grease gun aside; together, he and Mickey subdued me easily. I was determined not to give them the satisfaction of seeing my tears, but the thought of that grease gun squirting into my mouth caused me to yell again. I called out for Junior. I don't know why.

"I'll fix this," said Mickey. "I'll fix this god damn little shit." He disappeared for a few seconds, returning with something in his hand I couldn't see. "Hold his mouth open," he ordered.

Jack, his thumb on one side of my mouth, his fingers on the other, squeezed until I saw stars and gave in. A handful of cow manure, a fresh pie of it from the milking area, filled my mouth. Mickey was shoving, pushing his palm hard as if he meant to strangle me. Then he held his hand over my lips and I coughed and gagged and couldn't keep from swallowing.

"Bend him over that bale," said Jack. "God damn it, Teddy, you hurt my knee."

When the burning realization hit me of what Jack planned to do, I bucked like a roped steer. Mickey hunkered down and bit my ear hard. Then he whispered, "You're only gonna make it hurt worse fightin' it."

He was right.

I nearly went unconscious with the pain. It was a tearing, scalding pain as the barrel of the grease gun was jabbed up my rectum. Blinding, incredible pain. Then the muted pump of the gun, and I felt my lower insides filling up, tightening, bloating me. I was sobbing. Mickey took his hand from my mouth and I spat out a gob of manure and gagged some more.

I wasn't aware exactly when they left.

Maybe I passed out for a few seconds or maybe for a minute or so.

I curled up on the hay, my knees rucked up against my chest. My rectum blazed with every move I made, seemingly every breath I took. I reached back there with my hand and felt a blob of grease the size of a softball. I cried some more, and then, even though it was ninety degrees out, I began to shiver. I began to feel that there was something more than grease inside me; the blue-green gunk was soft and squishy. Whatever else they had lodged back there was not.

I squeezed my eyes shut as tightly as I could, gritted my teeth and began probing with my fingers. I touched something foreign, and at that instant I realized my tinkle bracelet was missing from my wrist. It took several painful minutes to retrieve it.

My bottom was on fire. Still naked, I did the only thing I could think of to help matters: I went back outside, climbed over the fence and soaked in the cow tank. Brutus shot a menacing glare my way, but it didn't matter. I had to put out my blazing insides and clean myself up and regain a modicum of composure before going to the house. When I stepped out of that tank my teeth were chattering and the chill of a hatred that would live with me for years had sunk deep into my heart.

"I just don't want to talk about it," I said to Judith.

I could still taste cow manure even though I'd brushed my teeth about a dozen times afterwards and gargled with salt water. My tinkle bracelet, despite my cleaning and bleaching efforts, continued to carry a faint whiff of nastiness. I had been walking around dizzy with anger. Judith was my only salvation, my passage into blissful repression.

She and I had plans to construct a globe, and I had everything ready. I pumped up a deflated basketball to which we were going to paste sheets of white notebook paper. From a cigar box of crayons I had kept since second grade, we had selected the colors we needed for the oceans and continents and individual countries.

"Sure, Teddy, we don't have to talk about it," said Judith, "but I feel like whatever they did to you is my fault. You were defending my honor that day when you shouted at them."

Those words—"defending my honor"—connected with every chivalrous cell in my body. I wanted Judith to say more; I wanted her to tell me that her heart was forever mine and that I was a thousand times more special to her than her Fiery Angel.

"A gentleman should always defend the honor of a lady," I said, but the words sounded silly, even to me.

"You're too much," said Judith, stifling a giggle.

Then I told her about the ghosts.

You could tell she was real upset, though pleased, I think, to learn that Oatmeal might be well again. Mostly, I was afraid she would be even more inclined to leave, to run away because she continued to believe that she was responsible for the ghosts being active. She also continued to believe that the ghosts would get stronger as long as she was nearby—they would somehow feed upon the strange power she had and get stronger. From insubstantial figures of dust to more than substantial figures of earth.

"Then we'll just stay away from there—from the Trogler place," I said. "We won't give them a chance to get stronger."

I think she liked my idea, but she wanted to know more about the Troglers. She wanted to understand who they were. I couldn't help her there. While we were talking, my mother came to the entrance of the mud room. Sometimes I felt that she sneaked up on us to try to catch us doing something vulgar or malicious, something she could use as evidence to my father that Judith should be sent back where she came from.

We helped her put away the laundry. She never even made eye contact with Judith.

"I'm going to the store," she announced when we finished. "Can I trust you two here alone?"

Such comments always made me want to punch my mother or to act in a way that would deliberately raise her suspicions even further. Judith never seemed to be offended.

"Could we go, too?" she said. "I'd like to visit the library."

My mother considered Judith's request for an uncomfortable span of seconds before nodding. I was puzzled by Judith's sudden interest in the library, but said nothing as we hurriedly folded up all our maps; then I had to plead with my mother to wait a minute for Judith to comb her hair and tighten her braces.

In the backseat of our 1946 Chevrolet Judith and I watched dust roostertail behind us on the country road.

"Teddy, can you drive this car?" she whispered, careful not to let my mother hear.

"Sure."

At least, I was pretty certain I could. My father had let me drive his pickup a little, and I could drive our tractor—the car would, comparatively, be a piece of cake, or so I reasoned.

"Good," said Judith, "because you might have to be my getaway driver."

I didn't know what else to say; I just stared at those plumes of dust and I wished to myself that I would never do anything to disappoint Judith.

Five

Onlie Begetter

Saddle Rock's library was a pathetic abode right in the middle of the only block of downtown. Its white-washed plaster wasn't holding up well; as the building settled, cracks forked like dark, miniature strikes of lightning forever trapped in those walls.

When my mother dumped us and continued on to the grocery, Judith and I soon found ourselves inside where Miss Harriet McAdams, the elderly librarian, not so much greeted us as warned us: "You young people be careful handling the books and don't make noises. This is a library. Are those braces going to make noises? We don't want to create a difficulty for others."

We were the only ones there.

Judith assured Miss McAdams that we would be quiet.

The library was one long, poorly lighted room. It was quite warm despite a floor fan that occasionally sputtered like an old-timey aircraft about to crash.

Judith didn't mind; she glided past the shelves—as much as someone with crutches and braces could glide—like a joyful apparition. For some reason, watching her made me think of the ghosts I had seen.

Meanwhile, I located an oversized book of world maps and sat at the only table, soon losing myself in deepest, darkest Africa, though some of the countries were brightly colored: aqua and yellow and pink. Minutes passed as I mentally journeyed from Africa to the whiteness of Antarctica and wondered whether it could really be as cold there as a Kansas January with the wind howling away. I sought imaginative warmth in the South Pacific, where I fantasized about being marooned with Judith on some uncharted island stocked, unbelievably, with food and drinking water; there we would live like the Swiss Family Robinson, building tree houses and swings and, miraculously, the ocean breezes, coupled with my love, would cure Judith's affliction.

A few minutes later Judith was at my shoulder, obviously excited about something. She whispered in a throaty voice of delight, "Teddy, you gotta come see what I found."

In the corner of the library farthest away from Miss McAdams' suspicious eyes, Judith had unrolled a newspaper between what looked like two long, thin rolling pins. It was the Topeka paper, and by its yellowing pages appeared to be pretty old. We hunkered down close to the floor.

"See this," said Judith.

I looked and quickly sucked in my breath and wasn't sure I could let it out again. The headline read, "The Saga of the Bloody Troglers"—and below the bold print were head and shoulders sketches of four people, as well as one of a dog.

"Geez, it's them!" I exclaimed.

Judith had to shush me, fearing that Miss McAdams would be drawn to our covert operation.

"Are these the ghosts you saw?" said Judith.

I nodded. The drawings were dead likenesses. The

old man—Rolf—the old woman—Senta—the young man—Siebert—and the witchy young woman—Romina. And the drawing of the dog—Hunter—was so lifelike it made me shudder and experience an auditory hallucination of his terrifying bark.

The long and short of the article was that the Troglers had gone on a bloody-crazed rampage, murdering Harold Suggs and his son, Dwight; then the madness escalated as, apparently, Romina Trogler, having newly given birth—and "hearing the voices of demons"—killed the members of her family and the family dog before committing suicide. Nothing was mentioned of revengeful actions on the part of James and Emmitt Suggs and others. The bloody chapter of the Troglers had ended. The book of their days closed. They had been called away by their own darkness. The fate of Romina's child was not mentioned.

Suddenly I wanted very much to tell someone else about the ghosts I'd seen. The sheriff or my father or somebody. Maybe somebody from the Topeka paper. Somebody. As if she were reading my mind, Judith said, "This has to be our secret, Teddy."

I reluctantly agreed.

"But . . . I mean, will their ghosts, you know . . . try to kill us?" I stuttered my question and, thankfully, Judith had a pretty quick answer.

"Not if I do what I have to do."

She looked hard into my eyes and it translated as two words: *Trust me.*

Just about then my mother arrived to retrieve us, apologizing to Miss McAdams for any trouble we might have caused her.

That evening in the mud room Judith and I talked some more about the newspaper article and the drawings and, of course, about what the ghosts might do next. I was lost because I didn't know the rules of the fantasy—I didn't know about ghosts, but I knew one thing: I was coming to believe in them. They existed. *Something* existed. Judith was reassuring in her view that the ghosts were not an immediate threat. Her Fiery Angel would protect us. But there was something more in Judith's crooked smile and mysterious air, something secretive and powerfully alluring.

She pushed her face close to mine and whispered, "Look at what I got at the library."

In an unabashedly forthright and perhaps immodest gesture she lifted up the front of her dress, reached into her panties and pulled something out. The flash of pink from those panties blurred my vision with an after-image for a second or two before I noticed that she was holding out a very small book for me to consider.

"I didn't see you check that out," I said. "What book is it?"

"I've always wanted a copy of Shakespeare's *Sonnets,* " she said, glowing like nothing I'd ever seen. Then she said, "I didn't check it out because I want to keep it."

I hesitated. I swallowed a big ball of saliva.

"But that means you stole it."

Judith's mouth was seized by a pout. Her lower lip curled down so seductively I couldn't think what to do or what else to say.

"No," she said. "I want this book more than anyone else does."

At that instant I realized Judith was, in her own way, amoral. She saw herself as outside morality and outside the law, transcending society's rules and strictures, choosing what to obey and what not to. Stealing the book of poetry was okay because she wanted it more personally and meaningfully than any other visitor to our library possibly could. As I watched her clutch the book—I think she believed that I would snatch it from her—I understood what Judith could do that I couldn't do: she was able to experience and shape the symbolic dimensions of her own reality.

It made her thoroughly human in my eyes.

She was no criminal. She didn't steal. She was no sinner. She didn't sin.

She ghosted through her life having somehow transformed herself.

I took a deep breath.

"All right," I said, "but whatever you do, don't let my mother find out you took it."

She threw her arms around me and hugged me tightly and kissed my ear. I sputtered like Miss McAdams' fan and knew for certain that some kind of crash was inevitable. But as long as Judith was happy, I was going to pretend that the future would take care of itself.

Heading into that weekend, I carried around a vague uneasiness not unlike a kind of emotional nausea. Yet, Judith's pilfered book seemed to give her face an arresting brilliance—I vowed to do nothing to dim it. She even hummed when I gave her the Kenny, and after her nap the next day she claimed that her legs were feeling much better and that she wanted to walk without her braces. I was skeptical.

"I'll still need one crutch," she said, but I had to admit that she appeared to be stronger. Although she wasn't ready to sprint, her legs were functioning better than I had seen them. "It's all because of you, Teddy."

Warmth spread through me in soothing ripples.

While I was basking in the undulations of so many

good feelings, my mother called me upstairs to help her move a heavy chest that once belonged to my grandmother. Thinking I ought to share some of my elation, I told her about Judith's progress. Her sour-faced response was, "This would be a good time to send the girl back to her mother before something goes wrong and she takes a turn for the worse."

When I went back downstairs Judith was gone.

For nearly longer than my nerves could bear, I really believed she had run off. Or, maybe, that the ghosts had gotten her. In panic, my heart in my throat, I dashed out of the house to look for her. I called her name and checked every building from the outhouse to the chicken coop. A candle flame flickering in the shadows of the barn discovered her for me. I was so relieved I was almost angry. I didn't ask where the candle came from—it must have been one of her treasures she had hidden away somewhere. She had enthroned herself on a bale of hay, and, seeing me, she said, "Teddy, I made it out here in a jiffy. Not much pain at all, and I'm not wearing my braces. I wanted a quiet place to read my book."

I thought about correcting her—it wasn't *her* book. But that seemed petty and, according to Judith's view of things, not really accurate.

"You scared me," I said. "Don't go off without telling me where you're going."

She pulled me down next to her and gave me a wet, full kiss on the cheek. Dear God, I wanted to climb on top of her and make love to her even though I had only the most nebulous notion of how to do so. I could feel her saliva on my skin and wished that my tongue were longer so I could enjoy licking it off.

"I can take care of myself," she said, a touch of petulance in her voice. "You don't have to be my shadow. I'm a big girl. In fact, I'm a young woman. Young

women should be more independent, if you want to
know my opinion."

"Yeah, but . . . I was just afraid something might
happen to you. What if something happened to you?"

I hated to sound like my mother.

"Oh, Teddy, I know what you mean, and that's why
I love you like I do."

I remember that my body suddenly felt as light as
puffs of dandelion heads when the wind breaks them
apart and they go floating off. Though David had spoken those same words to me, it was somehow different
hearing Judith say them. Better. More heart-stirring.

More wonderful. And, maybe, more frightening.

I was speechless. I was thoughtless. I was momentarily disconnected from reality.

I was mesmerized by her.

"Teddy, listen to some of these great poems. The
language is beautiful. I can't decide which is my favorite. They all are, I suppose."

I edged close to her on that bale and we rested our
backs against a wall of hay and the world narrowed
to just the two of us. The hay mow was our microcos-
mic Eden. We were its Adam and Eve. We were the
only beating hearts on the planet. I stared at Judith's
lips as she read and wondered what she would do if I
were to kiss her hard and long and tell her that I
wanted to be with her even more than I wanted to be
with David.

But I was a coward.

"'Shall I compare thee to a summer's day?'"

And thus she began to read and fill the remaining
hours of the afternoon with words at times unfamiliar
to me, yet spoken by her, through her, they seemed to
live and become embedded in my soul. Her voice was
magic. The voice of a beautiful fairy tale princess de-

livering lines from some benign wizard housed in the castle of her kingdom.

I listened and then I listened completely. I don't know how many of Shakespeare's sonnets she read that afternoon—dozens, I'm sure. She talked about them, explaining that she thought some were obviously addressed to a young man and some to a woman: "'Two loves I have of comfort and despair . . . ,'" and that it was neat that Shakespeare could be such close friends with both men and women, that he had a soul as big as the moon.

I smiled at her language. I let it fill me.

The only thing I could think to say was, "My English teacher, Miss Sisler, would love you to death if she had you in her class. She likes it when one of her students can talk about poems and writers."

I wondered why I had no poetry in me. But Judith smiled her heart-caressing smile and so it didn't matter.

"Here, Teddy, I want to show you something at the front of this book."

I could see by the slanting light that it was nearing supper time.

"We better go on in the house," I said. "I think I heard Pop's truck."

"But I want you to look at this first. It explains something I'm feeling."

I was hooked by that. And so I read what was apparently the headnote to the volume written by someone with the initials T.T. It was all in capital letters.

TO. THE. ONLIE. BEGETTER. OF
THESE. INSUING. SONNETS.
MR. W.H. ALL. HAPPINESSE.
AND. THAT. ETERNITIE.
PROMISED.
BY

OUR. EVER-LIVING. POET.
WISHEST.
THE. WELL-WISHING.
ADVENTURE. IN.
SETTING.
FORTH.

"What do you think, Teddy?"

I read through it again, hoping that I could detect
something I didn't pick up on the first time. But it
might as well have been written in a foreign language.

"I think it has a lot of misspelled words."

Judith laughed.

"No, silly. That's the way they spelled words in
Shakespeare's day. Don't you love those words, 'Onlie
Begetter'?"

I didn't exactly know what they meant.

"They're okay, I guess."

I had no idea where Judith was headed.

"But don't you see, Teddy, that's what *you* are.
That's the role you play."

I said the two words aloud, thinking that maybe the
sound of them would ring some sort of bell.

"I don't get it," I said, but I wanted to—desperately.

She put her finger on my heart and smiled and
said, *"You* are the onlie begetter of my happiness. You
beget—you bring about—my happiness. You are
good. You give me the Kenny and you do a hundred
things every day to make my pain bearable. You share
my secret about the ghosts. You help in so many ways,
and you've promised to help even more. The Fiery
Angel is my visionary guide, but you—you are my
Onlie Begetter."

My mouth was open and I think that my lips were
moving slightly. I probably looked like a goldfish up
against the glass of its bowl. I was in such a state of dis-

located puzzlement and joy that I could neither talk nor smile. It was truly as if Judith had cast a spell over me like the Good Witch in *The Wizard of Oz*. She reached up and touched my cheek and I closed my eyes because they were suddenly heavy as if I were about to fall asleep.

"Thank you," I said, though later, when I was lying awake next to Judith's cot I came up with pages more stuff to say. I wanted to ask her, for example, if I had become even more important to her than the Fiery Angel, my chief competitor, or were we about equal. "Thank you," I said again, "I'm glad about what you just said."

Judith shook her head, her eyes overflowing with seriousness.

"I'm the one who should be saying 'thank you.' I just hope, Teddy, that you'll always, always be my Onlie Begetter."

We got up to return to the house. We were almost there before I was able to whisper under my breath, "I will."

I don't know whether she heard me.

I remember the Saturday after that exchange. I felt close to Judith, and I was careful to distance myself from the threats to my physical and mental well-being: I had stayed away from the Trogler place and, more especially, had avoided Jack and Junior and their dark shadow, Mickey. It was a treat, in fact, on Saturday night to have them gone; Junior on a date, Jack and Mickey to wherever psychopaths hang out. On the other hand, I sensed that the ghosts weren't gone— just preternaturally attached to the haunted ground of their homestead.

My father always tried to make Saturday night kind of special, allowing everyone to choose his or her favorite soda pop, which he would then buy at the grocery and bring home. He would hook up an extension cord and bring the Philco radio out on the front porch where he and my mother would sit while Judith and I chased lightning bugs and June bugs and attempted to identify night birds calling in the distance. My father always chose root beer; my mother 7-UP, though she never drank more than a swallow or two of it. I liked Pepsi; Judith favored strawberry and could drink it without getting even a trace of red around her lips. My father listened to two radio programs religiously: *The Red Skelton Show*—which made him laugh uproariously—and *Gunsmoke* through which I think he fantasized of being Marshall Matt Dillon and maybe having a woman like Miss Kitty instead of his emaciated, neurotic wife. But I never knew my father's private world, and so I could only speculate.

Judith would listen to both programs with one ear, preferring to give attention to creating her own radio drama, usually centered on brave, plucky young women overcoming great odds to achieve great things. Her other program formats involved poetry readings, mystery stories, and world travels. In the latter category, she created a program entitled, "Travels With Teddy," starring a red-headed teenager accompanied by his female cousin who together managed to visit every country on the planet in the space of a year and do and see marvelous things.

Prophetically, Judith also created a ghost-hunting serial.

But the good vibrations of Saturday night disappeared one Sunday morning.

I suppose we should have seen it coming, given the fact that my mother devoted part of each day to ferreting out something that might cast Judith in a bad light. I was up before Judith that morning poaching our eggs when my mother marched into the kitchen and sat down. That in itself was surprising because she usually slept late on Sundays, as did my father and brothers. I noticed that she was holding something in her lap, but I went about my business, conscious of the fact that she was following my every move, a particularly unsettling glint in her eyes. Something was giving her secret delight, and I believe that it elated her further that her revelation would be painful to me.

She had me going. I burned my hand on the scalding water and left the toast in the toaster too long. When I couldn't stand any more of her silent baiting, I wheeled around to face her. A smile flickered at one corner of her mouth. She lifted something from her lap and placed it on the table.

It all came crashing down.

Her voice was calm and certain of victory.

"Teddy, wake up that girl and tell her to come in here."

My mother had found the book of sonnets.

My chest ballooned with a hot, nervous whoosh of air. I scrambled to control the damage.

"We just forgot to check it out," I said. "It's no big deal. There's probably not going to be a rush on Shakespeare's book in Saddle Rock this summer."

I think I might have smiled as a finishing touch to my impromptu defense. But the truth was that Judith had deliberately stolen the book; more significantly, the truth was that while taking the Shakespeare was a relatively trivial act, my mother would not treat it as such, and I feared the outcome of what would inevitably ensue.

My mother's jaw tightened. Her upper body trembled like a tiny volcano about to erupt, and then she shrieked—not merely raised her voice—she shrieked.

"Wake up that girl!"

I put out my hands in a calming gesture. She would have none of it, so I woke Judith. On sleepy feet, and with the help of one crutch, she dragged herself into the kitchen in her nightgown only to have my mother shout her back into the mud room to get herself decent. When Judith returned, I said to her, "I'm sorry, but my mother has been sneaking around and digging into stuff that's none of her business."

"I won't have a thief in my house," my mother shot back.

I could tell that Judith was locked in a bad case of morning pain. She glanced at me, and in her eyes was the unspoken, reassuring message that she could take whatever verbal punishment my mother had in mind.

And so my mother started in, raising and shaking the volume of Shakespeare like a hellfire and brimstone evangelist. Judith merely listened. She offered no explanation, though I found myself wishing she had attempted one. She just stood and took it all. There was not one drop of understanding in my mother's invective. The bitterness of her harangue dwindled down finally to three demands: first, that Judith and I were to get dressed and go with her to church that morning; second, that Judith was to confess her violation to my father; and, third, when the library opened Monday morning, Judith was to return the book and apologize profusely to Miss McAdams. The unspoken fourth demand was for Judith's summer with us to end.

When my mother concluded her spiel, Judith calmly walked over to her and took the book, tugging it away from my mother's grip. In the mud room, Judith whispered to me, "I'm not sorry, Teddy."

"I don't want you to be," I said.

Although I put up a mild protest, my mother succeeded in herding us to the church service. It was an hour that lasted for days. During the sermon, I imagined ways to hurt my mother, to exact an intimate revenge. It even passed my mind that I would like to see her haunted by the ghosts of the Troglers. But the best punishment I could come up with was running away with Judith. That might do the trick. That might drive a stake in my mother's vampiric heart. After our somber Sunday midday meal, my mother told my father that his niece had something she needed to tell him in private. I bit my tongue and said nothing because Judith squeezed my leg under the table, a move I translated to mean, "I can handle this."

I don't know what she told my father. They talked for a couple of minutes out on the front porch. When my father came back into the kitchen, he looked sad and perplexed, his hands hanging uselessly at his sides. Judith and I excused ourselves, and I gave her the Kenny. Her body was loaded with tension, and my rubbing and stretching caused her more pain than usual. Afterwards she didn't want to nap.

"I need to go out to the barn," she said to me. "Do you want to come along?"

I was dying to ask her whether my father would be calling up her mother. I was scared. More scared than I had been of my brothers and Mickey, more scared than I had been of the Trogler ghosts, the dog included. But what I said, there in the cool shadows of the hay mow, was, "I don't ever want to lose you."

"Teddy, Teddy," she murmured.

"I mean it."

"Your mother's right about the world," she said. "You see, don't you, that I have a hard time finding a place in it."

"My mother's not right about one damn thing," I insisted, but Judith shook her head.

"Here's what I have to do." She was holding the Shakespeare with both hands. "I have to memorize as many of these sonnets as I can because then they really will be mine. Not your mother nor Miss McAdams nor anybody else can reach into my memory and pluck them out. I'll carry all these beautiful poems around in my head like little pieces of gold. Only more valuable than gold. And I'll be able to hand them out to anyone who wants some beauty in their lives."

I think maybe I just stared at her for a few seconds.

I felt like a trespasser in her world. I believed I could never belong in it.

"But you've got to do it right away," I said. "We're going to have to take the book back tomorrow and there's no way Miss McAdams would ever let you check it out now."

"Will you help?" she said.

I melted down next to her and we began.

That next day Judith was magnificent at the library. With my mother standing just outside the front door, smirking like the villain she was, Judith went to Miss McAdams and confessed that she had taken the book. I stood off to the side attempting to look as supportive as possible. Miss McAdams drew up straight and as stiff as a board; the expression of shock on her face suggested that she'd just been informed of the most heinous crime conceivable—and that it had been committed against *her* personally.

Her chin jutting out in disdain, McAdams glared at Judith. When she finally spoke, her voice quavered and there was a deliberate pause between each word.

"You are an uncivilized young person. You are despicable. You must never set foot in this library again. And neither must you, Theodore."

"Don't worry, I won't," I said. "I wouldn't want to."

She barked out an indignant *huh* and gestured for Judith to put the volume of Shakespeare on her desk. Then she said, "Young woman, books are to be loved and cherished. They are to be engaged reverently. Someone who would steal a book is the lowest form of humanity."

I would have enjoyed socking the old bitch right in the mouth.

Judith steadied herself on her crutches. She had her response in hand.

"No one really *owns* Shakespeare's *Sonnets,*" she began. "The sonnets belong to anyone who has an eye and an ear for beauty and truth. The world claims it's wrong that I tried to take the book, so I've returned it. You can put it back on your shelves. But I still have it. I have it in my heart. I can enjoy it whenever I want."

McAdams shook her head as if she found Judith's remarks haughty and disingenuous. I reached out to help Judith turn around so that we could leave, but she had something more to say to McAdams.

"I'll share some of Shakespeare's beauty with you— you look as if you could use some. This is sonnet one-hundred sixteen: 'Let me not to the marriage of true minds/ Admit impediments . . . .'"

She recited the poem in that lovely, fairy tale princess voice. Then she glanced at me and smiled shyly and we left. We knew we had acted out of line. Ultimately, we knew we were in the wrong. Selfishly, we embraced that tiny scene of rebellion and empty triumph. I think, in our own separate ways, we both enjoyed flying in the face of propriety. I would say that we were seeking to be outsiders, but Judith believed that the only thing anyone really seeks is transcendence, though maybe in the end we all settle for transformation. And belief, for Judith, was sacred. Myself, I'm not sure that I believed in anything. I was born alienated from my soul, and I seemed destined to remain that way.

When we got home later that morning, Judith and I went to the barn and sat in the hay to take stock of our existence. Though she made a gallant effort, Judith had not been able to memorize a ton of Shakespeare's sonnets. Just a dozen maybe. We did not speak for a minute or so, and then I had to laugh.

"Teddy? What's so funny?"

"Miss McAdams. When you finished reciting that poem, she looked like a dog had peed on her leg."

"Teddy!"

We both laughed, though Judith much more softly. I started to ramble on about something, but she stopped me, shushed me, and we sat in silence. Judith, probably in pain, locked herself in a poised awareness. Thinking back now, I see that she taught me stillness. That morning there in the warm, fragrant hay, we got so quiet we could hear our souls speak. What did they say? What did they tell us?

Secrets. Terrible secrets.

Secrets so terrible that I couldn't bear to listen closely—and what I heard I forgot immediately.

But Judith did not.

That evening after I helped my father with the milking, I asked my mother why she hated Judith. As he often did at twilight, my father was out taking in the property, carrying a cup of coffee, strolling from building to building, his eyes alert for needed repairs or what have you. Jack and Junior were up in their rooms, and Judith, exhausted from the demands of the day, was resting in the mud room. My mother was sitting at the kitchen table, her hands surrounding a cup of coffee; she was staring off at nothing at all when I sat down across from her. I was determined not to sound angry.

"Just give me one reason why you hate my cousin," I said. "What has she done to deserve it?"

My mother did not appear surprised by the question, nor did she take it as an unwarranted challenge to her person.

"I remember," she said, quite calmly, "when you and I, Teddy, would take care of the home front. We worked the garden together, canned together, and often took an afternoon nap together. And we were. . . ."

She trailed off.

"What does all that have to do with anything?" I said, though, of course, in a way I saw where she was going. I thought it was a selfish direction. She returned to staring into her own introcosm, I suppose. Her face registered misery. But I wasn't going to let myself feel sorry for her because she had been cruel to Judith for no good reason that I could see. She blinked, and then turned to look at me, and I sucked in my breath knowing that what she would say would probably unsettle me.

"I don't have friends, Teddy," she said.

I started to dismiss that. Thinking better of it, I merely looked away and let her talk.

"Other women don't like women who hate this land. Other women belong here. They don't want to be around someone who doesn't belong here. That's part of why I started doing the things I did."

She was alluding to two winters ago when for most

of one week she would sneak out to the car and just drive off—we never knew where she went, and she didn't tell us, and it worried my father sick. He took her to see Doc Gillis and then to see someone in Emporia. During that time I drifted around on a dark cloud of concern. I thought she was going insane maybe. I thought I was somehow to blame. Jack and Junior were concerned, too, but hated to show it. Finally one day my father got us three boys together and told us, "Your mother is just sad these days. The doctors say women get sad like this. They can't help it. But I think if we all try harder to make her happy, she won't . . . she'll like being here more." So we did. For several weeks, we tried to be the Ozzie and Harriet family we listened to on the radio. I never really believed it made a big difference.

"What's this have to do with anything?" I said again. She was yanking my chain—she had that down to an art, similar to the way my father could always shame me.

"Teddy," said my mother, ". . . you and I used to be good friends. You were my helper. You stayed with me when everyone else had gone to town or to work and this old house would be so empty and I would be so lonely. But I always had my Teddy."

I couldn't keep from raising my voice.

"Ma, that's stupid stuff."

"Is it?"

Our eyes met. I was angry and frustrated and I needed to be hurtful.

"You're just mad because my cousin and I get along so well. You're just jealous and it makes you mean."

I got it out. What I thought was the truth. It sounded right, the words spoken out loud there in the kitchen, words that couldn't be taken back.

"That girl—that Child of the Devil—should never have come."

"Why? We're helping her. We're helping blood. Ma, I'm too old to do the stuff with you we used to do. Don't you see that?"

She looked at me with such sadness that I felt needle pricks of guilt all up and down my arms.

"Are you too old to be my friend, Teddy?"

I had to leave the house.

My dad was out by the barn leaning on the gate to the feedlot admiring Brutus. I wanted to go to him and to let him in on the exchange I'd had with my mother. I figured he would side with me because he liked Judith—she was blood. But as I approached him I sensed how contented he was, sipping his coffee, his elbows on the top rail, a man walking around inside himself and feeling good about being solitary.

I turned and headed for the driveway, not really knowing what to do with myself.

The ghosts called.

I could hear them in my head. Freaky soft whisperings. I tasted dust.

They needed me. More so, they needed Judith.

But I felt that I must resist them.

I remembered then that I hadn't brought in the mail that day. There wasn't much. No letter from Aunt Juanita; Judith had told me not to ever expect one. But there was a postcard, one of those cartoony ones of a big Northern Pike swallowing a boat with two comically horrified fishermen in it. I don't even recall the caption because I turned it over immediately. It was addressed to me.

It was from David.

"Dear Teddy (MLR)," it began. The MLR stood, of

course, for "My Little Red." Suddenly I missed David as I hadn't all summer. I wanted him to be with me in Kansas and not off in Minnesota or wherever. My hands were shaking ever so slightly as I read on.

"Having a fun time, but MISSING YOU! I'll be home before the 4th of July. Can't wait to see you."

He signed it "Shepherd Boy," his coded way of expressing to me that he and I had a special relationship—like a shepherd and a member of his flock. I read and re-read the card, and I smiled away every thought of my conversation with my mother.

And as the warm, soft, summer evening air embraced me, my emotions crowded Judith out of my world, too. I wasn't looking for poetry or transformation. Or revenge.

I wanted the flesh and blood touch of someone who desired me.

Six

The Oncoming Darkness

I saw eternity that summer.

Judith was my guide. Had I been smarter than teenage boys can be, I would have seen my fate, I would have seen metaphysical realities all around me there in the sheltered realm of the rows of corn, the green banners of the stalks streaming in the ever-present Kansas wind.

In the dragonfield.

I should have seen the dangers coming.

I just could not see to see.

The morning after receiving David's postcard and riding the waves of the suggestive promises it generated I tore it up. I suppose I had washed ashore on the beach of fickleness and liked it there. I hadn't committed myself to David. I didn't belong to anyone.

I had not slept beside Judith's cot; rather I had tossed and turned in my own bed wrestling with sexual fantasies of being with David and his eagerly seductive manner, his words, his touch, his lips, and whatever act of consummation excited the two of us most. When I woke very early I felt like a different person, one I didn't especially like, and I realized, soberly, that I had found something I was good at: abandoning anyone who cared for me.

David, Judith. My mother. Perhaps my father, too.

So I vowed I would change. Though I somehow missed the irony of it, my first act on the road to constructing a better, more caring self was to tear up David's postcard and throw it down the lefthand hole of the outhouse. Then I went back in the house to boil an egg for Judith. She would need her strength; we had plans to go to the dragonfield.

After breakfast, while the air was still almost as cool as the storm cellar, we headed out, Judith wearing shorts and a blouse, both of us barefoot. I remember that I carried that tarot card of The Hanged Man in the front pocket of my overalls—don't know why except that I liked looking at it and turning it upside down—one way the man was hanging by his feet, the other way he was dancing. It was something that never ceased to enchant me.

"I want to see Oatmeal," Judith announced as we reached the center of the field.

I resisted at first because the frightening encounter with the ghosts continued to echo in some empty chamber of my consciousness, but Judith assured me that we would be okay: We had the Fiery Angel to protect us. And so we clambered our way to the side of the Trogler manse, and I called out for the cat, suddenly eager for Judith to see that he had been healed.

"Teddy," said Judith, as we waited, putting our faces close to the opening in the crawl space, "did the young woman—Romina—did she have fire in her eyes?"

I thought a second and then responded that yes, she did. Witchy eyes. Judith seemed pensive, yet satisfied. We heard Oatmeal's weak meow.

"He's coming," I said, feeling a rush of happy anticipation.

Judith's smile was gorgeous. I let it wash over me. Then, as we were hunkering there, I said, "You're getting stronger." Because it seemed to me she was. Most of the time she no longer had to wear her braces, and though she needed one of her crutches, she could hobble at a pretty good clip sometimes.

"All because of you, Teddy. And the Kenny."

Her smile caused something in my throat to flutter. I felt as if I'd swallowed a butterfly and yet hadn't harmed it. Everything about being with Judith gave me a good feeling. At that instant I couldn't imagine how I might ever choose David over her.

"Oh, look," I said, turning my attention to the crawl space. "Here he comes. You're really going to be surprised."

But when the cat wiggled his head out through the opening, Judith gasped in horror. I reeled back unable to believe what I was seeing: instead of having two good eyes, Oatmeal had two burned-out sockets—like where cigarettes had been stubbed out.

I was sickened.

When the cat sensed our reaction, he ducked back inside, his meowing soft and mournful.

"*She* did this," said Judith. "With the fire in her eyes. She burned darkness into him."

I didn't know what to say. We stood up and I took Judith's hand.

"I swear I saw him with his eyes healed. I swear it. You believe me, don't you?"

Before Judith could respond, the side of the house began to tremble. I thought I heard the low growl of a dog, and then I distinctly heard a woman's voice. Judith heard it, too.

"Animus," said the voice. "Animus, is that you?"

I could see by Judith's reaction that she recognized the name.

The ghosts.

They began to sift out from the walls, dusty, amorphous, yet eagerly seeking shape.

"God, let's run," I exclaimed.

But Judith held me. And in a tone of consummate calm she whispered, "No, Teddy, no. Just stand as still as you possibly can. Don't move a muscle. Try not to even breathe."

We must have stayed like that for ten minutes. I know, of course, that it may have only been for a minute or two. But it seemed like a lifetime. We concentrated so intensely on being still that at one point I imagined that we levitated a few inches off the ground.

It was as weird and spooky as anything I've ever experienced.

And it worked.

The ghosts retreated.

We recovered in the dragonfield. It took some time. We were both shaken. But as I look back on things, I see that we were remarkably resilient, and Judith believed to the core that while she had awakened the ghosts of the Troglers, they could not harm us. Her powers—and the protective powers of the Fiery Angel—would negate the ghosts, the vengeance of the dead. Naturally, I asked about the name Animus, but it obviously made Judith uncomfortable, so I didn't press for an answer. I changed the subject.

As we made our way to our spot, I asked, "What are we going to pretend today?"

Because that's what we did in the dragonfield—we stepped out of ourselves and into another realm, and we'd talk about what it must have been like to live fifty years ago or a hundred. What if Thomas Jefferson were our president instead of Ike? What if there had been an atomic bomb during the Civil War? What would it be like to be a hawk? Or a snake? Or a fish?

What would it be like to walk around on the moon?

"Nobody ever will, I bet," was my prediction.

"I think somebody will," said Judith, "if they want to more than anything else."

Are we alone in the universe? we asked each other. We believed in ghosts, but we had deeper questions. Is there a Heaven? A Hell? Life after death? How will the world end? The immense mystery of such questions dizzied us, made us giddy, though Judith could wade deeper than I could into mystery without fearing she would drown.

I assumed that most kids asked those questions and thought those thoughts. Maybe even Jack and Junior—Mickey was a different story. It was much later in my life before I realized just how imaginative and intellectually curious Judith was. And, in those respects alone, how extraordinary she was.

"We're going to do something different this morning," she said, determined not to allow the sad scene at the Trogler place to get her down. Judith reminded me of a teacher some days in that she seemed always to have an agenda, a lesson plan; it was always evident that she'd thought about how she might use the day and not waste it.

I pestered her to tell me. But as usual, she kept silent on what she had in mind until we were fifty or so yards deep in the corn and had picked a likely site and playfully scouted a moment or two to see whether the dragon who occupied this particular field was still asleep.

"Dragons are sorta for little kids, aren't they?" I protested.

"Oh, no, Teddy," said Judith. "Dragons are fantasy

creations, and I think that means people—kids *and* grownups—have a need for dragons or they wouldn't have imagined them in the first place. We're just surrendering to the fantasy."

It made sense in a way. Most of what Judith said did, though I wondered whether her theory applied to ghosts as well.

"So, does that mean we created the dragonfield because *we* need it for some reason?"

Judith brightened.

"Gee, Teddy, that's good. You see what this is all about. You really do, don't you?"

Truth is, it was one of those stab in the dark, blindly lucky thoughts I got about once every six years, but it felt so great to impress Judith that I didn't care whether the Angel of the Lord or Edward R. Murrow or Vice President Nixon had whispered it to me.

We sat with our knees rucked up against our chests on the soft, loamy soil, everything quiet except for the blades of the cornstalks clucking when the wind stirred them and they rubbed together as if casual friends or maybe lovers. Sitting there, I felt we were hundreds of miles away from anyone else. It was just Judith and I, and as the stalks of corn grew slowly taller, she and I grew closer, our emotional spaces bordering and mutually dependent.

Judith slipped into her most serious tone.

"Teddy, I've never told you this, but . . . I've lived before."

"What'd you say?"

"I said I've lived before."

I studied her pretty face and watched as she brushed a long strand of that gorgeous, breeze-swept black hair out of her eyes, and I think I repeated her words to myself. Then I said, "You mean, Topeka? You lived in Topeka before you came here for the summer? Sure, I knew that."

She shook her head and tried to smile, but I could see that her revelation came wrapped in worry.

"I've lived before," she said again, and then glanced up into the sky. "What I mean is, I've lived as a different person . . . in a different part of the world and a different time in history. Quite a few different people, I think. And everywhere I've been there have been ghosts—and they've needed me."

It was like seeing a flash of lightning and waiting for the inevitable rumble of thunder and knowing the thunder will be several seconds behind the lightning. I knew her remarks were going to register with me, but not immediately. When they did, it was as if some ghostly thing had stuck a long, sharp, icy cold finger under my ribs and was probing around to find my heart. I think I involuntarily shivered.

"No, come on," I said, a wad of spittle trying to clog my throat. "This is your only life except for maybe if God brings you back from the grave and then sends you to Heaven or Hell."

She shook her head.

"I'm not joking with you, Teddy. This has nothing to do with God or Heaven or Hell. At least, I don't think it does."

My mouth went dry. I wished we'd brought along our thermos of cold water, but I had forgotten it. Judith had unnerved me and I didn't like it.

"Okay, then, prove it," I said.

"That's what I planned for us to do this morning."

She was beginning to scare me.

"Hey, I haven't lived any other life," I said more loudly than I anticipated. "I'm Teddy O'Dell and that's the only me I've ever been."

"Are you certain?"

"Sure. I'd remember being anybody else. Ask my folks, they'll tell you. You're sounding goofy—that's what I think."

I started to get up and leave.

"Don't you want to stay and watch?" she said. "I'm going back to another life I lived."

I was breathing funny. I hunched my shoulders because that cold finger was wagging around and up and down my spine. I sat all the way back down.

"Sure, I'll watch, but I bet you don't go anywhere."

What I remember most then is how quiet Judith got. She closed her eyes and cupped her hands together out in front of her as if she were going to catch water from the pump and take a cold drink.

"I'm going back, Teddy," she whispered.

I scooted a couple of feet farther away from her, but I didn't say anything. I don't know how much time passed because I was in some kind of bubble in which time didn't exist. Then suddenly, right out of the blue, Judith started speaking, not exactly *to* me, more like into an invisible tape recorder.

"I was a woman somewhere in Europe," she began. I smiled a kind of dopey smile because it was really a convincing job of pretending. "It was the medieval period, I think, and I had a straw hut at the edge of a deep, dark forest. One night I got frightened as I tended a pot of something I had fixed to eat, something I was heating over a small fire. I knew someone was coming. Men. A group of men. They were coming because they thought I was a witch. They said I kept company with wolves and ghosts and the devil. But I was not a witch."

She paused.

I was held in the grip of her story. I couldn't move. I didn't *want* to move, though this was stranger than anything else Judith had ever done. Then her face registered pain and anguish, and I thought maybe it was her polio stuff acting up, but it wasn't. She was breathing rapidly and her fists were suddenly clenched.

"They thought I was a witch because I gave people remedies. I had ways of preparing different plants to cure their sicknesses. I went about the countryside, and now these men were coming because they believed I was evil—" And just like that Judith shifted to the present tense. "And I can't stop them and they've broken into my hut. Their arms are strong, but I can sense how uncertain they are. I'm being dragged from my hut. I will be hanged or burned. Yes, burned. I see the flames reflected in their eyes. No, no-o-o, someone help. Please, someone help."

At the end of her narrative her voice pitched high and she hugged herself and rocked back and forth, and her face was pinched by dry tears. Then she blinked awake. Her breathing gradually calmed.

I was stunned.

I stood up on legs of soft mud.

"Judith," I said, "don't ever do this again. I mean it. You scared the holy shit out of me. You did. If somebody saw you doing this—some grownup, I mean—they'd lock you away."

She reached for my hand and gently pulled me down.

"There's nothing to be frightened of, Teddy. This is real. I'm not insane. I was that woman. She died horribly. She was burned at the stake, but I think she sacrificed herself for her village."

And she came back.

A deadrise from the past.

I just couldn't handle it.

* * *

I didn't go back to the dragonfield for several days. Judith went by herself. I don't know whether she also went on over to the Trogler place, but I think she did. Curiosity finally got the best of me. Or maybe, in part, I returned to the dragonfield because my mother was meanly suspicious of what Judith and I did out there. I delighted in making her wonder.

"I was a nurse in the Civil War," Judith explained the next time we were out there together. "And I was a soldier in France in World War I and I think I breathed mustard gas and my lungs were burning—my soul was burning—and as I lay dying on the battlefield I received a vision of the Fiery Angel, and he was a great comfort in my final minutes. He entered my body or my soul or both. A brilliant light. He can come and go as he pleases, it seems. I woke from the dead, and when I walked across the battlefield other men woke from the dead, too. That's what happens now when I walk over haunted ground—the dead wake. They are dust and, over time, they become earth—just like the earth upon which they died and into which they were buried."

I listened. My thoughts were thick like glue.

"You were a *man*?" I said, because nothing else came to mind.

She nodded.

"In most of my lives I've been a woman. But not every time."

She was often despondent when she spoke of her past lives, so many of them having involved pain and suffering and violence. Losing herself in the memory, she would connect and relive moments and then return and wait as if that former self might show up and speak to her like a friend she hadn't seen for a few months. Or as if she were a ventriloquist's dummy being controlled by a force from beyond. She seemed always to be waiting for something or someone. Hers was the long, sad waiting of animals locked up and forgotten.

Sometimes I would make the mistake of believing Judith had become transparent to me, that I could see through to the essence of her, that nothing blocked me from knowing her fully. I was like a housefly amazed when it smashes into the pane of glass it can see but not fly through. There was always something between Judith and me. Perhaps it was something that protected her from me.

As you might guess, once I had overcome the spookier sensations that I got around Judith in her past life episodes, I insisted that she show me how to call up my own experiences of having lived before. Patiently and assiduously she did so. But time after time I sensed, felt, saw, remembered nothing. Nothing at all. I began to feel that I was somehow abnormal. I began to feel like the boys at school who weren't even able to grow peach fuzz or like that one kid, Danny Dirkson, who had to give himself daily shots of insulin—I began to feel like the deformed bantam chicken my father had recently rescued from the others in its batch, the poor thing being nearly pecked to death because it was different.

Then one afternoon something hit me. I could do it. Judith cheered and hugged me. I was all smiles, and yet I was dutifully reverent in terms of the harsh circumstances and stoical demeanor of my former self. Eyes closed, hands cupped just as Judith always did, I began to see images and I described them.

"I was on a wagon train, and I think I was a scout or a trapper maybe and I was helping settlers cross a snowy mountain pass. We had broken camp one morning when the snow started coming harder and harder, a blizzard, a worse one than we get around

here. But on top of the blizzard, I had sensed that Indians were near, a savage band of them. And wolves,
too. A hungry pack of them. I knew the settlers would
be sitting ducks, and so I headed off in another direction to draw the Indians and the wolves and give
the settlers a chance to escape. My plan worked: I
killed a small band of the Indians and the whole pack
of wolves, but in the blinding snow I got lost. I wandered and wandered until I dropped that evening
from being so tired. I had just enough energy to build
a fire and try to wait out the storm. But during the
night I woke and there were wolves at the edges of my
firelight. A large pack of wolves with yellow eyes. Hungry wolves. The ghosts of the wolves I'd killed. Ghosts
of the Indians, too. I was surrounded. And then my
fire began to die down and down."

"Oh, Teddy," Judith whispered in awe.

"And that's when I became a killer of ghosts."

I shook myself from the vision and acted properly
dazed. Of course, I had made up every stitch of my
past life narrative. I didn't care. It pleased Judith, and
if something pleased Judith, if something gained attention for me in her eyes, then nothing else
mattered.

I wanted to be like her Fiery Angel.

I wanted to protect her from ghosts.

I was determined to fight the Trogler ghosts if it
came to that. I was determined to lay the once dead
to rest again. And, with Judith as my inspiration, I
foolishly thought I could.

But I could see in Judith's eyes an oncoming darkness.

I thought it was probably the ghosts. I knew somehow that they would get bolder.

Was it also because she suspected I was lying? I seriously doubted it. I think it might have had something to do with what she anticipated about her future, about doing what she must do. It was hinted at in the dragonfield. Sometimes when we were leaving its peaceful rows, she would claim that she saw traces of the Fiery Angel—tracks of light—nothing, however, that *I* could ever detect. And we would search for the elusive creature through row after row, never succeeding in meeting him face to face or catching even a vaporous glimpse.

Judith took her sensing of his presence as a sign that the day for her to leave was fast approaching. Her vision was calling her, and I was jealous—I wanted her for myself—and I was also frightened of that transpersonal realm Judith seemed to be able to enter. Would she leave me behind? And what about the ghosts?

Back in the mud room, we would haul out our maps and Judith would pore over them, often lowering her nose to within an inch or so of the roads and cities, studying them as intensely as Egyptologists study hieroglyphics.

"I have to find the way," she would mutter.

"The way where?" I would follow.

"The way to get to where I belong. To where I'm free. To where the dead won't listen for my steps. To where I can be so quiet I don't wake them."

Her words were as lonely and resonant as a school bell ringing in the middle of summer. What was most difficult is that I didn't know how to help her. I loved her, and yet I recognized how useless I was to her except for her romantic notion that I would drive her to where she would get away . . . and from there to where she would get away forever.

She would look into my eyes and say, "Teddy, when do you think I should go?"

My answer was always the same: "Tomorrow. I think tomorrow would be the best day to do it."

But I would never add that I planned to go with her. Each day I would wake and watch for some sign in Judith's behavior that the day had come. Our plans had a gossamer sketchiness about them: We agreed only that an afternoon departure held the most promise because my mother would often nap during that time of day and it would be easy for me to slip the car keys from her purse and swipe some gas money. I would take none of my earthly belongings, no vestige of my life with the O'Dell family; Judith would have consolidated her stuff into one suitcase and the road would be ours.

Yet days passed, and it seemed that the Kansas heat melted one afternoon into the next until time became seamless, and I grew restless, and then bored, and then worried, worried because David would be back in town soon. I didn't know what I would do if he showed up. I didn't trust myself.

There were other fears as well.

The Trogler ghosts were indeed getting stronger. Bolder. I saw evidence one day.

It involved my mother who continued her insidious attempts to run Judith off. Her ways were subtle and guileful; they made me paranoid at times, causing me to suspect that she might even attempt to poison Judith—lacing her iced tea perhaps. Dark scenarios flooded my thoughts. But my mother's most volatile weapon was her tongue and, especially, her constant nagging at my father to rid the house of Judith. Sometimes I would sneak to the door of the bedroom my parents shared and I would listen to the latest chapter in the narrative of complaints my mother voiced. Fortunately my father never succumbed to her twisted logic and repulsive fabrications. The truth is that I think my father enjoyed having Judith around; her beauty and manner lifted his spirits. Much as I did, he felt protective of her and often at the supper table he would ask her about her day, a gesture which never failed to send my mother dodging behind an ugly frown.

One afternoon I was surprised to find my mother had a visitor, though I'm not entirely certain she was aware of it. For me, it was a chilling scene, watching as my mother sat in the living room in her rocker and sewed at something in her lap. There, standing at her shoulder was a woman, poised as if to speak, yet holding back. It was Senta Trogler. I was not mistaken. Much more substantial than dust, the old woman looked, not threatening, but rather desperately lonely—it was as if she ached to reach into my mother's world and touch her, connecting with the possibility of a former friendship or just an acknowledgment that a neighbor had come to visit.

And then, perhaps because the woman sensed I was watching, she vanished. Seemed to crumble to dust and to disappear in the rising of an invisible wind.

My mother muttered something as if to break a lull in an inaudible conversation.

I slipped away, not exactly frightened, but definitely unnerved.

Then one morning very early I was surprised again—not by a ghost this time—this time it was the discovery that someone else in the house besides me and my father definitely liked Judith. For a score of days, Jack and Junior had been rising before dawn to drive to Cottonwood Falls to work at the largest cattle feedlot in the state of Kansas. Hearing them coming down from upstairs, I would scramble up from my pallet on the floor next to Judith's cot and duck out of sight. Junior, always grumpy and preoccupied, would march through the mud room first and Jack, often not fully dressed, would come dragging behind. After the first week or so that Judith had been with us, Jack and Junior gave little attention to her. The smutty remarks ended for the most part, as did the embarrassing pranks—including the stealing of her underwear and attendant display of it in plain sight: they had an affinity, for example, for throwing her brassieres and panties into the upper reaches of our big cedar tree, knowing I would have to brave the stickery limbs to retrieve the articles.

But on the morning I allude to I spied on Jack as he stopped at Judith's cot. She was asleep, her face turned away from him in the partial moonlight. My fists clenched as I watched because I assumed that Jack was planning an act of mischief before dashing off to join Junior. Instead, I saw something unexpected: Jack leaned down and reached out one hand—a ghostly, tender gesture—as if to touch her hair or perhaps her shoulder. He never made contact, but I could just make out his expression, and in it was an intimate diary of his feelings. Not pages of lust. Not a reflection of the kind of sexual abusiveness I knew Mickey wanted to commit. No, this was my brother, his body, his soul showing every sign of affection for Judith. A moonlight sonata of adoration. I saw it. I think he was in love with her, but to my knowledge, he didn't convey those feelings to her until later in the summer. Still, I worried. Could Judith possibly fall for my brutish brother?

And I wondered: Was this young man who had been called to eros the same one who savagely filled my rectum with tractor grease? I knew that it was. Further, I knew it was a testament to the power of Judith to enchant and transform. Increasingly, Judith directed those powers at the blank pages of her notepad. Most

of the stuff she wrote I never got to see, and she had a
peculiar habit of burning her verses when they satisfied
her. I would find tiny piles of ashes all over the property: in the barn, the implement shed, the chicken pen,
in the storm cellar, and even in the outhouse, the latter
prompting my father to issue a blanket indictment of
anyone who might accidentally burn down such an important facility. I don't believe he knew or even
suspected that Judith left ashes there. I certainly would
never have told, and I lived at times in mortal fear that
my mother would find out.

Judith allowed me to read two—and only two—of
her poems. The first was called, "An Ode to Oatmeal,"
inspired, of course, by the hapless creature that managed somehow to stay alive beneath the Trogler place.
The exact text of the poem eludes me, but through
the fog of memory I can see several of its lines:

> Your world is darkness beyond night.
> A realm where kindness finds no light.
> . . . .
> No human touch warms your soul;
> No angel voice whispers you whole.
> . . . .
> No eye of God seeks you out.
> . . . .
> You cannot see the love
> That makes a heart a heart.

I almost cried when I first read it. One day at twilight
we tucked the poem into the crawl space at the Troglers
and ran like fire (though Judith had a hard time doing
so) before any ghosts showed up. Breathless in the
dragonfield, we slowed to reflect upon the deed.

"You think he'll like it?" said Judith. "The poem, I
mean."

"I don't see how he couldn't," I said.

Then one afternoon in the hay mow while I was pretending to be napping but in actuality was fantasizing about holding Judith's naked body, she stopped writing on her notepad and said, "Teddy, what are you thinking about?"

I cleared my throat and drew a blank of humiliation for a heartbeat or two, covering myself by acting as if I'd been sound asleep.

"About someplace I've never been. Someplace neat."

"Like Arizona? Or California?"

"Someplace even better."

We exchanged coy smiles.

"What map is it on?"

"The one in my head."

"Oh, Teddy, you're too much."

She swatted at me playfully, and then I asked her whether she was writing a new poem, and she said that she was.

"It's a poem for you," she said. "Well, for us, really."

"You kidding me?"

She shook her head and those eyes flowed over me like a cool, gentle breeze.

"Here, you want to read it?"

I started to tell her that only one other person had ever written me a poem, but I was afraid she'd nose after that and I would have to explain who David was. I can't even remember the lines of his poem—Judith's is, as the saying goes, stamped indelibly in my thoughts. It was entitled, "To My Onlie Begetter":

Last night
I heard the moon
sky sing its song
to dawn.
To wake the sun.

Just for you
and me.
And the story of our day
was written on pages
of sunlight.

I took hold of her hand and thanked her and kissed
her fingers. I did it without even thinking. It surprised
her, and I believe it pleased her. But then she retreated into those more serious rooms of herself and
stayed there until she looked at me hard and yet with
a certain evident pity. All she said was, "You can't hide
it, Teddy. Your eyes can't keep secrets. But the world
doesn't want certain things to happen."

For the next few days I thought constantly about
what she said, giving her words every conceivable
reading. I kept her poem folded up in the pencil-
holding pocket of my overalls, nestled against the
tarot card. I left it there until sweat and dirt pretty
much obliterated the words, and then my mother's
wash water completed the destruction (and did bad
things to the tarot card as well). But nothing could
erase that poem from my heart.

Emboldened by Judith's verses, I gave extra energy
and attention to her Kennys, and one afternoon, perhaps as a result of my efforts, Judith announced that
she no longer needed her braces. I cautioned her to
wait until Mrs. Wallace could examine her before deciding in that direction, but Judith was adamant.

"I want to get rid of them, Teddy. I want them out
of my sight forever. What should we do with them?"

I didn't hesitate on that one.

"We could bury them."

Judith thought that was a grand idea and naturally then asked me where they should be interred.

"I know a place," I said.

It was out behind the implement shed. I should have known better than to suggest it, for it brought me face to face with a sadness—the one and only sadness—that I shared with my family. But I believed that I could brave any memory and detach myself from heart-tugging events of the past. I was wrong. Judith and I ceremoniously wrapped her braces in sheets of newspaper, and while she carried them in her arms like a dead child, I shouldered our shovel like a rifle.

"It looks like something else is buried here," Judith observed as she knelt down next to a cleared spot within a weed-infested area home to pieces of broken implements. She reached out and touched a small, plywood cross I had so lovingly nailed together for a burial that seemed to have taken place yesterday instead of last September.

My throat filled with phlegm.

All I could say was, "Gussie."

Judith stood up and probably detected how my eyes were welling.

"Who's Gussie?" she whispered.

"Well," I said, ". . . it doesn't matter."

I tottered for what seemed a lifetime before my knees gave and I collapsed to the ground and I wept as I had never wept. Months of repressed sadness came rushing forth like a creek after a toad strangler of a rain; my body convulsed, and I buried my hands in my face and the sounds I made clocked steadily from my soul. Heart-relieving sobs and cries for a living creature missed, for something gone forever. That's what that moment of necessary but embarrassing outburst taught me—some things in life are simply irreplaceable.

"Teddy, I want to know about this."

Through my sobs I think I said, "We'll never have another farm dog."

Judith took my head and shoulders in her arms and held me tightly, and it reminded me of how my mother would hold me years ago when my brothers would reject my efforts to play with them and I would run to her in tears.

In her soft, almost motherly voice, Judith said, "I want to hear about Gussie."

So I told her. Some narratives are pure catharsis. This one definitely was. I took Judith with me to a Christmas morning years ago when my father, melting snow dripping from his heavy coat, marched up to our decorated tree and set down a peach basket filled with a bright-eyed, frisky, black and white border collie puppy, a pretty female that a co-worker at Council Grove named Gus Bouton had given him.

"I think we ought to call her Gussie," said my father.

So we did. My brothers and I fell in love with her instantly, but not, as we would learn later, as deeply as my father did. Gussie was a member of our family for six years; she was our constant companion; she was a little sister to me and my brothers; she was the daughter my father never had—even my mother liked Gussie. Hyperbole is cheap and easy to dismiss, but I'd bet anything of value I possess that Gussie was the smartest dog in the universe. She was a watchdog without peer. Bottom line: She would have gladly given her life to protect any one of us. I remember that she could fetch a ball or a stick thrown into areas other dogs wouldn't dare venture; and she had absolute and total psychological control over every other animal on our farm. My father taught her to respond to the words, "Sic' cows, Gussie," and that's all it took for her to lay out full speed toward the pasture and barkingly cajole our Holsteins to the barn. She brooked no argument from them, sympathized with no excuses, had no patience with malingerers. In short, the roll call of her feats of intelligence and evidences of preternatural sensitivity was a long one and its entries were often cause for a member of our family to muse aloud, "Do you remember that time when Gussie . . ." and wax forth on some unusual or uncanny display of her animal smartness.

But Gussie developed one flaw. A tragic flaw. Looking back, we should have seen it coming. The best way to describe it is that Gussie acquired an addiction. She began chasing cars and trucks and even the school bus. It was as if some piece of wiring in that extraordinary brain of hers shorted out or perhaps some rebel strand of protein led a riot against an outpost of cells, creating an insatiable need for the reckless and self-destructive stimulation of nipping at the fenders and tires of every vehicle that passed our property. My father tried to break her of the habit; he would take a willow branch and whip her whenever he caught her indulging in her dangerous behavior, and on several occasions he borrowed a neighbor's pickup and drove by, and when Gussie gave chase he would have Jack or Junior toss a bucket of water on her as she ran within inches of them.

All to no avail. Gussie was hooked. Every roostertail of dust promised a fix.

The inevitable came on a cool, damp Sunday morning. Miss Opal Whittaker, a retired schoolteacher from Osage City, was heading home after visiting her sister not a mile down the road from us. Maybe because I was getting ready for Sunday school, I never heard a cry of pain, a thud or anything of the like. I remember hearing the knock at our front door and tracking cautiously down the stairs as my father greeted Miss Whittaker, who politely introduced herself even as she patted a handkerchief distractedly to her lips. And then I heard her say, "I've hit an animal, a dog, I'm sure, and it's in the ditch now and not moving . . . but not much blood. Is it yours? Its colors . . . I'm so terribly sorry. I tried to swerve—its colors are black and white."

My mother held back, but the rest of us moved through what seemed a netherworld of unreality to the ditch and the impossible to believe sight of Gussie's body. I don't recall much of anything that was said. My father tried his best to comfort Miss Whittaker before she went tearfully on her way. No one else appeared to want to touch Gussie, so I hunkered down close to her and petted her head, and when I did, my fingers froze. Her skull was soft where I touched, soft like a bad spot on an overly ripe cantaloupe. We lifted her body from the ditch with the matter-of-fact acceptance that farm life demands. We buried her, and then we would have tried to forget, but there was too much to remember. We were stormed by loss. For me and my brothers, the loss was of a loving, loyal companion. We lost a special pet. But for my father it was much worse: with the death of Gussie, he lost part of himself. My brothers and I grieved openly; but my father's grief was hidden and intensely private, and the only evidence of it came one evening when Junior entered the house soberly to say, "Pop's out there where we buried Gussie and he's crying." My impulse was to run to see that spectacle, but Junior stopped me. I'm glad he did.

When I finished my account for Judith, I wiped at my tears, embarrassment branding me like a hot poker, and freed myself from her embrace, though under any other circumstances I would have stayed in her heavenly arms until lightning struck me or the end of the world if possible.

"This isn't a good idea," said Judith, making reference to the burial.

She was right, of course. We gathered up the braces and the shovel and trudged away. But I should mention that Judith said one thing more. She pulled my eyes into her and softly murmured, "Would you like to see Gussie again?"

I remember nodding. I don't think I realized then what she really meant.

The next morning I woke to find Judith missing from her cot; I sensed that she hadn't been gone long, and so I raced outside with only one strap of my overalls clasped. I saw her almost immediately, but I couldn't figure out, right away at least, what she was doing. On her hands and knees, she was crawling up the dusty slope toward our broken windmill. When her arm—the one partially hidden from my view—slid forward, I could see that she had the braces, still wrapped in newspaper, and I knew then why she was creeping and what she was planning to do. Though I wanted to run to her and help her with the ritual, I held back and watched. She was inching up to the rotted planks covering the cistern. I knew how much she feared that cistern, how she had recounted a nightmare about it the third night of her days with us—the cistern had morphed into a hellmouth replete with blood-red lips and razored fangs, and the hand of some powerful force was dangling her over that horrid maw. She woke before she was dropped.

She approached the cistern with the glazed concentration of a snake charmer.

I held my breath. I wanted to shout, "Don't look down into it!" But I didn't. Couldn't.

Because the ghost stole my voice.

Head and shoulders rising up through the planks, the dusty ghost of Siebert Trogler, gripping a small sledgehammer, a blankly maniacal expression on his face, was there and visible for a score of heartbeats. Judith stayed magnificently silent. It became a standoff. And before another score of seconds passed, the ghost dissolved. I watched as Judith stuffed the braces through the rotted planks and let them fall upon the residue of the ghost and down into the hollow-sounding confines of the cistern. She sat back from the opening, and I could see that she was trembling; she put one hand over her eyes, then brushed it through her hair, shivered once and began inching away on her knees. I slipped away into the mud room to await her return. I assumed she would share her ritual, her victory over fear, her victory over one of the Trogler ghosts—her symbolic disposal of the braces—but she did not.

Naturally I became even more wary of the cistern from that point on. More wary of the ghosts. What did it mean that two of them had wandered onto our property? Could they become dangerous? As always, I waited for Judith to take the lead on issues related to the ghosts. Sans braces, she hiked around the property with the help of one crutch (and sometimes without it) and a grimly determined expression. I knew she wasn't escaping pain, merely trying desperately to keep out of its reach as much as possible, and thus she gave her attention to "things," real and live stuff that would allow her to take her mind off everything else. Everything except running away. One afternoon as I spread fresh straw in the chicken coop Judith squatted down to mess with a brood of bantam chicks, about five of them, each large enough to start pecking around for food on its own rather than clinging to the tail feathers of the mother hen.

"Teddy, I think this one's been abused by the others."

I looked over to see Judith holding a small bantie whose pink skin was shining through its black feathers in several places. I tasted the unfamiliar flavor of that word, "abused," making sure I could identify it before I decided to respond.

"They do that," I said. "If the other chicks sense something different about one chick, they'll bully it and sometimes even kill it."

Judith was appalled.

"How could they do that? Look, she's so smiley-faced and nice and pretty. Like Doris Day."

The bantie's meager comb did suggest it was a female, but to say the creature could smile or was nice seemed to me a stretch.

"Can it—can *she* walk all right?" I said.

Judith put the bantie down; she appeared fine, but a second or two later the wind caught the chicken coop door and rattled it just enough to send banties scurrying, half-flying, half-running to escape the imagined threat. Judith's bantie ran into my foot, and I guess I just sort of hopped to get out of the way, and when I landed, I crashed right down on the chick— on one of her legs.

Judith shrieked, "Teddy, you mashed Doris."

I had, indeed.

The damaged leg was as limp as a shoelace. I knew it was badly broken. I knew, further, that the creature's mobility would be so limited that it would be easy prey for stray cats or any other predators. I told Judith I was sorry. She held the bantie and talked to it, and we watched it hobble around for about an hour. I knew the bantie was doomed, but I couldn't bring myself to declare it to Judith. We went back in the house and I gave Judith the Kenny, and I assumed that the bantie had been somewhat forgotten. Sometime during the night, Judith woke me.

"The Fiery Angel came a minute ago and said I should take care of Doris."

I think I was miffed at the mention of the Fiery Angel.

"Do you always do what he tells you to do?"

It was, admittedly, a stupid question.

Judith's answer was delivered in that marvelous fairy tale princess voice she used on occasion: "I am only a spark in his holy fire," she said.

I had no response to that.

At supper Judith asked my father if she could keep Doris in a box in the mud room. My mother grunted in alarm.

"Norman," she said, "we've never allowed livestock in the house. Tell the girl we can't let her do that."

It was all I could do to keep from spitting at my mother. However, it wasn't necessary to offer support for Judith's request because I could see that my father had no intention of saying no to her.

In that way Doris took up residence in the mud room.

Judith cared for that pathetic creature as no mother hen would have; she fed her, watered her, cleaned up after her, and carried her around like a second purse. I was mad at the Fiery Angel for prompting Judith to lavish such care on a chicken. In fact, as the days unfolded I found that, more and more, I was swearing silent oaths naming the Fiery Angel as my invisible enemy.

That was foolish, of course, for I should have been mindful of the much more serious threat represented by the Trogler ghosts.

The dead were walking. Angry shades bent upon mayhem and revenge.

Seven

The Ever-Fixed Mark

In the deep summer nights I would dig for Judith like a treasure. Before I got to know her, I had always loved to bury things. But Judith taught me that unearthing was better. She had, for example, caused me to exhume my deepest feelings of love and affection, confused and conflicted as they were. She also caused me to disinter my appreciation for love poetry, something even Miss Sisler and David had failed despite giving their best efforts to change my negative attitude.

Judith led me to that hidden, lonely cavern of myself where the language of love echoed unabashedly, and when I returned to the outside world I knew that a poet such as Shakespeare could be part of my reality. Among the entries in Judith's memory store of Shakespeare's love sonnets, my favorite was CXVI—"Let me not to the marriage of true minds"—and I would ask her to repeat it probably every other day. At some point, I began to fantasize about being married to Judith and living on a farm with her surrounded by lots and lots of animals, especially bantam chickens. That I had no real affinity for farming made no difference. I embraced the vision with my heart and soul. I wanted Judith to be my wife; I wanted to worry about paying the bills with her; I wanted to have nightly sex with her; to have children with her; to listen to the radio with her; and to grow old and die in her arms.

"Who made up the rule that cousins can't get married?" I asked her one day.

She answered more quickly than I was expecting her to.

"God did. Or maybe God told one of those really old guys in *Genesis* or one of those other first books in the Bible to add it to the list of important things not to do."

"But it's not one of the ten commandments," I countered hesitantly, though I thought *maybe* it could be number six or seven.

"It doesn't matter, Teddy. The world doesn't want brothers and sisters marrying or cousins marrying. And it doesn't want you having more than one wife or more than one husband."

"I only want one wife," I said. Then I steered my next question closer to what was on my mind: "Do you think God would punish us if someday *we* got married?"

My throat tingled as I awaited her answer. She was twisting on a monkey fist made of baling twine.

"Somebody would. God or church ladies or someone like that. Cousins used to get married all the time, Teddy, but when they had children, the kids would be deformed or really stupid. They'd have great big heads and eyes that wouldn't stay open and mouths that couldn't stay shut and so they would slobber all the time."

In my fantasy of marrying Judith I suddenly edited out the part about having children with her.

"Oh," I said, trying not to sound too disappointed.

Judith sighed and said, "They say God punishes you for things forbidden."

That word, "forbidden," had an ominous ring to it for me.

"Do you think you did something forbidden and God got mad and made your legs crippled?"

I regretted the question. I knew she didn't like to talk about how her affliction had come about, and I didn't know where I was headed with my query.

Judith shrugged. Her face took on a seriousness that made her look shatteringly beautiful.

"If I did, I don't know what it was. Talked back to my mother maybe. Or maybe—well, I don't like church—that could be it. Or . . . or maybe God has nothing much to do with what happens to us."

She stared into my face with a certain defiance in her eyes that I had no intention of standing up to. I was on her side, in fact. I changed the subject, asking her to recite my favorite sonnet. The lines I liked best were those where Shakespeare describes love as ". . . an ever-fixed mark,/That looks on tempests, and is never shaken." Judith explained to me that a tempest was sort of like one of our thunderstorms—it seemed so neat to me that a storm wouldn't scare you away from loving someone. I said as much to Judith and she further explained that tempests might mean fights or arguments or that kind of thing. But I held onto the meaning I wanted: I knew my love for Judith was the ever-fixed mark; whether I would find the courage to say so one day was another matter. No thunderstorm, or even a tornado, would stop me from caring about her.

But I had a rival. Just as Shakespeare himself alluded to a "rival poet" in the lines of some of his sonnets, I, too, had a competitor for the affections of Judith—I didn't count Jack as such, though I should have, and I did watch him more and more carefully for signals of his intentions. No, my challenger was the Fiery Angel. He held Judith's heart in a way my hands and my mind weren't shaped for. It was frustrating because I had never even *seen* him. Would he be so big that I would be foolish to try to fight him?

Did he really exist?

All I knew for certain was that I wanted to win Judith over. She cared for me—she had said as much—and she called me her Onlie Begetter, and yet I unwisely wanted something more. I wanted to dazzle her. One warm summer morning I got my chance.

Judith and I were in the hay mow, and as she studied a map of the United States, she was digging at one of her ears with Slim, her treasured bobby pin. I told her that I was afraid one day she was going to poke a hole in her eardrum, but she was so transfixed by the map that she either didn't hear me or else she deflected my words immediately.

"I don't think it's Arizona after all," she said.

"What isn't?"

"Where the Fiery Angel is asking that I come to meet him."

"Why can't he just meet you here?"

Judith smiled at me with her arrestingly benign tolerance.

"Because, Teddy, probably this isn't the place I'm supposed to be. Least I don't think it is."

I let her go back to her map, biting my tongue to keep from saying something catty about the Fiery Angel. I was restless, with raging adolescent hormones. I felt like fighting or doing something I would later regret.

"Ever want to be a daredevil?" I said.

She shook her head.

"Well, I do. I feel like staring into the face of danger and spitting in his eye."

I was proud of the almost poetic nature of my statement.

Still scrutinizing her map, Judith said, "I think I hear Brutus out there pawing the ground. You could jump on his back and ride him like a rodeo rider— that would be a dangerous, daredevil stunt."

She shook her head again, this time a gesture indicating she wasn't being serious and that only someone about to run out of his day's supply of sanity would find any merit in her remark. But she set things to ticking in me. I stood up and said, "I'll be right back."

"Teddy?"

In one of my mother's rag bags, I found the reddest shirt I could. It would be my cape. I was going to play matador. Brutus would be my bull, my *toro*. No pretend bull, but rather the real, flesh and blood, savage beast I would toy with to the astonishment and delight of my lady love.

"You've got to come watch me," I said returning with the hole-infested red shirt and wearing one of Junior's old baseball caps.

"Teddy, what?"

"You'll see."

I headed out of the barn with Judith hobbling along behind. I was becoming intoxicated with every drink of the possibilities I was envisioning. I hesitated at the top of the fence to make sure Judith was watching.

"Teddy, what do you think you're going to do?"

In precise terms, I didn't have an answer for her. Brutus was standing at the far end of our feedlot; he was chewing his cud indifferently, probably thinking of some sexy-bottomed lady cow he'd like to mount. The full force of my stupidity didn't hit me until I jumped down from the fence and started walking toward Brutus waving the raggedy shirt.

"Teddy, you have gone crazy!"

There was both genuine fear and amazement in Judith's voice, and though I knew I was investing heavily in foolishness, I felt good. I had Judith's undivided attention. I could feel it on my back like a concentrated ray of sunlight. I had stolen the show from the Fiery Angel and it was my opportunity to perform.

"Hey, bull. Hey, bull," I called out.

But Brutus didn't even turn his magnificent head.

"Teddy, get out of there! I can't believe you're doing this!"

Part of me couldn't either.

I picked up three or four pieces of dried cow manure and tossed them at Brutus—only one piece struck him. Slowly he cranked his massive head around, not stopping his chewing, but eyeing me with enough suspicion that I felt he wouldn't totally disregard me. Judith continued haranguing me in the distance; I guess I must have tuned her out, especially when Brutus shook his head and repositioned himself so that he was facing me.

Then the scene acquired more spectators.

It was weird. Very, very weird. But there they were, not completely distinct, but definitely there: the Troglers—Rolf, Senta, Siebert, Romina . . . and Hunter—pressed against the fence looking a bit as if they were certain I was about to join their ranks. I assumed that Judith saw them, too. It didn't matter. A line had been crossed.

I felt a dull, rushing sensation similar to being underwater, and yet at the same time I could feel the earth beneath my bare feet, warm, dusty earth, substantial and somehow reassuring. Brutus and I drew a bead on each other. He didn't appear angry or to have any mad bull traits that I could detect. If anything, he seemed puzzled by the sight of a fourteen-year-old boy in the feedlot willing to die. As he stared at me, I tried to recall the moves I'd seen a

matador make on a newsreel clip once—something
like an elegant dance but with a partner who instead
of wanting to embrace you, had in mind ripping your
intestines out.

I lifted my cape and the word, "Toro," leaped from
my mouth.

I still felt pretty good. Pretty courageous.

I stutter-stepped forward until I was within twenty
yards of Brutus. I thrust out my chin and tried to look
haughty and disdainful. I flapped my cape, holding
it out where I imagined the bull would direct his
charge. The ghosts looked on, shapings of dirt and
not quite substantial. And so did Judith.

"Teddy, I'm going to be mad at you if you get hurt!"

The lovely Judith, I reasoned, would revise her comments once she had seen my bravery, my skill in full
bloom. All my thoughts of how foolish I was being had
evaporated. But Brutus wasn't performing his role.
He appeared to have no intention whatsoever of coming at me. It occurred to me that maybe he was the
wrong kind of bull. Spanish and Mexican bulls were
black; Brutus was just an ordinary, albeit huge, whitefaced bull. Maybe it was like trying to charm a water
moccasin when what you needed was a cobra.

Maybe Brutus was just too damn big and lazy.

I kicked up some dust and shouted at him.

Still nothing.

I glanced over my shoulder and saw Judith on the
top rail; her face showed signs of pain and anxiety
and, as always, a remarkable beauty. That beauty pro-
vided a shot of adrenalin. I took a chance and faked a
run at Brutus. It surprised him. He took a couple of
steps back and readjusted his eyeing of me.

He never pawed the ground or snorted, but something in the way he lowered his head and kept me in
view gave me a sudden start. My grip on the shirt was

sweaty; the warmth of the morning was pressing in on me, and I realized that I had waded into the center of the feedlot where escape would be difficult. And I hadn't brought a sword (of course, I didn't have one) or any other kind of weapon.

"Teddy, just back away from him very, very slowly, and maybe he won't do anything."

Judith made good sense. I lowered the shirt momentarily, and I could picture myself inching backward and reaching the safety of the fence and perhaps the embrace of Judith, an embrace she would offer despite her disgust with me.

Suddenly Brutus bobbed his head. I could hear his breathing; it was chesty and agitated, flecked with impatience. I sensed that he might be ready to do something, and I wasn't prepared for what happened next. The ghost dog's barking exploded like powerful shouts, purposeful barking designed to prompt the bull. I turned to face the ghosts, but they crumbled, and so did the barking, muffled and throaty.

But it was too late.

I couldn't believe how quickly Brutus moved.

I thought again of how they say that in moments of extreme fear one's sense of reality slows. Not mine. It seemed to me that everything found warp speed. Brutus filled my vision before I could blink twice. Vaguely, I could hear, as if it were coming from somewhere in another realm, Judith scream. The rust-red and white blob that was Brutus thundered straight for me; sheer survival instincts allowed me to dodge out of the way of his head and horns and most of his body. I dove and landed hard on my stomach in the dust, a surprising pain crescendoing up my leg and into my chest and finally my brain. I yelled so loudly that, despite the degree of pain, I could hear my voice echo around the rim of our silo and spin off into the pasture.

Brutus had stepped on my foot.

My mouth went dry. I tasted something bitter; it was like holding an aspirin on your tongue too long before swallowing it without a glass of water. I must have blacked out, much as I probably had when Jack and Mickey greased me.

I next remember an intensely bright light in my face. It was as if the sun were only a few feet above me. It had fallen into my eyes. And I could smell Judith's perfume. She was impossibly near. She blocked out that bright light and helped me sit up.

"Teddy, did his horns get you?"

Judith's fear and concern were palpable. She was looking all over me—for blood, I guess. Then pain began again to move through me in ripples, throbbing, burning, stinging.

"It's my foot," I whimpered.

"Oh, God, Teddy."

I reached for it, but when I saw it—saw it in detail—I decided not to touch it: it was mostly skinned with an ugly, red stain shaped like a messy lipstick kiss from huge lips. The skin on the top of my foot and up a ways on my ankle was peeled back grotesquely like a boiled chicken's. The foot had already started to swell, raising dark, purplish lumps the color of egg plant.

"I don't think it's broken," I said. "But it hurts like hell."

Judith stuck her pretty face right into mine. "If I had a switch, I'd whip your rear end for doing such a crazy thing. Why'd you do this?"

"So you'd stop talking about the Fiery Angel."

She was speechless—at least for a few seconds. In the meantime I remembered Brutus. I glanced around hurriedly. Then I saw him back where he was when I had first climbed down into the feedlot.

"Well, for your information," said Judith, "it's the Fiery Angel who's probably going to keep you from getting stomped as flat as a cow pie."

It wasn't what I wanted to hear. I recalled that intensely bright light and wondered about its source. I also gritted my teeth.

"I don't need his help."

"Can you stand up?"

"Yeah, I think I can."

I braced myself against Judith and nearly fainted when I tried to put weight on the foot. I groaned. Judith held me, and at about that same instant I noticed Brutus had turned our way and looked annoyed.

"Teddy, I'm going to let you sit back down."

"Are you going to just leave me here with Brutus?"

She helped me lower myself into the dust and then she stepped between me and the bull.

"I have a mind to," she said.

What happened next did not lodge in my memory in a clear, frame-by-frame sequence. It was gauzy and nonlinear. I recall that in a frightened tone I pleaded with her to get out of the feedlot. I recall Brutus swinging his head, globs of foamy saliva dripping from his mouth. We had pissed him off—or rather *I* had (with the help of Hunter's barking) and Judith had come to my rescue.

This hadn't been the plan at all.

In white-knuckled, cowardly fashion I began to crawl toward safety. Judith was not responding to my calls to save herself; in fact, she was stubbornly holding her position even as Brutus issued a low, bellicose warning of his own which sounded as if it shook loose from his groin and spiraled up into his throat before being launched from his tongue.

Judith merely raised her one crutch and aimed it at Brutus, pointed it right between his eyes. I continued my pathetic crawling, all the while scrambling mentally to think of some way to explain to my father how it came to be that our cousin was trampled by a bull. Every foot or so I would hesitate long enough to renew my plea that Judith get the hell out of the feedlot.

She didn't need my advice.

She charmed that bull.

I don't know any other way to describe it—how she did it, I will never know, though to add insult to injury, she later gave more credit to the Fiery Angel. The standoff between her and Brutus ended when the massive creature turned and meandered over to the water tank. And while my bullfighting days came to an end that morning, I could not imagine that my humiliation ever would.

Judith wouldn't speak to me the rest of the day. Of course, my mother blamed Judith for my wound; it was a hot, tense ride into town to see Doc Gillis who wrapped my foot and chortled over the narrative of how I received the injury—as you might assume, my revised version did not include the barking of a ghostly dog or the role of the Fiery Angel. Nothing was broken. Just badly bruised. My ego more so than my foot if I were to characterize matters accurately.

Back at home Judith loaned me her other crutch and thus we became odd twins, and I was quick to point out to her the symbolic import of the situation, the new bond that had been forged between us. I tried several times to thank her for rescuing me, but she was apparently so disappointed by my stupidity that she would simply turn away and shake her head.

At supper that night my father expressed his consternation and Jack laughed his head off. I noticed that he stared a bit longingly at Judith when I described her bravery. Junior, on the other hand, was indifferent to my plight; he was obviously floating miles from the rest of us in an atmosphere of worry about something in his own life. Again, I didn't mention ghosts—my family wasn't prepared for Otherness.

The next morning, my foot very sore but not on fire, I caught up with Judith in the dragonfield; she swatted me on the head and made me promise I would never, ever again do anything as idiotic as attempting to fight a bull. I wanted to kiss away the glaze of anger on her lips, but I figured that she would swat me a second time—and probably use her crutch for emphasis.

We skirted the whole issue of ghosts.

I was growing increasingly worried about them; if Judith was, she didn't often give herself away.

"You know, I can still drive," I said, hoping to reassure her that if her plans to escape materialized anytime soon, I could be counted on to help. "It's my clutch foot, so it won't matter a lot."

Suddenly, and this took me completely by surprise, she began to laugh.

"Oh, Teddy, you're too much."

I bathed in her laughter and in her smile. A breeze jostled the corn and clouds scudded across the sun, and it felt good to be with her, good to be alive.

"I wasn't great at showing off, was I?"

She shook her head. Then she frowned.

"I was really scared," she said.

She reached over and stroked my wrist, the one with the tinkle bracelet, and when she touched me images rose in my head, stuff that came, I think, from my bottomless desire for our lives to become inextricably bound.

I felt the surge of boldness that all liars feel.

"Like another time," I said. "Like when you saved me before."

"Before? When?"

I had the entirety of her beautiful face. I was holding it tenderly with my words. My mind was filling rapidly like a grain bin fills with milo or wheat after harvest in a Kansas summer. I was about to make something up, and I knew it had to be convincing. I knew it had to sell. It just had to.

"In another life," I said.

"We've been in another life *together?* Oh, Teddy, are you sure?"

I nodded gravely, confidently.

She edged up close to me, and my thoughts started winging wildly like birds uncertain of their flight pattern.

"Yeah, I'm real sure."

"When? Where? I want to know all about it."

I spoke without breathing.

"It was in . . . Kentucky."

I thought of that state because Junior and Jack always talked about what a good college basketball team they have.

Judith's eyes were filled with interest; she nested herself to listen, and I began talking, narrating—making up stuff, grasping at pieces of flotsam and jetsam in my stream of consciousness.

"About a hundred years ago. You see, I was a scout for a wagon train of settlers heading west, and we were in Kentucky. Seems like I've been a scout several times in the past. I had—I was scouting ahead for the best trail and—to look for Indians. Yeah, I knew there were Indians, unfriendly Indians that threatened the

wagon train. Then, you see, a band of them—I don't
know what tribe—a hunting party I think it was—well,
they saw me before I saw them and they started chasing after me, shooting arrows and yelling their war
yells. I ran. I knew the forest because I was a real good
scout, and I got away from them, but they—they
wounded me."

"Oh, Teddy."

What bullshit I was spreading!

"Yeah, an arrow. One of them got me with an
arrow—in . . . in my foot. The same foot Brutus
stepped on."

I hesitated, not wanting to meet Judith's eyes because I thought she would detect my whopper of a lie.
But apparently she didn't. Emboldened, I kept my
story going.

"I was hurt pretty bad, bleeding a lot. And that's
when—that's when *you* found me."

Judith was spellbound.

"Was I with the wagon train? Who was I?"

I just kept talking, hoping the lie had a life of its
own.

"No, . . . not with the wagon train. No, you see, you
were—you were an Indian." I paused to catch my
breath, dizzied by the pulsating goofiness of my tall
tale. "You were a young woman and a member of the
tribe that shot me, only instead of running when you
found me, you know, running and telling the other
members of the tribe where I was, well—you helped
me."

My fabrication gave me a brief out-of-body sensation. When I fell back into my flesh and blood, I was
gulping air and my chest was hot and tingling, and I
wondered if maybe—like Pinocchio—my nose was
going to start growing. Judith shook her head in awe.
She was buying it, buying every pound of it. I was like

a bowling ball rolling downhill—nothing was going to slow up my tale. I was shooting for a strike.

"You put some stuff on my wound, stuff you carried in a little deerskin pouch, I think it was. You stopped the bleeding, and you wrapped my foot in some kind of leaves. And I told you that you were brave and kind and when we—when we looked into each other's eyes, we fell in love. Right there, we just both knew it. Love at first sight, sort of. Love like the ever-fixed mark."

I held my breath as Judith gazed off into nothingness and whispered, "We were soul mates. We were meant to be together."

"I think so," I followed, "because here's what happened: Your tribe caught up with us and killed us, but . . . well, we came back as ghosts . . . and . . . and we were lovers for all time."

Before I knew what was happening, she slung her arms around my neck and pulled me forward and kissed me full on the mouth. I remember only that my face felt funny—tight with joy, tight like a balloon about to burst. Then she grabbed my wrist and said, "Teddy, I want to see if I can make contact with that life, with those ghosts wherever they are."

"What do you mean?"

I felt an icy fork of terror jab into my spine.

"I mean, I want to go back to that same moment of being the Indian woman and tending to your wound and falling in love with you."

My God, her smile was gorgeous. She was so excited she was almost panting. But I was on the edge of panic.

"I don't know if that's possible," I said.

Judith, however, insisted that she rest her hands in the palms of mine and that we close our eyes and concentrate. She was convinced we could have some kind of instantaneous past life revisitation. My heart felt as heavy and lifeless as a big clinker of coal.

We tried for better than ten minutes, I would guess.

"Maybe my foot's hurting so much I'm just not able to concentrate," I said.

But Judith shook her head, and once again I found myself holding my breath. I felt that she had caught me in the lie. I felt naked and exposed.

"No," she said. "I believe I'm the one who's keeping the memory from coming back."

"Why do you say that? I mean, maybe you are, but. . . ."

"I've blocked it out. I'm sorry, Teddy, but I think I've blocked it out because I knew even then that there would be obstacles in our love. The world would try to keep us apart, and so I just erased the experience from all memory."

I started to breathe normally again.

But I felt terrible. Judith was on the verge of tears. She was blaming herself.

"Maybe it'll come back to you," I said.

A small smile flickered at her lips.

"Maybe. I hope so. I'm sorry, Teddy. I'm sorry I spoiled things."

"No. No, you didn't."

I held her hand for a long time. I held it until the sun drove us from the dragonfield. I felt lousy and wonderful all at once. I hated to see Judith sad, and yet I still carried her kiss of elation on my lips. And there was something more. While I felt that I was an imposter—that I hadn't legitimately entered Judith's transpersonal realm—I suddenly believed I had the power to make her believe.

A power to create fantasy.

And be the ghost of myself.

And wait for the good hard light of tomorrow when Judith and I would run away together.

Then one morning tomorrow arrived.

I woke early to a grey-eyed rain, and so did Judith. My hands were sticky and I could smell myself, and I felt too embarrassed to meet her eyes directly. Busy writing poetry or some kind of notes, she gave no indication at breakfast that our escape day had dawned. Maybe as we ate our eggs she did not know. She also didn't let on if she knew what I had done during the night. The house was silent. On the stove, in my father's much-loved, much-used, blackened coffee pot, were the dregs of his morning coffee. A cereal bowl, corn flakes stuck to its sides, was in the sink; it belonged to Jack. I guessed that Junior hadn't felt like eating. As usual, I had heard my brothers thunder down the stairs and had hidden, and perhaps I had listened to their exchange more closely because of what had happened to Junior. Neither had much to say.

Junior's girlfriend, Phyllis Penner, had discovered she was pregnant.

Awash in darkly uncertain emotions, Junior had broken the news to my parents the night before, and I had stolen down from my room to eavesdrop on the somber scene. My brother cried. My mother, not unexpectedly, managed somehow to include Judith as part of the cause for Junior's problem.

"Nothing about this family has been the same since that girl came here and brought the Devil with her."

My father dismissed her reasoning, of course, but I knew that Judith probably overheard her. Had Judith become inured to the verbal pain my mother dished out? I suppose she had—still, I couldn't keep from hating my mother every time she directed hurtful

comments at the young woman I loved. I felt sorry for
Junior. From what I could gather, he wanted to marry
Phyllis, but her parents would not hear of it. They
planned to send their daughter off to relatives in Missouri where she would have the child and then
apparently put it up for adoption. Junior was torn. My
father quietly, strongly urged him to finish his senior
year of high school and see how things looked then.
Weather and the future, he explained, change before
a man can rest his mind on them. He took Junior outside where they stood under the yard light and talked
for probably an hour or more. My mother muttered
off to bed. I don't know what my father and Junior
said to each other. Things of cosmic importance
under a starry, Kansas sky, I'm sure. From my vantage
point I watched as my father draped his arm around
Junior's neck, and Junior folded against my father's
shoulder like a frightened little boy. It was a moment
of high drama Shakespeare himself could not have
bettered.

Father and son, a companionship of new ghosts
after the death of innocence.

In a way, my mother was right. Our family was not
the same—not because of the arrival of Judith—but
rather because we had lost whatever closeness we had.
We were five separate individuals living separate lives,
sharing virtually nothing, wanting and expecting little of each other. I think my father tried to keep the
bond intact (the scene with Junior was evidence). So
did my mother in her own neurotic and feckless way.
But we had pulled in different directions for too long.
In part, it was natural: Three boys heading toward
manhood can't stand on common ground with their
parents forever, and yet I realized that we were all selfish and had been that way for years. My father gave

every effort to be our center, but the center could not hold. It seems it never does.

The O'Dells were almost as dead and ghostly as the Troglers.

When my father and Junior solemnly trudged off to their beds, I limped to my nighttime area next to Judith's cot. She was asleep, I believed, though tossing some because it was so warm and our electric fan so pathetic. Finally I just unplugged it and thought about Junior and listened to the wind kick up in front of an approaching thundershower. I imagined I could hear Oatmeal and the preternatural barking of Hunter. I thought that perhaps Oatmeal belonged with the ghosts, so lonely and in pain. But unlike them he refused to die. In one corner of the mud room Doris was clucking raggedly with her beak closed. I could hear a distant train chugging through town, and I listened for its hauntingly solitary departure whistle. Then my thoughts gravitated back to Junior and Phyllis, and I could imagine them in the backseat of Junior's old car, laughing as maybe they undressed each other and kissed, kissed until kissing wasn't enough. I tried to imagine what followed.

I could feel an erection straining against my underpants.

The air in the mud room took on a sultry edge. Judith tossed and turned once or twice more, and then suddenly she sat up. I was lying so that I faced her cot, but I pretended to be asleep. Through squinted eyes I watched as Judith tugged her cotton nightgown over her head and then dabbed it at her neck and forehead. Even in the shadows I could make out her body, naked except for white panties that seemed to glow. I could not keep my eyes from her breasts as she leaned her head back, causing those full breasts to jut out so invitingly. I feared I would choke on the phlegm of

desire rising from my chest into my throat. Having
folded up her nightgown and put it aside, Judith lowered herself down again, her back to me, and settled
into sleep.

But I couldn't.

I waited a lifetime of seconds for Judith's breathing
to slow and thicken, signals I knew meant that she had
fallen asleep, before I took my pillow and sandwiched
my hard penis with it. In my thoughts, I wove my way
into Judith's womanly flesh. I wandered in the uneasy
maze known to every sexually inexperienced male
where imagination attempts to locate pieces of a marvelous puzzle and make sense of the mystery of sexual
urges. The sides of the pillow were Judith's thighs; I
buried myself between them. I moaned as sensation
left imagination far behind and infinite yearnings
rose and I battled to keep as silent as possible. Then
pleasure transcended all other concerns and realities,
and I danced on the edge of ecstasy, danced faster
and faster, and I was blending with the shadows and
escaping time, soaring inwardly, my pulse singing fire,
my body pumping, my tinkle bracelet rattling melo-
diously.

But my passion fountained, spewing well before I
could prepare myself to fully enjoy the magic I had
conjured. The dreamy texture of sexual fantasy dissolved into a wet, sticky, effusive mess. I was jolted
back to reality. My sensations crashed. I raked my sore
foot against the leg of Judith's cot and stifled a yelp;
fortunately, though only a matter of feet away from
me, she did not waken. I cleaned up as well as I could
in the virtually lightless room, and then I collapsed,
still breathing rather heavily, and touched myself even
as I grew flaccid and shameful and sweatingly satisfied.

After breakfast I told Judith I had to go to the barn

to clean out the milking stalls. She continued writing on her notepad, and so I said, "You writing a poem about Doris?"

She shook her head.

"No, I'm just writing to myself about how you and I are like spirits."

I approached her remark with caution.

"Spirits? You mean, like ghosts? That kind of thing?"

She shrugged disarmingly.

"Maybe. Or maybe spirits in the sense of not quite real people who have to be in a place where they don't belong. It's a blessing when spirits know each other."

Images of the Troglers slipped through my thoughts like an inner slide show, but then I decided I was pleased that Judith included me in whatever she was talking about.

"Oh," I said. "Yeah, I see what you mean."

On the way to the barn I had to admit that, as usual, I had only the foggiest notion what she meant—that business about "not quite real people"—it baffled me because, if anything, when I was with Judith I felt I had a better grasp of what was real and what was not. She made things real. When she looked at things, they became real—the sky, trees, the barn, rocks, chickens—she saw the particularity of things and embraced them not as something ideal or as something symbolic, but as that which could be experienced by the senses.

Everything except the Fiery Angel.

And perhaps the Troglers.

In the barn I spent the better part of an hour scooping manure and laying out a fresh floor of straw and seeing that our big feed sacks of milo and bran were full. Keeping cow shit away from my bandaged foot was tricky. I did a lot of hopping. As I worked, I let my thoughts float off like bubbles or balloons released at the county fair. Mostly I thought about Judith—I vowed not to masturbate so close to her again—but at other moments I thought about Junior and my father and even about David. I dreaded having him and Judith in my life at the same time. It smacked of having to make a choice, and I knew I wouldn't be able to run right through it and escape the dangers—it was too much like trekking over quicksand.

I also believed I wanted Judith far more than I wanted David.

By the time I finished the stalls, the sun was out, eye-blisteringly bright and promising to get hotter than sin. I was hobbling toward the house when I saw something that stopped me dead in my tracks: Judith was halfway up the rungs of the windmill. More unsettling was this: The ghost of Romina Trogler was at the top. At first, I gave my entire attention to Judith; I was afraid to call to her because I thought it might startle her and she would fall. She was hanging on with one hand, and with the other she was shielding her eyes from the sun; she was squinting hard, and yet I could detect a sweet, beatific smile on her face. Was she looking at Romina? I couldn't tell.

Somehow she must have known I was below because she suddenly spoke and her remarks seemed to be directed at me.

"Sometimes he hides in the sun," she said.

"Who does?"

She looked down with an expression of surprise, not because I had said something, but rather that I didn't know the source of her reference.

"The Fiery Angel. Can you see him?"

She glanced up again and pointed. The ghost of Romina Trogler disappeared. I looked higher. All I could see was the sun, but I pressed with my eyes until I was nearly blinded.

"I can't see nothing."

Thankfully Judith began her descent before much time passed. I helped her from the final rungs and out over the rotted mouth of the cistern. I gleaned the area for any sign of Siebert Trogler. Had the cistern become his hiding place?

Then Judith said, "The Fiery Angel likes to do that—get right in front of the sun so you can't see him clearly."

"So what's he doing? Is he just hovering up there for no good reason? And why was Romina up there?"

Judith shook her head.

"Teddy, it means it's time. This afternoon I need to leave. The Fiery Angel is calling. The ghosts are getting braver."

I was unprepared.

I'm not sure why, but I wanted to protest. I even started to suggest that she had been out in the sun too long. I didn't, because her voice, her manner, her words were compelling. And besides that, I loved her. I wanted to leave with her regardless of who or what was calling her. And I told myself that I wasn't afraid of the ghosts.

Back in the kitchen my mother was sitting at the table locked in one of her mesmeric gazes, the cup of coffee in front of her no longer giving off steam. The ghost of Senta Trogler was sitting with her, or was, at least until my presence apparently caused her to dissolve in a powdery puff of dust.

My thoughts were too committed to the escape plan to give much attention to either my mother or her ghostly companion—in fact, I would have paid them no mind at all were it not for what I saw near my mother's coffee cup.

A small heap of ashes on a plain, white paper napkin.

I felt a nauseating wave of terror wash over me.

In the mud room I smelled smoke. My mother had discovered one of Judith's burnings, but I knew she wouldn't say anything until my father got home. She would merely taunt us by putting the ashes on display. I was glad when she left the table, and I hoped that she would follow her usual pattern of taking a nap at some point in the afternoon.

"Should I bring along Doris?"

Judith had finished packing as I put together a few sandwiches and retrieved a couple of hard-boiled eggs from the ice box. I also made a thermos of tea.

"She'll just be one more thing for you to worry about," I said.

Judith had the bantam pressed against her cheek.

"I don't want to leave her. I can't bear to think what would happen to her."

I wasn't going to argue; besides, I needed to think about other stuff. While we were waiting in the mud room for my mother to fall asleep, we got out our maps and pretended to study them. I say pretended because I sensed that neither of us was concentrating on them.

Breaking an awkward silence, Judith whispered, "I'll never forget you, Teddy. You're good. You're a dear heart."

What she said angered me. I don't know why. Maybe because I was disappointed that she didn't see that I wasn't about to let her go by herself, that she didn't see how much I wanted to be with her. I got up and went and rifled through my mother's purse. I took the car keys and some money. All she had was about two dollars. That would give us most of a tank of gas, but it seemed to me we ought to have more road money, and so when I came back to Judith I said, "Money's going to be a problem," and I showed her a dollar bill and almost another dollar's worth of change.

"I have money, Teddy," she said. "I always have secret money."

She picked up her small, black patent leather purse and hugged it to her stomach. I almost accused her of stealing the money from somewhere. I didn't know how much she had, and I was mystified as to why her secretive ways irritated me.

"I'm going to check to make sure she's asleep—then we'll go," I said.

It didn't seem possible that we were really going to do this. Wouldn't someone stop us? Could it really be this easy?

The door to my parents' bedroom was open a crack, enough space to let me see that my mother was lying in a fetal position with her face toward the wall. The ghost of Senta Trogler was standing there staring down at my mother who looked small and fragile. I listened until I heard my mother's faint snoring, then I surprised myself by whispering, "Goodbye," and the ghost of the old woman became a small heap of dirt. Why had she been there? Truth is, I no longer cared.

I imagined one day getting over being angry with my mother, but not anytime soon. I knew, of course, that she would blame our running away totally on Judith. I wouldn't be around to present the truth of the matter. My only other regret was that this would hurt my father. He didn't deserve to be hurt. Jack and Junior wouldn't miss me, but my father was another story. I had thought about leaving him a note; however, the gap between language and reality was too great for me. Leaving was one of those untellable things. It opened up an inner chasm, and I couldn't tightrope walk over it.

"Let's go," I said to Judith.

"Teddy, I have a favor to ask of you."

I was nervous. I wanted to get going before my mother woke or I got cold feet.

"We'd better hurry," I said. "What is it?"

Her eyes—those extraordinary eyes—were filling, and she touched my wrist and said, "Will you tell your father I'm sorry. I just had to do this. It's not his fault. He's been good. I felt welcome in his house when he was around—tell him that, would you?"

"Sure."

I grabbed her suitcase and the sack lunch I'd fixed and she followed with Doris cradled in one arm. I vowed that I wouldn't look back at the house, but by the time I got to the car it felt like there was something wedged across my throat and that I wouldn't ever be able to swallow again if I didn't turn around. So I did. It was just a Kansas farmhouse, a plain, two-story, white clapboard farmhouse—probably thousands like it in the state. But it was the only home I'd ever known.

I sighed so deeply that it made my shoulders ache.

Then we loaded up. Suddenly I knew how Junior must have felt—a wrenching of whatever had always kept him bolted down. I wasn't leaving. I was coming loose, and if Judith hadn't said something right then as I positioned myself behind the wheel and put the key in the ignition, I might have aborted the escape.

"It's a second blessing," she said, "when one spirit has another spirit that will help her get to where she belongs. I'm twice blest."

I glanced over at her. She looked radiant.

"Me, too," I said.

I hesitated long enough to issue a silent prayer to the gods that the car would start and we wouldn't have a flat tire or the radiator wouldn't boil over on us. When that ignition roared to life on the first try, Judith and I cheered, and she leaned over and kissed me on the shoulder in the usual spot, and I suppose at that point I totally dismissed how crazy, how absolutely insane we were to be running away, me with no driver's license, little money, no clothes except those on my back, and no real idea of where we were going or how we would live.

But we were on our way.

I had some trouble with the clutch and not just because I had a sore foot. I kept whispering that I was sorry each time I would grind the gears and the car would buck and lurch. Judith didn't seem to mind. She began reciting Sonnet XXX: "When to the sessions of sweet silent thought . . . ," and said that because I was her friend she could not really ever have sorrows.

I asked how her legs felt, and she said fine and thanked me again for giving her the Kenny all those times. Everything was going well. I made a slow turn onto state highway 56 heading west to Council Grove. It was the only route that Judith and I had agreed on. She claimed she would get a sense of where I needed to take her once we got out away from Saddle Rock. But all I could think of was how I was going to break the news to her that I planned to go with her, to be with her wherever she decided was her destination.

I was rehearsing a spiel to myself about halfway to Council Grove.

Judith had her face up close to the windshield studying the sky as if she'd never seen it before. We had the windows down, so she almost had to shout.

"We're flying, aren't we, Teddy? We're dancing across the world. Two spirits."

I smiled.

Before I could say anything, Judith got all excited.

"Look, Teddy, look right up there. It's the Fiery Angel. He's showing us the way. Look right up there. Can you see him?"

I had to crane my neck so that I wouldn't be blocked by the rearview mirror. I was gawking right into the early afternoon sun, and I could see no shape or substance that resembled anything like an angel or some special configuration of light.

"I don't see—"

I had leaned back, and in doing so had cut a glance at the rearview mirror.

And saw someone in the backseat.

The ghost of Romina Trogler.

I heard her voice. I think Judith did, too.

"Come back, Animus," she said, the voice magically sounding over the wind song at the windows. "Come back."

Mid-sentence, I freaked.

The front tire was suddenly riding on the soft sand of the shoulder, a shoulder that sloped at a sharp angle toward a deep ditch. Surrendering to panic, I did everything wrong. I braked and steered hard to the left and the end result was that we skidded across the other lane and onto the opposite shoulder. Judith was thrown against her door. I heard her cry out, and I heard Doris squawk. The car stalled and began rolling down into the ditch. Because I had slammed my chin against the top of the steering wheel, I didn't react quickly enough, and so the car rolled back until it unceremoniously toppled onto the passenger's side and I landed on Judith.

I think Doris flew out the window.

The ghost of Romina Trogler was nowhere in sight. She left behind a fog of dust.

My head was hurting, and Judith was moaning. I knew she must be in a lot of pain. The only other thing I knew was this: Fate had apprehended us and the ghosts were in control.

Eight

A Feather for Each Wind that Blows

"What do they want?"

I gotta admit I was scared. We were in the mud room, and I was trying to pin Judith down because I thought she knew everything that needed to be known about the Trogler ghosts. The episode of putting the car in the ditch and the role the ghost of Romina Trogler had played in it changed a lot of things for me. Made me realize some stuff. First, that maybe I had stowed too much trust in Judith's assumption that the ghosts weren't strong enough to be a threat. Embracing her reading of things, I suppose I had naively seen the ghosts as merely fascinating phenomena—and not much more. Maybe, just like the Troglers, I was waking up.

Picking at a monkey fist, Judith looked pale and drawn. But she managed a whispered response to my question: "Revenge." Then she drew herself up and frowned, adding, "At least I *think* that's what they want. And they need to be stronger. And . . . I think *I'm* the one they need. But, Teddy, I don't have all the answers. That's why I had to try to leave."

I wasn't satisfied.

"Who's Animus? I bet you know, and you're not telling me. You think I'm just a kid. You think I can't handle knowing about all this stuff."

She shook her head.

"That's not true."

"Well, then, who is it? Romina Trogler obviously thinks it's you."

"Perhaps it is," said Judith. "I don't have all the answers. Why can't you accept that? There's a lot that's a mystery."

I just couldn't believe that. So I kept after her.

"What I really don't understand is this: If the Fiery Angel is such a big, wonderful spirit or whatever, why didn't he protect us?"

Judith began to cry quietly. I was swinging between fist-clenching anger and heart-tugging empathy. I didn't know what else to do and so I left the room.

A couple of days later, at the urging of Judith, I walked back to the scene of the accident to look for Doris. My foot still hurt some, but not as much as my heart. The long walk gave me time to think about a lot of things. Aside from what Romina Trogler did, I blamed myself for a lot that had happened: putting the car in the ditch, losing Doris, generating hostility at home, and, most of all, hurting Judith.

Fate and the ghost had not only apprehended the runaways, they had also been grimly insistent that we should pay a price for our foolhardy attempt. I paid through guilt; Judith through pain. I sensed that over time my guilt would fade, but Judith's physical condition had roosted for the worse and all the progress she had gained through the Kenny had apparently been lost. The day after the accident my father took a day off from work to drive her into town to see Doc Gillis, who, in turn, called for Mrs. Wallace to come up from Emporia. Judith's polio-like symptoms had returned with a vengeance, making sleep impossible for her and any kind of mobility extremely difficult.

When Mrs. Wallace and Doc Gillis took Judith into the examination room, I stayed in the waiting area with my father. His face was the color of ashes and his eyes rimmed moistly with some kind of emotion I could not read. He sat and buckled forward, his large hands clasped in front of him. There was much I wanted and needed to say, different varieties of apology mostly. I couldn't stand his silence; I would have traded it for his anger in a heartbeat.

"Can the car be fixed?" I said.

He sighed. It took him a long time to respond.

"I 'spect so. Tie rod is bent. Everything looks to be in working condition otherwise. Scratches and small dents—I can hammer out most of them. Front side window is cracked. Probably let it stay like it is."

"I'll pay for whatever it costs," I said. "Emmitt Suggs needs somebody to help him put up some extra hay from his last bailing. He said he'd pay me fifty cents an hour."

It was true. Suggs, a farmer who doubled as our mail carrier (or vice versa), had first asked Jack, but he had enough work elsewhere so Suggs gave me a shot at the job. Of course at the time I didn't realize we'd be loading those bales into the small barn at the Troglers.

At first, my father said nothing in reply to my offer. I began to feel that I had said something foolish, that maybe what little money I would make wouldn't begin to repair the car. Eventually he cleared his throat and worked his jaw; I could tell he was searching for the right words, but they were staying out of reach. He found them after a considerable pause.

"My God, son," he said, "didn't you figure for even a minute how stupid a thing it was to take off like that with your cousin? What's wrong with you?"

My mouth went dry. I could hear my heart thrumming in my ears. The only response I could manage came out in a hoarse whisper.

"I'm really sorry."

Then I did exactly the thing I didn't think I'd do: I told him about the ghosts. It just spilled out of me, but as it did it morphed into shapes and colors and configurations I had not anticipated. In short, everything I said and maintained sounded silly and foolish. Worse yet, it sounded boyish—like a little boy rattling on about, of all things, ghosts.

When I stuttered to an inglorious halt, my father stared hard at me. There was the rough, ragged texture of gravel in his voice when he spoke: "So that's your story?" He shook his head as if he couldn't possibly be more disgusted with an explanation. Then he pointed toward the examination room. "That poor girl in there. I just . . ."

He seemed so bereft, so filled with sorrow and helplessness that it was impossible to follow up with words or actions to lessen his pain. I could only sit there and suffer at the center of things. At that moment I felt as if I could not possibly imagine what was going to happen to any of us. We would go on, I assumed, but in what direction? How would it all play out? Could we freely choose to take a certain road? Was some dark Fate in control?

Or were the ghosts?

I watched my father's face flush hotly when Doc Gillis motioned us into the examination room. Judith was on her back on a table. She looked scared, yet determined. I couldn't tell whether her resolve was to beat her pain or to escape from the present company of people. I pushed a smile at her, but she turned away as if embarrassed. I had convinced myself the two medical folks were going to pronounce that Judith would never walk again. I was prepared to challenge that—I'm not sure why—my love for her was part of it.

I still hadn't told her just how I felt.

Mrs. Wallace was looking down at Judith as she started explaining things to my father and me.

"I'd like to check her into the Newman Hospital in Emporia. They have a couple of good doctors who could tell us if she needs more intensive care, the kind she would get in Wichita or Topeka."

"That sounds best," said my father.

I moved around to the other side of the examination table, and this time Judith smiled shyly, though I could see that her jaw was set like a limestone fence post.

"But she really doesn't want to," said Mrs. Wallace. "She says that if you call her father, he'll come for her and she won't need to go to the hospital."

My father shook his head. His eyes had the sheen of exhaustion that a marathon runner has at the end of a race.

"I just don't know if we can find the man," he said. "I'll try to get a hold of my brother and see if he knows where he is. Her mother has . . . she's not able to tend to her daughter just now and so you probably know that this young lady's been staying with us."

Mrs. Wallace nodded.

Doc Gillis caressed Judith's cheek with his skeletal hand; he smiled kindly, but I think it was all Judith could do to keep from shuddering. Mrs. Wallace talked awhile longer with my father, and I said to Judith, "Maybe if you said one of your sonnets it would make you feel better." And so she did—in a weak voice, she recited the one beginning, "When in disgrace with fortune and men's eyes . . . ." A good choice, I thought. Best of all, when she finished she frowned at me and added, "I got to find a better getaway driver."

I laughed and, of course, Doc Gillis had no idea what we were talking about, but laughed along, and then Mrs. Wallace said that we needed to let Judith get dressed. Doc Gillis gave us a stack of *Time* magazines for Judith to read while she was recuperating. After that we drove home. My mother had been curiously silent about things. I should have known that she wouldn't let the matter pass without leveling her rage at Judith and me—or at least at Judith. When my father and I had helped Judith onto her cot in the mud room, we turned to find my mother standing in the doorway trembling. Her hair was a mess, and she had her hands all twisted up in front of her face like one of those mythological women who've been cursed by Zeus himself or who'd sprung from his head. Or both.

"Kathleen?" said my father. "Kathleen, babe, calm yourself down. It's no good saying anything."

But she did anyway. Although she didn't take a single step into the mud room, I stationed myself protectively between her and Judith. My father held his arms out in front of him like a wrestler preparing to meet his opponent. My mother's expression shifted from mythological fury to Old Testament vengeance as it notched up and up until she spewed out a spray of spittle and then screamed, "I hate you girl! I hate you and I hope you turn worse and die! Child of the Devil! Ours is a house defiled by you!"

I draped myself over Judith; her eyes flashed an odd

light, and I wished I could have kept her from hearing my mother, but I couldn't. In the pause that followed my mother's outburst I heard my father say, "Now Kathleen, you don't mean that. Not one word of it."

But she did. I knew it and Judith knew it.

And my mother's horrid words became embedded in the walls of our sad, sad house like some kind of grotesque mildew or fungus that couldn't be removed or even painted over without its ghosting through over time.

Tomorrow came, and I held my breath.

I only vaguely realized it then, but being lowered down into the cistern to retrieve Judith's braces characterized much of the summer: a descent into the darkness of self unsure what I would find.

"See 'em anywhere?" my father called out, his voice touching off an echo.

He was handling the rope, letting me down about a foot at a time. He had tied one end of the rope to a gunny sack filled with old rags and straw. I locked my legs around the sack and gripped a flashlight in one hand. With every heartbeat I expected to meet the ghost of Siebert Trogler, the sledge-wielding young man who seemed to favor those confines. I was afraid, and yet I almost *wanted* the ghost to appear so that my father could see it. Then maybe he wouldn't think I was crazy—maybe he wouldn't be so disappointed in me.

It felt ten degrees cooler than above ground as the darkness of the cistern welcomed me, but my chest was tight with an uneasiness that bordered on fear. It was twilight and a few small, brown, agitated bats had been darting and winging their way around our windmill. My father thought perhaps they lived in the barn, but he didn't rule out the possibility that they nested in the cistern. I had seen the bats before; Judith had been frightened of them because she believed they would get tangled up in her hair—one night, in fact, she had a bad dream about that actually happening. It wasn't just the bats and the darkness of the cistern that had me upset, though. Right before my father and I started on our mission to retrieve the braces, he telephoned his brother, John, for the third time in as many nights. I sat in the mud room with Judith. We could hear snatches of my father's side of the conversation, and as we listened, Judith held onto a leather monkey fist and seemed to be praying—to her Fiery Angel, I supposed. It hurt to admit it, but I didn't want my father to succeed in finding Judith's father. I didn't want her to leave. I didn't want to lose her.

My father's beaming smile signaled, for me at least, the bad news.

"Your daddy's going to come for you the last Saturday in July. He's working out in Colorado," is what he told Judith, and she just about leaped from her cot to hug my father's neck. I feigned my delight for her. But an odd feeling swept over me. A question: Why hadn't Judith's father asked to speak with her?

"Oh, Teddy, I knew he wouldn't forget. I'm in his thoughts. I knew I was. Colorado. I'm going to be living in Colorado. Maybe that's where I belong."

No, I wanted to say—you belong with *me.* And I had to bite my tongue hard because I wanted to ask her why her father hadn't come for her before this and why he had abandoned his wife and child in the first place. Judith's gorgeous face full of smiling warmth kept me from it. I loved her too much at that moment to puncture her joy.

She needed her braces—that was the task at hand—
she needed them until she could get around better.
Learning that her father would be coming for her in
several weeks fired her determination to regain the
progress we had made before the accident. When I finally located the braces they were still wrapped in
newspaper, yet partially buried in a layer of mossy,
slimy residue that coated the backs of my fingers as I
called for my father to lift me out of the cistern. The
smelly muck at the bottom lingered in my nostrils for
days afterwards.

"I won't need these for very long, Teddy," Judith
told me when I presented her with the braces. I noticed that my father kept quiet. I thought maybe he
was hiding something, maybe just his feelings—I
couldn't be sure.

"You ought to go slow," I said to her.

Then she punched me in the heart with those
beautiful eyes, eyes pleading for me to understand.

"You'll do the things I'll need to get better, won't
you, Teddy? You'll help, won't you? I need you until
my father comes."

I think I would have spent the rest of my days at the
bottom of the cistern if she'd said that's what she
needed. But as for her father—I suddenly hated him
with a blinding passion.

"Sure, I'll help."

Her smile battered me some more, and after she
hugged me I staggered away with the warmth of her
magnificent breasts still tingling my skin even through
my overalls.

I found traces of Doris near the site of the accident.
Feathers mostly. I knew they were hers. The black
sheen of them and the tips of red-orange. A coyote

probably got her or maybe even a stray cat or a hawk. I found a few eagerly chewed bones and bloody strings of flesh and sinew. I picked one of the feathers and decided I would take it back to Judith, knowing she would latch onto it as a keepsake or a lucky omen or sign that Doris might still be alive. Judith lived on hope. It was blood for her. When I had tucked away the feather I planned to give to her, I gathered up the rest of them and held them in the palms of my hands. The incessant Kansas wind blew into my face and threatened to scatter the feathers so I held them against my stomach and stared out at the rolling blanket of grass that was the Flint Hills. I thought about the escape, and I wondered how far Judith and I would be had I not skidded into the ditch.

The Fiery Angel was partly responsible.

Even more so, the ghost of Romina Trogler.

I remember how I landed on top of Judith when the car rocked over onto its side, and I remember being angry with myself and then feeling lucky that a farmer stopped and then drove to the closest house and got another farmer to come with his tractor to pull the car out of the ditch. I remember Judith moaning softly in pain, and, when the farmer had taken us home, I remember how she asked about Doris.

I knew even then that Doris didn't have a prayer.

A lot like Judith.

I knew even then that the world had predators. Judith had hope and courage and beauty and intelligence, but not enough feathers, not strong enough wings to fly above all the evil. I would never be able to protect her from all the dark forces capable of crushing her. I would never really be able to help her escape from what needed escaping.

I took my handfuls of feathers and I tossed them high above my head, and the wind caught them and lifted them into a delicate spiral, and where they landed I do not know.

I saw David on the Fourth of July.

My father drove Judith and me to town to the park, an area consisting of a ballfield and, out beyond the outfield fence (a rust-colored snow fence which had been bent to the ground in places) some playground equipment: a set of swings, a merry-go-round and a picnic pavilion. My father parked along the third-base line and helped Judith get comfortable in the back of the pickup, propping a pillow behind her head and putting a blanket near her in case she needed it later in the evening. I sat back there with her, and we watched other cars and pickups pull in and we listened to both adults and kids laughing and talking loudly to drown out the sound of exploding cherry bombs. I noticed that Judith held the single, black feather I had brought back from the remains of Doris, and I wondered whether her tendency to be easily startled would turn her evening into a nightmare.

Members of the American Legion were in charge of the fireworks. A node of them clustered out where second base normally would have been, plotting the evening's strategy, I suppose. Another nest of them was over at the picnic pavilion going at a truckload of watermelons, halving and quartering them with large knives, the melon pieces to be given out free of charge to spectators. My father was not a member of the American Legion on account of his not having been in the military during World War II or Korea. Being tagged a draft dodger and bearing the nickname "Dodger O'Dell" had never seemed to bother him—at least as far as I could determine. I went through a period of hating his nickname and being ashamed of his not having been a soldier. I asked him once why he didn't go to war, and he said, "Teddy, not every man can be an Audie Murphy. Someone had to stay behind and raise crops to feed the country." I tried unsuccessfully to buy his message. I think Jack and Junior had trouble with it, too.

My mother didn't ride in with us to see the fireworks, though my father asked her if she wanted to. She shook her head sullenly and said she was going to bed, and my father tried to joke with her about turning in before the chickens did—my mother wasn't amused. She had gone into herself, and there, in some realm the rest of us couldn't or wouldn't want to visit, her frequent companion—I believe—was the ghost of Senta Trogler. Most of the time my mother was simply absent from the day, sleeping or at least secluded in her bedroom—she called it *her* bedroom, even though, of course, she shared it with my father. Late at night I would occasionally hear my father talking to her, his tone a sublimely pathetic cadenza of pleading and prodding. But as far as I could tell, she did not respond much. She increasingly avoided the mud room like the plague, and she would not set a dish for Judith at the supper table, nor would she wash Judith's clothes or, in fact, acknowledge my cousin's presence in any way except to vilify her. My mother, or some shadowing of her, continued her domestic chores robotically. I caught her once or twice standing at the clothesline merely staring off at the horizon. Was it possible, I asked myself, for someone to become a ghost without dying? Judith claimed that she imagined my mother to be like a bird which had unaccountably forgotten how to fly or had lost its will to fly and was only blankly engaged with the new reality of being grounded, a stranger to earth.

My mother became a stranger to us all that summer.

In his own way, Junior donned the role of stranger, too. Apparently desperate to see Phyllis, he took off in his car early one morning: destination Missouri. He returned after midnight, the driver's side of his car dented badly and the engine throbbing and howling like an animal in pain. From my eavesdropping, I gathered that he had found the home of the relatives who had agreed to keep Phyllis, but when he insisted upon seeing her, they drove him away like some Old Testament abomination. For days after the incident, he did not go to work, choosing instead to sit in his broken car like a zombie or to take long walks around our pasture and over onto the Trogler's property and down to their pond to throw huge clods into the water and send up impressive splashes. I wanted to warn him about the ghosts, but decided not to. My father tried to talk with him; I don't think he had much success, or no more success than he had with my mother.

At supper one evening my father said to us, "Junior's being blown around by some strong winds. He's like a piece of straw or a feather or a speck of dust. His life will calm down in time. Just like the wind. Meanwhile, stay out of his way. He'll get through this and move on. It's what you have to do."

Those comments amounted to as much personal philosophy as I ever heard my father deliver at one offing. Much of it had the ring of truth to me. Maybe it did to Jack, too. I know that Junior's situation affected him; he wouldn't let on that it did, of course. Unfortunately, Junior's depression spun Jack toward more conflicts with himself. He continued to hang around some with Mickey Palmer, though I think his private miseries, including his affection for Judith, weakened the bond of meanness they had shared. Jack and Mickey showed up at the park for the fireworks, and when my father wandered off to shoot the breeze with a neighbor of ours, the two of them circled up to Judith and me, a yellow-eyed, up-to-no-good, jackal-look in their eyes. Mickey especially. He even grinned like a jackal.

"Teddy boy, you back here wetting your finger in this young lady's pussy? Shame on you."

I bristled. "Nobody invited you guys. Why don't you go and kick a cat or something—nobody wants you around here."

I sounded brave, but I was scared. Mickey dismissed my remark with a smirk and a casual sweep of his hand. He zeroed in on Judith; she kept her jaw firm, not allowing him the perverse pleasure of seeing that he might have unsettled her. There was an ugly wanting in Mickey, in the way he propped his elbows on the tailgate and licked his bottom lip as he leered at Judith. I knew it was just a matter of time before he acted on whatever passionate abusiveness he was reining in. Jack held back. I could see more than ever before the feelings he had for Judith; those feelings confused him. But he was committed to an imprisoning duplicity and he couldn't do much in the presence of Mickey to give himself away. When Jack spoke, he pretended that we were beneath contempt.

"Come on, Mick, let's leave these twerps alone," he said. "They ain't worth it."

Mickey's face was tight with a predatory intensity. But he relented at Jack's words and smiled sweetly at Judith.

"Listen here, cripple cunt," he said, "keep that

pussy warm and wet and one of these days I'll give you what little Teddy isn't man enough to." He winked at her and clutched eagerly at his crotch and bulged out his eyes. He darted his tongue in and out.

Then he slithered away on the heels of Jack.

All I could do was shake with the usual rage and dodge Judith's eyes.

"Teddy, I'm not really bothered by them," I heard her whisper. "My father's coming. I'm safe with you until then. And don't blame Jack—it's that Mickey who's bad. Jack is . . . he has a heart that wants so much to love. I wish he and I could be friends. More than friends."

What I heard in her voice staggered me.

I began to imagine that she was falling in love with my brother.

I was scared and jealous and angry. Thankfully the night soon gave over completely to booms and colorful sprays of twinkling sparks, and I sat close to Judith and smelled her perfume and we joined the chorus of o-ohs and a-ahs and cupped our hands over our ears and craned our necks to trace the moments before the sky gave birth to elemental twins—color and noise. At one point Judith said softly, "It's as bright as my Fiery Angel."

During a break in the shooting of the fireworks, David walked up from nowhere and stood at the tailgate about the same place Mickey had. When I saw him, I thought he was a ghost; my throat started to tingle and I reflexively moved away from Judith as if I didn't want him to see me beside her.

He did not disappear or evaporate.

"Hi, David," I said. "You're back. I got your card. The one from Minnesota. It was neat."

He was wearing a new shirt, plaid, short-sleeved, but he hadn't buttoned it and so his bronzed chest and stomach were visible. He seemed taller, his shoulders broader than when I had last seen him in May. His hair was longer, though neatly combed as always, and he was wearing jeans and tennis shoes. I thought he was strikingly handsome.

"Who's she?"

He gestured with his chin toward Judith.

I scrambled to the rear of the truck and then looked back.

"Oh, yeah, well, she's my cousin from Topeka. She's been staying with us."

David studied her a few seconds.

"She's wearing braces. How'd she get crippled like that?"

Judith cast her eyes down and then off to one side as if she weren't interested in what we had to say. She smoothed at her shorts with one hand and ran her fingers through her hair with the other. It felt odd to be talking about her—as if she were an object rather than a person—and yet the presence of David held me like a spell, and I lapsed into the rhythm of his comments.

"It's not polio," I explained. "But something like it."

I guess I was thrown off balance so much that I didn't even introduce the two of them. David turned to me and my face got hot as if some mechanism under my skin had been activated.

"Why do you want to sit with her?" he said.

His tone pinched hard at me, and I knew his words hurt Judith. But the fabric of my loyalty tore quickly, and I heard myself say, "I don't. Who said I did? I really don't."

"All right, good. Let's go mess around by the playground equipment. I've been thinking about us every day this summer."

"You have?"

Breathing hard, I hurried at his back at he strode away. I said nothing to Judith.

While everyone else remained glued to the fireworks display, David and I sat on the small, rickety merry-go-round, letting the toes of our shoes drag lines in the dust as it spun slowly. David had an aura about him, some kind of indefinable energy that made me both nervous and excited. I asked him about his vacation and whether he caught any fish and whether the mosquitoes in the north woods were really as big as sparrows like I'd heard.

"I'd rather talk about you," he said, after my questions apparently became tedious.

His eyes cut through the shadows to examine my face, to admire it, it seemed, the way one might admire the luster of a gem or the polished sheen of a new saddle. I was ravished by the attention he heaped upon me. I found it irresistible. He made me feel that I was surrounded by a strange, magical light. I was astonished by how good I felt about myself because of him. When I managed to respond, my voice was as insubstantial as sawdust.

I must have sounded like a ghost.

"What's there to say about me?"

It seemed like a whole minute passed before he spoke.

"About how special you are. About how I think you're ready for us to be closer."

"Closer? How?"

He glanced over his shoulder. Thirty yards away men from the American Legion were handing out slices of watermelon under the pavilion. Elsewhere little kids were farting around, chasing each other, laughing and screaming innocently. The world of Saddle Rock had its eyes on everything but us.

"Let's go over there," said David.

And so I followed him to the rather deep ditch that bordered the far side of the park.

"It's kinda hard to see the fireworks from here," I said.

David appeared unconcerned about that.

"I want to lay in the grass and look up at the stars and be right by you. Just you and me."

The grass in the ditch was about a foot tall, its blades moist with summer evening dew. It smelled sweet and it tickled my back and my neck, but I didn't mind.

"I wonder how many stars there are," I said. "Couple zillion maybe is my guess."

But David was quiet, so quiet I thought I could hear his breathing in those hushed moments between the colorful explosions, the crowd reaction and the anticipation of the next display. He asked about my tinkle bracelet and I lied. Then he held my hand and squeezed it, and he said, "I've told you I love you, Teddy, my little Red. I've never told anybody else that. Not even my mom and dad."

"Thank you," I stammered.

I didn't know what I meant. I was happy and chilled at the same time; I felt as far away from myself as those stars above us were from earth. What I can look back at now and see is that my budding bisexuality divided me as thoroughly as one might slice an apple or a peach in half. It was as if I had two personalities: number one, heterosexual, number two, homosexual, and they were about as much at home in one body as fire and water.

"I know you may not love *me*," David whispered, "but one of these days you will, I think."

He rolled over and started kissing my cheek and chin; I closed my eyes, and he kissed my eyelids and then my lips. When my body suddenly stiffened, he pulled away. Then, after a few moments, he took my hand and put it on his stomach and rubbed himself with it as if it were a washcloth. I felt as if I were beginning to float out of my body—it scared me, it delighted me. Then he unbuckled his belt and unzipped his jeans and took my hand again. My fingers were numb; I swallowed hard and tried to take my hand away, but David held it there. Soon he was squirming and letting out tiny moans of pleasure.

I stared up at the stars.

I wondered if God were watching.

The night had grown quiet. A moon was rising bold and bright and muscular, and it almost yanked my heart out of my chest before I realized that the fireworks had ended. Car lights were switching on; engines were turning over. We got up out of the ditch, David on legs that threatened not to support him.

"Teddy? Teddy, where are you? Time to head home, son."

It was my father calling out from a distance.

"David, I'll see you. I got to go."

He grabbed my wrist and said, "There's a tent show coming to town next Wednesday night. They're showing *King Kong*. You'll be there, won't you?"

In what light there was, I saw droplets of spittle on his lips; there was a weird glimmer in his eyes. He was trembling.

"Yeah, sure," I said. "I'll be there."

Then he released me and I started running toward my father. David yelled after me, "It's a neat movie. I saw it in Minnesota. We'll sit together, okay?"

"Yeah, sure," I hollered back.

My heart was a fountain gushing bright, colorful emotion.

At that moment, there were no ghosts in my life.

During the ride home, my father and Judith talked about the fireworks and I kept quiet. I wasn't certain who I was. In my thoughts I kept playing back all that David had said, words that made me smile inside but caused me to frown as well. When I got out of the truck, Judith said, "Teddy, I want to ask you something."

I reluctantly followed her to the mud room. She plopped down on her cot and said, "You really like that boy a lot, don't you?"

"You mean David?"

"That's what you called him. I can tell you like him."

I was annoyed by her remarks, and I could feel the annoyance sweeping across my skin like prickly heat.

"So what if I do?"

She was stroking Doris' feather and looking serious.

"Maybe it means I'm not as important to you now. But I still need you, Teddy."

"No, you don't."

"I do, Teddy. I do. You're my Onlie Begetter."

For some reason her words stung like a barbed-wire scratch.

"All you need is your father and your damn old Fiery Angel," I shouted. "And maybe Jack, too. I think he's the one, so you two just go on and be in love. I don't care."

"Oh, Teddy, why can't I have a lot of different loves in my life?"

I didn't have an answer.

I wanted to hate her, but I couldn't, and that was more than I could bear. I couldn't hold her gaze, and so when I caught sight again of the black feather she was holding, I said, "That crippled bantie you love so much is dead."

I was breathing hard. I glared at her. She was incredulous.

"Doris is dead? But you said that maybe she—"

"Well, I lied. Something got her."

Judith's face crumpled like a paper bag. I wanted her to cry.

I ran from the room feeling good, feeling that David would have been proud of me, and my good feeling lasted almost until morning; yet by the time the sun rose, I was so disgusted with myself that I wanted to die.

And become a ghost.

And haunt every piece of ground I had ever walked upon.

Shakespeare understood.

He wrote a sonnet—I forget the number—that begins, "Two loves I have of comfort and despair," in which he casts a mini-drama of someone being caught between his love for a "man right fair" and a "woman, colour'd ill." And the long and short of it is that the speaker just doesn't know how it's going to work out. Can one have both "angels"? I don't know what Shakespeare thought about that, but I had the feeling I was slipping down a greasy funnel—I cared for David *and* for Judith, and yet caring for them pulled me apart and shoved the pieces of myself into a swirling abyss. I was perplexed. I needed an answer from the outside because I couldn't find one in the chaos of my thoughts and the labyrinth of my heart.

The next day I woke before Judith did. I assumed that she would occupy herself while I began my work duties for Emmitt Suggs. She would be fine, I reasoned, if she simply stayed out of my mother's path. But then I asked myself: Had I been any less cruel to Judith than my mother had? Perhaps I was the one she should avoid. I couldn't understand myself. In a gesture of self-loathing I kicked the dirt between the corn rows in the foggy dragonfield as I sauntered toward the Trogler place. I regretted the power David held over me. I didn't like the person I became around him; in fact, I wanted to murder that part of myself. Most of all, I wanted to finish my assigned chores as quickly as possible and race back to Judith to apologize.

In the haunting patches of rising fog, the Trogler place looked sinister.

Were the ghosts of the Troglers watching? I assumed they were. Would Hunter come charging at me viciously? How much strength had the ghosts acquired? Enough to be really dangerous? I reminded myself that if they materialized and seemed to act in a threatening manner I should remain as still as possible—but would I be able to do that without Judith by my side?

It was preternaturally silent as I approached the crawl space to see whether Oatmeal was up and about. Truth is, I hoped I wouldn't hear him. I hoped he was mercifully dead. Wrapped in tinfoil, the chicken drumstick I had brought just in case the cat was still alive and hungry would be my lure. I folded back the foil and edged it into the darkness. I called out "Kitty, kitty," and held my breath. A weak, wracked-with-suffering meow reached out to me. The blinded Oatmeal, impossibly thin, stumbled forward, barely enough energy to bite at the meat. Saddened, I turned away at the sight of him. Once again, I thought it would be best if the creature died or if, instead of feeding it, I, or someone else, would put it out of its misery.

At the far corner of the house, I noticed that daylilies were blooming as if there were nothing whatsoever unusual about the property—as if a normal flesh and blood family lived there rather than a family of ghosts. The blooms were yellow shading to gold, the stalks as hardy and green as if they had been coddled in a plant nursery. I made a note to myself to pick a few for Judith on my way home. And then, as I was admiring the flowers, I heard a truck pull in, and I was reminded of my resolve to work and earn some money so that I could pay my father for the damages to the car.

Emmitt Suggs greeted me with a firm handshake. He was a short, wiry man with a flushed face and dirty overalls, heavy boots, a cap and deep blue eyes—eyes that understood the mysteries of farming the land. The flatbed truck he drove carried a half load of alfalfa bales. Seeing them, the green bulk of the tightly packed rectangles, I momentarily questioned whether I could handle the task of bucking them. Right off, Suggs slipped me a hayhook and opened the passenger door for his spotted pointer, Duke, to get out. And it was odd: The dog immediately started nosing around as hunting dogs do, his tail whipping back and forth, but then, not many seconds later, he issued a low in the throat, apprehensive growl.

"This fog got you spooked, fella?" said Suggs.

The man snickered, but then exchanged a glance of startled puzzlement with me. For the entire time that we spent unloading the hay, Duke gave the Trogler house a wide berth as he practically became Suggs' shadow. I knew, of course, that the dog sensed the ghosts. However, I didn't say anything. By mid-

morning the heat of the day had shoved the fog from
the scene, and Suggs and I—with Duke cowering near
his master—had unloaded most of the bales. I kept
trying to sense anything ghostly in the small barn, but
nothing manifested itself. Except dust and the pleas-
antly pungent aroma of green alfalfa and a tight
burning in my biceps.

They were watching from the house.

The ghosts. Old Rolf and Senta. Siebert and
Romina.

Once or twice I even heard the slightly muffled
bark of Hunter.

At one point Suggs and I took a water break. We
perched on bales in the open air of the flatbed and
mopped the sweat from our brows. That's when I saw
them. The father and mother glaring out through vacant panes on the ground floor; their son and
daughter from upstairs—God, it was scary to see them
and to know that *they knew* I could see them. If Suggs
could, he didn't let on. He did, however, say, "Did it
sound to you like there's a dog barking in the house?"

"No, sir," I lied.

Suggs shook his head as if he thought he'd been
hearing things, and then, as he brushed his eyes up
and down the rear of the derelict house, he said, "Bad
memories in that sorry place. My brother and his
boy . . . well, I don't know. Some days I think it'd be
better if I'd tear it down. You know what I mean?"

I nodded. And maybe I did know. Suggs, obviously
in a darkly reflective mood, continued, and it was
equally obvious that he wanted, needed to confide
something. I felt uneasy as he picked at the dirt under
his fingernails. "Most folks don't know this," he
began. "But my brother, Harold, had . . . oh, an eye
for women, despite the fact he was married and had a
son. Well, you see he got that Trogler girl pregnant,

and the whole family pretty much rose up against him. They were killers—plain, cold fact, and they killed Harold and little Dwight, and so something had to be done. You understand that?"

He glanced at me the way adults will do when they're being real serious with a kid.

"I guess so."

"James, my other brother—the one that didn't come back from the war in the Pacific because the Japs got him—he and I and a few others, we decided something had to be done, and so we did it."

I sort of shrugged nervously, and then a curious light came into Suggs' eyes. It was like he had just realized something and needed to pass it along to me.

"Your daddy—now he's a good man—and I got no way of knowing if he's told you this, but he came here, too. He was with us. He was in on evening the score with the Troglers. Your daddy and I, we's the only ones still living who know the whole story."

For a run of seconds I was literally blinded by the shock of the revelation.

I wanted to toss my doubts back into the man's face, but I knew intuitively that he was telling the truth. And the truth left me speechless. And very, very scared.

When we finished stacking all the bales in the barn, Suggs thanked me, and though I hadn't worked more than four hours, he gave me a five-dollar bill. Had I not still been in shock, I would have felt rich. He gathered up Duke, who was only too glad to leave, and drove off as if he'd spent as much time around the Trogler place as he cared to.

Beyond everything else, I felt a staggering wave of guilt.

You see, I believed that I should have warned Suggs about the ghosts. I sensed that he was in danger, that

he shouldn't come around there again—the ghosts
would be getting stronger. They wanted revenge. And
they would start with him . . . and they would include
my father. I said nothing because there was just something in those hard, flinty, no-nonsense eyes of Suggs
that probably wouldn't have allowed him to accept my
warning. He would have laughed it off with the
thought: *This shit ass kid trying to scare this old fella? God
damn if he will.*

I probably would have thought the same thing.

So I picked three day lilies, and as I was leaving I felt
the eyes of the ghosts on me. Eyes that clawed at me.
I heard Hunter growl deep below the crawl space.
And I wished I had said to Suggs that his notion that
the Trogler place should be torn down was a good
one.

I wanted to see my father. I wanted to jump into his
arms and hug him hard.

I wanted to protect him.

I did not think of much of anything as I walked
home, flowers in one hand, five-dollar bill in the
other. When I got there, Judith was not in the mud
room. My mother was on the phone talking with Mrs.
Penner, I guessed, the two of them having formed a
curious bond since the bad news about their offspring. Mrs. Penner—I think her name was
Alma—came with her husband one evening when he
arrived to take Brutus off our hands, and she struck
up something of a friendship with my mother. When
Mr. Penner and my father finished loading up the
bull, their wives were on the front porch all teary-eyed
from their whispery conversation. I didn't mind seeing that my mother had a friend—other than the
ghost of Senta Trogler—nor did I mind seeing Brutus

trucked away where he would not crush my foot ever again with his more than ample weight.

On my way to the barn in search of Judith I saw that Junior was under the rear end of his car wielding some kind of wrench; it looked as if the vehicle had squatted on him like a huge dog. Jack had been in the barn; he brushed by me and joined Junior. I found Judith in our fortress of hay sitting like an Indian next to a campfire. I assumed she'd been talking with Jack, and that assumption made my chest burn. She was engrossed in a map she had spread out on one of the bales—a map of Colorado, no doubt. I almost called to her, but something stopped me: the sight of her beauty, in part, and yet something more. She seemed at that moment a vision of hope, a young woman pregnant with an acceptance of life, and as I stared at her, vaguely, ever so vaguely, I projected that one day she might give birth to my salvation.

If I didn't lose her.

I had to stifle a giggle as I watched her study the map and dig at one ear with Slim. She also had a stack of *Time* magazines by her as well as her much-read copy of *A Room of One's Own*. I stood there for maybe half a minute disgusted with myself for having hurt her. I knew that I would do or give anything if she would forgive me. With that uncanny inner radar she had, she sensed my presence, looked up half startled and then smiled. I quickly hid the day lilies behind my back.

"Hi, Teddy. You get your work done for Mr. Suggs?"

My lungs filled with something more than air as I approached. I didn't mention Jack.

"Yeah, sure. Boy, those bales were heavy, and Mr. Suggs's dog, Duke, got scared. I think because he smelled the ghosts. Oatmeal—he's still alive. Barely."

But I couldn't bring myself to share Suggs's revelation about my father.

Judith had seen through my behind-the-back deception; her eyes twinkled with that awareness, and perhaps she even knew that I planned to apologize. I almost wished that she would be angry with me.

"I've been wandering around Colorado," she said. "I thought I might be able to tell where my father is. Colorado has lots of mountains, but it also has areas like Kansas, flat with not many towns. You ever been there? Ever been to Colorado?"

"I've been nowhere," I said, then added hesitantly, "How are you feeling? Your legs hurt you?"

She smiled and brushed back several strands of her beautiful hair.

"Not so bad, really. Maybe if I could ask you to do a Kenny and we could walk some so I could strengthen my muscles I'd get better soon. I want to be walking fine when my father comes."

My stomach was churning, and I was squeezing the day lily stems so tightly that they were turning to pulp.

"Sure, I'll help you. I can give you a Kenny any time you want, and I . . . ." Right then I noticed that she had that single black feather in her hair and maybe that set me off; suddenly a rush of emotion seized me like a rip tide and words seemed to be pulled from my tongue before I could think about what I was saying. "Judith, I'm sorry. I am. I'm sorry for running off from you at the park and for telling you about Doris being dead and just plain for being mean . . . because I don't want you to feel bad, and I'm sorry you have to be with our messed up family, and I'm sorry I couldn't help you escape from here and from the ghosts. And I brought you these flowers from the Trogler place because I thought of you when I saw them."

I took a breath and Judith beamed. She took me in
her arms and held me, and I was afraid I would start
crying. When we leaned out of the embrace, I lifted
the flowers to her and her eyes filled and she whispered, "I'll pretend they're roses—roses with yellow
flames. Roses and fire. You're my fire, Teddy. My
Onlie Begetter."

She touched my cheek and kissed me on the lips.
Not a deep, passionate kiss, but at least one that
seemed to stay there for hours.

"I promise I won't be mean to you again," I followed.

"Teddy, you know something? I asked the Fiery
Angel to bring you back and, see, he did. I told him I
loved you and needed you, and here you are, and with
lovely flowers."

But what about Jack?

She carefully broke off part of one stem and placed
the day lily over one ear. I really wished it could be a
rose. In my imagination, it was. I looked at her and
felt as if I were parachuting into Heaven.

"You're beautiful," I said.

For the moment, I wasn't annoyed by her mention
of the Fiery Angel; for the moment, he didn't seem
like my enemy. For the moment, I forgot about Jack.
I forgot about what Suggs had told me. I felt as if I
were on the road into the open, accepting things, seeing into the heart of life and love and myself.

"Oh, Teddy," she said, "you're too much."

After lunch the next day and over my protest that it
was too hot to be out doing stuff, Judith and I went
slogging around the property, her determination win-
ning over her pain. She fought with her crutches and
braces until she got the upper hand; we cut a path

through the dragonfield and then down to Trogler's Pond. We sat in the shade of the willows and worshiped from afar the monstrous cottonwood before heading back, ending up at the distant pasture gate where we rested some more and watched a few cars and trucks pass by on the highway.

As always, Judith calculated how far it was from there into town.

"Too far," I said.

"It depends," she said.

"On what?"

"On how badly you want to get there."

"It's just a little pissant town. You've seen it. Why's it such a big deal?"

She shrugged. I didn't know what secret she was harboring, but I knew that before the summer was over, she would set sail on it. Would I be with her? I wondered. When we got back to the house, I gave her the most thorough Kenny I ever had. I applied the heat packs firmly yet gently, and she held up as the pain faded and partial relief set in. Then I removed the packs and used my hands. Her slightly sweaty skin felt marvelous to the touch. She was lying on her stomach and, as usual, she had a sheet covering down to her upper thighs, but I rubbed as high as I dared. As I was doing so she whispered, "Move up farther, please."

I swallowed a mouthful of saliva and did as she requested, running my fingers just beyond the edge of the sheet and brushing against her panties. Suddenly she reached around and took one hand.

"Up here, Teddy."

My hand was on her bottom; the silky feel of her panties aroused me. She moaned softly as my fingertips pressed small circles and my knuckles kneaded her flesh through the material. My tinkle bracelet purled like water dancing over a creek bed.

"Is this the right place?" I said.

"It's perfect. It feels real good. Keep doing it, please."

As I brought my other hand up onto her bottom, I feared that my mother would walk in or, even crazier, that David somehow would. Or maybe even Jack. Would my brother and I get in a fist fight over the girl we loved?

"I'm not hurting you, am I?"

"No, Teddy. You're doing just right."

I rubbed and pressed until my knees threatened to buckle from a combination of fatigue and unreleased desire. Perhaps she sensed that I was flagging, for soon after that she pushed up from the cot smiling the smile of a goddess. When she turned to face me, the sheet escaped her grasp and for just an instant slipped down, exposing her full, bare breasts.

"Oh, sorry," she said, covering herself.

My face reddened. I choked out the words, "I hope you're not feeling too much pain."

"I'm not," she said. "Thanks to you."

She got to her feet and kissed me on the shoulder.

I left the room so that she could get dressed. My thoughts were flickering with images of caressing and kissing Judith's breasts. It was a different kind of desire from what I felt around David; I imagined it as a different color, a different texture, and a different flavor. Though they spun me into a new world of confusion, I needed both kinds of desire. But I didn't know how to make room for them.

I drifted into the kitchen where Junior had poured himself a glass of iced tea. Out of the blue I said to him, "You about to get your car fixed?"

To my surprise, he answered in something other

than a tone of disdain: "It's close. I'm thinking I'll give it a test drive here in a minute."

I nodded. Junior suddenly seemed older to me, as old as most adult men I knew. The summer had changed him in ways I did not understand, but I liked the impression I was getting. I could almost hear myself having a serious conversation with him, relating my conflict over David and Judith. What would his response be? Wouldn't he be disgusted with a little brother in love with another boy, as well as in love with his female cousin? Wouldn't he think I was sick and needed a psychiatrist? I entertained those same thoughts some nights when sleep wouldn't come. I felt that I had no one I could talk to. At least Judith had her Fiery Angel—I had no one. I didn't even feel that I could recite my narrative to my father, especially not after my sputtering about the ghosts. My mother, of course, was out of the question as a confidante.

And I wondered if Junior knew about our father and the Troglers.

Junior's voice brought me out of a reverie of confusion and near despair.

"You being careful in there, Teddy?"

He gestured toward the mud room. All I could do at first was frown. When our eyes met, I realized that I was looking at my father: the same muted light, the same moist and plaintive concern in those eyes. It was ghostly. I didn't say anything, so he followed up.

"Whatever you're doing in there with your cousin— what I'm saying is, be careful."

I flushed and was on the verge of some forceful denial both that we were doing anything requiring us to be careful and that I would go against social taboo in feeling affection or desire for my cousin. Judith's entrance saved me. She said hello to Junior, and for an uncomfortable run of seconds he studied us. He read our text well, but what he said was, "You guys wanna go for a ride? I need to blow the carbon out of my jitney."

We sat in the front seat with him, Judith in the middle, and we felt like big shots. Riding with one's older brother was heady stuff. When he got his Ford out on the highway, he really gunned it. The acceleration snapped us deliciously back into the seat; all three of us giggled. We raced toward Council Grove, out beyond the spot where I had put the family car in the ditch, and out of the corner of my eye I saw Junior smile broadly for the first time in I don't know how long. We turned around at the Council Grove drive-in theater, but we didn't roar back as fast as we had come. Junior's expression took on a more somber cast. As for Judith, she was quiet; I caught her stealing a glance at the late afternoon sun as if she might be searching for the Fiery Angel hovering somewhere above us.

When we crossed the Rock Creek bridge, Junior turned in on a narrow road bordering a field of alfalfa. I felt a pocket of cool air in my stomach because I didn't know where he was going, and it made me apprehensive. He drove about a quarter of a mile and then stopped and turned off the engine.

"You know where we are?" he said.

I had no idea and I'm sure Judith didn't either.

"The middle of nowhere," I muttered.

From the parking spot Rock Creek was visible below and off to the left; it was a nothing little muddy creek, though occasionally someone pulled a good-sized catfish out of it.

"This is where my girl and I did the deed," said Junior.

Embarrassed, I sneaked a peek at Judith. Her expression did not give her away. I was shocked that Junior would say what he did. I felt uncomfortable until he continued on, and I realized that more than anything else, he just wanted to talk. He was desperately lonely. Judith and I listened as he told us about the initial disappointment and yet elation at learning he had impregnated Phyllis Penner and of the devastation of not being allowed to see her, that forces beyond his control were denying them even the possibility of a future together.

"I'm telling you guys this," he said. "I'm leaving as soon as I can. Going as far away from here as I can get. There's nothing here. Not for me."

He babbled on like someone cursed. We listened, mesmerized.

Before it got dark, we drove into Saddle Rock. Judith asked him to stop by the railroad tracks where a freight waited to unload a few cars of coal; she got out and looked into several of the empties and pressed Junior for details about train routes.

We made one last stop: the Trogler place.

"Haven't been here in a long time," said Junior.

"I think maybe the place has changed," I volunteered.

We three stood in the abandoned living room. I could feel the ghosts stirring. Watching. So could Judith. She stood very still. I kept looking at Junior as the eager emptiness of the room settled around him. Could he feel the eyes of the ghosts? I think he could. And then, when we heard Hunter growl low beneath our feet, Junior visibly shuddered.

"Christ," he hissed. "This place gives me the heebie-jeebies. You guys oughtta stay away from here."

There were several more dusty, ghostly beats of silence before Judith spoke.

"We can't," she said.

* * *

That evening I filled our washtub for Judith so she
could take a bath. I closed off the mud room to give
her some privacy, and then I sat at the kitchen table
and lost myself in a fantasy of being where I could
watch her bathe. I imagined her nakedness enveloped
in a blue flame.

I imagined her surrounded by fire and roses.

Junior came in and sat with me, and I suppose he
sort of read my thoughts. The only thing he said was,
"Don't get yourself in the mess I did."

I understood.

Then he shook his head and sort of chuckled.

"Jack's hot for her, too. But you probably know that
already."

I shrank into myself as I nodded.

During the night Judith woke very upset. The
Trogler ghosts had been walking around under the
house and slithering up into the kitchen hoping to
vampire more energy from her, but, according to Judith, her Fiery Angel was keeping them at bay. For the
moment at least. I sat with Judith on her cot and she
told me about a bad dream she'd had. She was in a
strange, yet vaguely familiar house and someone was
trying to burn her and someone was trying to save
her. She thought it was me.

"Couldn't you tell for sure?" I said.

"No, but I think I wanted it to be you."

"And not Jack?"

She didn't respond to that; instead, she pulled me
gently down with her on the cot, and I held her, and
she fell asleep on my shoulder. That night she was
mine—not the Fiery Angel's, not Jack's—mine, and

mine alone. I felt as if I were embracing a body filled
with sunlight on the coldest day of the year. I wanted
her warmth to stay with me forever. I wanted the light
of her being. I thought of David, and I told myself that
perhaps he was just a beautiful sunset that I had mistaken for a dawn.

Nine

'Twas Beauty Killed the Beast

The summer of 1955 spawned many untellable things.

Looking back, it seemed transcendent stuff—scenes either of deepest fear or deepest love played out in a splendidly dappled realm of darkness and light unreachable through words, scenes one can describe but not convey, moments worthy of being lifted from the forbidding gothic pages of *The Scarlet Letter* or, more especially, a tale by Poe. Scenes that leave indelible traces along the pathways of the heart.

The ghosts would not go away.

I wrongly assumed they would because the supernatural hadn't entered my cozy, safe Kansas life before. To me, the ghosts were simply a darkness passing—like a bad thunderstorm or a three-day blizzard or a hot, dry, crops-withering spell. But I misjudged things. The truth finally settled into my marrow the morning Judith and I designed a pedestal for our basketball globe of the world; it was a comically crude stand made of cardboard—yet we were proud of it. And that same morning, we debated whether to try to coax Oatmeal out from under the Trogler crawl space. We decided against it, opting instead to seek out our barn. I had reluctance in my step and dread weighing on my shoulders because it was the day the tent show was to come to town. My father promised to take Judith and me—David had said he would be there. I was torn, and Judith sensed it.

"No need to hurry. No need to sparkle. No need to be anybody but one's self," she said to me as we took up our places in the fortress of hay. "That's from Virginia Woolf," she added. Judith was trying in her own inimitable way to cheer me up, I suppose, or at least to jog me out of my self-absorbed funk.

She lighted a candle, and when I failed to respond to her quotation she began telling me of a vision that came to her in the night; it was the Fiery Angel racing toward her across a twilit sky leaving footprints of fire and, upon reaching her, lifting her into his arms— only when she smiled up into his face, she saw that it was her father.

"Isn't that strange?" she said.

I nodded. But my mind would not release me from the anxiety I was experiencing. And questions: Would I have to choose between Judith and David? Was I losing Judith to Jack? And I was worried about my father—a vague, imprecise pattern of worry emerging from what I knew about his involvement with the Troglers.

"Oh, Teddy," Judith broke in. "I forgot to bring our map of Colorado. It's back in the mud room. Would you go get it, please?"

Lost in thought, I returned to the house and shuffled through Judith's stack of maps until I found Colorado, but as I started to retrace my way through the kitchen I heard my mother humming. As an instinctual reaction on my part, I hid myself at the doorway and listened. I could not distinguish a tune in my mother's humming. It was a weird snatch of not-quite music, and hearing it made the hairs on my forearms prickle. I positioned myself so that I could see her without being seen.

She was not alone.

Continuing her humming, she came hesitantly across the room dressed in her bathrobe, as was her morning custom, and she was carrying a purple bath towel. The ghost of Senta Trogler was guiding her by an elbow. My mother appeared at once distracted and yet centered and resigned; Senta Trogler looked hollow and way past crazy. Waiting for the two of them at the utensil drawer was the ghost of Romina Trogler who rifled through its contents, creating a lot of noise, as my mother watched. It sounds nothing to tell, but being there, observing the threesome, was a totally arresting, totally frightening experience, especially when Romina, her manner darkly knowing and forceful, retrieved a single utensil and handed it to my mother.

Our largest butcher knife.

My mother stared down at the weapon for an inordinately long time before she took it and wrapped it in the towel and let Senta escort her from the room. I'm not quite certain what happened next. I know that I made a gasping sound, and when I did Romina wheeled and caught sight of me. She held me with her eyes. I couldn't move. She lifted her forefinger and pointed it at my forehead.

All I recall is a gauzy warmth spreading down over my face.

My next moment of awareness was of being in the barn handing the map of Colorado to Judith.

I'm pretty certain Romina did something to make me forget the incident until later.

My heart was beating as loudly as a hard rain on a tin roof when we arrived in town that evening and waded in with others to the ticket stand just outside an impressive stretch of butterscotch-colored canvas on the street next to the American Legion building. The canvas surrounded a seating area, but left a sky full of stars as the ceiling. My father handed me two dimes and said, "If this movie gets too scary, you kids come on down to the grocery. I'll be shooting the breeze with whoever's around."

He hung a serious look on me, then winked. He smiled at Judith and touched her shoulder.

"I won't get scared," Judith whispered to me. "It's just a movie."

"It's *King Kong,*" I countered. "I've heard it can really scare little kids. Not like us. But first and second graders."

Judith's smile of acknowledgment made me feel fluttery. She had fixed herself up to be especially beautiful, wearing a dark blue dress I hadn't seen before; the evening, with a shimmering, almost full moon blessing the scene, magnified her beauty.

"Let's sit down close to the screen," I suggested.

Judith wasn't wearing her braces, but she needed one crutch, and I didn't mind too much that she put her hand on my elbow so as not to get jostled by the crowd. I tried to make it not so obvious that I was glancing around for David. I think Judith knew. But did she know that part of me hoped I wouldn't see him? We sat in the middle of the second row of wooden, folding chairs about forty feet from the giant white screen. Behind us, the projection truck was thrumming and hissing, and the fibrous light from the projector gave everything a magical aura. Though I had attended only two other tent shows in the past, I explained how things worked as if I were an experienced moviegoer.

"They'll run a newsreel and a cartoon before the fea-

ture. The boys who get here early and help set up chairs
get in free. I saw *The Wizard of Oz* here last summer."

"That's a good movie," said Judith. "I've seen it, too.
I liked Dorothy because she had spunk. Don't girls
help set up chairs, too?"

I frowned at her question.

"I don't think so."

"Too bad," said Judith. Then, half in surprise, half
delight, she pointed at the screen. "Look at what
somebody's doing."

Pairs of hands were casting shadows on the brilliant
white screen: rabbits and ducks and human faces before deteriorating to obscene, middle-fingered
gestures and sexually explicit configurations I hoped
Judith wouldn't call attention to. I should have known
who the creators were. Jack and Mickey, laughing as
only the truly disturbed can, emerged from somewhere beneath the screen and dashed toward the
front row. But I noticed that when Jack spotted Judith,
he separated himself from his fiendish friend.

"I think they just escaped from the loony bin," I
said.

"Jack's not really like that," said Judith.

I felt my heart shrink. When I looked away, I saw Junior; he was sitting by himself. He looked lonely, but
I knew he probably wouldn't want to be seen with us,
so I didn't suggest that we go sit with him.

By the time the newsreel cranked up, a large and
exotic collection of night bugs was spinning a geom-
etry of many-angled rounds in and out of the
projector's spray of light. The trumpeting strains of
music pulled me back to the screen just as I was cran-
ing my neck one last time to catch a possible glimpse
of David. Could he be sitting with someone else? I
wondered. I told myself I didn't care one way or the
other. A resonant voiceover suddenly reached out to

us. The borderline raucous crowd stuffed itself into
sleeves of silence, watching as President Eisenhower
teed off for a round of golf somewhere in Georgia before the scene shifted to splashy headlines about the
Communists brewing up trouble in just about every
part of the world. Communism and polio—the twin
terrors of our planet in that moment of history. Some
would have thrown in the bomb and rock and roll as
additional threats to humanity, but Bill Haley and the
Comets didn't seem too lethal to me. And the bomb
was simply unthinkable.

Worse than ghosts.

The cartoon was a good one—Tom and Jerry. I
heard Judith giggle a few times, and when a breeze
lifted from the south I could smell her perfume. I also
felt the warmth of her thigh next to mine until she de-
murely moved it. My thoughts were sticky with
confusion. I turned to catch her profile: What I saw
jabbed at me with fear.

The ghost of Romina Trogler was sitting on the
other side of Judith.

She ritched her head back behind Judith and
smiled at me. It was weird.

I didn't know what to think or do. To my amazement, Judith seemed calm.

And I wondered: Who else can see the ghost?

Unnerved, I swung back to the screen. The main
feature was about to start and still no sign of David. In
fact, the expedition to Skull Island landed before he
slipped into the chair beside me, slightly sweaty and
out of breath. He was wearing some kind of cologne
that warred with the whiffs of perspiration odor.

"Thanks for saving a seat. It's just starting to get to the
good part. The natives are going to kidnap the blonde
lady and offer her to Kong. Wait'll you see him."

His eager smile sliced my heart up into pieces and

juggled them. I'm not sure why, but I fought off returning his smile. I started to tell him that I really hadn't saved him a seat, stopping only because he leaned close, gesturing toward Judith, and whispered, "Why'd you bring *her?*"

I jerked my head away from him and said nothing. It suddenly angered me that David was trying to come between me and Judith. He was jealous of her, and I thought that was silly. I cared about both of them— why couldn't both of them exist in the plenty of my affection? It was frustrating.

On the screen, the natives were chanting their mantra: "Kong! Kong! Kong!" Fortunately, my first view of the huge ape gave me a reprieve from my anguish; he was mesmerizing. He appeared to be taller than our silo, and his roar was terrifying, grabbing me all the way down to my groin, and those eyes—primitive and malicious and yet somehow innocent and even hopeful—sucked me into the deepest well of my fascination. I tensed with each of Kong's roars, and then tensed even more with each of Fay Wray's penetrating screams. Never had I heard anyone scream quite so convincingly. Some of the girls in our crowd echoed those screams, and the boys gasped, then hooted, then tried to laugh off how truly unsettled they were.

Judith didn't scream, but thinking she might be frightened by what was unfolding on the screen, I inched my hand over onto hers without looking directly into her eyes. I noticed that the ghost of Romina Trogler had left. At about the same time, David sought out my other hand, and so there I was, currents of affection surging through me. When I was twelve, I had gone to the drive-in with my folks, and we had seen the Boris Karloff *Frankenstein* and I had been enthralled by the laboratory scene in which the creature receives lightning-generated bolts of electricity to bring him to life. I was feeling those same bolts. But then I saw something on the screen even more emblematic of my situation: Fay Wray, having been offered up as a sacrifice to Kong, was tied between two posts like a mock-crucifixion. Despite her frenetic struggle and some of her best screams, she could not free herself. I knew how she felt, for there I was, bound between two souls who had kidnapped my heart. But to what was *I* being sacrificed?

Love?

Family?

The ghosts?

The movie stirred me as none other ever had, and I slipped readily into fantasies of protecting Judith from Kong and also of being there with David, living and thriving on that island like jungle versions of Huck Finn and Tom Sawyer. I watched with eyes as intent as clenched fists as the film bore down to its thrilling conclusion and somehow I was no longer a viewer—I had become Kong clinging precariously to the top of the Empire State Building as those insidious planes peppered him with bullets until, bloodied and weakened, he could not endure. He could not hang on any longer. A crushing sadness gripped my heart when he fell. I fell with him. The man who had brought Kong back to civilization pronounced that beauty had killed the beast. I didn't know how I felt about that.

When the reel flickered off, I think I suddenly felt nothing.

Judith was wiping away a tear; David seemed agog.

"I told you it was a good movie," he said, grinning. "Didn't I tell you it was?"

I turned and Judith met me with a smile, her eyes brimming.

"I felt sorry for King Kong," she said.

"Me, too," I said.

"They came and took him from the place where he belonged," she added.

"Yeah, I know."

As we melded with the crowd and shuffled our way to the exit, David grabbed my arm and said, "Hey, Teddy, come over behind the American Legion with me. There's something I gotta show you."

"What is it?"

"You'll see. Come on."

I was reluctant.

"Maybe for a minute," I said. "My father's waiting to take us home."

David was tugging at my arm as I found the glow of Judith's face and told her to stand just outside the canvas wall and I'd be back. I wanted to ask her about the ghost of Romina Trogler. Maybe most of all, I wanted to know whether Judith was afraid of the ghosts. When I told her to wait, I couldn't read her expression. Was it merely disappointment? A touch of jealousy? Or had she tapped into the deeper layers of my choice to go with David? What did she know? What untellable things?

I followed David to the shadowy side of the American Legion building. He was holding my hand, but I didn't want him to. Not really.

"What you got to show me?" I said.

"What? Oh, . . . well, nothing much. I just had to be with you by myself. Not with *her*."

Had he seen the ghost of Romina Trogler? Apparently not.

I freed my hand from his.

"I gotta go," I said.

"No, wait. See that star up there?"

I traced the imaginary line of David's pointing finger into the bowl of tiny twinkling diamonds above us.

"There's millions of 'em," I said. "Which one?"

His voice got soft and kind of goofy.

"Whichever one you want."

I shook my head. I didn't like his tone, and he wasn't making sense.

"I better go," I said.

"Teddy, I love you," he said.

Before I could fend him off, he was hugging me and kissing my cheek and ear. He was trembling like a wet puppy.

"David, I don't like this," I said.

I pushed at his throat. The look of surprise and hurt that suddenly flamed around his eyes caught me up. I felt bad. I wanted the shadows to swallow me, and yet, more than that, I wanted not to be tied up, not to be emotionally helpless. I wanted to be as far away as one of those unimaginably distant stars.

David's voice was hot and throaty.

"It's that girl, isn't it? It's your cousin. You like her instead of me. Is that it, Teddy? Her instead of me?"

My voice was thin and watery—no match for the fire in his.

"No. No, . . . I mean, sure I like her. She's my cousin. She's blood. We've done stuff together. I like both of you."

And I wanted to say more. I wanted to talk about the ghosts and the Fiery Angel. But I didn't. David was shaking his head as if in disbelief, as if he couldn't begin to understand what I was saying and that I didn't embrace his feelings.

"But Teddy, she doesn't love you the way I do. Not the same way. She just can't. A girl couldn't."

I began backing away from him, and I had my hands up at about shoulder level, and for some reason my fingers had folded into limp fists. And in my thoughts—with the rhythm and intensity of the natives' mantra—my own mantra voiced itself: "Wrong! Wrong! Wrong!" I stared at David and kept him at bay as I tried to connect with that mantra. It was difficult. It was confusing because I didn't feel that the affection David and I had shared was immoral; I didn't believe we would be damned or anything like that. It was more that I couldn't be exclusively his. I couldn't be who I was without the existence of my feelings for Judith. It would be wrong for me.

"Wrong," I whispered.

I could see how much that single word stung David. Tears blossomed at the corners of his eyes and his voice was suddenly strained and moist.

"I need you, Teddy. I don't want to live without you. If you won't love me, I'll die. Do you understand that?"

When he came toward me, I clenched my fists.

"Stay back," I said. "You can't have me. I don't want *anybody* to have me."

"You don't mean that. You're my little Red. You're mine, and I'm yours. That's the best way. You've got to like me better than you like her."

He kept coming and reaching for me with spidery webs of insistence.

"Wrong," I said aloud, and in the next instant I punched him a hard blow to his shoulder. It surprised both of us. I was gritting my teeth and quaking like leaves on a cottonwood in a strong breeze. Then I started walking fast away from him. He was clutching at his shoulder, and he was saying, "I can't live without you, Teddy. I'll die. I will. I'll die." Then he crashed to his knees and slumped into the wall of the building. As he repeated the words over and over, his voice pitched high and out of control, and I feared that somebody would hear him.

I ran fast from the shadow of myself, and I didn't look back.

In the mud room, twisting and turning and falling at last into a fitful sleep, I woke to Judith's whisper. "I think that Trogler dog is after Oatmeal. We have to help our poor kitty."

I listened, and from out across the darkness I thought I did hear a mournful cry blanketed by the rough, mean barking of a dog.

"All right," I said.

As I slipped on my overalls, it seemed that *King Kong* and the episode with David was just a bad dream. Confusion had become my normal state. The world had turned me upside down and inside out. I grabbed a flashlight and an iron poker, but I had virtually no volition as I followed Judith through the dragonfield on a moon-washed night, dew already starting to bead up on the cornstalks.

The Trogler place looked deceptively harmless.

Judith spoke in a worry-flecked voice as we approached the crawl space: "I can't hear anything now, Teddy. You think we're too late?"

I had no idea what to think. I wanted to be asleep. No, I wanted a new day, a new life.

I wanted simples—simple needs, simple desires, simple thoughts.

We hunkered down and quietly called the cat and listened for a long time before Judith gasped in what sounded like joy: "Oh, Teddy, do you hear that? Oatmeal's purring. Oh, the dog didn't get him. He's purring."

She hugged at my shoulder, but, honestly, I couldn't hear the cat. I said I did. It was an easy lie. Why spoil Judith's moment? I told myself. Besides,

maybe my various conflicts had partially deafened me.
I shined the flashlight into the crawl space, catching
a blur of movement, enough to show both of us that
the cat was most definitely alive. With that I said,
"Well, I guess we can go back home now."

Then it started.

From beneath the haunted ground. Then out from
the haunted walls.

"Animus! Animus! Animus, come home!"

It was an irresistible call. Scratchy. Throaty. Seduc-
tive. I felt it in my groin, and when I saw how arrested
Judith was, I pulled at her arm. "Let's get out of here.
Let's go."

I was surprised to find that I couldn't budge her.

"But Teddy I can't. I can't. And neither can you."

I hated the voice I heard—not Judith's voice at all.
No sweetness or warmth. It was the flat monotone of
someone under a spell. I yanked at her again, but it
was no use. She was headed around to the front entrance, and all I could do was trail along.

The front room was surprisingly pitch dark.

It was as if not even moonlight could enter the
place. My flashlight beam captured circles of the
emptiness—dust motes and silence. I could hear our
breathing and our footfalls and that was about it. Just
to break the unnerving quiet I said, "I saw Romina at
the show. You saw her, too, didn't you?"

I was sweeping the beam around the walls and over
a mound of milo, and then, still waiting for Judith to
respond, I swung the light up at the ceiling where a
rope dangled down from a gaping hole. The end of
the rope reached to within a few inches of the floor
we were standing on. I found myself studying the
rope, wondering what it was doing there and what it
was connected to.

And that's when the flashlight winked out.

Judith shrieked, and I think I did, too, and then I felt her fingers—much colder than they usually were—clamp onto my wrist in the darkness.

"Teddy, listen!"

We heard the voice again. Romina's voice. No mistaking it.

"Animus, come home. Come home. Come home."

What happened next was really weird. About four feet up from the floor on one wall a soft, yellowish, ghostly light appeared, casting an oval of illumination. Within the illumination an invisible hand was writing something on the white plaster.

Animus come home. Come home. Come home.

The script continued in a spooky repetition until it reached a corner, and there the ghost of Senta Trogler stepped from the wall. She honed her stare in on Judith. I raised the poker, but I knew that I lacked the courage to do anything. The scene was mesmerizing. The script, in the nimbus of light, snaked from wall to wall.

And the other Trogler ghosts emerged.

Old Rolf with his wicked sling blade and hideous face.

Then, above us, peering down through the hole from which the rope extended, Siebert leering down at Judith, looking even more malicious than Mickey Palmer ever did. Then the growl of Hunter as the dog pawed its way up through the floor behind us, blocking our exit. Each ghost radiated a light, each was surrounded by an aura.

"Teddy," Judith whispered. "Don't move. Stay still. And don't be afraid."

I was petrified.

The writing stopped. Silence reigned.

Then the ghost of Romina rose up through the floor directly beneath Judith's feet. The spookiest part

is that the ghost seemed to halt her rise in the area of
Judith's stomach, and I could see my cousin's body go
somewhat limp. All I could suddenly think of was that
she looked like a ventriloquist's dummy—the ghost of
Romina Trogler was in control of her.

Then I was scared and angry. And I made a mistake.

I should have stayed as still as I could, but I lunged
forward in a pretty stupid attempt to protect Judith.
The next thing I knew the end of the dangling rope
coiled around one of my ankles. I smashed at the rope
with the poker like I was smashing at a bull snake in
the chicken coop.

My feet were suddenly jerked up.

The thud of my shoulder and side of my face
against the floor made me see stars.

I cried out in pain and terror, and the room swung
and the floor fell away and I was weightless for a moment and as blood rushed to my head I thought I
would lose consciousness. I don't remember much except that when I was a good five or six feet off the
floor my tarot card fell out of my overalls and yet before it could flutter too far from me it flamed into a
wad of dark ashes.

I heard Judith scream something as I thrashed and
bucked, dancing a strange dance, dancing hard and
fast and seeing a blur of movement that was the approach of old Rolf, his sling blade raised for action,
and then glancing up above me where Siebert was
inching down the rope gripping his sledge.

I was going to be murdered.

I was going to die.

Just before I closed my eyes, I saw the eruption of
blue beneath me. I didn't know what it meant. My
eyes shut tightly, I braced myself for death. I heard the
whsst of Rolf's sling blade, and I could feel the rope re-

leasing me and I heard the crash of Siebert's sledge near my head.

And I was embraced by a blue flame—like warm, gentle, protective hands.

You're safe.

Those were the words branded in my thoughts, but I have no idea where they came from.

Then a woman's voice: "You're safe."

"It was the Fiery Angel, Teddy. I know it was."

"Maybe so," I said. "But I definitely heard a woman speak."

I asked again about the identity of Animus; I'd never heard a name like that, but I could sense that Judith didn't want to say anything about it, though I continued to believe she knew more than she was willing to say.

She was on her cot, snuggling under a sheet and gazing at me. I couldn't stop trembling, and I really didn't want to hear about the Fiery Angel, though I was certainly thankful for whatever force rescued us at the Troglers. Could be I just wouldn't let myself believe in the Fiery Angel. Not the way Judith did—which was like the way some people believe in Jesus.

I think maybe Judith could tell I didn't want to talk.

"Teddy, they'll go away when I do."

Of course, she was talking about the ghosts. All I could do was nod. She knew that I didn't want her to leave.

"Teddy," she followed, her voice thick with need, "could we hold each other? I don't think it would be too wrong if we just held each other."

That word "wrong" resonated. I felt empty and bewildered. My shoulder and one side of my face ached. At the same time, I wasn't going to turn down another chance to lie with Judith in my arms, those warm, firm breasts against my body. I slipped off my overalls so I was wearing only my underpants and joined her.

"Thank you, Teddy," she whispered. "Do you feel all right about what we're doing?"

I didn't know what I felt beyond the way a certain area of my body was automatically responding to the pressure of Judith's thigh. She put her head on my shoulder—not the sore one; I closed my eyes and tried to block out David's cries of anguish and Kong's cries of pain and Fay Wray's screams of fear.

Mostly, though, I tried to block out all the images of the ghosts.

"I feel all right. I really do," I said.

I pretty much stopped trembling. I began to feel . . . well, *safe.*

In almost no time Judith was asleep. Even her snoring was lovely to me.

I slept some, but deep into the night I woke. Restless, my thoughts sharp and cold like a hailstorm, I was feeling a tremendous sense of having forgotten something. I began to imagine that someone was lurking in the shadows—not one of the ghosts, but someone—and yet I knew there really wasn't anyone. And I realized even more intimately than before that whatever beauty our sad house, our sad family, had possessed, it had been killed by an unknown beast, a beast that couldn't be gunned down the way Hollywood scripted.

I lay there with Judith in my arms for a couple of hours more. Near dawn, sleep cornered me again and I was about to surrender when suddenly the blade of memory was at my throat; I saw again my mother receiving a butcher knife and concealing it in a towel. Not a dream. Not something I had imagined. Not something I could explain away.

It was real.

I knew I should tell my father.

I knew I should try again to tell him about the ghosts.

Because I knew this: The ghosts had given the knife to my mother so that she could kill my father.

Ten

Answers

Instead, I opened my eyes and I listened to the pre-dawn darkness.

I pressed Judith closer to me.

And I thought about blood.

And I thought about how frightening the world is when you're upside down.

And I thought about death.

Mid-July of 1955 found me sitting in a hospital waiting room in Emporia, Kansas, about to come face to face with someone star-cursed and demon-haunted—misfortune's shadow. And what I could not grasp was that others believed that I, as well as Fate, had played a role in another person's demise. Thankfully, not *everyone* condemned me.

"You shouldn't blame yourself," Judith whispered as she and I sat there with my brother, Junior, who had buried his face in a magazine. Junior was neutral on the issue of my guilt.

I guess I was in shock or, at least, deeply confused by what had occurred.

It did, however, take my mind off the ghosts.

I stared into Judith's beautiful eyes and said, "You, too. Don't pay any attention to what my mother said this morning. There's something wrong with her."

Judith nodded and looked down at her hands.

"Everything will be fine after my father comes," she muttered. "After I've gone away. It upsets your mother that I'm around. She'll be fine after I'm gone. I told the Fiery Angel about all of this, and I believe he'll make sure that things are fine."

I shook my head. It didn't seem like this was any of the Fiery Angel's business. This was family business. I hadn't told Judith about seeing the ghosts encourage my mother to take up the butcher knife, but I had mentioned to my father that I thought my mother might do something strange. I had swallowed back what really frightened me. He told me not to be alarmed. He would see about it, and I suppose maybe he talked to her. I knew I should have related all that I'd seen to him. And how do you tell a man that you've had a flash of shadowy intuition that his wife wants to murder him? I had no proof. All I had was a vague, nebulous sense that my mother was becoming a puppet for the revenge of the ghosts upon my father.

They were after an intimate revenge.

But of nothing could I be certain.

What set my mother off on her jag of rage was receiving the call that morning from David's mother who explained about her son being in the hospital as a result of self-inflicted wounds. She said that David was begging to see me, and whatever else was exchanged in that call it led my mother to assume a suicide attempt. She read darkly into my part in it and, not surprisingly, made Judith an accomplice, if not the root cause, of David's act.

"They told me that girl is wicked! Child of the Devil! She's a witch! She's walking-around, living, breathing evil—that's what she is! Turned my Teddy evil! Killed the spirit of this family! I pray that God will strike her down, and if He doesn't, they told me I was to do it! They gave me a sword!"

I was the only one who knew her ravings carried allusions to the ghosts of Senta and Romina Trogler. I was apparently the only one who suspected that while she might be cursing Judith, the blood she planned to spill was my father's. Then again, I began to fear that Judith might well become a target, too.

My father wrestled her around the waist and held her fury in check until the woman collapsed against him in tears. She was completely crazy—couldn't my father see that? Couldn't he sense that she was being controlled by the ghosts?

"She'll be leaving soon, Kathleen. I don't think whatever's happened here is her fault, but she'll be leaving soon, and I'm not going to throw a blood relative out of my house when she's got nowhere to go."

Before the emotional storm passed, I told my father that Judith had nothing to do with whatever idiotic thing David had attempted—of course, that was not entirely true, but I wanted to reassure him so he wouldn't change his mind and send her away. My father was tired and heavy with sadness, like a disaster victim surveying damage to his property.

I wished that I could make him feel better.

I wished that things would not get worse—but I suspected that they were going to.

In the waiting room I thought about suicide, about why anybody would try it, and about exactly how David had wounded himself. It all made my stomach queasy. And when David's mother, a pretty woman with thin lips and a grim expression, approached me, I felt I might need to seek out the restroom.

She nodded at Junior, who lowered his magazine to acknowledge her.

"Hello, Mrs. Packard," he said. "Sorry to hear about David."

She squeezed out a smile and then glanced from me to Judith and then back to me.

"Teddy," she began, placing fingers against her throat as if she anticipated her voice would fail her, "David . . . he would like to see you."

"All right," I said. Then, more out of nervousness than politeness, I added, "This is my cousin from Topeka." I didn't say her name because my brain got caught between "Judith" and "Ilona" and so neither got voiced.

David's mother flicked her eyes at Judith, but very quickly looked back at me.

"Do you think you can see him without upsetting him? It seems you're the reason he's upset, and when I talked with your mother this morning she claimed she didn't know what you did to David and so—"

"Nothing," I blurted out. "I didn't do nothing to him. Honest, I didn't."

I was quivering all over and couldn't stop it. David's mother was rigid with doubt. I think she was no more than a heartbeat away from slapping my face or clawing at my eyes—mostly, though, she was beside herself with confusion and pain.

"If you can see him without upsetting him . . . I just don't understand why he would . . . do you have any idea why he would try this? He's always been a smart, sensible . . ."

Her words seemed to disappear down her throat like a frightened animal seeking its den. I stood up and looked at Junior and then at Judith, and then I began to follow David's mother to his room. I couldn't imagine what I was going to say to him. I wanted nothing more than to turn and run back to Judith and Junior and head home.

Holding my breath, I slipped through the door.

He looked like a ghost.

Pale and very weary, his eyes red and his wrists bandaged, David was propped up against the pillow. He was sipping orange juice through a straw. He brightened when he saw me and then to his mother he said, "I want to talk with Teddy by myself."

His mother hesitated and took a deep breath.

"Well, that would be fine, I suppose. I'll be right outside the door here if you need anything. Just right outside this door."

When she left the room, David said, "My parents want a shrink to examine me."

"A what?"

"A shrink. Don't you know what a shrink is?" My blank expression caused him to follow up. "It's a psychiatrist. My parents think I must be mentally disturbed. But I'm not. It's just that . . . I need you."

I felt as if I were smothering. I stared at David, and all I could say was "What did you do?"

"Oh, you mean *this*?"

He grinned shyly and held out his wrists as if he were proud of them.

"So you tried to cut yourself read bad?"

"Come over here and see. Come on, I'll show you. I used my dad's razor."

I felt as if I had the flu. But I was mesmerized by the partial sight of a deep gash neatly stitched up when David tugged away an edge of one bandage.

"You must have bled a lot."

"Yeah, you should have seen our bathroom floor."

"You really wanted to kill yourself?"

I knew I shouldn't have asked that—it just slipped out. I couldn't understand David's high spirits. I couldn't understand much of anything about the moment.

"Yeah," he said, and then, more soberly, "yeah, I think I did. Or . . . I wanted to show you I meant what I said. I meant it, Teddy."

"Sure," I said.

We talked a few minutes longer, or rather, David talked and I listened. He talked about books he'd been reading and he talked about how he thought he might end up being a writer one day.

"A lot of writers have attempted suicide," he said.

It's funny, but I suddenly wondered whether if David had succeeded—if he had killed himself— could Judith wake him up from being dead the way she woke up the Troglers? Could she wake up all of the dead or just a few? I realized that I didn't know precisely how her talent worked.

I was relieved when David's mother poked her head in and suggested that we wind up our conversation because her son needed some rest and that she had called in a special doctor to talk with him later. David waited for her to duck back outside and then he smirked and reached for my hand. I felt something for him—I just wasn't sure what.

"Will you think about us, Teddy? Think about just the two of us and not of your cousin or nobody else. I still love you, Teddy, and maybe I did a real stupid thing, but I did it because I meant what I said. You'll think about us, won't you?"

I told him I would.

He lifted my hand to his lips and kissed it softly and rubbed it against his cheek as if it were fur or a kitten or a puppy. I pulled my hand away more quickly than I intended to.

"See you," I said.

"Bye, little Red. I'll be thinking about you. You're mine. You know that, don't you?"

I stopped.

"No. No, I'm not. I'm not yours."

His face changed in the blink of an eye—from love to something like hate—and his voice changed, too.

"You are," he said, almost in a growl. "If you say you aren't, I'll make you pay, Teddy. I'll hurt you. I'll make you pay. You'll see. You've let that witch mess up your mind, Teddy. Everybody says she's a witch. Keep away from her. You're mine—can't you see that? If you won't love me, I'll make you wish you had—I swear I will, Teddy."

His voice scratched high and scary.

I hurried out when I saw his eyes flame. He morphed into a small and angry and mangled creature, and the moment I was outside his door I wondered why I had come. I wondered why it was so hard to find the right place for people in my life. And I wondered if he would make good on his threat.

On the way home, Junior rambled on about what could happen to David: unsettling stuff centered on wasting away in a mental institution somewhere, and then something about David not really meaning to commit suicide or he would have succeeded. I blocked out much of what he said. Judith held my hand and said nothing. I appreciated that. When his ramblings ended, Junior started singing Bo Diddly tunes, including "Who Do You Love?," "Road Runner" and "You Can't Judge a Book by Its Cover." Judith giggled at them, which seemed to cause Junior to sing even more loudly. We rocked and rolled home, all three of us laughing by the time we pulled into the driveway.

I had temporarily pushed David out of my life.

The ghosts, too.

What Judith and I found in the mud room erased our good mood.

Our basketball globe had been savagely stabbed at and ripped in a bloodless attack. Judith, shaken by the sight of it, stole away to the barn. I followed after I showed Junior what had happened. He shrugged it off, but I think he knew as well as I did who murdered our globe. And I think he was scared some about the danger Judith and I might be in.

When I got to the barn, Jack was talking with Judith and sort of drumming the point of his javelin on the hay-strewn floor. He had stayed home that morning to help my father work on the pickup. He seemed pretty shaken up. I didn't like to see him there standing close to Judith, and so I asked him what he wanted. He blurted out something that almost knocked me over.

"Ma tried to stab Pop with a butcher knife. I saw it. She meant to hurt him real bad."

He looked at Judith and then at me, narrowing his eyes as if to make certain we wouldn't challenge his words.

"What did Pop do?" I said.

"Took the knife away from her and . . . I don't know, talked to her, I suppose. I don't know. I split."

Judith touched his arm.

"I think it will be all right soon," she said.

But Jack was working his mouth and poking his javelin harder, and when he spoke again there was almost no emotion in his voice.

"Things have gone crazy in a hurry."

He was right about that.

When evening fell I asked my father to come outside so we could talk. I was real nervous. I told him what I thought I should tell him: first, that Jack had shared what he had seen and then that Emmitt Suggs had told me who was involved in delivering a violent justice to the Troglers long ago. And, finally, I told him about the ghosts and how they'd been in control of my mother, how they'd probably gotten her to try to stab him. It was their revenge, pure and simple.

My father listened patiently. Seemed like he considered his response quite some time before he finally said, "Son, I'm not proud of what I did back then with the Troglers. I got caught up in something—and I've lived with thoughts of what I took part in every single day since then. God as my witness, I have. But this is not about ghosts—it's about guilt and regret. I did wrong. And your mother—for her it's always been about not being where she thought she belonged. I tried to do everything to make her happy here. But I brought her to this."

"No!" I exclaimed. "It's not because of you."

He just smiled sadly and hugged my neck.

All the next day I kept one eye ever vigilant for further signs of strangeness in my mother. My attention never left her when she was anywhere near.

Evenings of the days that followed my father took to listening to the radio and keeping close to my mother. Our Saturday night radio family gatherings had ended. Now my father would sit in his rocking chair in the living room and maintain the volume very low; my mother would sit across from him sewing in another rocking chair or, more often than not, reading her Bible. I say reading, though in my spying on her I rarely saw her turn a page. I discovered that for whatever reason she had broken off her friendship with Mrs. Penner; I discovered as well that she would occasionally slip down into our storm cellar, where I would hear her whispering in a weird, gossipy tone.

At first, I thought she was down there talking to herself.

Then I found out that the ghost of Senta Trogler was with her—they were like twin crazies—both, in their own way, dead and haunting the rest of us.

I wanted to tell my father about her friendship with a ghost; I wanted him to do something about my mother—I'm not sure what. Get all of the madness out of her, I guess. Or perhaps just get her to admit that she had destroyed our globe; instead, my father accused Jack of putting stories in my head about ghosts and the like. Judith came to Jack's rescue, defending him against the charge. My confusion deepened: I knew, despite Jack's attempts to keep his feelings hidden, that he was in love with Judith; and I was having to consider the possibility that she had warm feelings for him. Beyond that, I could see that my father did not wish to believe the darkest possible narrative concerning my mother and her sanity. At the same time, he wanted to protect his family from harm—and that, of course, included Judith.

This was a heavy cross for him to bear.

As for me, I wanted to become more than Judith's Onlie Begetter—I wanted to become her guardian.

I thought I was prepared to walk through fire or wade through blood for her.

I believed I might be able to die for her.

One morning Judith took a broom and swept God out of her life.

It was, in fact, the morning after we were forced to hear the Reverend Lex Macready, a honey-tongued, young evangelist, speak at the high school gymnasium. My mother, her mental faculties scrambled, had insisted upon our attendance; my father had caved in to her irrational request, and thus Judith and I had been delivered to the speaking engagement against our wills. In what struck me as spineless behavior, my father had disappointed and angered me. He had embraced the cold, passionless spirit of my mother's predatory morality.

The timing for an encounter with a man-child of God seemed all wrong because in the days following my visit to David in the hospital and having his threat thrown in my face, and in the wake of my renewed determination to protect Judith from the violent threat my mother posed, I wanted answers to all sorts of questions: questions about love and sex and family and the future. Questions about ghosts in my life and why those ghosts might want me in their lives. My father, goaded on by my mother and, I think, haunted by his murderous involvement with the Troglers, was also issuing unspoken questions. It was all too complex for me—I wanted simply to know who I was and where I belonged. I wanted to be able to look into tomorrow and see myself with all the clarity of a photograph. I craved a life in focus. Ironically, I came to believe the Reverend Macready offered me an answer. Offered one to Judith as well, but, of course, she had become more content to ignore the questions.

Before the summer ended, I would change my mind and let go of the quest for answers; I would learn that the need for mystery is greater than the need for answers.

The casual events leading up to our forced encounter with the Reverend Macready seem easy enough to trace now. They began that next Sunday afternoon when my Uncle John pulled into our driveway scattering banties and shouting dust. My father met him on the front porch; the rest of us crowded up close to the scene with what must have appeared to be xenophobic puzzlement on our faces. I, for one, believed Uncle John had been drinking.

He announced to us that he was on his way to Alaska to work on some highway project. Then he pressed his look over my father's shoulder directly at Judith and said, "Girl, here's the sad truth: Your mama has run off with a fella she met at that place in Topeka she went to. She's gone off with him and you hadn't oughta 'spect to hear from her. Not never again."

We all sort of edged away from Judith to give her room to respond. I felt sorry for her, and when my mother grunted out an ugly sound, I turned and gave her a nasty stare before bouncing my attention back to Judith. Her eyes were moist, but her jaw was firm.

"My father's coming. He said he would. I'm waiting for him to come so I can go to Colorado where I think I belong. My father's coming, isn't he?"

I held my breath. I studied the slack, rubbery expression on Uncle John's face. I feared what he might say.

"Oh, I 'spect he will. If he said he would, I 'spect he will. All's I came by to tell is not to look to hear from your mama, and I'm sorry 'bout that. Appears she's left you on your own. I can't be no help neither 'cause I'll be gone."

My father had his hands on his hips and donned that opaquely serious mask every farmer has at his disposal when he needs it—the look of cold, hard business.

"Well, John," he said, "this young lady here will be fine. She's more than welcome til her daddy comes for her. We appreciate you stopping in to tell us about Juanita. I'm hoping she'll come to her senses. We'll see."

Then, in a rare moment of both lucidity and civility, my mother issued my uncle a barely audible invitation to come in for some iced tea, but he declined and was soon departing the summer afternoon for points north. I expected never to see him again. Or my Aunt Juanita, for that matter. The porch scene broke up with my father muttering softly to Judith that things would be fine. He gave her shoulder a paternalistic squeeze. I saw how he truly did care for her; like me, he was her protector. But there was an aching sadness in his expression generated by what I guessed was some secret anticipation of events to come.

That afternoon, secrets were riding on the wind.

Restless, a touch bewildered, Judith and I went first to the barn and then by twilight into the dragonfield; we shunned the Trogler place because Judith said it was dangerous for us to go there. As always, she claimed that the only possible response to the ghosts was for her to leave; otherwise, a battle loomed, one the outcome of which she feared. And because she feared it, so did I. But the fabric of things for me, emotionally, began to tear even more as the sun slipped away. Something happened. The sacred space we had created was violated. It occurred when I was hunkered down among the corn rows watching Judith burn a small pile of her latest poems. She was explaining once again that she didn't care about what her mother had done—didn't care to see her again as long as the Fiery Angel directed the steps of her father to Saddle Rock to rescue her. Nothing else mattered.

I swallowed hard at what seemed her indifference to our friendship.

Then Judith went into one of her past-life trances. I was studying her face and her uplifted hands and the swell of her breasts—she always looked so sexy in a trance—and I was probably smiling as she began to

speak in the weird tone of voice of whoever she had
returned to. When the usually ceaseless Kansas breeze
suddenly, inexplicably died down, I sensed something.

Then heard it.

The whistle of Jack's javelin before it stabbed into a
corn row ten yards away.

"Hey," I barked out. "Dang you." I scrambled to my
feet in time to see a figure running down one of the
rows, the blades of corn whipping against his body. Of
course, had he been trying to kill us rather than just
scare us, he could have. He was that proficient with
his aim. Judith bolted from her trance and clutched
at my arm. She glanced from the javelin to the escape
of the distant figure.

"Was that Jack?" she said.

I was breathing hard, my anger seething out
through my nostrils so ferociously that I couldn't
speak. But I had heard something more. Something
in Judith's voice: the lilt of a growing affection for
my brother. I had seen a dozen or more subtle signs
of it over the weeks even as Jack had donned a brave
denial. He was jealous. He was in love with Judith.
And he was becoming her mythic spear thrower.

They had been talking about us.

Something in the halting rhythm of the scene made
that evident.

In fact, they were still feasting upon us when Judith
and I entered the kitchen from the mud room and
found all four of them there at the kitchen table. Only
it appeared that Junior might be defending us because we heard him challenge my father.

"Besides that," he said, "you don't have all the answers."

I don't know what Junior was responding to, but when Jack saw us he pushed up out of his chair and stole away as guilty as Cain. I assumed he had been spreading poison with words just as he often set out poison on peanut butter and crackers for the rats that infested our chicken pen.

As I stood there taking in the somber trio of Junior, my father and my mother, things began to crystallize, or so I thought. I read it that Jack wanted Judith for himself and so he had told my folks something vicious, something touching upon the relationship Judith and I shared, something about our dragonfield behavior—any number of possibilities might have been offered and colored darkly. All of them lies.

My mother would believe chapter and verse of such a treacherous volume.

"What's going on?" I said.

Junior shook his head and spit out a sound of disgust as he got up to leave. Then my father began. "Your mother believes . . . ."

I held Judith's hand as I listened, hatred leaching from my every pore as my father stumbled over words accusing us of everything from lasciviousness to consorting with demons.

"I didn't raise my sons to be immoral."

Glancing from Junior to me, that's how my father finished his spiel.

"Jack's telling you lies," I said.

But Judith was quick to protest: "No, Teddy. Jack wouldn't."

I sank into a realization that she was probably right. My father said something more; his eyes locked onto our hands, but we held our grasp. I wanted to shout into my father's face: *How can you listen to a crazy woman? She tried to kill you—the ghosts are telling her to kill you.* My mother was shivering like a wet dog, shivering not from a chill, rather from some puritanical fervor that had seized her, twisting her mouth into hideous shapes. She lowered her eyes, a gesture combining shame and disgust. Her fingers tapped nervously at a flyer in front of her. In bold letters it read as follows:

THE ANSWER
COME HEAR IT FROM
THE REVEREND LEX MACREADY
WEDNESDAY NIGHT, HIGH SCHOOL GYMNASIUM

In the barn that evening I argued with Judith that we should run away.

She wouldn't hear of it.

"I can put up with anything until my father comes," she said. "I have the Fiery Angel and I have you, Teddy, as my protector. You're my Onlie Begetter. And Jack has become my friend, too. He's not with that awful Mickey anymore."

I gritted my teeth. But then she kissed me on the shoulder, and I melted like a chocolate bar in the hot sun.

When Wednesday evening arrived, Judith looked gorgeous in her pink dress, and I was pretty spiffy myself, and so it was that my folks carted us off to a man-boy evangelist to be saved or exorcised or whatever. Truth is, my mother was the one who needed the exorcism. The Trogler place, too—a whole pack of demons called it home.

An unforgettable evening was about to unfold.

I was barely in the door to the gathering before I sloughed off my anger and opened to the spectacle of promised joy and transfiguration. I almost felt as if I were betraying Judith. But I couldn't help it. I knew that something there was going to touch me, move me and force me to see . . . *possibilities*. That's the best word for what I carried from those sweaty and exciting moments of my life.

Macready's "people"—older, handsome, well-dressed, well-groomed men—welcomed the citizens of Saddle Rock and the surrounding area to the high school gym, smiling as if smiles were inexhaustible. They handed out tiny Bibles and a program overviewing the ministry of young Lex Macready; the latter was tricked out with screaming lines of scripture and photos of Macready preaching the Word, healing the sick and lame, and kicking at demons and evil spirits as if they were footballs to be booted over a crossbar. I thought it was a grand document. I deeply envied Macready even before I sat down to hear him. His men had lined up a couple of hundred folding chairs on the gym floor. My folks, Judith and I sat smack in the jump ball circle and took in the stage, where the floor had been covered with some kind of white, fluffy material, cottony like clouds, and the steps leading to the stage sported a red carpet. Giant oscillating fans set up at angles to the audience thrummed eagerly, though ineffectually, against the summer heat. On stage, there was a podium and palm plants in huge pots, and stretching across the width of the stage a tinsel-lettered banner (with large, silver letters that twinkled like Christmas) reading, THE ANSWER.

I thought it was all breathtaking.

I couldn't wait to see and hear Macready.

But they made me suffer through tenderly seductive piano music, a baritone solo of "Rock of Ages" and a long, prologue sermon by an older man who spoke of young Macready as if the boy and Jesus were school pals and as if God had reached down from Heaven with a nozzle to fill the lad with premium, soul-saving, miracle-producing, demon-chasing, affliction-healing power.

Then Macready was on stage in the blink of an eye, appearing as if by magic.

I think the audience gasped. I certainly did. Everyone around me ceased fanning their hot faces. But when Macready materialized, everybody else in the world gradually became invisible to me. Only he and I were there, and when he began to stride back and forth across the stage I knew what he was doing: He was walking around inside me, inside my doubts, inside my disaffection with self, inside my frustration over Judith being out of my reach at times, inside my confusion over sex, inside my desire to part company forever with my family and inside my fear of the ghosts.

He was walking around inside the future of who I wanted to be: somebody famous. Somebody the world would admire. I was glad he didn't know. I took a deep breath and watched and listened as the show unfolded.

In my first blush view of Macready, I fell in love with him.

Then I began to study him: First of all, I could tell he was about my age. He wore an apricot-colored jacket and trousers, a tie red-orange as a ripe tomato and white bucks. His soft, brown, sparrow-feather hair was neatly combed; his eyes were hazel, I believe. He was even more handsome than David.

"I have the answer, friends!"

His opening shout branded my chest.

He strode to one end of the stage. "I have the answer, friends!"

He strode to the other end of the stage. "I have the answer, friends!"

He returned to the podium and perched an elbow there. "I have the answer, friends!"

An anticipatory silence like morning fog over a Kansas pond filled the auditorium.

"The answer . . . is *God!*"

I had never heard the word "God" sound so good. I had never seen anyone quite so magical as Lex Macready. His voice, with just a touch of a Southern accent, was almost otherworldly. He was hypnotic— every nonverbal gesture, every intonation, every mesmeric casting of his eyes over the audience—he was a master. He was a boy with a man's ethos. He threw a net over the crowd; we were like fish. He hauled us in and we flopped, but we were caught. And we believed. That is, most members of the gathering believed Macready's message, but I . . . I believed in Macready's performance.

Quite honestly, I recall very little of his actual sermon. Shining pieces of it—like brilliant, yet cheap jewelry—lodged in my mental filter. I recall his blasting out a passage from *Ephesians*: "Put on the whole armor of God, that you may be able to stand against the wiles of the devil. For we wrestle not against flesh and blood, but against principalities, against powers, against the rulers of the darkness of this world, against spiritual wickedness in high places." And I recall his posing of that marvelous question from *2 Corinthians:* "What communion hath light with darkness?" He returned to *Ephesians* to punctuate his attack on darkness: "Be ye, therefore, followers of God, as dear children . . . For ye were sometimes darkness, but now are ye light in the Lord; walk as children of light." And he reminded his enthralled audience to ". . . have no fellowship with the unfruitful works of darkness, but, rather, reprove them."

He was an actor.

He was Superman sans cape.

He could leap depressed souls in a single bound and bend the steel of apostates.

He understood the deepest wish of his audience: to believe. He had the figurative taste of blood in his mouth; his heart vibrated with the potential for transformation. But more than anything else, he was simply this: the center of attention.

Like a sun god.

And, oh, how I envied that. I wanted it. Maybe I wanted what Macready had more than I wanted Judith. I think I did. I leaned forward on the edge of my seat and I watched an indescribable metamorphosis take place. I watched young Macready, a Bible in one hand, flap his arms as if he were about to sprout wings and launch himself into the air. I saw light from some hidden source surround him. And I saw fire. And suddenly, I saw something more.

Lex Macready became a fiery angel.

I glanced furtively at Judith, but I could not read the soft smile on her lips.

Fiery angel.

At that moment I believed that I, too, could become a fiery angel, my own fiery angel.

"Onlie Begetter," I whispered to myself.

Judith heard and turned her curious smile my way.

At that moment something started growing inside me—but I didn't know what it was. I turned my attention back to Macready. He was suddenly speaking sotto voce and without the benefit of the microphone, and yet everyone in the audience could hear him—I was certain they could.

"God has given me the power to heal," he said. "It's God's power, not mine. If you have need of healing, I'm asking you now to come forward. Come forward. Come right on up here on this stage and be healed. God wants you to be whole. God is the answer."

A heavyset woman I had never seen in Saddle Rock mushroomed up from the front row. Two of Macready's men helped her ascend the steps. Macready reached for her and gently turned her so we all could see her, and he said, "What is it, my child? What needs to be healed?"

The woman, a middle-aged farm wife-type with ruddy cheeks, spoke in a scratchy voice.

"There's a lump of cancer in my throat."

She squeezed about where her vocal cords would be, and then she started to cry very softly. Macready got her a chair and sat her into it so that she faced the audience. He was smiling and nodding, acting magnificently in my view of things. Stepping around behind the woman whose tear-stained face shone like the tinsel letters above her head, Macready said, "Will y'all bow your heads and pray for this precious soul as I lay my hands on her? Let's invite God's miracle of healing to fill this auditorium."

It's funny, but I realized right that moment how it was the first time I'd ever heard someone in real life speak with a southern accent—I immediately envied it. I didn't bow my head, though, and I didn't pray, and I don't believe Judith did either. I wanted to watch every second of Macready's performance. I didn't want to miss a thing. He put his guts into it. He squeezed his eyes shut tightly, as tightly and fiercely as someone constipated and intent upon coaxing a difficult bowel movement—that was the image that came to mind.

I saw spittle spray from Macready's lips as he pressed at the woman's forehead as if he were trying to remove a stuck lid on a Mason jar. I sat there in flames. I have no idea whether he healed that woman—in fact, I couldn't have cared less, nor was I concerned about the baby boy a young mother carried onto the stage. The child's heart beat funny, she explained, and doctors said it would not live long. There was an old man with cataracts and a nearly deaf woman who had been kicked by a horse. All that mattered to me was getting to see Macready perform.

I wanted to dash on stage and wipe his sweaty brow and kiss his pouty lips.

"Is there anyone else this evening?" he intoned. "Anyone else afflicted who needs God's healing grace? I am His instrument. God is the answer. Come forward and you will see."

What happened next was a complete shock to me.

Dumbfounded, I watched as someone began to walk up the steps to the stage: David.

I thought I might faint as I listened to David respond to Macready's question about the source of his suffering. Still visibly weak, David faced the audience and said, "A demon tried to make me kill myself."

The crowd convulsed in horror.

And David continued. "The demon—really there's two of them—they're here right now."

Again the crowd reacted in muted exclamations of shock and unease and something bordering on terror. Macready had to calm them, in fact, before he could speak.

"David," he said, "would you show us where they are? God has the power to deal with demons. He has the answer. He *is* the answer."

Not a muscle in my body moved as I sat there, stiffer than a board, waiting. Out of the corner of my eye, I could see that Judith was drinking everything in, studying it, disdainful of it.

Then David pointed directly at me.

"There. Right there. It's Teddy O'Dell. He's got demons in him and so does she. His cousin—she's got demons, too."

My father clutched my mother in his arms, and the whispers and half sentences around me and Judith began to sound like angry hisses. Judith rustled beside me. Then, astonishingly, she got to her feet. She glanced down at me, her smile gentle and mischievous.

Macready was gesturing for us to come. People were drawing back from us as if we might cause them to combust with a mere glance.

"I'm going up there, Teddy," said Judith.

"What?"

She nodded at the startled look on my face and began making her way to the aisle. There was a Red Sea parting of folks as she did. I went, too.

I don't recall my feet making contact with the gym floor or the stage, but I went, cupping Judith's elbow as she clopped up the steps. She waved off Macready's offer to help her negotiate the final step. I shot one look at David, but he shrank off to one side and behind Macready. His face simmered with sweat and anger and what else, I don't know.

The audience was preternaturally silent.

Then Macready, clearly nervous and a bit shaken, said, "God is the answer for you young folks." But there wasn't much conviction in his tone. Judith wouldn't shake hands with him. I did because I wanted to feel his touch. When I grasped his hand, it felt as soft as sheep's wool.

All I could think to say was, "I'm not really a demon and neither is my cousin—but she's crippled with something like polio."

I think the audience murmured, though, quite frankly I had blotted them out.

I noticed that Macready hesitated when his eyes met Judith's. He asked her her name.

"Judith," she said. "I'm Shakespeare's imaginary sister."

My heart was suddenly a hot rock in my throat. I didn't know what Judith was up to. Macready's lower lip danced nervously. He smiled blankly. He had no idea how to get a fix on Judith: was she just kidding or was she crazy or perhaps retarded? He held his smile as if it were something slippery like a bluegill. But I could tell that he was losing his nerve. His voice suddenly sounded hollow: "Would you like for God to cast out your demons? They've crippled your body."

"No demons," she replied. "And I'm not crippled. I'm broken."

I heard a click in Macready's throat. Vaguely I heard the audience a thousand miles away. Macready inched toward Judith.

"I can heal you," he said. "I mean—God can. If you believe."

Judith smiled confidently.

"I believe in the Fiery Angel—he protects me from ghosts. Protects Teddy, too. And there's something more I ought to tell you." She hesitated. Macready's jaw had fallen slack. Judith bore right into his face and said, "I wake up the dead."

Then she closed her eyes and raised her hands, palms up as she had so often in the dragonfield in making contact with a past life.

Macready stepped back with what sounded to me like a frightened groan.

I had to wade in. I had to say something.

"She can," I said. "She woke up the Troglers. She's not crazy or nothing. She's just real different, but she's in pain, and I give her the Kenny all the time. It helps some. She's in a lot of pain sometimes. She needs to be healed."

Macready was deep in fascination and fear. His lips

were moving and his eyes were frozen in a stony stare. The audience had lapsed back into total silence. They watched, as I did, as Macready lifted his right hand and extended it toward Judith's shoulder.

And he whispered, "You have darkness in you." Then, wild-eyed, he turned to face me even as his fingers hovered a few inches from Judith's shoulder. "Have no fellowship with the unfruitful works of darkness."

I shrugged nervously.

Judith stood her ground. Her chin jutted out defiantly. I think she knew that Macready's fingers were beginning to tremble. He tried to catch himself; he was like someone who has lost their balance and has started to fall and can't help themselves. He muttered something about demons.

Then his fingers met Judith's shoulder.

Instantly she spoke: "Your father is dead back in Louisiana, but I can wake him up. Do you want to see him?"

I felt a strange blast of heat at that moment. I have never felt anything like it. And then I saw Macready's eyes roll back and saliva dribble from the corners of his mouth. Two of his men lurched forward, but not in time.

The audience gasped.

David looked at me with hatred in his eyes.

What happened, happened with alarming suddenness.

The Reverend Lex Macready fainted, collapsing in a heap of frightened little boy at Judith's feet.

Judith wielded that broom as if she were killing snakes.

The dust of long ago seasons rose in sluggish puffs,

the dust of all the ghosts in her life, from the floor of the mud room and from the haunted ground far beneath our feet. Judith was engaged in some kind of symbolic act I could not relate to; I could not read its text, and, in fact, it would have remained a total mystery to me had she not explained that she had had it with God and men of God. "They don't belong in my life."

After Macready's service, the crowd had naturally buzzed and thrown daggers of disapproving looks at Judith and me. My father herded us away as quickly as possible; my mother refused to ride in the same vehicle with us, opting instead to accept a fellow church member's offer to take her home. As Judith and I followed my father out the gymnasium door, one of Macready's men shouted that God was angered and would curse us for exercising our demonic powers on the young evangelist. I remember part of what the man shouted: "You ought to be stoned in the town square to demonstrate that the God-fearing residents of Saddle Rock don't tolerate demons among them."

It wasn't a pretty thought.

And certainly this: We had not seen the last of the Reverend Macready.

I turned off my mental movie of the Macready incident because the dust was getting to me, and I started hacking like a two-packs-a-day smoker.

"Haven't you swept enough?" I said to Judith.

Teeth gritted, she relented.

Then I saw that she was in pain, severe pain. When she suddenly lost her grip on the broom, I reached for her. She cried out. Her legs wouldn't hold her. I caught her and she held me so tightly that I thought she was going to break a rib.

"They don't have the answers, Teddy," she murmured.

"I know."

"Will you protect me, Teddy?"

My heart rose up with her question. So many things occurred to me simultaneously. It seemed that maybe I had become as essential to her as the Fiery Angel; that maybe she loved me more than she loved Jack; that maybe I really could protect her from the ghosts if she believed in me. That maybe I could defeat the demon hunting Macready if he came after us—and I sensed that he would.

It seemed that the mud room got very dark, as dark as from some kind of weird eclipse.

"Yes," I said, holding the only person on the planet I truly loved, and I tried as hard as I could to pull her inside me so that we could be one.

Eleven

Words Tongued with Fire

Not too many days before Judith's father was to arrive, we rescued a mirror and a book. I rescued the mirror; Judith rescued the book. The mirror, a small, oval-shaped hand mirror of pink plastic made to resemble the texture of conch, was in a box of stuff Junior was throwing away. I asked him if I could have it and he said, "Sure, I don't give a fuck. But it's cracked. That's why I didn't give it to Phyllis."

I think there's an old Kansas superstition about cracked mirrors and bad luck in love relationships. I told Junior I didn't mind what condition it was in—I just thought it was pretty, and he told me I could have any of the other shit in the box, too—mostly it was memorabilia from his months going steady with Phyllis: a ceramic raccoon, a brilliant red, heart-shaped cushion, a volume of the wisdom of Henry David Thoreau, a large pair of spongy dice that had once dangled from his rearview mirror and some other items I can't recall. Judith latched onto the volume of Thoreau and was soon assailing me with lines such as ". . . for a man is rich in proportion to the number of things which he can afford to let alone." Thoreau momentarily supplanted Shakespeare and Virginia Woolf

as the author she most liked to quote. When I gave
her the cracked mirror, she was so touched that she
dropped Thoreau for the rest of the day. In the barn,
in our cozy fortress of hay, she took the mirror and
held it up to her face and invited me to share her reflection.

"See," she said, "I'm not a vampire."

For some reason, when she alluded to vampires I
thought instantly of Lex Macready.

"No," I said, "you're beautiful."

She giggled.

"Oh, Teddy, you're too much."

But while Judith was able to move on with her life
and erase Macready from the blackboard of her
mind, I was not. He haunted me every bit as much as
the Trogler ghosts did. The self he had awakened
stalked me. His presence burned within me more
darkly than that of the Fiery Angel.

In the wake of the Macready incident, the new min-
ister of the Christian Church—a graduate student at
Kansas State University in Manhattan—and two other
men from church came out to the farm one evening
and talked nervously at Judith and me about what had
happened. Their language was vague and their tone
serious. My father listened with the kind of grave demeanor he wore the day the vet told us one of our
milk cows had a stomach lining that was devouring itself. My mother did not join the somber gathering,
choosing instead to skulk self-righteously at the doorway or flit through to offer the men coffee, which they
politely turned down. I wanted to stop the proceed-
ings and point at her and say, "What about her? She
listens to ghosts and they told her to try to stab my father with a butcher knife." I should have, but I didn't.
As the uncomfortable session drew to a close, one of
the men, Herbert Gorman, hesitantly suggested that

Judith and I should be separated—he made it sound
like we were animals in heat. Further, he said that perhaps Judith should be sent back to whatever home she
had. Her summer visit, in his eyes, was over.

Neither Judith nor I said anything. She was magnificently above the inquisition. But I could tell that
my father was slightly angered by the nerve of this otherwise timid little clutch of men, because through a
clenched jaw he explained that Judith's father was
coming for her in a matter of days, on some not-too-
distant Saturday, and that we, as a family, would tend
to the situation ourselves. He thanked the church fa-
thers and sent them off before my mother could offer
them some other form of refreshment or encouragement. I was cheered by my father's attitude, and I
regretted later that I didn't tell him so.

Early one afternoon I couldn't find Judith. I
headed to the dragonfield, and from there I was on
my way to the Trogler place, scared that maybe the
ghosts had called her to them. In a sense, I think I was
right about that. Crouched low among the stalks of
corn, I saw her emerge from the rear of the old ghost-
infested house.

Jack was with her.

Seeing them together, I felt like scorched earth.

What had they been up to?

Jack, tossing his javelin out in front of him and then
chasing after it, had given Judith a hug and a kiss before darting off toward the pond. I was heartsick.
Then I noticed something else: Judith was walking
fine. She was walking without her braces or her
crutches.

She'd been healed.

Part of me wanted to run to her and express the joy

I felt in seeing her move about so freely; yet another part of me was mad and hurt and deeply puzzled. I felt she had been disloyal to me, and so I turned away and sneaked back through the dragonfield not allowing her to see my exit, and I wandered to the far end of our pasture, to the spot where Rock Creek elbowed onto our property. Gussie's spot. I waded in the cool water, and I fought back tears, tears that made me even angrier. Finally I decided I needed to confront Judith about Jack. Besides, I was also curious about her apparent healing.

I found her in the barn, her face buried in a small book. I assumed it was Thoreau or maybe some other book she had salvaged from Junior's box of throwaways. I was spectacularly wrong.

As I approached her, I tried to sound upset, but I couldn't generate the kind of energy I wanted. "I saw you a little while ago. With Jack at the Troglers'. And you're walking—no crutches. No braces. What's going on?"

She gestured for me to come sit with her.

"I'll tell you later," she said.

Of course, I wanted to know right then. Perching beside her on a bale of hay, I tried to sneak a peek at the reading material, but, to my surprise, Judith pulled it out of sight.

"Hey, what's the deal?" I said.

She stared at me. It was a funny, startling, silent moment like the effect of a sparrow or some other small bird flying into a room and landing on someone's shoulder. We locked eyes in the hush surrounding the situation. Then I realized that I had caught Judith at something—she had a blush of guilt on her cheeks. I figured it involved Jack or the Troglers or her healing, but I was wrong. Eventually she grinned nervously to break the oddly muted scene.

"This is a very peculiar book," she said.

"Let me see it."

She hesitated. Then shook her head.

"First I want to show you where I found it."

We got down from the hay, and I followed her to the rock wall just opposite the milking stalls. There she reached down almost to the straw-covered ground, worked one rock free from its place and said, "Right here. Tucked back in here. I think it's Jack's book, or maybe it belongs to Jack and Junior. Mickey, too."

The space behind the rock revealed two packs of Lucky Strikes, a can of Prince Albert tobacco and a small box of cigarette papers. I had known for a long time that Junior and Jack secretly smoked. I just hadn't discovered their cache. My father was dead set against them picking up the habit, but I think maybe he knew that they were cultivating an addiction to the wicked weed. However, it was the book rather than the tobacco items that had *me* breathing funny.

Interest and fear were firing in me like spark plugs. When we returned to our bale of hay, Judith handed me the book. I swallowed a mouthful of air. What it looked like was a comic book, only it was maybe six or eight inches wide and just three or four inches tall. Its cover had been torn off or fingered to death, and its pages were crinkled from repeated wetting and drying—rain had probably seeped into that wall. I could feel Judith's breath on one cheek as she leaned close and examined its pages with me. At first, I saw nothing special. Cartoony panels of characters, the first strip showing a salesman knocking on a door and being greeted by a housewife—I think the guy was selling vacuum cleaners—and being invited in. The housewife left the room, but when she returned . . . when she returned she was clad in a see-through negligee, her large breasts no match for the filmy ma-

terial and her pubic region dark and seductively op-
probrious. She wasn't in the mood, it appeared, for
buying a vacuum cleaner. She seemed to want another kind of demonstration and, accordingly, started
undressing the salesman. He didn't object.

My eyes began gobbling up the panels.

Followed by a slow, deliberate digestion of them.

I was shocked, but at the same time, looking at the
sexually explicit drawings with Judith on my shoulder
generated silky coils of delight spinning up into my
groin.

I whispered, "Gee whiz."

In a more serious and matter-of-factly inquisitive
tone, Judith said, "Teddy, what's 'fellatio'?"

I frowned as I stared at the next panel and its de-
piction of the housewife on her knees in front of the
salesman—who was sporting a large erection—and in
the balloon caption rising from her was some ditty
tricked out in words rhyming with "fellatio." I was
spared having to admit I didn't know the answer to Judith's question, for the trio of panels on the next page
clarified much.

I closed the book.

"We better put this back," I said.

"Why?"

"Because if they find out it's missing, they'll blame
us. Or blame *me* at least. Besides that . . . it's nasty. It
should be hidden."

"From whom?"

I heard my stomach gurgling. Heat was radiating
throughout my body.

"Well, . . . from *myself!*" I exclaimed.

That word of emphasis dropped into a deep well of
momentary silence.

Then Judith laughed. She laughed hard. She tried
to put her hand to her mouth to suppress her laugh-

ter, but it spilled out at the corners. I was flaming with embarrassment. When Judith composed herself some, she said, "I think we should look at it, Teddy. It's normal, healthy curiosity to want to look at it."

At that moment my brain had the consistency of scrambled eggs.

"Okay, I guess."

We gave the book nothing short of scholarly attention. It was as if we had been bound together closely with strong rope, helpless to free ourselves from our captors—those eye-arresting panels that depicted the housewife and the salesman in every imaginable sexual intercourse position.

"Let's go back to the first pages," Judith suggested when we had perused a couple of dozen scenes of sexual gymnastics.

She leafed back to the fellatio panels, gave them a head-tilting examination, and then squared around to face me. With obvious reference to the panel in which the housewife had virtually swallowed the salesman's penis, Judith said, "Teddy, would you like it if I did that to you?"

I was stunned. I had what I recall being some kind of weird, out-of-body experience. I floated above the scene like a huge bubble. I knew the proper thing to do was say "No" as firmly as possible. But I couldn't bring myself to battle my hesitation. I had about as much fight in me as a melting snowman.

"Are you serious?" I said.

"Well . . . we like each other and we're not strangers. Those two," she continued, pointing at one of the panels, "probably have never even met, and the salesman acts like he really enjoys what she's doing to him—look at his face. And I bet they're not even in love."

I wasn't sure I was following her line of thinking.

"Yeah, but isn't it kinda . . . I don't know . . . *sinful?*"

Judith was perturbed.

"More Bible junk," she muttered. "I just don't understand why everybody gets so upset about sin. Sin, sin, sin. What is it, anyway? The Fiery Angel has never whispered anything in my ear about sin. I think that Macready boy got to you. Don't you see, Teddy, you and I are cousins, but if you love me and I love you, why can't we be intimate even though the world doesn't want us to?"

That word "intimate" made me shiver. A good shiver. I didn't even care if I didn't know exactly what it meant. But then, out of nowhere, the image of Jack roared into my thoughts. "Do you want to do these things with Jack, too?"

She had her hands on her hips and a moue on her face.

"Teddy, why can't I love both of you?"

"Because . . . because Jack's a shithead."

I was proud of my thrust of rough language—the summer had helped me to acquire it.

"No, he's not. There's another side to Jack—a good side. I like him."

"But you gotta like me more."

What I wanted to say was that I loved her. Love? Yes, I did love Judith, though I couldn't say it. And I didn't have a response for the angle she was taking on the matter, so our conversation died. I sensed that she was disappointed that I didn't want to share her with Jack. We kept looking at the book. It had a few really disgusting parts such as one that showed a farmer humping one of his milk cows. There was also a disturbing series of panels depicting sadistic bondage and a violent rape—those made my stomach queasy, and I could feel Judith trembling as she eyed them before turning away and kind of shuddering.

We forgot about the time.

Judith and I got lost in a world that wasn't on any map.

Unfortunately, Jack discovered us.

"Hey, what're you doing with that? It doesn't belong to you."

We snapped to at the sound of his voice. He approached with the slither of an angry copperhead, and yet he was also embarrassed, and I think he felt he needed to be protective of Judith.

"I bet Pop doesn't know you have this," I said.

Jack kept coming, his anger bubbling like boiling water beneath his skin.

"I'm going to kill you, Teddy."

I reached for a hayhook and tried to stand my ground. I was determined to protect myself and Judith, and I was surprised suddenly to hear her voice.

"Jack, I'm the one who found your book," she said.

It seemed as if, right that instant, Jack was hit with a strong gust of wind. He actually staggered a step or two. He blinked at Judith.

"It was hidden," he stammered. "What did you think you was doing? A girl like you—you shouldn't be looking at a book like this."

His voice had softened. I could feel how painfully confused he was.

Judith pushed off the bale of hay and handed the book to him.

"Here. I'm sorry," she said, then added, "You know how much I want to be your friend, Jack." She kissed him on the cheek and started to brush by him to leave the barn. He caught her arm. What happened next threw me for a loop. I saw tears welling up in Jack's eyes. But whatever those tears meant, everything changed when Mickey ducked his head into the barn. He had pulled up in his new car—a 1955 Ford Crown Victoria his uncle had bought for him—and I think he'd come to show it off and maybe mend his broken friendship with Jack.

Mickey grinned as he surveyed the scene.

"What's up, Jacko? The cripple cunt going down for ya?"

Right then the air in the barn changed; it acquired an ugly ticking. I wanted to run. I didn't care if it would make me look like a coward. I couldn't take my eyes off Jack. He was staring up into Mickey's face and he was trembling. When he spoke, it was in a flat, toneless manner that made the hairs stand up on the back of my neck: "Get out," he said. "Get the hell clear on out of here."

Mickey stared back at him. His grin rotted into a wretched chuckle.

"What do we have here, Jacko?" he said, his eyes glazed with defiance. "You and your dick of a little brother found you a whore? Both of you fucking this bitch?"

I tightened my grip on the hayhook.

Anger crackled across Jack's body. He took a couple of steps forward and spit right into Mickey's face. And when Mickey, stunned by what Jack had done, raised one hand to his cheek, Jack slugged him hard in the stomach. Mickey doubled over, his mouth frozen open in a large O.

That was it for me. I scrammed.

From the safe harbor of the far, outside corner of the barn I waited and listened to the fight that ensued. It didn't last long. Shouting profanities, Mickey stumbled out, his lip bleeding just like you see in the movies, and threw himself into his car. He spun out with unequaled fury, spewing gravel and terrifying banties.

When I stepped out into the open, he flipped me the finger as he tore away.

I waited another minute and then sneaked just inside the barn door.

Judith was in Jack's arms, looking into his face and caressing a bruise low on his jaw.

Hayhook still in hand, I stepped back out and looked down at my feet and prayed that the ground would open up and swallow me and that my ghost would never, ever be awakened.

Judith had blood all over her the next morning.

Honest to God, I thought she was dying. I had no sooner noticed the blood on her nightgown than she stirred, and, almost breathless, I heard myself say, "I'm going to call Doc Gillis for you."

But Judith grabbed my wrist.

"No, Teddy, not about this," she said, suddenly aware of the blood on her gown. "I should have been ready for this."

"Hey, you're bleeding," I said. "We gotta get you to a doctor."

As morning light began to fill the mud room, I could see that the blood wasn't as bad as I had imagined. It had apparently trickled down the inside of one leg and soaked into her gown. I assumed it had something to do with her polio-like condition, but I had no idea what.

"It'll be all right, Teddy. I just need to clean myself up. You need to leave for a few minutes."

"Does it hurt?" I said.

My head felt as if a tiny milk churn was going full speed where my brain should have been. Judith gently pushed me from the room. I stood by the telephone and tried to catch my breath and calm my nerves. When Judith finally called me back, she was cradling a Kotex pad as if it were a small, white bird she intended to release at any moment.

"Did you know I'm laying an egg once a month?" she said.

Then it hit me. I had heard bits and pieces about menstruation at school—I think maybe David had even explained to me. I had simply failed to connect Judith's bloody gown with her time of the month.

"Oh, I forgot about all that," I said, relieved. "I thought there was something terrible wrong."

"It's not so bad," she said. "I get cramps that hurt some, but not as bad as my other pains used to be." She held the Kotex out where I could see it better, and I swallowed back a little of my embarrassment. Then she continued. "These you put in your panties to catch the blood. It's like putting a furry, sleepy little animal down there. You get used to it."

My face was blazing. My throat got so scratchy that I knew I couldn't respond. Judith smiled very sweetly.

"It means I'm a woman, Teddy. I could have a baby."

"Yeah," I managed to say, "I guess that's how it works."

She nodded. I think she was trying to be adult and forthcoming.

"You probably know this," she said, "but if you put your binker in me, and you squirted your seed into me, then we'd make a baby—unless your seed didn't meet up with my egg. If it didn't, the deal would be off."

My embarrassment had no bounds. I wished she hadn't used the word "binker"—it made me feel like a little boy.

"Yeah," I said, "I guess that's how. . . . ."

Judith suddenly hugged herself. She was beaming.

"If we had a baby together, Teddy, I bet it would have your red hair. You have pretty hair. Or with Jack, it'd have brown hair, like the color of nice dirt."

Her smile was a thousand stars twinkling.

The rest of the day I thought about two things: one, how much I hated the thought of Judith and Jack having a baby together, and, two, how neat it would be to be a father—to have a small boy with my red hair (just like in my first grade school picture). I walked around holding the hand of my fantasy offspring. I forced myself to imagine that it wouldn't be strange or deformed. I thought even more about my seed, and I wondered whether it resembled radish seeds or kernels of corn. Was it red like my hair? Or like Judith's blood?

But I went to sleep jealous of Jack and thinking about his dirty comic book. In the panels I became the salesman and Judith the housewife and the word "fellatio" flowed through my thoughts, materializing as an exotic dancer swirling and spinning until it dissolved in darkness, and the night became a flowing stream and I was lying at the bottom of it thinking about sex as a gentle expression of love. Yet the disturbing panels depicting the rape caught me up as well in treacherous eddies. I found myself thinking about Lex Macready and I felt cold. I thought about Jack and I felt cold. I found warmth only when I thought of Judith. I lay there at the bottom of the night knowing somehow that I would never want a woman as much as I wanted Judith. And from the dreaming corner of my consciousness I heard her whisper, "I know that."

In that realm darker than darkness, I forgot about the ghosts.

And that was a mistake.

A drought was sinking its teeth into the north central landscape of Kansas, threatening to devour the Flint Hills with a drying, wilting heat, drooping our stalks of corn and our wills to exist. Even the mornings were hot and dry, the baking heat so in contrast with the cold I was often feeling within.

One morning Judith offered relief.

"I can make it rain, Teddy. I can raise a storm. Romina gave me the power."

We were in the mud room.

"I doubt it," I said, though the mention of Romina intrigued me because Judith had continued to dance around any revelation about her newfound health and the role that ghosts had played in it. While I continued to massage her muscles a little each day, she really had made a remarkable recovery from her polio-like symptoms—the Kenny simply wasn't much needed.

"Here, watch," she countered. "It may take a while to get it to start raining, but I can do it." She closed her eyes and raised her hands out in front of her, palms up; she blinked a few times and took tiny, funny gulps of air. Then she sort of purred like a cat before suddenly opening her eyes wide. I just shook my head.

Despite what I had seen of her growing affection for Jack—and his for her—I couldn't stop wanting to be near her. To touch her. I didn't want her father to come get her. She, of course, sensed that I was blue, so she made up new installments of "Travels with Teddy," continent hopping from South America to Asia and back to North America, landing—no surprise to me—somewhere in Colorado. She recited a couple of Shakespearean sonnets and a line from Thoreau about hearing the beat of a different drummer and we talked about movies and famous people and past lives. She told me that her father smelled like pomade and ripe apples and pipe smoke—good smells, she claimed—and that when she woke that morning the Fiery Angel was sitting at the end of her cot smiling down at her.

"I guess I musta missed him," I said.

"He's careful about not being seen," she said.

She picked up the mirror which I had given her and studied her face. She seemed to keep it with her almost constantly. We were having a really pleasant time, though I thought at one point I might have heard distant thunder. Mostly, I was trying not to think about sex, about Jack's sex book or about anything else related to sex. But it was hard because I wanted to know what it would feel like. Would it be better than masturbation? And maybe I also wondered if God would send something horrible to visit me as punishment for thinking about sinning with my cousin—maybe a plague of silver-dollar–sized pimples all over my body or maybe He would make my penis rot and fall off.

I wondered what Lex Macready would say about my unclean thoughts.

I envied Judith for not being bothered by God and sin and possible damnation.

We were embracing each other's company, just really delighting in being together, when I made the mistake of asking Judith if she thought her father would mind if I went with them when Saturday rolled around.

"Oh, Teddy, . . . you already have a place where you belong."

"Here? Are you kidding? I hate this place. I want to go with you to Colorado." Then, because I couldn't help myself, I added, "I bet you'd like it if Jack went with you."

Judith looked sad and maybe a little perplexed. She gazed deeper into the mirror. Her expression was one that just about broke my heart, not to mention send-

ing me into a dark carnival ride of confusion. I figured maybe she was going to mention the Fiery Angel
and offer some goofy line about his role in her life
and how that life didn't really have a place for me. I
wish I hadn't mentioned Jack.

Her response was even more mysterious than I expected.

"Teddy, you need to stay around here because . . .
there's so much more you need to learn about yourself.
Important things. And you have to learn them here."

Boy, I had no idea what she was talking about. I
shook my head again.

"What is all this?"

She looked more serious than I'd ever seen her,
and in the next instant she took my hand and said,
"Come on. We're going to the dragonfield before my
storm comes. I have to tell you a few things."

Out amidst the tragically dry corn stalks we sat on
the warm dirt like a couple of Indians in a pow-wow.
Judith told me she wanted to explain how she'd made
such a remarkable recovery from her affliction; part
of it, she claimed, was a result of my giving her the
Kenny, but much of it was the ghost of Romina
Trogler who had healing powers. I can remember my
stomach gurgling as I listened.

"I went to her because of the Fiery Angel. He directed me to. The ghosts—especially Romina—they've
gotten stronger. You can hear it in their words. You can
hear it when they talk. At first, their talk was just ghost
talk—angry and frustrated—but as they kept getting
stronger, as they changed from figures of dust to figures
of solid earth, their talk changed, too."

I just listened. I had no idea what to say, though I
know I must have had doubt written all over my face.
Dark clouds were gathering in the west; Judith

scanned them, a touch of satisfaction in her expression, before she continued.

"Now the ghosts speak words tongued with fire—beyond the language of the living. It's hard to resist those words. Do you understand that, Teddy?"

"I guess so," I said. For some reason anger and frustration were building within me, burrowing up, it seemed, from the ground beneath me as if some earth demon were at work determined to possess me.

"I made a promise to Romina," said Judith. "I promised that if she healed my broken body, I'd stay near the Troglers so they could continue getting stronger—and be able to get revenge on those who murdered them. But, Teddy, I was lying. I'm not staying. I'm leaving with my father when he comes. Besides that, I think the ghosts are already strong enough. They're very, very dangerous."

For just a moment I stopped thinking about myself.

"The ghosts," I said, "they want Mr. Suggs and they want my Pop, don't they?"

Judith nodded. "And you and I—they want us, too, but in a different way." She hesitated, then added, "I know what can stop them."

"The Fiery Angel?"

"Well, yes, . . . I think maybe he can. And something else."

"What?"

"It's this: Since the ghosts are made of earth and not flesh and blood and bones, then it seems to me that water would destroy them. Water would dissolve them."

"Oh," I said, repressing a giggle, "that's sounds silly. Ghosts turning into mud." I think maybe I laughed out loud.

"You have to be serious about this, Teddy. You have

to go back far in your life and find the truth. So do I.
Let's hold hands and go back together."

She had reached for me, and I'm not sure why but
her gesture really lit my anger.

"I'm not. I won't. I'm not doing that." And then I
let her have the truth. I told her that before, when we
had talked about past lives, I had made everything up.
"It's stupid stuff!" I yelled at her. "I don't believe it and
neither should you!"

She was crushed, I could tell. I softened my tone a
notch.

"So now I guess you hate me, right?"

"No. I could never hate *you*."

The air was roaring with a splendid, unsettling
calm. There was a full-scale thunderstorm on the way,
though I wouldn't allow myself to read Judith as its
source. I got up to leave, my first steps taking me in
the direction of the Trogler place.

"Teddy, don't."

I kept walking. I could hear Judith behind me, hur-
rying to catch me.

"Teddy, Jack knows about the ghosts. Jack knows
what's going on."

I wheeled around. It was the kind of moment in
which nothing sensible comes out of a young man's
mouth. I proved it.

"Well, why don't you just go and suck on his dick! I
don't care!"

"Teddy, wait. Don't go to the Troglers. Jack said . . .
he said don't let my kid brother go there ever again."

That did it.

With the first heavy drops of rain pelting the earth
around me, I began to run. While she didn't chase
after me, Judith shouted at my heels, "Please, Teddy,
no! My storm is coming!"

I was wet and sweaty by the time I burst into the

front room of the Troglers, shaking like an almost-
drowned dog, shaking as much from anger as from
the sudden chill of the rain. Thunder shook the walls;
lightning played menacingly among the empty
rooms; and the wind soughed indifferently, rattling
every aging and derelict inch of the place. I bit the
sides of my cheeks hard to keep from crying. I sat
down in the middle of the front room and waited
until the thunder and lightning had subsided and a
gentle rain had replaced the initial downpour. Almost
directly below me I could hear Oatmeal mewing. I
likened my condition to his. God, I was miserable. I
was pathetic.

But I wanted to see the ghosts. That was the weird
part. I suddenly had a mission.

I got to my feet, trumped up my courage and
shouted, "Don't hurt my Pop!" And I kept shouting
my plea until my throat was raw and my voice ragged.
Then I started to cry. I couldn't help it.

When, minutes later, I heard the voice of Romina's
ghost, I knew that Judith was right about one thing: It
was a voice you couldn't turn away from.

"Animus? Animus come home. Animus."

It came from out of the everywhere.

Strange as this will sound, the voice, the words, the
rhythm of it all—it was like a lullabye. I couldn't leave.
In fact, for a few minutes, I fell asleep.

Emmitt Suggs woke me.

"Son, are you all right? I heard someone call out my
name. You all right? You call my name, did you?"

Suggs looked pretty scared. Even in the shadowy
front room I could see how flushed his face was and
how filled with near terror his eyes were. It was late
morning yet gray as slate out. The rain—Judith's

rain?—continued to fall, not heavily. The air had an eerie cleanness to it. Just a hint of a breeze. I told Suggs I was fine. I don't know, maybe he could see that I'd been crying. I'm not sure. He told me he'd stopped to pick up a few bales of hay, but when he'd stepped out of his truck he'd heard a voice. He thought he'd heard someone call his name. He was unnerved by it, that was obvious, and I think he felt I'd been playing a trick on him.

I should have told him to leave. Get the hell out of there. Run for his life.

But I said nothing of the kind as he hunkered down next to me. A curious thoughtfulness dropped over him like a net, and he began looking around and talking about his brother and about my father. Talking like he had no choice but to do so.

"My brother, Red, he was a good man, a strong man. He got tempted—that's all it was. By that strange girl. Wicked girl. He fell in with darkness. But he was a good man—and you ought to know that."

It was a theme he'd essayed before. I just listened as he continued.

"And your daddy—Norman O'Dell—he's a good man, too. The best kind of man. Not a murderer—not that. Not evil."

I stared into the man's moist, frightened eyes. I tried to clear my throat, but my words came out all raspy: "They want to hurt my Pop," I said. "And they want to hurt you, too."

Suggs swallowed. Nodded ever so slightly. It was the response of a man who is not surprised to hear of approaching horrors, but terrified just the same. I watched as he began to tremble. Then he took hold of me and helped me up, and I sorta helped him up, too, because his legs were weak and shaky.

"Let's us get on out of here," he whispered.

An awful calm gathered around us.

And I knew it was too late to leave.

Romina's voice was like iron bars materializing to block every exit.

"Suggs must die. Suggs must die."

In a futile gesture, Suggs spun around, fists clenched. The words echoed as if we were at the bottom of a canyon or a deep cistern.

"Get gone, son!" he exclaimed to me.

But arms held me. A body pressed against me from behind. It smelled of sour earth; its voice was soothing and disquieting and burning all at once. A voice that initially took away all desire to struggle.

The defiant figure of Suggs diminished in the presence of the ghosts.

I don't believe he ever had a chance against them.

Their hate, their fury, their desire for revenge was palpable—thicker than smoke.

And I was helpless.

Senta Trogler was the first to come at Suggs, her eyes dead and staring right through the man, a hypnotic effect. Suggs dropped his raised fists, unfolded his fingers and relinquished all his volition. His arms fell to his sides as if they were those of a stuffed cloth doll.

The smell of earth—too old, too cold and barren and dead for anything to grow in—filled the room. Siebert Trogler approached Suggs from one side, Rolf Trogler from another. A long awaited need for revenge seemed to power each step the ghosts took. Suggs momentarily freed himself from the old woman's mesmerizing stare, but it did him no good. He swung around to meet old Rolf—and so he never saw Siebert raise the sledgehammer, never had a chance to fend off the crushing blow to the back of his neck.

Suggs crashed to his knees, barely conscious. Threads of saliva hung from his lips as his body heaved like a sick animal.

Fire in his eyes, Rolf cut low into the gloomy, sunless air with his sling blade. It tore into Suggs' arm, slicing it open at the biceps. Blood pulsed out with the energy of Rock Creek rising after a big rain. Suggs groaned—a sound beyond pain. Rolf swung again as Siebert and Senta looked on. The second bite of the blade ripped across Suggs' back, welling up blood to soak the man's shirt and overalls almost instantly.

I remember praying that the Fiery Angel would save him.

Closing my eyes. Closing out the horror. Praying. Praying.

And then the image of my father possibly being where Suggs was flashed into my thoughts, and that was enough for me to reach into myself and gather all the fury I had—and I broke free of Romina's hold.

"Get out in the rain!" I cried. "You gotta get out in the rain!"

But, of course, Suggs, being barely conscious, offered little response, and so I scrambled to him and began pulling on him with every ounce of strength I had. For a few seconds, the ghosts simply watched, surprised perhaps at what I was attempting. I heard smug, eerie laughter. I could smell them—never had earth smelled so rotten or so vile. And then, somewhere beyond the laughter of the ghosts, I heard the menacing growl of Hunter.

And I felt a sudden gust of icy air in my gut.

But I kept tugging at Suggs until I managed to drag him to the back door.

No further.

Romina's voice yanked me back. I was like a calf in a roping contest. She had me. And the ghosts had

Suggs. It was horrible. His groans. His pathetic efforts to fend them off. All the blood. The vengeful laughing of Siebert and Rolf. The cold, dead stare of Senta.

Then the worst part.

Suggs raising his head, looking for me to help, blood streaming from his mouth and nose, blinking his eyes in pain and disbelief.

Before Hunter tore into his face and finished him off.

Eventually I wrestled free, or maybe I was released, and ran from the house.

But for days a warm spot pulsed in my forehead. Romina had touched me there. To make me forget what I'd seen if only temporarily.

There was a blessing in that.

And yet the horrors were underway.

Earth had called from hearts of revenge.

Summer days of death held sway.

Twelve

Where Summer Ends

Forgetting can be beautiful.

But the soul wants to remember.

Late afternoon Suggs's wife, Francine, found the body of her husband—what was left of it—at the Trogler place. Being a strong and stoic Kansas farm woman, she calmly reported the matter to the sheriff who, that evening, swarmed down upon our household. He described the murder in terms that made you believe only a wild animal could have been responsible. He said he had a prime suspect.

My brother, Jack, was arrested and taken away.

My father almost had to be arrested, too, and Junior as well, because they hotly defended my brother against a flimsy bit of testimony offered by Mickey Palmer, who had told the sheriff that he had heard Jack threaten Suggs because Suggs owed him money for some work earlier in the summer.

Mickey was getting his revenge.

It was an ugly, chaotic scene at our sorry farmhouse what with Jack being handcuffed and my father flushed with rage and Junior at his shoulder shouting that Mickey was making up stuff. At one point the sheriff drew his gun.

My mother wailed. Frightened and angry and shaken to her soul, all she could do was blame Judith: "She made him do it—she turned my Jack evil! I will *not* spend another night under the same roof with that girl—that *Child of the Devil!*" And thereupon fainted and later had to be hospitalized. We didn't know it at the time, but we were soon to learn that my mother had stomach cancer.

Judith and I, stupefied and helpless, watched the scene unfold from the doorway to the mud room.

Through the dark panoply of events, Jack appeared resigned to his fate.

Of course, he knew he was innocent of the charges, and yet there was something more in his manner— something almost magnificent, as if he were accepting a kind of martyrdom for the family. God, I envied him. I wanted to change places with him so that I could be the center of attention. I came a hair's breadth from confessing to the murder myself.

As the sheriff escorted Jack away—and my father and Junior continued to raise their voices in protest— Judith, starting to cry, tore away from my side and ran to Jack and embraced him. It was as if they were the last two people on earth, as if they needed each other more than any other two people had *ever* needed each other.

Coldly distant from the energy of their closeness, I felt staggeringly alone.

My father and Junior took my mother to the hospital, and the next morning they would leave early to try to get Jack out of jail and to see how my mother was. I had heard them sitting up late talking about things. Though I wanted to join them, I did not. Too much of a coward maybe. Truth is, part of me didn't mind seeing Jack taken away from Judith.

When I woke the next morning Judith was sitting

on her cot staring into her cracked mirror. She looked beautiful. She stirred something deep in me, something down there in the bowels of my desire. I wanted to hold her and kiss her and see where the affection would take us.

"Teddy," she said, when she saw I was awake, "I'll be leaving tomorrow, but there's something I'd like to give to you. It'll be my way of thanking you for being my friend this summer—for being my Onlie Begetter."

I figured maybe she had written me another poem.

"You don't have to thank me," I said. Then I hesitated. "And I'm sorry about Jack. I hope you get to see him again before you have to go."

I mostly meant it.

"This is not about Jack," she said. "It's about you. It's about us. You and I know Jack is innocent. You and I know the ghosts killed Emmitt Suggs."

I nodded, and it's weird but right then I got a flash of something—of Siebert smashing his sledge into the back of Suggs—not more than that. It was enough to excite me into saying, "We got to go tell the sheriff it was the ghosts—yeah, I know it now. I think I saw it. . . . and I . . . ."

But my words trailed off.

"You did see it, Teddy, but telling the sheriff won't do any good. No one will believe us. When I leave, things will eventually return to normal. The ghosts will weaken and turn to dust again."

"But what about Jack?"

"Jack has my love. No matter what happens, he has my love, and I have his. Nothing they can do to him will change that."

My head was swimming.

Then I bristled.

"I don't want anything from you," I said. "Just keep it—whatever it is."

She smiled tolerantly.

"Let's go to the barn," she said, deflecting my remark. "We'll take a blanket and a candle and my mirror."

At the Troglers' there must have been a half dozen cars—law enforcement officials and even someone from the Topeka paper—poring over the crime scene.

We left our empty house and trekked to our barn and ensconced ourselves among the bales of hay, spreading the blanket and lighting a single candle. We held hands and put our faces together so that we could see each other, see both of us in the mirror's reflection.

"I need something pure and loving, Teddy, before I leave."

Those words—"pure" and "loving"—seemed miles above me, rather like hawks almost out of sight circling, circling, then lowering to find prey. Only there was no threat in the words as Judith spoke them.

"Sure," I said.

"Teddy, my Fiery Angel said that without love the Earth will die."

I was feeling an odd surge of nervousness, and so I said, "It needs rain, too, and sun." Then I felt stupid.

Judith smiled a lovely candlelight smile.

"What I want us to do is for love and with love. Do you understand that?"

"Sort of."

But obviously I didn't, and what she did next took me completely by surprise. She began unbuttoning her blouse. She unzipped and removed her shorts and undid her brassiere, and I heard myself give out a soft, hollow whistle with my tongue between my teeth. Then she reached out and unclasped the straps of my overalls, and I began to tremble. She leaned forward, and the feel of her full breasts against my naked chest took my breath away. We held each other, and she whispered something about physical and spiritual junction and the seeds of transcendence and something about cosmic energy flowing between us.

We kissed.

The vibration of our bodies was delicate, perhaps as much emotional as physical. My arousal was complete in moments, and I was kissing her hard. She lay back on the blanket and slipped off her panties, and I clumsily removed my underpants, snagging and pretty much dislocating my big toe in my hurry.

"Teddy," she said, as I gazed down at her and the candle flame danced nearby, "desire is a sleeping snake, and we have to understand that it can be dangerous. Let it rise quietly and peacefully and lovingly. We have to be patient."

But patience wasn't on my mind. I was no more able to be patient and to slow and direct my desire lovingly than I could have stopped a waterfall. When Judith took my penis in her hands, my body jolted as if I'd been jammed by a cattle prod. I thought fleetingly of Jack's perversely sexy comic book, and then Judith's touch wiped out everything I was thinking.

"Slower, Teddy. Please. Slow and gentle."

I was as jittery as a droplet of water in a hot skillet.

She guided me to the wetness between her legs, and I lost control. The eyes of a waking serpent drove me; I jerked and thrust at the command of the creature. I couldn't help myself, and I couldn't stop, not even when Judith cried out in pain and pushed at my chest. I grunted when I slipped out of her. My ejaculation spewed out harmlessly onto the hay. The shock of the frustrating culmination shook me hard. I slumped onto my knees and rocked back and forth gulping for air, sweat beading up along my hairline. And then in the shadows I saw an expression of utter dejection on Judith's face.

"I'm sorry," I said. "I'm sorry, sorry, sorry."

I was ashamed. I was disgusted with myself. In those dreadful moments after our awkward sex, I felt that I was a failure. I would have welcomed somebody beating me, breaking me.

Most of all, I wanted to tell Judith that I loved her. But I couldn't.

We got dressed.

I assumed Judith would want to go back to the house, eager to get away from me and wait out the time remaining for the arrival of her father. I'm sure she thought of Jack; I'm sure she believed Jack could have loved her properly, given her satisfying sex.

"Don't say you're sorry," she said. "It wasn't your fault or mine. The Fiery Angel got in our way."

Her words angered me.

"Well, dang it, why did he?"

We were sitting facing each other again, and she smiled and reached out and stroked my cheek and her hand felt like the wing of an angel.

"I need your help, Teddy. Say something to the Fiery Angel. He's all around us here. Make him understand that I need his strength to escape the ghosts."

I glanced to either side of me as if half expecting to see some flaming presence.

"I don't think he'd listen to me," I said.

"Would you try, Teddy—you're my Onlie Begetter. I know you want to help."

I did. My God, I did.

"I don't know how to."

Judith closed her eyes. The morning wind died

down. The gods of the day seemed to press closer. And after several seconds, I began to feel something: horror and dread and a fiery rise of joy. There were torches of light behind my eyes.

Suddenly I saw Lex Macready onstage.

I shuddered because I was beginning to grasp something. I was beginning to see a way that I could help the woman I loved. Yes, I was indeed her Onlie Begetter, and I felt a fable singing in my blood.

"Judith," I whispered.

She kept her eyes closed, but she said, "Yes, Teddy. Is the Fiery Angel coming? Am I going to be strengthened? Is he coming?"

Her questions floated in the air like magical bubbles.

Until I said, "Yes, he is."

She smiled.

"I'm ready," she said.

I cleared my throat. I knew, as I had never known anything else quite so certainly, that if I failed, I might lose Judith forever. So I did something very foolish.

"I'm going to call the Fiery Angel into me now," I said. "I'm your Onlie Begetter, and I can do that."

I closed my eyes tightly, as I had seen Macready do it, and I lifted my hands, palms up, and there, in the musty, shadowy barn, I began the performance of my life. I invited the spirit of the Fiery Angel into me. I knew it was all a show. I never believed it was anything more. I strutted onto the stage of myself, and I tried as hard as I could to become something I wasn't.

And it worked.

When I spoke to Judith again it was in a throaty whisper.

"Judith, I'm here. I've been called to help you. Touch my hands."

I could feel her body trembling.

What did she feel when our fingers met? Fire and ice and joy and wholeness?

I have no idea.

"Oh, yes," she whispered in return.

Fingertip to fingertip, I could almost believe we transcended sexual intimacy. The world moved on and left us absolutely alone.

When I opened my eyes, Judith's shadow-strewn smile told me that I had somehow eliminated much of the ghosts' control of her. I had annealed her. Judith believed it, and it did not matter what I believed.

Judith had been transfigured.

And I embraced a new view of myself: the Onlie Begetter and the Fiery Angel had become brothers in soul. I had brought them together.

And I had no idea what a mistake I had made.

For our private ritual had been witnessed by a force that wanted and needed the two of us in ways I could not possibly have understood at that moment, a force that would take advantage of what we had created.

Soft as a whisper, fast as a shout, the ghost of Romina Trogler passed by.

My heart lay as if it were a pile of dust in my chest.

When I woke the next morning on the floor beside Judith's cot, waves of regret, like nausea, were sweeping through my thoughts. I regretted that I could not believe what Judith believed. I could not embrace the fable I had created for her—I feared in fact, that I had committed myself to a profound duplicity. I also regretted that she did not want me to go with her, for I knew even then that I would never be the person I desired to be if Judith were not in my life.

In the early morning light, Judith, sleeping soundly, looked beautiful beyond words, and yet I felt something verging on terror, or an uneasy wonder at the least, when I sensed that there, in the witchy pall out of which day would come, I might be gazing down upon a ghost and not a real woman at all.

Then I heard Oatmeal.

The desolate mewing drifted past the dawn, coming impossibly my way. Curious, I stepped out of the mud room and sat on the steps and was greeted by a thick fog, its droplets pleasingly cool. And the mewing. I assumed that the fog would burn off quickly, and yet this seemed nothing like the denser hazes and mists we sometimes experienced in our part of the world.

I peered into that fog. I listened more closely, certain finally that the mewing was Oatmeal's and that the disfigured cat was coming home. Almost home. When those words lifted free in my thoughts, I shivered involuntarily, for they seemed guided toward me like a missile. And then I saw that someone was approaching through the fog.

"Who's there?" I said.

But even before I could make out her facial features beneath the dark scarf she was wearing, I knew that Romina Trogler was approaching. Her ghostly, earthy smell preceded her. She was carrying Oatmeal, stroking him gently, a hint of a smile on her face.

I couldn't move. I sat on the back steps as if paralyzed.

And waited as the woman glided soundlessly forward and placed the cat in my lap. I tried to say something—thank you, maybe—but it was a mouthful of gravel instead of words. She said nothing, merely held that faint, mysterious, somehow knowing smile, and in that moment I believe we communicated something deeper than words.

I glanced down at Oatmeal. He seemed stronger, and though his bad eye was as hideous as ever, the other one seemed fine. I whispered nonsense to him and petted him and rubbed his fur against my cheek the way people do with cats, and the more I petted him, the more he relaxed until he was purring. I smiled. I looked up.

The ghost of Romina Trogler had disappeared.

Funny, but for just an instant, I think I was actually disappointed to see that she was gone.

Of course, then I hustled inside to show Judith how the prodigal cat had returned. She was delighted. We spent several warm minutes expressing our affection for the cat; I think, in fact, we sort of wore it out, because after not too long it fell asleep on Judith's cot.

"I have to start packing," said Judith. "I have to be ready when my father comes. Do you want to help?"

"I guess maybe. Sure."

But then she said, "I hope your father and Junior will bring Jack home this morning." She brightened. "It'll be just like Oatmeal coming home, and if your mother can come home, then your whole family will be together again—won't that be swell, Teddy?"

I had chosen not to tell her that the ghost of Romina Trogler had returned Oatmeal. And I couldn't tell her that I didn't think I had a family anymore. Not one I belonged to. I didn't know where I belonged.

"Nothing's swell," I muttered as I pushed out the back door feeling sorry for myself, maybe even wanting to hurt myself or at least to rise above what I was beginning to see as a dark, meaningless fate.

The fog was dissolving.

I was restless and miserable in a way only boys can be.

I thought what I needed was a new vantage point on things; accordingly, I decided to climb the silo. Inside its cool, silent hollowness my every move generated a muted yet eager echo. Every step raised old, pungent-smelling grain dust. For some reason, in that setting I imagined myself a ghost. The thought of haunting my family burst upon me, leaving me breathless with anticipated joy. Then I looked up at the circle of sky at the top of the silo. I was eager to do something foolish. Proud to say, I managed not to slip on the dew-moistened rungs and felt the heady thrill of triumph when I reached the summit and hooked my elbows over the rim and looked down upon the world.

Everything was smaller, even my life.

My heart was swollen from the exertion and from my self-pity, too.

I stayed up there a long time just thinking about people. More so, thinking about the ghosts, especially the ghost of Romina and the weird symbiosis I felt with her. And here I'll tell you what scared the crap out of me—what made me almost fall. In fact, I actually lost my grip on the rim and slid down three rungs before I caught myself and scrambled back to the top.

You see, what happened was this: It all came back.

I remembered.

I remembered the murder of Emmitt Suggs.

Every horrifying detail.

I was trembling so severely that I could barely hang on; I knew—and the good angel of my self sat on one shoulder insisting—that I should scamper down and tell the sheriff what I knew. Wouldn't not doing so be some kind of crime? I was scared. Every possible choice—telling, not telling—going, staying—it all unsettled me.

I fought back tears and was about to lose the battle against their threatened onslaught when I saw Judith come out of the house and raise a hand to her brow so that she could squint into the sun. I felt warmth pulse in my throat because I assumed she was looking for me. I began to feel braver. Then excited—and the rush of excitement almost caused me to fall.

"Hey," I called out. "Up here."

When she finally located me, I waved as if I were stranded on a desert isle and she were my rescuer.

"Teddy, you won't fall, will you?"

I laughed. Suddenly no longer frightened, I felt terrific, and I wasn't sure why.

"I might."

I was giddy.

"I'd never forgive you."

"You wouldn't have to. I'd probably be dead."

Man, I was wired.

Then she said, "I don't want you to die before I do, Teddy. Promise you won't?"

In what had been a light and teasing exchange, her sentiments speared me just as certainly as if Jack had fired his javelin at me. I stopped giggling. Dropped my smile. I felt cold and empty.

"I'm not coming down," I said.

I was clenching my teeth and holding onto the rim of the silo so tightly that my arms quickly began to ache. I was thinking and feeling everything and nothing. Judith was soon directly below me looking straight up and shaking her head.

"Not even to say goodbye?"

I felt tears welling again and I was angry, angry with myself, angry with Judith, angry with the ghosts, and angry with a world that seemed so totally indifferent to my pain. Then I said what I had to say.

"I'm not coming down unless I can go with you when your father comes."

"Oh, Teddy, don't be silly. The sun'll fry you, and this winter you'll freeze to death."

My God, her face—even tricked out in a frown and seeing it from such an odd angle—was incredible.

"I mean it."

I saw her shoulders heave as if she were carrying some invisible weight. She let several seconds pass before she said, "No, Teddy, I have to go alone. I can't take you or Jack. I have to go alone. I have to find where I belong."

"But maybe I belong there, too. Maybe I belong looking for that place with you."

"You belong to yourself."

"But I don't want to. You need me—I know you do. You need me more than you need Jack or anybody else. I want to belong to you."

She had her hands on her hips as if she were growing exasperated with me. She gathered herself for one final bit of rhetorical strategy.

"No, Teddy," she exclaimed, "don't you see? Don't you understand any of this?"

I guess I didn't.

By early afternoon hunger and the sun drove me down.

My father was trying to make a phone call; Junior was at the kitchen table eating stale popcorn; and Judith, all packed, was sitting patiently on her cot holding an apparently sleeping Oatmeal in her lap. She glanced up and smiled when I entered the room, but I could see she'd been crying.

"I was worried about you," she said. Then she glanced down at Oatmeal.

"I got so hot it burned the stupid out of me," I said.

She forced a soft laugh, yet looked sad, and the combination of that laugh and her sad expression brushed over me, throwing me off balance.

"Are you still going to be famous some day?" she said.

I nodded. I was staring at Oatmeal. "I'm planning to."

"I bet you will if you want to enough."

"I do."

We really didn't know what to say to each other. Every word that came out had tears flecked in the lining.

Then she said, "Oatmeal really has come home."

Slowly it dawned on me. A fresh round of tears gently squirted from her eyes, and she muttered something about the cat's death meaning something. I think she meant that it presaged something.

Finally I said, "I know where we oughta bury him."

Although the ground was pretty hard next to Gussie's grave, I fought at it with the end of the shovel. We didn't need much of a hole. When we had covered him up, I said that he'd been a good cat and I hoped that the foot Mickey kicked him with would get blood poisoning and have to be cut off. Judith shook her head—I didn't know what that meant.

Back at the house, Junior told us that Jack and my mother would both be home that evening. Jack remained under suspicion I think; my mother would have to return to the hospital the next week for tests. Her stomach had sharp teeth.

My father, who had been talking on the phone, walked over to the kitchen table where we were all sitting and he tousled my hair; then he looked down at Judith, and you could tell he was searching for a way to say what he needed to say. I guess I was expecting him to say goodbye. But what he said was, "He's not coming."

The strangest part was that Judith, a deep expression of resigned sadness on her face, an expression like the one I'd seen on a painting of the Virgin Mary when they took Jesus down from the cross, said very softly, "I know."

I felt everything collapsing inside me.

Junior got up, patted Judith's hand, and wandered outside.

I heard my father say, "I'm very sorry." He wanted to say more, but right at that moment he couldn't and so he left the room. I wanted to run after him and ask him how he knew. Had Judith's father called?

But instead I turned to Judith.

"Maybe he'll come tomorrow. Maybe he just couldn't make it today. Could have had car trouble. Lots of cars overheat in hot weather."

She shook her head. When she spoke, her voice was weary.

"The ghosts won't let him."

"But they can't do that. They can't stop him."

Judith's eyes deflected my words.

"I'm going to take a nap now, Teddy."

She sounded like an old, very tired, very discouraged woman.

"Okay, sure," I said.

I felt so sorry for her I just about couldn't walk out of the room on my rubbery legs. My father was nowhere in sight. Junior was looking back through the screened door.

"Our cousin has real shitty luck, doesn't she?" he said.

I sat out on the front porch until the late afternoon light burnished everything. I got up when Judith clopped through the screen door and said that she was going down to Trogler's Pond. I said I'd go with her, but she told me she wanted to go alone. I saw that she was noticeably more crippled than she had been.

I ran to the silo and climbed to the top as fast as I could. I followed Judith's tortuously slow trek all the way to the pond. I watched for ghosts. I kept wondering whether I should have not listened to her and just gone along with her in case she needed me. I think I feared what she might do. That's what was on my mind when a large white car—a Cadillac, I believe— pulled in the driveway. I scrambled down in a hurry because for some crazy reason I thought it was Judith's father.

It wasn't, of course.

It was Lex Macready.

My surprise was intense. When he got out of the car he was wearing dark glasses and a powder blue suit. He looked pale and wan. There was a hint of a pained smile when he recognized me. He was accompanied by two of his well-dressed goons, heavyset men with soft, pale, powdery faces and hard eyes.

Macready dismissed my greeting.

"I want to see that young woman, your cousin. Where is she?"

"She's not here," I said. "She's down in the pasture."

Removing his dark glasses, Macready approached me. I was shaking. He stared into my face and tonelessly explained that he had not been able to preach effectively since his visit to Saddle Rock and his encounter with Judith.

"We were in Arkansas last night, and while I was on stage an angel enveloped in flames was on stage, too. A dark angel sent by that young woman, I believe. That demon, your cousin. She's filled with darkness. She sent that dark angel to still my tongue. I knew last night that I would have to confront her or I might never preach again. I would have to run the spear of my faith into her wicked body. God is the answer."

I couldn't speak. I wanted to defend Judith, but I didn't know what to say. Macready reached out and touched my shoulder and his fingers felt reassuring. I knew instantly that I was his.

"Take me where she is," he commanded.

I said I would.

Macready's goons followed on our heels. I suggested that they watch for burrs and cow flop. Along the way I lied and told Macready that Judith's father was coming for her and, for some reason, I added that when she was gone I would never see her again. I wanted to gaze into his eyes, but he had slipped on the dark glasses again.

"I pray to God that's true," he said.

Even as we approached the pond, I knew I would regret betraying Judith. I couldn't help myself—such was Macready's ability to cast a spell over me. He touched that male-to-male something in me only David had touched. I think I wanted to be Macready's lover, though the likelihood of that, of course, was remote.

We walked away from the lowering sun. Its palette of summer colors was magnificent: reds, a violent orange, yellows that vibrated, and an underbelly of ethereal pink. Judith was in the pond, the water up to her waist. She was standing out in the middle, her back to us. She was naked.

She seemed a vision. She seemed unreal and yet more at home there, a water and sun goddess, than those of us watching and feeling uncomfortable with ourselves. I was staring at her, imagining that she was calling the twilight into herself when I heard Macready say, "Put that away. It won't be necessary."

I wheeled around to find one of his goons tucking a revolver back inside his coat.

"Hey," I said, "what's going on here?"

I was instantly mad as hell.

"Don't be alarmed," said Macready, and I relented.

He removed his glasses. As the sun began to sink by perceptible degrees, he and I stood together. I saw fiery lights dancing around Judith's body and then I imagined serpents surrounding her, and I glanced at Macready.

"You see them, too, don't you?" I said.

I was shocked that he did.

Then he looked at me, and his face and his voice were deep in sadness.

"She makes it impossible to do what I need to do," he said. "The darkness in her."

Feelings welled up in me, and I said what I had to say, and what I said did not surprise Macready.

"I love her."

He continued gazing at her for a few moments, then held my eyes with his, firmly and securely.

"You will be cursed until the day she no longer walks the earth. But if you forsake her, you're almost home."

Those words again.

I can't describe the effect of them—the warmth, the promise, and yet . . . and yet another part of me rose up and met his offerings.

"I'm her Onlie Begetter," I said. "She needs me, and I need to be somebody's center."

"You need the Son of God. In *John* 10: 7-9 He said, 'I am the gate; whoever enters through me will be saved. He will come in and go out, and find pasture'."

I wanted pasture. I believed I knew what that meant.

At that moment images of the murder of Emmitt Suggs erupted in my thoughts. I couldn't keep myself from confessing all that I had seen—everything about the Trogler ghosts and Judith's role in waking them.

When I finished, I was shivering. Macready clutched my shoulders and we embraced.

Choosing at last to acknowledge our presence, Judith turned and looked at us over her shoulder. But her expression was one of indifference; she paid us only a moment's attention.

"She belongs in the fire," said Macready. "The eternal fire of damnation. Her dark magic. Her fellowship with ghosts and dead spirits. One day God will bring her to the flames, and I'll be there to witness it."

I shook my head. I couldn't stop trembling. Something like defiance suddenly raged within me.

"She can save herself," I cried.

Macready was in my face. His breath was cool and his manner calm. Softly, very softly, he said, "But can you?"

Thirteen

When Judith from
Her Darkness Rose

That night Judith stole away.

She left just as I was poised to tell her that I loved her, that I would willingly devote myself completely to her. That Lex Macready had not seduced my soul to follow him and his God of answers to some home in the sky beyond the stars or even to some kingdom within.

Macready and his goons had left vowing one day to burn all the demons and all the darkness and all the evil from the shadowy creature they feared. Yes, they *feared* Judith, and that gave me a secret joy. When they were out of sight, I took off my clothes and waded, buck naked, into the pond, joining Judith under blossoming stars. As we stood in the water, a dull blue flame enveloped us, and everywhere but in our tight circumference the pond was as calm as I had ever seen it. Against and around our bodies, however, the water churned and stirred mysteriously. We lowered ourselves into the surprisingly warm and turbulent water until only our heads bobbed free and we laughed until the surface grew placid, and then we got out and dressed. I held Judith and she cried but didn't say why.

I assumed it was because her father hadn't come. Maybe I was wrong.

She didn't ask about Macready's visit. I didn't volunteer anything.

On the bank of the pond, Judith said, "I have to go up there." And her eyes cut in the direction of the Trogler place.

"Are you crazy?" I exclaimed. "You wanna get killed like Emmitt Suggs did?"

"I'm to blame for that."

"No, you're not. The ghosts were getting revenge for what happened a long time ago. They want revenge on my Pop, too, and what's going to stop them from killing us if we go in that house now?"

She turned to me, and even in the thickening twilight I could see her shy, knowing smile.

"You will, Teddy—you and the Fiery Angel."

I felt caught in my own foolish trap. That nonsense I had pulled about bringing the Fiery Angel into me—my brain must have been the consistency of creamed corn when I had done that.

"Why don't we just run away instead? Me and you—just take off and go and leave the ghosts and, like you said, maybe they'll just die if you're not around for them to draw strength from."

But then she nailed me.

"I have to try to make things right. I'm the one who woke up those ghosts—Emmitt Suggs has been murdered. What if your father is next? What about that, Teddy?"

Every word I had in mind to speak curled up and died in my throat.

Hand in hand, we walked through the Troglers' orchard.

We heard voices there. I think the trees whispered
things, but I ignored them. We walked past the small
barn. The voices buzzed around us like a swarm of
bees. Judith didn't flinch. We walked past the cistern,
and from just beneath the rim of it the ghost of
Siebert Trogler popped up, a live bat squirming in his
teeth. I jumped, but Judith squeezed my hand. Heat
lightning from nowhere flashed near the horror of
that ghost, and I wished that I had the courage to
push him down into the distant water where he would
dissolve into harmless mud. But I did not.

Siebert let us pass.

It was like a vesperal walk.

At the back door we were met by a posted sign:

KEEP OUT!
BY ORDER OF
SHERIFF

I had seen one like it around at the front door, too.
The problem was curiosity seekers, for word of Suggs's
grisly murder had spread and so, naturally, cars and
trucks had driven by in a macabre procession—grim
folks seeking grim scenes. The Trogler place had
drawn them like a magnet. The sheriff needed to dis-
courage them from daring to sneak inside the
premises and take a look-see for themselves—maybe
behold blood stains, maybe taste murder in the air.

We entered the darkened, silent house holding
hands, my breath working in ragged, labored puffs.
The rooms had never seemed so empty to me. Judith
led the way. We stopped somewhere near the center
of the living room, and we sat down on the floor. I
suddenly felt that something momentous would occur
before we left. Nervousness lining my voice, I said,

"We shouldn't do this. We shouldn't be here. What are you trying to do?"

We were sitting in the dark room, sitting like Indians around a fire in their tepee.

Except there was no fire—at first, no light of any kind.

"We're going to end things," said Judith.

And I couldn't read her tone. Did she mean force a final battle with the ghosts? Did she mean surrender to them? Sacrifice ourselves to them?

"How?" I said. I could smell the death of Emmitt Suggs. I could smell his blood. I could feel the faint echoes of his screams.

"With our love—and with the power of the Fiery Angel."

"No," I begged. "No, I don't want to do this."

Judith held my hand with surprising strength. I could not pull away from her.

"We have to, Teddy. Now we have to stop talking and concentrate. The ghosts are on their way."

And she was right: I could sense them—smell them, hear them, taste them—they were coming. A sickly yellow light rose along every inch of floor molding.

"We can't fight them," I challenged. "We can't do this."

"Yes, we can. Call the Fiery Angel from within you. I'll help. We'll call him, and he'll lead the ghosts back into the realm of the dead. He'll whisper his words of fire to meet their words of fire, and he'll soothe their desire for vengeance and make them sleep again the sleep of the dead."

"No, it'll never work."

"It has to, Teddy. It has to."

She pressed my hand. The ghosts—all of them—walked out of the walls and surrounded us.

"Oh, God," I murmured.

"Stay very still," Judith whispered. "Call the Fiery Angel."

I tried. And though I had participated in a lie, though I had been false to Judith in my claim to a certain intimacy with the Fiery Angel, I concentrated. Together, Judith and I willed something there, something I cannot begin to explain. Our efforts seemed to keep the ghosts at bay, and then I began to feel the results of the bond of the need to evoke the supernatural that I momentarily shared with Judith—Judith, the woman I loved.

First, a heat rose around us from beneath the floor. Then a blue light.

A blue flame.

Light and heat so heavenly I wanted to die in it.

But the ghosts were not ready to surrender. They were strong.

In the end, too strong.

It was the voice of Romina Trogler that won the hour for them. Yes, I believe that was it.

"Animus," she called. Then, more insistently: "Animus, you're home. You're home."

I could feel the blue flame pulsing a protective shield for us. I could hear Judith's breathing. She believed in that power ringing us, keeping us from harm.

"Don't let go of this," she said.

I'll never know precisely what the *this* referred to. Perhaps it didn't matter, for, in the final analysis, I could not hold on. The ghosts knew. They silently slipped down beneath the floor, and the blue flame spread to meet them.

And the haunted ground under us shook and the old house creaked and the sky thundered and there was lightning behind my eyes. The only other thing that I remember about those indescribably terrifying minutes was that Judith gasped, and I did not know, at that instant, what that gasp meant.

Except that she let go of my hand.

And there was, quite suddenly, silence. And darkness.

I thought that my heart had stopped beating.

The blue flame had been snuffed out.

The room lost all heat. There, in the middle of summer, the air began to feel like January.

"Go!" Judith shouted. "Go, now, Teddy!"

I felt her push at me; she shoved me to my feet, and, together, we fled that house of night.

Back in the mud room, we tried to sleep. I think I had deluded myself into believing that some magical force generated by me and the woman I loved had destroyed the ghosts. As Judith and I lay in the darkness, however, I soon realized that I was wrong.

I heard Judith quietly sobbing.

"What is it?" I said, crawling onto her cot with her.

We held each other, and when she had found her voice, she said, "He's gone. The Fiery Angel is no more. But the ghosts are still there."

I wanted to protest: How could she *know* that? And yet I was almost certain that somehow she did. I remained helplessly silent, but there, locked in our embrace, Judith trembled. She nuzzled close to my ear, and in a very intense whisper she said, "Teddy, don't *ever* go back there. The voices will call you, but don't *ever* go back. Promise me you won't."

I whispered, "Okay, sure."

Truth is, I would have promised anything.

I must have slept very soundly, though I did dream—of a mammoth blue flame swallowing me like

a whale might. It was a warm and blissful dream.
When I woke it was past dawn.

And Judith was not there.

She had once again consolidated all her belongings
into one suitcase, and that suitcase was missing. I
raced outside and began looking everywhere for her,
eventually dashing down into the pasture to the far
gate leading to the highway. There, by the barbed
wire fence, I found indications that she had probably
been there. Her footprints suggested she had headed
either for the highway or for town. I breathlessly informed my father what had happened and we
immediately struck out in his pickup to find her. We
drove up and down Highway 56, and we cruised every
street in Saddle Rock. I told my father that I thought
she might have hopped a freight train. He doubted it.

But back home, he called the sheriff and also Santa
Fe railroad officials, and then there was nothing more
that we could do except wait. The sheriff wasn't likely
to be much help, seeing that Jack had cursed him and
thrown a tin water cup at him last night when my father came to free him. For his misbehavior, Jack
would remain in jail for one more day. I actually felt
kind of sorry that he didn't get to say one last goodbye to Judith. My mother, having been released from
the hospital, was sleeping—the ghost of Senta Trogler
probably hovering nearby.

My father and I sat out on the front porch on the
emptiest, most dreadful Sunday morning I have ever
spent. We said virtually nothing to each other, though
I recall my father trying to be reassuring. I know that
he was amazed Judith could have negotiated the distance into town, let alone hop a freight. But that was
because he didn't know her as I knew her.

Around noon we received a call from Walton, Kansas, a little town down on Highway 50. Some men who worked at the grain elevator had found Judith in one of the empty boxcars. They had taken her to the hospital in nearby Newton because she was disoriented and could not walk. My father and I didn't hesitate to go for her. Junior agreed to stay with my mother while we went after our runaway. On route, I kept having to choke back tears, and, at one point, my father, his voice filled with regret, whispered, "I should have taken better care of her. She's blood."

At the hospital in Newton, a nurse took us aside at the registration desk and explained that Judith was doing pretty well—bumped and scratched some, but resting and that we could see her. While my father stayed back to talk some more with the nurse and to arrange to have Judith released, I bought her a cold bottle of strawberry soda, and just outside her room I practiced over and over to myself how I would tell her that I loved her, that I would always love her. I remember stepping very cautiously into her room and finding her propped up in bed looking tired and yet beautiful.

"Hey," I said, "were you headed for Colorado?"

She smiled weakly and nodded.

Then I said, "Pop and I were worried that you'd get hurt or something. Jack has to spend another night in jail. Here, I got this for you."

I handed the bottle of strawberry soda to her, and I thought maybe she was going to cry. "Thanks. You remembered what I like." Then, her bottom lip quivering, she added, "The ghosts wouldn't let me get away. Teddy, we have to go back and fight them."

"Don't think about that now."

She drank two sips of the soda before exhaustion began to hold sway. She closed her eyes. I just stood there and watched her for the longest time. Eventually I leaned over and kissed her on the cheek and whispered, "I love you."

But I don't think she heard me.

It was still hot when we got back to our farm that evening. We were windblown and sweaty from riding with all the windows rolled down, and I thought Judith looked unusually peaked. I knew she hadn't gotten much sleep. The doctor had given her some pain pills, nothing, however, strong enough to handle the throbbing in her legs.

When we had climbed out of the truck, I recall vividly that my father hugged Judith and told her again how sorry he was that she had felt like she needed to run away.

"You're blood," he said, because he obviously continued to think that was important.

"I'm glad," said Judith. "Thank you. You're very kind."

"We'll try to make things better so's you won't want to take off again like you did. We wasn't good hosts—that's a fact. I'm real sorry. This'll work out better this time." And he iterated how sorry he was her father hadn't come for her, seeing how she was so eager to be with him.

"It wasn't your fault. Not anyone's fault maybe," she replied. "It's just the way things are. I'm not someone my father wants around. I'll have to keep looking for where I belong."

Then, when he noticed how much pain she was in as she tried to walk, he picked her up sweet as pie, just as I'd seen him lift baby calves, and he swept her into our house.

Junior, who opened the screen door for them, chuckled at the sight.

"Pop looks like he's carrying his bride over the threshold."

It was the right thing for him to say, I thought, because there he was, my older brother who wanted to have a bride of his own, a family of his own so he could show the world that not every family had to be broken beyond repair. Like ours.

As for me, I admit to having been jealous at the sight of Judith's arms wrapped around my father's neck. I lugged her suitcase along behind them. I felt weak. Felt like a sissy. I wondered whether I would ever be strong enough to take care of a family of my own. Like Judith, I wondered where I belonged.

Wherever it was, I believed she should be there, too.

I never lost that belief. Maybe it's the only one I've ever had.

The return home was not exactly victorious, and not everyone in the welcoming party was glad to see my cousin. Arms folded across her ailing stomach, my mother had struggled out of bed to meet us in the kitchen. Despite her sickly nature, she had the meanness of a gunfighter in her eyes. She glared at my father as he gently put Judith down. No doubt my mother had hoped she would never see my cousin again.

You could tell she wanted to hurt and humiliate Judith one more time.

"Brought *her* back, did you?"

"Now Kathleen, babe, there's no call for this. You knew full well what the deal was. Did you expect me to turn her over to the Salvation Army or some such thing? I still feel like we might be hearing from Juanita any day, but until then we're not throwing this young lady out on the street. Would a God-fearing family do that?"

My father's words hit my mother right between the eyes. Slowed her down some if not stunned her. And the stuff about being "God-fearing" was the clincher. However, my mother was too filled with venom not to coil up and strike again. And she had fangs.

Pointing directly at Judith, she said, "That girl is wicked and no good. I've said it over and over. She's poisoned Teddy. She's poisoned Jack. And look at what Junior's gone on and done—brought disgrace to the family and himself. And that girl's especially poisoned you, Norman, and you can't see it."

I continued not to understand how Judith had influenced Junior's behavior, but then, of course, I realized that my mother wasn't playing with a full deck. You could tell. It was scary and sad. But she had no right to take out her feelings on my cousin. On the woman I loved.

My father was shaking his head. He was bewildered. He was at the end of his patience, and yet he continued to talk softly and with understanding.

"Kathleen, I've never known you to be a hurtful person. But what you're doing and what you're saying is hurtful. It cuts at me to see this happening. And I think . . . I believe you owe this young lady an apology."

That's when something snapped.

When all hell started to break loose.

It was a fascinating moment.

Hearing my father ask her to apologize, my mother started trembling. Her face got pale, pale and white as milk with the cream skimmed off. Standing next to me, Judith turned away from the metamorphosis my mother was undergoing. I glanced at Junior and saw that he was shooting daggers at my mother and gritting his teeth. My father had his hands out as if he expected to catch the woman if she fainted or pitched into conniptions of some sort.

My mother's lips drew up in a firm, ugly line.

"Norman, I want you to choose. You decide which

it's going to be. You choose right here between me,
your faithful wife and mother of your children, between me . . . and that girl."

Our kitchen got smaller. The walls moved in. I
swear they did.

"Kathleen, you can't ask . . . this isn't about choosing. You've got things all cockeyed."

"Have I?" Still trembling, my mother drew up and
took a deep breath; she seemed, momentarily, to get
taller. "You're all against me, aren't you? Every last
one of you. I suppose Jack would be, too, if he were
here. You all hate me."

"No, Kathleen, we—"

"Damn you all, you do!" she screamed.

My mother began nodding in a frightening way. I
can't exactly describe it. Hers was an expression of absolute determination. She knew precisely what she
must do—none of us, however, could guess what it
was going to be. Her voice sounded strange, too. Like
an Old Testament voice. Otherworldly. Judgmental.
Supernaturally certain.

"We have suffered a witch to come into our home,"
she said. "A demon. That young Reverend Macready
has come back to Saddle Rock. He will lead us to destroy her. God will set her to the flames. She's evil; the
Child of the Devil. Filthy and horrible." Then she focused on me. "My little Teddy used to love his mother
and take care of her—that girl stole him from his
mother. That girl turned him completely against his
mother. Taught him sin. Showed him the ways of
darkness."

I wanted to shout in her face, but my response
came out more like a squawk.

"No, she didn't either."

Everything seemed to close down then. No movement. No more words for maybe a half dozen

heartbeats. My father broke the spell when he took a step toward my mother and said, "This is enough, Kathleen."

Then the worst part.

My mother's laugh was chilling. I've never heard anything like it—a mad cackle—and I'd never seen her move so quickly as she did there in the shadowy light of our stifling kitchen. She wheeled around to the silverware drawer and had a butcher knife in her hand and raised it as we looked on in horror.

She yelled and rushed forward and stabbed at Judith twice before Junior tackled her.

That's what he did. Like a defensive player sacking the quarterback. They crashed to the floor and my mother fumbled the knife. Judith, barely escaping the blade, shrieked and ran into the mud room and I followed, but from the doorway I watched as it took both Junior and my father to subdue the woman. My mother. She bit and kicked and jerked. She recovered the knife and stabbed at my father; she stabbed at Junior. She cried out in anguish as they wrested the weapon from her, and her face went all shrunken and pathetic. They got her to her feet and she swayed as if blown by an inner wind. Finally, on the verge of collapse, she mustered enough energy to speak calmly.

"The both of you—you let go of me so I can pack up and leave here where I'm not wanted."

"Kathleen, babe, my God, don't do this."

I felt deeply sorry for my father. He looked as if one fist of thorns had smacked him in the mouth and another in the stomach. He was holding my mother from behind, and he kept holding her as he maneuvered her from the room like a greased pig. When they were gone, I watched Junior sit down on the floor and bury his face in his hands.

Despite his best efforts to smooth things over and assuage the crazed person my mother had become, my father could not talk her out of leaving. After the two of them had driven off to the Gorman's house in town, Junior fixed us some bologna sandwiches and I boiled a few eggs and made iced tea. We ate at the kitchen table pretty much in silence at first. Then when Judith and I went back to the mud room, Junior sidled after us.

"She's lost it," he said. "Pop might as well face it. That woman's mind has cracked open like an overripe watermelon. Topeka's the place for her. Why can't Pop see that?"

Judith's words brimmed with confusion and an aching sadness.

"She didn't really want to hurt anyone. She's in a lot of pain. Pain in her mind and her heart and her soul. She needs everybody's love and she needs for this house to be where she belongs again."

Then I said, "I hope she never ever comes back."

"Oh, no, Teddy, don't say that. She's your mother and she loves you. And she loves Junior and Jack. And she loves your father. She's scared of this storm in her life."

"You're wrong about something," said Junior. "If that woman could have, she'd have stabbed you to death. Pop and me, too. Her mind's completely gone."

I was upset and frightened, and I had no idea what was going to happen to all of us.

"What do we do now?" I said.

Junior had me sit on Judith's cot with her; he hunkered down in front of us.

"You guys take care of yourselves the best you can, okay?"

We sort of nodded, I believe, and I could tell he had something more to say. He reached out and tapped Judith on the back of her hand.

"Could you help me with something? A big favor is what I need."

Neither Judith nor I knew what he was talking about.

"If I can," said Judith. "Yes. I'd like to."

He motioned for us to follow him to the phone, and then he explained how he was going to call the people Phyllis was staying with in Missouri. If he could get through to her, he was going to plan out a way for her to escape with him and drive back to Saddle Rock and demand that their parents give them permission to get married.

"If they say they won't, we'll run off and do it anyway."

I remember when he said that I about shouted with joy.

"I don't see how I can help," said Judith.

"Here's the thing. See, these people won't let Phyllis come to the phone if they know it's me. But if you call and tell them you're Phyllis's friend, Wendy Wentworth, it'll be fine. It won't be much of a lie, and it'll be for a good cause."

"Yeah," I said. Then I stopped myself. It was Judith's decision.

She thought about it a moment.

"Since it's for love, I'll do it," she said. "I think you and Phyllis belong together."

"I think we do, too," said Junior.

So Judith did it, and we waited until those people brought Phyllis to the phone. At that point Junior shooed us out of the room. Judith and I were giddy as we sat on her cot. We hugged each other because we were happy for Junior. It was fun helping him.

It made us forget about how dark it was getting outside.

And how dark it was inside my family.

Most of all, it made us forget, for a time, the battle
with the ghosts—the final, inevitable battle.

Five minutes later Junior jigged into the room. It
didn't take a genius to see that he and his love had a
plan.

"I'm headin' out at dawn. I ain't tellin' Pop ahead of
time, so you guys don't rat on me." Then he looked
right at Judith and said, "Thanks, cousin." He leaned
down and planted a soft, sweet kiss on her cheek, and
that surprised me, but for some reason I wasn't jealous.

"You're welcome," she said. "I hope you have better
luck with your plan than I had with mine."

Just a little while after that my father came home.
He stepped quietly into the mud room and forced a
smile onto his deeply stressed face.

"This'll all be fine soon," he said to both of us, and
then more to Judith he added, "Your Aunt Kathleen,
she's just very upset. I'll have to try to get her some
help. What she did—try to forgive her. That's all I can
ask."

"I do," said Judith.

My father nodded. He left the room quickly because I think he was about to break down and cry.

I fixed Judith a tub of cool bath water and she
soaked in it while I gave her privacy. The scene with
my mother came back hauntingly as I sat at the
kitchen table. Nothing made sense. Nothing except
being close to Judith.

After her bath she was lying on her stomach with a
big towel wrapped around her when she asked me to
come in.

"Romina Trogler brought back my affliction," she
said. "I need a good Kenny from my Onlie Begetter."

I smiled and said, "Sure."

I heated some strips of wool, careful not to get
them too hot.

She asked me to turn off the light and then she slipped out of the towel and lay back down on her stomach. She was completely naked. For several minutes I couldn't get my breathing to even out as I placed strips on her marvelous flesh. Then I removed the strips and started rubbing her down. She moaned with a mixture of pleasure and pain. I was aroused. I delighted in every second that my fingers had contact with her calves, her thighs, her bottom, her back, her shoulders. Everywhere on her.

I made it an extra long Kenny.

When I finished, Judith sat up, one arm and hand covering her breasts, and kissed me on the shoulder and asked me to take off my clothes and get under a sheet with her. I almost tore my overalls shedding them so quickly. When we realized that a sheet was just too hot for a sultry night, we tossed it aside and Judith lay in my arms, her breasts radiating warmth against my chest.

"Thank you for everything," she whispered.

My penis was uncomfortably erect in a few seconds.

"You're welcome," I said. "But I haven't done much."

Her fingers tracked down from my chest over my stomach before discovering my erection. My whole body jerked as she stroked one finger over the length of my penis.

"Oh, sorry," she said when I convulsed violently.

"No, really . . . it's fine."

She nuzzled at my throat and relaxed, and I started talking about how afraid I was I'd never see her again when she hopped that freight and how glad I was when we found her. And then I decided it was time to make love to her. Slow, thorough lovemaking—not the boyishly eager, clumsy attempt like before. So I began kissing her forehead and her nose, and I began reassigning my hands to the sexual areas promising the most pleasure for both of us.

And that's when I realized that Judith, exhausted from the day, had fallen asleep.

I woke just before dawn when I heard someone sneaking quietly into the kitchen.

It was Junior.

There was just enough light for me to see him raise a finger to his lips to caution me against making noise. He smiled shyly and whispered, "Headin' out on my rescue mission."

"I hope you bring her back," I said.

He poured himself a big glass of milk and drank it down in one long gulp. Then I followed him out to his car.

"Teddy," he said, "don't think about how fucked up we are. This family, I mean. It'll drive you as nutty as our mother is."

"I won't think about it," I said.

"You understand why I have to do this, don't you?" I did.

Once again he reminded me of my father. I saw a lot of goodness in Junior's face. I saw that what he was doing was difficult but that he had learned to trust what was difficult. I was only beginning to. And he understood sorrow. I'd had a taste of that myself. But there was another helping or two of it to come.

"Yeah, sure," I said. "I'd do what you're doing. I wouldn't care what nobody thought."

He squeezed my shoulder.

"You know, Teddy, I'm really sorry about the bad shit Jack and I have done to you over the years."

"No big deal," I said. "That's what little brothers are for—to beat up on."

He chuckled at that.

He was standing with the driver's side door open, his boot propped up on the running board; he was looking out at the barn and the pasture beyond. It was a little foggy.

"This hasn't been the worst place, I guess," he said. "Just not the best."

I agreed.

Then I happened to notice his .20 gauge shotgun leaning against a door in the backseat.

"You going to use that?"

"If I have to. I sure as hell don't want to."

I knew it would have to be a totally crazy situation before he would. I lost myself for a few moments thinking about whether I could shoot anyone. I had fired Junior's shotgun at coffee cans—the kick bruised my shoulder. Jack had one just like it. I thought about what that shotgun would do to someone's body. I thought about all the blood.

I shivered.

I looked into Junior's eyes and I said, "Be careful."

"Got to be." He hesitated. "And listen—stay away from the Trogler place, okay?" Then, with a wink, he added, "And don't you and Jack kill each other over our cousin."

Blushing, I nodded.

My brother waved as he drove off to fight ghosts of his own.

I was real sorry to see him go.

Fourteen

We Belong Dead

Later that morning my father brought Jack home.

Judith was happy to see him. Very happy. Jack, looking a lot like James Dean, was smiling shyly and trying to act cool. But I could tell how much he loved Judith.

Hand in hand they walked out to the barn. Judith glanced once over her shoulder at me, but I could not read her expression—I guess she was doing something she had to do, something she really wanted to do. I could imagine what was going to take place in the barn.

My world fell away.

More than anything else, I wished I could die—just an easy, painless death. Like falling asleep. Death was better than losing Judith. Had I possessed the courage to do so, I might have ended my life right then. Instead, I sat on our porch frozen in a block of misery.

My father joined me.

"Junior's gone off, hasn't he?" he said.

I shrugged. I didn't care about anything other than my smashed and broken heart. My father, misreading things, assumed I was thinking about Junior. He put his big hand on my shoulder and said, "He feels like

it's what he's got to do. He feels like it's what a man
would do."

Of a sudden then—like out of nowhere, like lightning on a cloudless day—I felt a jolt of panic. Maybe
it was a case of my self-pity opening up some hidden
realm, some door into a different dimension. Whatever it was, it let me see the ghosts; more so, it let me
see the bloodied body of Emmitt Suggs, only when
the vision zoomed in for a close-up of Suggs what materialized was the face of my father.

"I'm scared," I said.

And you could hear it in my voice.

"Of what, Teddy? Goodness sakes, don't be scared.
Junior, he'll be fine."

"Not that," I said. "I'm scared of somebody hurting
you bad."

He sort of laughed, but he was also moved deeply
by my words.

"Nobody's gonna hurt your ole man. Don't you
worry none about that. And don't you worry none
about your mother—we'll get her back all the way
well. You'll see."

He sat with me a little while longer, and then he got
up and said he had to go to work before they decided
to fire him. After he left, I sat there on the porch another twenty minutes or so trying as hard as I could
not to envision Jack and Judith making love.

I hated both of them. I felt betrayed. I wanted to die
of my broken heart, and I wanted my death to devas-
tate Judith—the death of her Onlie Begetter.
Drowning in that sea of self-pity, I suddenly saw someone pedaling a bike up the road toward our farm.

It was David.

I guess I was too heartsick to know what to think or
do.

David looked thin and pale in a plaid, button-down

shirt and blue jeans. I saw that he was wearing new sneakers. Smiling as he put down his kickstand and started to approach, he was carrying a paper sack that had been tied to his bike rack. He was sweating along his hairline. I didn't exactly welcome him with open arms.

"What are *you* doing out here?" I said as he plopped down on a step below me.

"I came to visit my favorite guy."

He was breathing pretty heavily from the biking. When he said something more, something about how hot it was and how his bike had a low tire, I began to notice that his voice was more effeminate than I recalled. I didn't like that voice, and I especially didn't like the way he put his hand on the knee of my overalls and tried to rub his fingers up my thigh.

"You picked a bad time to come," I said. "You better go on home."

My feelings for David had died. But words to that effect escaped me, and I was angry because they did. Angry at David. Angry at myself. Angry at Judith and Jack. Angry at whatever had initially triggered my attraction to both sexes.

"Why?" he said. "What's goin' on? I thought you'd be glad I came."

I was eyeing the paper sack. Then I noticed the bandages on his wrists, much smaller ones than he'd worn at the hospital.

"You're not trying to kill yourself no more, are you?"

I gestured toward his wrists.

"Nope. My shrink says I was just mixed up. But, hey, I'm gonna have the coolest scars. Wanna see?"

His wounds were jaggedly stitched up in black thread like you might sew up a hole in a sock with, and I was repulsed by the fact that in some ways that

ugly stitching was connected to me. I wanted no part
of those wounds and the scars they would produce. I
wanted no more ugliness. I wanted only the beauty of
Judith in my life, and I didn't have it because she was
in Jack's life and I couldn't understand how she could
possibly love both of us.

"Mixed up, how?"

David hesitated.

"About my sexuality."

He swallowed that last word as if it were a live worm;
he squinched up his face, and then I said, "I didn't
know that could make somebody try to kill themselves."

But that wasn't completely true. I shared some of
David's confusion even as I was irritated by his presence and ashamed of the feelings I once had for him
and similar feelings for Macready.

"My self-worth has been damaged," he added.
"That's what my shrink said. I'm trying to understand
that, but it doesn't matter as long as I have you."

He made a move as if he were going to kiss me. I
scooted away.

"Stop it. I don't want you to do that. I'm not *yours*.
I'm not anybody's. You better go on home."

He looked hurt. His face collapsed. He glanced
down at the paper sack he was holding, and I think
maybe his lower lip quivered. Then he wiped his fingertips across his sweaty forehead.

"Could I have a glass of cold water, please?"

I shook my head.

"I wish you'd just go on home," I said before re-
lenting. "Okay, I'll give you the water, but then you got
to go. My cousin—she's not feeling good. There's nobody else to take care of her, so I have to."

I said those words as firmly as I could—the lie
didn't really bother me. I wondered why David being

around upset me so much. When I brought him the water, he thanked me and drank deeply.

"Water from a well always tastes better than town water," he said.

"I guess so. Yeah."

He finished the glass and looked at me, bruises of hurt feelings around his eyes.

"Don't you want to know what's in this sack?"

I shrugged. All I wanted was for him to leave. Eager to get my reaction, he pulled something out of the sack with the flourish of a magician. I couldn't help noticing that there was apparently more than one thing in the sack.

"I saw this at the dime store in Emporia and knew you'd like it. I bought it with my own money. It's for you."

He had me there. The gift itself tugged at my addiction to new things, things that cost money, things you could only hope for maybe at Christmas. It was a miniature pinball machine on the theme of wild-fowl hunting, replete with tiny ball bearings you shot into a slanted array of plastic catchers each carrying a numerical value, each representing a different game bird: a mallard duck, a pheasant, a quail, a Canadian goose, and a ruffled grouse. The small paintings of each bird were exquisite. I tried not to show how neat I thought the gift was.

"What else is in that sack?"

David wrinkled up his nose and shook his head. "Just something. Nothing."

As I studied the pinball game another moment or two, David, his voice awash in hopefulness, said, "What do you think? Do you like it?"

"It's okay, I guess."

Suddenly it appeared that David did not know what else to say. He stared at me. He reached for the leg of

my overalls and stroked it. I felt hot needles in my
throat. I wanted to say something that would just
make him go and never come back. I wanted to keep
the gift, but I also wanted to break it. I wanted to put
it down on the porch and stomp on it. I wanted to
hear it crack and shatter.

"Teddy, nobody likes your cousin. You know that,
don't you?"

His eyes were steady and there was a ferocious lean
to his body. I was not really surprised by what he said.
Still, it angered me.

"Who's been talking about my cousin?"

He glanced away. I saw his chest heave.

"People at church mostly."

He meant the Christian Church. Our church. Or,
rather, my mother's church. Not mine.

"They're all crazy," I said. "What do they say?"

"About how, you know, how wicked she is. How
she's broken up your family. And what she did to that
Reverend Macready. And that maybe she had something to do with Emmitt Suggs gettin' killed. And how
your own mother hates her, and people are talking
about doing something." He paused to catch his
breath. "Doing something to make your cousin go
away forever."

It sounded like maybe he had practiced saying a lot
of what he said and that made me even more upset
for some reason. And that word "forever" terrified
me.

I stood up. The pinball game dropped and rattled
down a few steps before David retrieved it.

"You don't even know!" I shouted.

I held my fists at my sides. I gritted my teeth until
they hurt.

David stood up, too.

"Teddy, she's bad. Don't you see that? The people at church—"

"God damn it!" I screamed.

That felt good. The release.

David was holding the pinball game and the sack against his chest; he was blinking rapidly as if trying to process my anger and scrambling to think of what to do or say next. He didn't want to lose me—you could see it in his expression—but it was too late. Too late for many things.

"She's changed you, Teddy," he said.

"No, she hasn't. And she didn't have nothing to do with what happened to Emmitt Suggs. And if you wanna know the truth, I hate everybody at that church, and I hate my mother, too."

David looked at me in disbelief. Then he reached for me one last time, and I almost gave in. I knew his touch. I knew what being with him felt like. What it had felt like *before*. Before I truly became Judith's Onlie Begetter. Before I lost her.

"Stay away from your cousin, Teddy. I'm the only one who really cares about you. She can't care about you the way I do. She just can't."

He kept pleading. Each word was like barbed wire being pulled through me. Finally, when I could stand it no longer, I cupped my hands over my ears. My body thrummed and I felt sick like I was going to throw up.

"Go to hell!" I cried out.

That finished it. David stepped back a couple of feet. His mouth went slack as he gazed at me, gazed as if he no longer knew me, and I suppose that was true. Then, very softly, he said, "You're the one, Teddy. You're the one who's going to hell. Because of that girl."

He turned and started for his bike. I almost called

to him to stop. To come back. But I didn't. Couldn't. Then he did stop. He was still hugging the pinball game and whatever was in the sack. He walked toward me, and I could see anger in the set of his jaw. He was seething. I instinctively raised my fists; I could feel tears welling at the corners of my eyes. I could see that he was also fighting back tears.

"You can keep this," he said, his voice flat and tone-less.

He tossed the game up by the steps.

"I don't want it," I said.

It was a standoff. We looked at each other the way boys do when the language of their emotions is far too difficult to translate, when only some violent phys-ical action will gain closure. I was still thinking he might try to fight me, but I wasn't sure what we would be fighting about. Instead, he rushed up to the game and drove the heel of one of his sneakers into it.

The plastic broke in a screech that made me shiver.

Several of the tiny ball bearings leaked out onto the ground.

"There," he said, "that's what I think of you and your shitty cousin." His face morphed. Turned to stone. He stood there as if he realized the next thing was unthinkable. Because it was. "If we can't be to-gether, Teddy," he said, his tone a chilling matter-of-factness, "then we belong dead."

Then he reached into the paper sack.

And every instinct in me shouted to run.

I ran through the dragonfield without looking back. I ran to the rear of the Trogler place.

I could see the road. I could follow David on his bike. I prayed that he would go on back to town, but I think I knew he wouldn't.

When he caught up with me behind the ghostly house, he was holding a small revolver with both hands. My mouth was dry; my heart was drumming in my ears.

"Don't," I said. His eyes scared me into a whimper of words. "Please, please . . . don't. Please don't."

He walked up to within maybe twenty feet of me.

"I mean it, Teddy," he said. "You'll see. You'll see."

I opened my mouth to say something more. All that came out was, "Please."

David was not in the world: hurt and anger and things unsayable had taken him to a place beyond reason.

"You made me do this, Teddy. You made me."

And I heard the gun fire.

There was a hard, fiery pinch in my chest.

I staggered. I heard David cry out as if he were suddenly frightened by the return to reality.

I slumped to my knees. I glanced down at a blossoming rose of blood where my heart was. I couldn't breathe. Couldn't think. All I heard was David running away.

I put my hand to my heart as if I were about to say the Pledge of Allegiance.

I crumpled backwards.

Dust swirled around me.

The sky was blue.

Then no color at all.

I couldn't feel the sun.

For a fleeting instant I could hear the wind. Then couldn't.

The last thing I heard was the final beat of my heart.

Fifteen

Fear in a Handful of Dust

I don't know how long I was dead.

Time lost all meaning while life leaked from my heart.

Dying sort of surprised me: It didn't hurt that much—a steady, eager pain but not as painful as, say, stepping on a rusty nail when you're barefoot, especially if you count Doc Gillis giving you a tetanus shot in your rear end. In fact, I didn't feel that anything really, really terrible had happened. It was like something kind of ordinary. At first, I imagined myself simply being a piece of freshly fallen fruit—maybe a crab apple or a pear.

Then instead of rotting or being picked at by birds, I turned into dust.

I lifted from my body as particles of dust on something like wind only not quite wind. Maybe it was the breath of God.

I swung up high like a kite.

It was glorious and sad at the same time.

As a small cloud of dust, I dropped down into the Trogler house. That was the sad part. The scary part.

You see, the ghosts wanted me—me as a handful of dust.

I heard their words of fire: needy, angry, forlorn.

Was I really becoming one of them?

They told me I should stay dead. They told me that in time I would get stronger—that I would become earth again and live in a different realm, somewhere down in a haunted place I could not imagine. All the ghosts embraced my dust, except Romina.

I didn't understand.

What did she want that the others did not?

I drifted through the rooms. I saw all the years of their lives in that house—saw time pass in an instant. Saw a little joy and many tears. And blood. Much blood.

Then a surprising sensation of being sucked out of the house, right up through the roof, and being aware of falling, falling, falling and hovering just over my body, being aware as well, that beyond me the ghosts were very angry.

All except Romina.

I settled down onto my body as a patina of dust.

Then a jolt of pain.

I had been a ghost, but I had returned to my body. My heart hiccoughed to life.

I could feel an odd pressure in my chest.

I blinked once. Twice. I was alive.

Someone was poking a finger into the hole in my heart.

Someone was stopping the bleeding.

Suddenly my chest heaved and I coughed and then I focused on my savior: Romina Trogler, smelling of earth and sour not-quite-life, not-quite-death. She almost smiled. Mostly her face was passionless. I stared at the dark mole above her lip. Though I couldn't make out the word, she was whispering something. A name, I believe.

I felt her remove her finger from the hole in my heart.

I lay there cold, not exactly asleep, not exactly awake.

Gradually I became very, very scared, for I sensed something dark about the future.

Late afternoon I sensed the ghosts were near. I think they wanted to kill me, and maybe they would have right then and there with me pretty helpless still recovering from being shot in the heart by David and being brought back to life by Romina.

Why would she do that?

She was keeping her family of ghosts from killing me—I believe that.

The ghosts disappeared when, drifting out from the dragonfield, Judith's voice calling for me drew near. I heard her cry in something close to terror when she found me. Jack was with her, javelin in hand.

"Teddy! Teddy!"

Her face was down only an inch from mine. I was weak, but I managed to whisper, "Help me up, okay?"

But she paused.

She was looking at me very strangely. She saw something. Knew something.

Jack said, "God, he's been bleeding. What happened to him?"

Judith shook her head. Then she held my face in her hands and said, "Teddy, listen carefully: I'm giving you something. Please don't try to give it back. Promise you won't."

I promised.

What happened next I can't really describe other than to say what it felt like: It *felt like* Judith reached her hands into my chest just the way you would put your hands into gloves, and she held them there for what seemed like a minute only probably wasn't.

I saw flaming roses when she did that.

I saw the blue light of the Fiery Angel wink out again.

I saw the color of darkness.

I saw my own shadow, shaped just like my body.

Then Judith and Jack helped me up, and suddenly I knew what she had done: She had given her powers to me. I looked hard at her to make certain I was right. She sort of bit at her lip and so, yes, I was right.

I didn't want her powers.

But I had promised I wouldn't try to give them back.

"Come to the house with us," said Judith.

"You think he needs Doc Gillis?" Jack followed.

I was shaking my head.

"I'm okay. I'll be okay. Just want to be alone."

They looked kind of sad as they left me—you know, almost maybe the way Adam and Eve looked when God ran them out of Eden. I think they felt guilty— Judith and Jack, that is—and I didn't mind if they did. Mostly, though, I really did need to be alone. To think. To figure out who I had become and what I must now do.

I walked toward the Troglers's pond. It was hot, but the heat didn't bother me.

I decided I wanted not to hate David.

Or Judith and Jack. Or my mother.

I stared up at the top limbs of the massive cottonwood, and somehow, my eyes raised until I was on the edge of dizziness, I suddenly knew: *This is what I must do, and I must do it—fight the ghosts.*

Protect my father.

Protect my family, even though I did not belong to it.

Eyes locked onto that magnificent tree, I felt something surge in me. My fingertips hummed. I lifted my hand and pointed at the clear, blue sky above that cottonwood and I clenched my teeth and I jabbed my finger into the air.

A fork of lightning danced a few feet above the top-most branches.

I smiled.

For a moment or two I was tempted to direct a lightning strike right at the Trogler place. But I resisted.

Then I ran to test my powers further.

I ran to Gussie's grave.

I was close to being giddy as I stood by it and took a deep breath and shut my eyes and let the capacity to wake the dead course through me. When I finally opened my eyes, the dusty shape of Gussie was there.

God, I was happy.

And so was Gussie, I think.

I didn't wake Oatmeal—just thought he needed to stay dead longer. I spent the rest of the daylight hours running free with my ghost of a dog, thrilling to the sound once again of her bark. Then I returned her to her gravesite and she sank into the ground like the sun sinking below the horizon.

That evening Judith was with Jack—it hurt to see them together and in love, but I knew I would have to accept it. I knew I had to think about other things.

The ghosts were calling.

They wanted blood.

To Judith and Jack I said, "Things are going to get very bad, but it'll soon be over."

Judith kissed me on the shoulder, and Jack gave me kind of a hug, and then I left the house and as darkness was falling in earnest, I climbed.

I climbed the silo and stared over across the dragonfield at the Trogler place.

I saw fire and storm and death.

All of it headed into my life.

Sixteen

How the End Came Quickly

I woke the next morning and could feel that the day was already dying much too fast. A haunting light greeted me. The wound to my heart had magically healed—the gunshot wound, that is—not the other wound, the one caused by Judith and Jack.

I felt free but sad.

I had lost Judith. She belonged with Jack, and yet could they ever really be together? Could I possibly help them find a happily ever after? I wanted to. The best part of me did. But first things first.

The ghosts were calling.

I went out into our pasture to prepare myself for a battle that could not be avoided. Gussie joined me. It felt good traipsing to the far corner of our land, to Rock Creek. I waded across it at a fairly deep though narrow spot, then turned to caution Gussie about getting wet. But she knew. She understood. Smart dog. She leaped over the water, and when I waded back, she leaped over again.

We spent the day roaming.

I ignored the calling of the ghosts for as long as I could.

I wandered back to the house late afternoon to

have some supper with Judith and Jack and to wait for
my father. I did not know it right then, but only four
hours of my life as I had known it remained. My universe was winding down.

Hour One

The end began at sunset when, after helping Judith
and Jack put away the supper dishes, I stepped out onto
the porch, and there was my father petting the ghost of
Gussie. When he heard me approach, he turned and
looked up, his eyes moist, his lips quivering.

"It's Gussie, isn't it?"

I nodded.

You should have seen my father—he was so happy.
And so was Gussie.

I wanted the moment to last forever.

Then, more soberly, my father said, "Folks in town
are all riled up. That Reverend Macready boy has
rounded them into a mob. I've been told they're coming out—they want your cousin. Things could get
ugly."

I said nothing.

I had a passing thought about Macready—to me, he
wasn't the real danger.

Twilight slipped closer. Everything was peaceful, on
the surface at least. A half moon was rising; the first
stars began to appear. I remember sighing, breathing in a deep feeling of serenity.

My last of the night.

The ghosts were calling again.

I knew it initially because of the low growling in
Gussie's throat. I glanced at my father, and I saw it
there, too—in his face. He was hearing their tongues
of fire. I sensed that he wouldn't be able to resist, but

still I whispered, "Don't listen to them, Pop. Stay here and they can't hurt you."

I didn't know that for certain. Just wishful thinking perhaps.

Then I saw her, standing out there by the old cistern: Senta Trogler, staring her zombie-stare right at my father. Gussie barked an alarm. Too late, though. My father rose from the porch. I reached for his arm and then felt Senta's gaze on me, and, slowly, I released my grip on my father. Gussie stopped barking. Boy and dog were dazed by Senta's stare. And my father was called away.

When I snapped out of the spell the old woman had put me under, my first thought was to get Judith to help. I swallowed back that idea, for I sensed that what I had to do I would have to do alone. I began to race across the dragonfield to the Trogler place. Finding the house empty, I ran past the old well and the barn and through the orchard to the pond and there, in the fading light of day, my breath caught in my chest: Senta was holding my father with her eyes. He was standing near the edge of the pond, and, seemingly, he could not move.

The scene had all the trappings of a bad dream: surrealistic movements, a feeling of helplessness and despair, and the not-quite-audible words of Senta in my head. Then a moment of clarity as I saw what Senta was doing. As she held my father mesmerized, old Rolf, his razor-sharp sling blade in hand, walked up from the ground beneath the orchard and approached, his eyes, buried in that hideous face, fiery with a desire for revenge.

I tried to scream, but just as in a bad dream, I could not.

At my side, Gussie whimpered in fear.

The dark outline of the huge cottonwood loomed

above all of us, indifferent to the danger my father
was in.

I knew that he was doomed unless I could draw the
ghosts into the water, where their earthen selves
would dissolve and merge with the muddy pond bottom. I watched helplessly as Senta and Rolf moved
hungrily toward my father. Believing it would do no
good to rush them and try to fight them off, I closed
my eyes and attempted to will Judith's powers into action.

But nothing arose.

And so I ran, splashing out into the center of the
pond, and I thrashed about as if drowning. And I
cried out to my father for help.

And it worked.

It broke the spell.

The primitive need for a father to help a son held
sway.

Hearing, seeing me in trouble, he plunged into the
water to save me. And I was, in turn, overjoyed to see
that my sudden thrust of inspiration might just have
the result I wanted, for Senta continued to approach,
so intent upon my father that she did not stop at the
water's edge but entered—until she was far enough
out that she could not return.

Her cry of anguish was horrible to hear.

Old Rolf could not rescue her.

My father and I watched as she weakened, stumbled
forward and finally surrendered her earthen body to
the mud of the pond.

I cheered.

But then I saw that old Rolf held back.

My heart sank.

"Pop, stay right here in the water—they can't get
you here."

I was wasting my breath. Suggesting the impossible.

As my father led me out of the pond, I knew that it wasn't his way to listen to me. He had to face the Trogler ghost—there was no other way. I tugged and pulled at him, but it was no use.

"Teddy, this is about settling the past," he said.

On the bank of the pond, man and ghost faced each other.

God, I was terrified.

My senses were a neon jangle.

Off to one side, Gussie barked flatly, too frightened to attack.

My father strode defiantly out of the pond to meet his nemesis, and maybe my father could have been a match for him were it not again for the ghostly tongue of fire—the old man's words, things unsayable for anyone other than a wraith. Hearing those indecipherable words, it appeared simply that my father suddenly had no volition. He could not defend himself.

The sling blade rose and fell, cutting into my father's shoulder.

The spilled blood gleamed in the twilight.

I ran as if to tackle old Rolf, but he was much stronger than I anticipated. He threw me down, and I watched as my wounded father writhed on the ground.

He would die horribly. Right before my eyes.

Rolf loomed over him, the years of thwarted revenge reaching an end.

As the old man raised the sling blade again, my fingers began to hum. I felt little pinches of static electricity, and then I felt a welling of something like hope. And just as suddenly the first stars drew my eyes to the top of the monolithic cottonwood.

I blinked hard.

This was it.

I pitched myself like a ball— with every ounce of will and energy that I possessed.

And the sky blazed.

Two bursts of lightning. One stroke high, torching the top branches. Halting his swing, Rolf glanced up to see the coming night set on fire. Then the second stroke axed at the tree about a third of the way up, and you could hear that ancient cottonwood shriek and pop and groan, and the slow, majestic, terrifying fall of it seemed to suck away all of the air around us. The monstrous trunk and the large branches hit the surface of the pond and exploded like an atomic bomb.

The splash was incredible. It was like a preternatural tidal wave. A wall of water rose as if erupting from some deep pool at the center of the earth. It was beautiful.

I heard Rolf cry out.

The water slammed down upon him and my father, but my father—flesh and blood—survived it. The earth that was the eldest Trogler softened, and his body, limb by limb, broke apart, melting into mud as I scrambled to my father's side.

Two ghosts down.

But the most vicious ones were calling—voices flaming and insistent.

Voices demanding blood and vengeance.

Hour Two

With the touch of my fingertips, I slowed my father's bleeding, but he still needed first aid.

"Teddy, it's me they want. Go on and let me get this over with."

I didn't listen to my father. I wasn't about to let him

serve himself up to the other ghosts. No way. As I was bending over him, Gussie nudged up close, and my father smiled and petted her weakly. Then Judith and Jack showed up, and I told them what had happened. Judith took it all in calmly—she understood. Jack wore a mask of disbelief.

When we had helped my father to his feet, Judith and Jack were going to take him back to the house. Judith caught my arm and said, "Don't try to fight them alone." I shook her off, and then she turned to Jack. "Stay and help him."

But I cried, "No!"

I wasn't ready to forgive Jack. I didn't want his help.

And I held my ground, and Judith's face was hard and sad as she and Jack struggled some to assist my father away from the scene.

Alone, I felt the weight of the night.

I stared once out at the fallen cottonwood. It looked like some prehistoric reptile soaking in the darkness. Then I heard Gussie barking up by the Trogler place. I made my way through the orchard and past the barn, but I slowed at the well. For good luck maybe, I picked up a small rock and tossed it in and waited to hear the distant, muted splash.

I entered the house. Gussie wouldn't. That was okay.

This is what I must do, and I must do it.

I waded through the silence of the rooms, each of which was filled with that sickly yellow light I had seen before. Like a diseased light. Like haloes gone bad. It was the Trogler light—repulsive, death-generated.

For a few moments, I tried to disregard the whisperings that broke the intense quiet. Deep in the earth below the floor, below my feet, I could hear her—Romina—her soft chant: "Animus! Animus!"

And there was also a distant, rolling growl—
Hunter's—like approaching thunder.

I quaked as I stood in the center of the front room.
I was waiting.

Within the wall I faced I could hear a wheezing,
near hysterical laughter. I knew it was Siebert. He was
taunting me. He was making me wait to die. He was
drinking away my courage. I sensed that a moment
neared in which I must run, in which my cowardice
would seize me and I would bolt from the house and
run as far away as possible.

To anywhere but here.

I waited.

Silence reigned again.

I was so scared that I began to hiccough almost un-
controllably. It seemed absurd.

Everything did.

And when the wall exploded—Siebert hammering
his way with his sledge into my presence—I screamed
so hard that I was dizzied. The burly young man was
surrounded by a savage light. His smile was pure madness.

Maybe it was that smile that prodded my survival instincts into action.

I ran.

I ran out of the house, foolishly stopping at the well
to see how close he was in his pursuit. And then surprise: Siebert wasn't chasing me. But I could see him.
The light of the half moon captured the gleam of one
eye in the corner of the paneless kitchen window.

He was watching me. He blinked and the white of
his eye retreated for a heartbeat.

We looked at each other for what seemed like five
or ten minutes.

It was almost as if, standing there, locked in that intense exchange of looking, I would fall asleep for a

few seconds, then rouse myself. In our staring, we shared a strange intimacy. And that intimacy told me things and forced questions.

Siebert is going to kill me.

Why doesn't he come after me?

Why am I not escaping?

I could not move.

I struggled to find voice, and when I succeeded, I yelled out, "Come on, you bastard!"

And he did.

My senses were activated to a supernatural level as he charged out of the haunted house. I heard the gossamer songs of mosquitoes. I smelled sour earth. I felt my body vibrating. I saw particles of moon dust. I tasted blood. It was one of those moments when nature has withdrawn from reality and become a dream again and is waiting on the promise of night to disappear into space.

Then another surprise. Siebert lowered his sledge as he approached; he slowed dramatically, and I would swear that he was listening to a voice inside his head, a voice only he could hear. I was standing next to the well, and my heart was beating so rapidly that my ribs ached.

When Siebert had stepped to within ten feet of me, I measured my chances once again of running. But I didn't run. Instead, I fixed my sight upon Siebert's lips. He was murmuring something. And what he said, confused me, astonished me.

"Romina's child," he said, tonelessly. Then repeated the words with slightly more emotion. Then he smiled and the smile blossomed maniacally. "Romina's child," he said, and in a matter of seconds they had become ugly words.

He raised his sledge and worked his mouth, but at first no more words came out.

Something about his manner caused me to drop my guard.

Suddenly he shouted, "Behind you! Hunter!"

I stiffened, but wheeled around to face the dog.

It wasn't there.

Siebert's sledge narrowly missed me. I felt the sickening wind from it.

And then he was on top of me.

Hour Three

It was the sensation of the pond in winter. Of skating upon the surface and hearing/feeling the ice cracking, then breaking. The crashing through and the stab of cold water. Only in this case it was cold earth—cold, heavy earth. It squeezed the air out of my lungs.

Siebert's stinking breath nauseated me.

With my eyes watering, I gasped for air as he ritched back and swung his sledge again, again narrowly missing me, grazing my left ear. I screamed and did the only thing in self defense I could possibly do—I rucked up my knees and kicked at his crotch.

And connected.

He howled and bent over, and when he did I went for his face. I tore at it. I gouged it. Globs of dirt that had been his cheek came free in my grasp. Dropping his sledge to one side, he roared and pushed at my hands. We struggled.

And he was too strong.

I managed to get to my feet, but he had me. He had me by the throat. I could feel myself losing consciousness though I fought mightily to keep from being strangled to death. Above me stars seemed to wink out. My eyes were bulging and my screams were raspy—then faded to silence. I fell away from him and coughed as I tried to find breath.

He was standing over me.

He held the small sledge with both hands, poised to make a vicious chopping movement. I was too weak even to roll to one side. My throat burned and my vision was blurry. But I could imagine the end: My brains would be bashed out. I could imagine it—everything but the pain, and I hoped that it would be brief. Like killing a farm animal: Make it quick. Don't let it suffer.

I heard a whistling sound, and I suppose I thought it was the sledge.

In my helpless state, terrified, I blinked.

Siebert hadn't followed through with the swing of the sledge. He was standing there, making gurgling noises. He lowered the sledge, and he looked down at his chest. Beyond me, beyond my vision, I thought I heard Jack. Then Judith. Shouting. Shouting.

I looked again at Siebert. My vision cleared.

He was staggering backward.

Jack's javelin had plunged through his chest and was stuck in the ground behind him. It was as if that spear had been hurled from the stars. I watched in disbelief as he worked the javelin free, then stutter-stepped forward and fell heavily in a heap next to me.

And then I momentarily lost consciousness.

When I came to, Judith was patting my cheeks. Jack was saying something I couldn't decipher. I tried to speak. Tried to tell Jack thanks—thanks for saving my life—but my voice was ragged, and I couldn't think of individual words.

"You have to get up," Judith was saying. Fear spilled from her voice.

Then I heard Jack—even more fear in his.

"God, he's not dead!"

I rolled to my feet and pulled Judith back as Siebert, revived, stood shakily and met Jack's fists. I jumped into the battle as best I could, and when one of my punches landed high on Siebert's chest, I knew what we had to do.

It all came clear to me.

"Knock him down the well!" I shouted. "We gotta knock him down into the water!"

That's when I went for the ghost's legs while Jack waded into his upper body, and between the two of us, we did it. Siebert tottered. Crashed backward. Jack grabbed his javelin and jammed it into the ghost's eye. Then into his heart.

Judith helped us pull and lug his body to the edge of the well. We yelled triumphantly as he tumbled into the depths, tumbled and tumbled until the eventual splash overjoyed us to the point that I believe we could have levitated.

Smiling, Jack turned in the partial moonlight and started to reach for my hand—to shake it, I think. And that's when I heard Judith's cry, "No, watch it! The dog!"

But it was too late.

Hunter, clambering furiously up out of the ground, was on Jack before he had a chance to protect himself. Judith and I tried to help. We tried to beat at the animal to keep it from killing Jack. The bites were cold-blooded and crazed, ripping at Jack's arms and legs, and when my brother lowered his hands from in front of his face, the dog went for his throat.

Judith was sobbing and screaming and hammering at the animal with her fists. I tried to jab at it with the javelin, but it turned and snapped at my wrist, opening a gash there. I could tell that Jack was losing strength, losing the capacity to fight back. I gritted my teeth and ran and tackled the dog, knocking it momentarily off my brother.

But then I became the target of the animal's ferocity.

It was all over me. Teeth and claws and savagery.

Until I was rescued.

By Gussie.

The two ghostly dogs went at each other, whirling, snapping, eagerly, instinctively intent upon seriously wounding, if not destroying, the other. As the dogs fought, Judith hustled Jack into the Trogler place for shelter. For safety. And to tend to his bites and scratches.

Standing ineffectually to one side, still holding Jack's javelin, I simply couldn't find a way to help Gussie, and as they continued their battle I became vaguely aware of car lights approaching out on the road from town—many pairs of them. Fleetingly I recalled my father mentioning how riled up folks in town had become. They wanted Judith.

They wanted to get her.

But there was not time to think about that: Gussie was losing. Hunter had her down and was starting to rip at her throat. Once again I tried to spear him. Came close enough to distract him and that gave Gussie a chance to escape.

I yelled, "Run, Gussie, run!"

She was running before the words got out of my mouth.

But Hunter was quickly in hot pursuit.

Dropping the javelin, I followed until my bleeding wrist slowed me and, finally, I had to stop and apply my powers to stay the flow of the blood. I was dizzy and scared. Up ahead I could hear Hunter giving chase—in full cry—gone away like hounds after a fox.

By the sound of the barking, I knew that they must

be in our pasture. Sadness punched at me because I did not believe Gussie could escape. It seemed hopeless. Everything did. As I continued running in the direction of the chase, I found myself wanting to take a detour to our house and see about my father and the wound given him by old Rolf.

I thought about the ghosts.

Rolf and Senta and Siebert had been destroyed.

But Romina remained.

And at the Trogler place Judith and Jack would also be threatened by the mob once those townsfolk discovered Judith was there.

I was getting weak, too weak to think.

Gussie and Hunter were swinging in a desperate circle at the far corner of our pasture. In the partial moonlight they were liquid shadows. As I watched the chase continue, I regretted not having brought Jack's javelin. I looked around for a big rock, but could find only little ones. When I glanced up from my search, I saw that Gussie was heading for Rock Creek.

I think I must have screamed out for her not to go there.

I ran to a vantage point on the scene and, from a distance, here's what I saw: Gussie laying out as fast as she could run, but straight toward the creek. I was murmuring "No, no!" I didn't want to see Gussie plunge into the water even if it might also mean the end of Hunter.

But that's when our Gussie did something real smart.

She jumped.

She lifted high and far and when she landed on the other side of a somewhat narrow run of Rock Creek, I cheered, and I watched as her savage pursuer splashed into the water, barking, growling, eager to close upon his prey.

But the water caught him.

With Gussie barking victoriously and looking on, Hunter began to thrash and weaken and dissolve until his body crumpled, bobbed once below the surface, then back out and then, howling in anguish, sank once again below the surface.

And was gone.

Hour Four

The mob had gathered.

From the front room of the Trogler place, we could see them: eager and angry, determined. I could hear Macready calling for Judith to come out. I could see a number of Saddle Rock citizens there with them, amassed like the townsfolk you see in old horror movies, only they were carrying flashlights instead of torches; some had the headlights of their cars trained on the house. The eerie brightness was impossible to stare into. And yet I could recognize some who had joined Macready in his mission to drive out the demon he had convinced himself Judith was. I could see Mickey Palmer. And I could see my mother standing there as well, huddled next to the Gormans.

I saw David. He was close to Macready. I wondered whether he knew I had survived his attempt to kill me. And then I saw another car pull up; someone wielding a shotgun jumped out: It was Junior. He had returned with Phyllis. He must have sensed that I was in trouble, or at least he knew that a mob gathered in front of the Trogler place must involve our family. I was cheered to see him.

"Teddy, Jack's got some bad wounds," said Judith.

My brother was on his back. When he spoke, his

words were slurred: "I'll be okay. Don't worry about me."

In a way, I wasn't. I was worried about the ghosts. And I was worried about my father. Returning from the pasture, I had stopped at our house and found my father on Judith's cot. I think she had bandaged his wounds. Loss of blood had weakened him, but he smiled when he saw me and Gussie. And he warned me that the mob from town was dangerous. He didn't want me to go back to the Trogler place, but I left Gussie with him. I had to leave.

There was one more Trogler to face.

Judith wanted to surrender herself to the mob, but Jack and I wouldn't let her.

Worst of all, I could hear Romina whispering in the walls.

"What does she want?" I said.

"You and me, Teddy," said Judith. "You see, she thinks I'm the spirit of the brother who died when her mother gave birth to her—she thinks that the death of her twin brother was the beginning of darkness for the Trogler family. And she wants you, too."

It was obvious she had more to say, but something kept her from it. In the meantime, the mob continued shouting and throwing rocks and threatening us in every way they could. I knew there wasn't much time. I had to do something. Fast.

Then it began to become clear. Looking at Judith as she tended so lovingly to Jack, I suddenly saw a warm, blue light surround them. They were meant to be together. I swallowed hard, and maybe Judith intuited what I was thinking—I believe she did—because she reached for my hand, and the moment we touched I knew exactly what I must do.

I stood back away from them.

There was only one way for Judith and Jack to share their love forever and that was as ghosts.

I raised my hands out in front of me. I concentrated.

I brought tiny, shivering, jangling strikes of lightning to my fingertips.

"Teddy, no!" Judith cried.

"It's for you," I said, "for you and Jack."

I struck every wall with fire, and then, with the haunting whispers of Romina Trogler chasing after me, I ran from that house of ghosts as it exploded into flames. I could hear the angry mob gasp and then roar their approval.

Out behind the house, I watched, tears streaming down my face, as the Trogler place was completely engulfed in a matter of seconds. The fire blossomed like a rose. I was sad and horrified: I was losing a brother and the woman I loved, and yet it was the only thing to do. The best thing.

The only thing that counts: Doing something for someone you love.

But there was more.

The ghostly voice—words tongued with fire—was in my head: "Animus! Animus!"

A few yards from me, dark and shadowy against the backdrop of flames, Romina Trogler approached. I couldn't see her face clearly, but her voice held me, a voice filled with wanting and needing. Maybe there was love in it, too. I was swirled in the mystery of life created in those moments.

I screamed for help.

Then I heard a man's voice: "I'm here. Son, I'm here."

Behind me, moving out from the dragonfield, were my father and Gussie. My father was holding his shoulder.

"Pop!" I said, but when I tried to run to him I couldn't. Romina Trogler had me under some kind of spell, I think.

"Teddy," said my father, his tone strange—a hollowness to it generated by fear and desperation, "you gotta hear the truth about this."

I didn't know what he was talking about.

"Pop, she's gonna kill me. Help me, please."

"No, Teddy . . . she won't."

When he said those words, I felt chills course through me. I looked into the shadowy face of Romina Trogler, and I knew that I was on the cliff edge of revelation.

"Who is she?" I said to my father.

As he stepped closer, he spoke very quietly. "She's your mother, Teddy. And Harold Suggs was your father. When he was killed, and when the Troglers were killed—"

"No!" I shouted. Then more softly, "No." And I recalled the moment that Siebert had called me "Romina's child," and I thought about Judith trying to find a way to tell me who I was.

Romina Trogler reached out both hands to me. It was almost too much to resist.

"Animus. Animus, my child."

My heart was on fire, blazing as furiously as the flames bringing down the derelict walls of the Trogler place. I was shaking my head. But I managed one last cry of defiance: "No, stay away from me!"

Romina Trogler was lunging for me when the shotgun blast filled the night.

I saw part of her shoulder tear away from her body.

"Run, Teddy!"

It was Junior.

The ghost of my real mother crumpled to her

knees. Something swept over me—a wave of compassion as I have never felt—and I knelt by her.

Our eyes met.

Then I glanced up at Junior and then over my shoulder at my father and Gussie.

The ghost of my mother could not smile. She was releasing me. I don't know any other way to describe it. She was allowing me to choose: Go to the realm of ghosts with her or stay in the world I had always known.

I looked at her, my heart beating in the rhythm of hers, and I whispered, "I'm sorry," letting my words slide into her darkness.

I stood up and I backed away and I told Junior to take my father and Gussie to his car. Most of the members of Macready's mob had driven off, satisfied, I assume. The flames that had claimed Judith and Jack flickered in the breeze.

And when I was alone with the ghost of my mother, I brought a storm onto the scene.

Wind and lightning and, most of all, sheet after sheet of heavy rain.

A toad strangler.

And as the rain soaked my body, washing away my past, cleansing me of the horrible immediacy of the moment, I watched as the woman who had brought me into this haunted life was beaten down by the fury of the rain, then, by rapid degrees, disintegrated, the earth calling her to earth again and then to nothingness.

Epilogue

Haunted Ground

I never got famous.

Never married.

For years I have worked as a hospital orderly in Emporia. Though I have been tempted to, I never use any of my fading powers beyond the boundaries of our farm. If I had any writing ability maybe I could write up the story of the O'Dells and the Troglers and sell it to the movies. Of course, it would have to be packaged as fiction—no one would believe it really happened.

My mother died in 1975, her stomach cancer (with a touch of help from me) had gone into remission. But she was weak and bitter despite a modicum of health; it was as if she waited for Nixon to resign and Vietnam to be over before she passed on. I nursed her until the end.

My father, 86, is feeble, but once or twice a week we walk the property, the haunted ground that we have always known. Gussie, made of that sacred earth, joins us, pleasing my father to no end. I brought Oatmeal back, too—you never had to warn that cat about not getting wet.

Junior and Phyllis visit often. After moving away for

years, they came back to Kansas right before my mother died. They live on a farm just west of us. Rock Creek runs through it. They have two daughters, Melanie and Meredith, who call me "Uncle Teddy," and I think that's cool.

Within weeks after the fiery end of everything that the summer of 1955 had become, I was faced with a decision. Judith had been buried in the family plot next to Jack. The jealous part of me didn't want to do it, but one morning I woke them. They blew in the wind as dust at first. Then, over the days to come, they fed upon me, becoming stronger, more substantial. Earth strong. Their affection for each other strong, too.

I have never stopped loving Judith.

No other woman could possibly measure up to her—my beloved.

After we buried my mother, I woke her, too, because my father was so lonely for her.

In time, my father will pass.

And I'll wake him, too.

It's a family joke, of course, that no one comes out on a rainy day—no swimming in Trogler's Pond or wading in Rock Creek. No baths.

I have only a summary account of the remaining cast of characters from that summer: David became a writer, I've heard. I never saw him again after high school. Mickey Palmer was a star basketball player in college, became a lawyer, and now is running for a state representative position. Lex Macready went back to Louisiana, gave up his ministry and, according to reports I've received, manages a successful car dealership.

I often think about my real parents.

When I do a blue flame haunts my thoughts. I once looked up and visited briefly with Alma Suggs, the widow of Harold Suggs. But I found it painful and confusing to listen to her talk of my real father—she called him "Harry" and did not believe, could not believe, that her husband ever fathered an illegitimate child.

When I think of my real mother, I sometimes hear a voice: maternal, longing, yearning—"Animus," it whispers. I can't resist it, though there is no way to embrace it. I long to look into her eyes and feel the blast resistless between mother and son.

I walk through the dragonfield to the spot where the Trogler place was razed long ago. Corn is planted there now. I walk around and an immense loneliness settles upon me.

I listen.

But over the incessant Kansas wind the only sound I hear is the voice of my own darkness.

I have learned that, alive or dead, we are all ghosts—and we haunt ourselves.

ABOUT THE AUTHOR

Stephen Gresham lives in Alabama and is currently working on his next horror novel to be published by Pinnacle Books in 2004. He loves to hear from readers, and you may write to him c/o Pinnacle Books. Please include a self-addressed stamped envelope if you wish a response.

He may also be reached via e-mail at:
greshsl@auburn.edu

Feel the Seduction of
Pinnacle Horror